David Ridgway

THURSDAY

Limited Special Edition. No. 6 of 25 Paperbacks

David is a graduate of the University of Life. He had a variety of jobs, always in selling, before starting a career in financial services. He has served as a magistrate and a local borough councillor, before being elected the Mayor of Kirklees in 2012. Married with three grown-up and successful children, David is now retired, giving him time for his grandchildren, his garden and his writing.

To my wife, Karen, for her support over the past 44 years and Jeanette, for her unstinting encouragement, proofreading and advice.

David Ridgway

THURSDAY

AUSTIN MACAULEY PUBLISHERS™

LONDON • CAMBRIDGE • NEW YORK • SHARJAH

A CIP catalogue record for this title is available from the British Library.

ISBN 9781528978118 (Paperback)
ISBN 9781528978125 (Hardback)
ISBN 9781528978156 (ePub e-book)

www.austinmacauley.com

First Published (2020)
Austin Macauley Publishers Ltd
25 Canada Square
Canary Wharf
London
E14 5LQ

Synopsis

MAIN THEME

In February sometime in the near future, a big storm comes across the North Atlantic with a record-deep, low-pressure system. The hurricane winds push the sea southwards down the North Atlantic and into the North Sea, as well as bringing snow to Scotland and north-eastern England.

A second, equally low depression has raced across the Atlantic, but further south, past the Azores, before moving north-east up the Bay of Biscay and past southern Ireland. This is causing gale-force winds to blow eastwards, pushing the sea up the English Channel.

Neither depression can progress because of an anti-cyclone over Western Europe, which has been causing deep frosts from Holland right over to Russia.

The southern depression is centred over Oxford and the northern depression is centred 200 miles to the north-west of Stavanger.

In addition, it is season for the spring tides.

Early on the Thursday morning, the tide begins to flow. As high tide is reached, isolated flooding occurs in Devon, Hampshire, Northern France, Belgium and Holland. There is also some coastal flooding on the Yorkshire coast, East Anglia, Essex and the Thames Estuary. The surge up the River Thames is broadly held by the Thames Barrier, but the height of the tide breaks all records around the southeast coast.

As the tide starts to ebb, the westerly wind up the Channel seems to intensify, as does the southerly wind down the North Sea. The effect of this is that the tide does not recede for the next 6 hours and early in the afternoon, the tide begins to flow once more.

The Thames Barrier is breached and a massive wave of water flows up the Thames and this tidal surge is noted even beyond Teddington Lock.

MAIN STORY

David Varley is an A level student, aged 18. He first predicts this weather event but is ridiculed by his teacher and his father. His father, Michael, works in the city and has been called to an overnight conference on Wednesday, scheduled to return Thursday evening.

David has a girlfriend, Jackie, although the relationship has been drifting of late, caused by the enforced necessity to revise and the distance between their homes. David's mother, Sarah, comes from West Yorkshire, but no longer works for a living. Instead, she is involved with local community and charitable groups. Her parents, Christine and Robert Sykes, live in Huddersfield.

Because London is at threat, David goes to find his father to bring him home. He contacts Jackie and, together, they travel up to London.

CHARACTERS

David Varley.

Michael, his father, a broker in the city.

Sarah, his mother.

Jackie Bleasdale, his girlfriend, dark-haired, slight, pretty and provocative. Her parents are Annabel and Kevin. He is a chief superintendent based at Scotland Yard.

John Dickinson, his pal at school.

Christine and Robert Sykes, his maternal grandparents in West Yorkshire.

OTHER CHARACTERS

Mr Smith, David's science teacher at Richmond Academy.

Martin and Jennifer Havers, who farm in Hadleigh, Essex on the Thames estuary. They have three children Charlie (and Paula), James (and Megan) and Helen. They live at Thatched Barn Farm. The children have moved away. James is practical, Charlie is not.

Fred and Dinah Shemming. He is a fire officer on the Isle of Dogs. They have two sons.

Rajinder Singh, the owner of a corner shop in Poplar.

Alice works for Michael Varley.

Andy Greene, a cabbie based in Kennington. He is a widower and has a lucrative side-line hobby, photography.

Sebastian Fortescue-Brown, a hotelier in Kensington.

Betty is his chief cook and bottle washer, married to Jack the hotel's handyman.

Tim Watson, hotel's accountant.

Milton Pryde, a West Indian driver on the Underground. His girlfriend is Pamela.

WPC Elizabeth Drury works for Chief Superintendent Kevin Bleasdale.

Preamble

There can be no doubt, looking back, that it really happened on Thursday. On Wednesday, still no one believed that it could happen and by Friday, of course, it was all over.

There had been years of media build up, following the news in 2018 that the Thwaites Glacier in Antarctica was showing signs of instability and retreating at an unprecedented rate. Of course, the doomsters had been predicting global warming disasters for generations. And, more recently, they had added other immediate disasters to their joyful list: economic collapse in the Far East, AIDS and population migration from Africa, Covid-19 and political unrest throughout Europe.

Everyone was massively over informed. We all knew that something *might* happen, but surely not in our own backyard.

The winter had been unusually long and unpleasantly wet. The previous summer had been poor with very few consecutive days of sunshine. Naturally, the farmers had complained about the harvest, but no one really listened to them because it had all been said before. Anyway, the farmers still had their big Range Rovers, so things couldn't be all that bad, could they?

Surprisingly, Christmas had been clear, sunny and cold giving everyone hope that the New Year would show an improvement. Any improvement was long overdue after all the autumnal rain.

But Mother Nature isn't like that. She's real contrary when she puts her mind to it and she had put up with far too much and for far too long. Yes! We were foolish to believe that the weather would improve. By the second week in January, the rain was back. The land was already waterlogged and those two weeks over the Christmas and New Year holiday had hardly had any effect on the high level of the water table.

Depression after depression swept in from the Atlantic. Rivers burst their banks and football matches were postponed. The transport system began to creek under the pressure. Everyone was depressed.

Despite the scientific journals predicting that the collapse of the Thwaites Glacier and its near neighbour the Pine Island Glacier will raise sea levels by at least a metre, except for some very broad comments in the quality press, there was little coverage. An international team of glaciologists was despatched to that remote part of Antarctica in late 2018 and their early reports indicated that the retreat of both glaciers was already irreversible. Each subsequent year, there was a slight but measurable rise in sea levels and around the world the predicted frequency of devastating storms was unfolding month by month.

By Tuesday in the third week of February, everyone was feeling miserable, well accustomed to trudging to work through the incessant rain. The false smiles and false hopes of the weather forecasters then turned serious as they told us of an even deeper depression which promised high winds and even more driving rain, especially in the south and east of England.

And they were right!

Coupled with the annual spring tides, the first specific depression arrived at just the wrong time. It deepened drastically, causing the westerly gales to intensify in the Channel. Structural damage was reported all along the South coast, trees were blown down and local power cuts added to the confusion.

Then, early on Wednesday morning, the tide began to flow as normal. Being a spring tide and backed by severe gale force winds, the television news programmes were able to show some spectacular sights of waves breaking over sea defences. Rather more seriously, there was flooding in the low-lying coastal towns, the worst hit being Weymouth. We should have realised something was amiss when the tide didn't really go out. By low tide in London at ten o'clock on Wednesday morning, a remarkable amount of water had not ebbed away as normal. Mind you, not many people noticed because the weather was so awful that most had gone to work with their heads bowed down and their umbrellas turned into the wind.

But it was on Thursday when the real problems began. The tide had turned about an hour before midnight and begun to flow back in. The low depression was now centred over Oxford. Very unusually, a second depression had crossed the northern Atlantic, past the northern tip of Scotland and was centred off the western coast of Norway near Stavanger. This caused severe southerly gales in the North Sea, which following the intensifying westerly gales in the English Channel, created a swift and intense build-up of sea water. The coastline of Northern France, Belgium, Holland and Denmark bore the initial brunt.

By high tide in London, scheduled at half past four in the morning, the sea had already breached the sea walls in parts of Norfolk, Suffolk and Essex. The Thames Barrier had already been activated to cope with the high tides on the Wednesday, but this did little to help the situation on Canvey Island, out in the Thames Estuary. However, the high tide came and went and the concrete seawalls around that strategic island had held out and everyone breathed a little easier.

The news bulletins at last began to report with some accuracy on the growing difficulties in East Anglia. As the people awoke, they were told of flooding in Holland and along the Channel coastline. All ferry crossings were cancelled, because of the gale force winds. With the passing of the high tide, the danger was expected to recede like the sea water, but the Environment Agency advised that the gale force winds were expected to remain and even to intensify so much so that the next high tide, just after 5.00 pm, there could be severe flooding. People were advised not to leave home or travel, except in cases of absolute emergency.

Scotland, meanwhile, had experienced exceptional snowfall, with enormous drifting in the fierce northerly gale force winds. There had been many disruptions to the power supply. By mid-day, as it was becoming blindingly obvious that a massive weather calamity was unfolding north of the border, the news bulletins announced that all major communication links with England had been broken. But the weather pays no heed to manmade national boundaries and the excessive snowfall, just like Bonnie Prince Charlie in 1745, extended as far south as Derby and Nottingham.

Low tide in London on Thursday morning was scheduled at about eleven o'clock. The effect of the easterly gales in the channel, however, had been to force the sea eastwards and this had restricted the natural ebbing of the tide.

As the tide flowed back in, the build-up of water on both sides of the Channel was immense. The channel ports were inundated and thousands of acres of land were flooded, particularly in northern France and Belgium. There was immense disruption to transport and power supply. In the North Sea the seawater, being forced southwards by the second depression off Norway, met the unnatural build-up of sea water that had been unable to flow away when the tide should have ebbed down the English Channel. A sea surge was created about 10 feet in height and travelling at around 200 miles per hour in a southeasterly direction.

As the surge met the continental shelf off Holland, it slowed down very quickly, but its inherent energy created a wave, rather like a tsunami, of some 50 feet in height.

The centuries-old Dutch dyke system was simply overwhelmed as incalculable millions of tons of seawater inundated the polders and low-lying farms. The coastlines of northern Germany and western Denmark were also severely flooded. These disasters were soon followed by the sea defence systems being overwhelmed around the southeast coastline of England. From Norfolk down to Essex, the surge simply flowed over the seawalls.

By midday, the nuclear power stations Sizewell A and B and Bradwell had all ceased operations. Following the advice of the Environment Agency, their safety codes had been activated and the power production had been rendered safe.

Across the country, however, the National Grid was struggling. With the loss of much of the network in Scotland, the Grid had been overwhelmed and by ten o'clock in the morning, virtually the whole country was experiencing power cuts. The landline telephone system came under considerable pressure and the railway service became intermittent. The last news bulletins to be issued advised the public to stay calm and wait until the water receded, after the high tide had passed. The Environment Agency had given this advice more in hope than expectation, of course. It was certainly lacking in detail.

The hurricane force winds continued to sweep up the Channel and down the North Sea, before joining forces and moving eastwards across northern Europe to wreak considerable structural havoc throughout northern Germany, Poland and even as far as western Russia. The rain was now spread in a belt from Iceland and Scotland in the north, through Ireland and down to the Bay of Biscay, Southern France and Northern Spain.

The sea surge made landfall in Holland at just after one o'clock GMT. It continued to flow in both directions along the European coastline. It entered the Thames Estuary at about half past one and travelled westwards up river at about 20 miles per hour. As the riverbed shelved, so the sea surge had slowed, but the inherent energy created a 40-foot wave over and above the increased amount of water that was already in the flooded river. Behind it, the tide continued to flow and, unbelievably, the water levels continued to rise after the passing of the wave.

Famous landmarks simply disappeared; others could be seen as islands, appearing isolated in a brown swirl of dirty water. Much of Tower Bridge stood proudly above the surface, but many older tower blocks had simply collapsed and their foundations were washed away by the scouring pressure of the water. There was no sign of the London Eye, but the Royal Standard still proudly flew over the roof of Buckingham Palace giving hope to all those who could see it. St James' Park was completely flooded. The Houses of Parliament and Big Ben were marooned like a darkened cruise ship, surrounded by water, debris and floating corpses.

During the evening, the depressions started to fill and began to drift away to the east. The wind slackened and, finally, the rain stopped. The clouds began to rise and small gaps began to appear. High Tide came at five o'clock in the afternoon, after which, the water in the Thames and the floods on both banks, began to recede. With such an enormous amount of water forced into so small area between the east coast of England and continental Europe, the outgoing tide would drain off the surface of the land very rapidly, bringing further calamitous disasters.

Chapter 1
Monday – Ten Days to Go

Out in the Pacific Ocean, the weather systems had been affected by the El Nino effect. The warm water on the surface of the sea had been blown far to the west by the trade winds and the subsequent La Nina had then reversed that process. The warm water had now reached the American western seaboard and weather systems had subsequently built up bringing high winds and heavy rain to San Francisco, Los Angeles and as far north as Seattle, Vancouver and Alaska.

"Come on, David," shouted Sarah. "You'll be late for school."

As always, Sarah was in charge of getting the breakfast and ensuring that Michael, her husband, and David, her son, would leave on time for David to get to school and Michael to get to work. It always seemed that bit more difficult on Mondays, but it had been this way since she had given up work to look after her baby, some 17 years earlier. An elegant woman, good looking and just starting to show some signs of grey in her hair, Sarah had never regretted her decision to become a housewife and mother. When David was old enough to go to nursery and then to school, Sarah found that she now had the time to join her local gym in order to keep fit. She had kept her figure and maintained her good looks with regular massage and facials. She maintained her sanity by volunteering in the local library.

It was the same every weekday morning. Michael and Sarah would always be up, eating breakfast and ready to start the day, but not David. David had other agendas. Clever in class, he was able to indulge himself in thinking his own thoughts, to the extent that he was often mistaken as lazy. He appeared to be a dreamer but was always the first in line when things needed to be done. Many did not understand him, despite his ability to demonstrate an extraordinary loyalty to those who gained his respect or interest.

David Varley was seventeen and well on schedule for passing his 'A' levels, but whether or not with distinction remained to be seen. He was certainly capable of achieving exceptional grades and university entrance, but his real interests lay in other directions, and he was clever enough to do sufficient work to keep his teachers off his back, but not necessarily to achieve his full potential. Jack Smith, his science teacher, was the only one who recognised this lack of focus and despaired that David's refusal to engage a determined concentration would see life's opportunities slip wastefully away.

All his life, David has been able to absorb knowledge, especially in subjects that interested him. He only needed to read or hear a fact once and it was stored forever. He learned at an early age, however, that no one likes a wise guy. That had been a salutary lesson. Years before, when still at Preparatory School, one of his classmates, John Dickinson, was asked in History which wife Henry VIII had beheaded. It was part of the homework reading from the week before but, as usual, Dickinson hadn't done the reading and didn't know. When the rest of the class was asked, David's hand went up and the teacher pointed to him.

"Anne Boleyn, sir," came the prompt reply.

"Clever clogs," whispered Dickinson. "Showing me up again. I'll see to you at break."

And he did. David's knuckles were bruised, his knees and shoes were scuffed from falling and his blazer was torn. He vowed never to be beaten up again and ever afterwards kept his knowledge well under control. He learned to avoid confrontation but was always ready to help a pal and to right a wrong. Strangely, this incident was also the start of a very close friendship with John Dickinson.

On the rugby field, however, it was a different story. All the pent-up emotions from the classroom were released and David was developing into an accomplished full back, with that rare ability to combine strength with courage, enhanced by exceptional strategic thinking. He was always in the right place at the right time and seemed to know when he should run or just rely on his kicking. But he remained modest about his skills, preferring others to take the accolades. And it was the same on the cricket field in summer. David was a reliable fast bowler, regularly tying up the opposing batsmen, as well as scoring sufficient runs to support the team.

In short, David was a team player, a good lieutenant rather than a leader, reliable and loyal. Indeed, his closest friend, John Dickinson, who had become a natural leader and excellent sportsman, regularly relied on David to help him through his classwork. In return, he pushed and encouraged David on the rugby field not only to enhance his skills but also to build up his physique.

At age 13, both David and John had passed the Common Entrance to Richmond School, which was reasonably convenient for both their families. Now both were 17, facing their 'A' levels and a planned move to university.

The autumn term was pretty intensive, with the school year being focussed on the exams scheduled for the coming spring. As soon as the term started, however, the weather turned cold and wet. In class, David continued to coast through his work, gaining sufficient grades to avoid any unnecessary attention from his teachers but leaving enough time to help his pal Dickinson. The rugby matches started with quite decent pitches, but as the weeks passed, these became more and more waterlogged and match after match was cancelled. To keep fit, the boys went running, but the rain doggedly kept falling and the water table kept rising, until local rivers burst their banks and flooded the low-lying fields.

David asked Mr Smith, the science teacher, what was causing the rain to persist for so long and this opened up a new interest – meteorology. The weather, what causes it and why. Mr Smith took the enquiry seriously and suggested that David do some additional work, looking into the phenomenon of the El Nino and how it affected weather creation and whether global warming accentuated or diminished its power.

"Do me a four-side essay, showing what you've discovered. Bring it in on Monday and we'll look at what you've written."

So, as his parents were shouting for him to come to breakfast, David's thoughts were far away in the Pacific, wondering why the movement of the sea currents on the west coast of South America should cause the rain to keep falling in England.

"I'm coming," he called, grabbing his jacket and running down the stairs.

"What were you up to yesterday evening?" his father asked, after breakfast, as they got into the car. "You missed the rugby on TV."

"Mr Smith's given me this assignment. To look into reasons why the weather has been so awful. I was researching the El Nino current and seeing whether there is any connection between it and the rain we've been having.

"Did you know," he continued, "that the melting Antarctic ice could have an effect on sea levels and that could change our weather patterns forever?"

"I hope this has something to do with your 'A' levels, David. You should be concentrating on your grades, rather than wasting your time on matters outside the curriculum."

"Well, I'm hoping to put it all into some form of presentation and see if I can get it included in the General Studies paper. Mr Smith asked for a 4-side essay, but I've already written 25 pages. It's really fascinating!"

"Mm!" His father wasn't really convinced but knew better than to argue, because David would only withdraw into a place where he could sustain a polite though disinterested level of conversation, while giving full rein to his thoughts.

Michael dropped David off at the corner of the road near the school. As he drove away, he saw David meet up with John Dickinson and walk, together, towards the school gates.

"Have you done your revision?" John asked.

"Not really. I thought the assignment was pretty simple, so I expect I'll be able to blag it. I was spending a lot of time on an assignment that Maquis gave me." Maquis was the school's nickname for Mr Smith because in each boy's first year, he would be taught about electric current and resistance. The Maquis had been the French Resistance in France in the 1940s and Mr Smith was married to a delightful, dark-haired Parisienne.

"What about?"

"The weather and the possible links to the El Nino effect in the Pacific."

"What's that then?"

"Have you ever wondered why the weather seems to be getting more and more difficult this winter?"

"Not really," replied John. "All I know is that it's causing too many cancellations of school matches. The pitches are so waterlogged that it'll be weeks before we can play again. And for that to happen, it's got to stop raining today."

They both looked up to the west, where the rain clouds were heralding yet another day of rain.

"And it's windy as well," he muttered.

David knew better than to start explaining his research to his pal and they both wandered off to Assembly.

As the head teacher was announcing the additional programme of the day, including running for all the senior school, David was beginning to wonder what might happen if the rain never stopped.

Well, he thought, *'never' is pretty endless, so it's bound to stop at some time.* Little did he know that Mother Nature had a real event up her sleeve.

Chapter 2
Tuesday – Nine Days to Go

Five thousand miles to the west of Great Britain, in the Gulf of Mexico to be exact, a new weather system was being created. Back in the autumn, the trade winds had reversed and La Nina had pushed the warm Pacific water back towards the coast of South America. The subsequent weather systems had brought flooding to the west coast of the United States and the prevailing winds seemed to be even more intense than normal.

These systems had now passed across North America, bringing very heavy snowfall in Canada and the northern states, plus tornados and heavy rain in Texas, Arkansas and Florida.

A new system, spawning in the Gulf of Mexico, was accentuated by very warm air moving from the Atlantic along the northern Brazilian coast before turning northwards into the Gulf. Here it encountered the cooler air over the North American landmass, making the wind speeds rise and the rainfall increase.

"And now over to Jon Mitchell for the local weather forecast." The news presenter faded and Jon's cheery face came on screen with a weather map of Yorkshire and Humberside behind him.

"The only forecast I can promise is that there will be rain and then more rain," he smiled. "There's no let-up in the string of low-pressure systems moving across the Atlantic and, one after the other, these are either moving up the west of Ireland and over Scotland bringing rain, with snow over the hills, or they are taking a southerly route up the English Channel, bringing rain and high winds to southern England.

"The upland Pennines are already waterlogged and further rain could cause local flooding along the river valleys. The Environment Agency has issued flood alerts for the Aire Valley, the Calder Valley and the Don Valley.

"With the spring tides coming early this year, the City of York is under considerable threat and the City Council has advised people, living in areas prone to flooding, to take valuables upstairs."

Robert and Christine Sykes were only paying scant attention, while Robert was serving up the evening meal. Christine was reading the local paper and finding precious little of interest.

"Anything interesting?" asked Robert.

"Don't know why I buy it," grumbled Christine. "There's a bit here suggesting we should take our furniture upstairs."

"Jon Mitchell has just been saying the same thing on the telly," said Robert.

"Well, thank God, we live on a hillside. Not much chance of flooding here."

"I'm glad we don't live in Marsden, though. Just think what damage would happen if Butterley Reservoir overflowed."

"There's no real chance of that happening," stated Robert. Despite an intense public campaign back in 2015 to save the iconic Victorian, stone-built spillway, Yorkshire Water plc had built a new concrete spillway. It had seemed to the campaigners that Yorkshire Water's sole motive was to remove a popular local tourist attraction that had received very indifferent maintenance over too many years and was in need of considerable renovation. The new concrete spillway was a scar on the countryside. But, to date, there had not been any intense rainfall to test the new concrete structure.

"Why should a 'once in 50,000 years flood' happen now? It's rained before and it'll rain again," he continued.

"But the land is so waterlogged," said Christine, "All over the country. Even where Sarah and Michael live down in Richmond, the river's swollen and travelling in and out of London is getting worse."

"Mm! Serves the buggers right for living down there!" muttered Robert. Louder, he said, "I was never happy for our lass to be persuaded to live down there. It might be well and nice to visit, but I'm always happy to get back home, where people are real and there's a decent fire to welcome you."

Robert put a plate of beef stew, boiled potatoes, carrots and broccoli in front of Christine. She grunted her acknowledgement, reached for the brown sauce and squeezed a goodly portion onto the side of her plate.

"You know perfectly well that she always wanted to use her degree and she did get a really good job in London with that Advertising Agency. She and Michael have made a good home for David and he's doing well at school. I don't know why you're always complaining about them being so far away. We see them often enough."

"After we got married," Robert replied, "My mum and dad lived in the next village, not 200 bloody miles away. That was good enough for us. Your mum and dad lived in the same street and I agree that was a bit of a pain. Always popping in and telling us what's what."

"You see, you're never satisfied!" Christine crowed as if she had won this minor skirmish. "My mum and dad were too close, but your daughter is too far away!"

"Mebbe you're right! It's just that they're not in Yorkshire and our David is turning into a right southern Jessie. Rugby Union, indeed. Why can't he play League like the rest of the lads in this family?

"Anyway, she doesn't work for Saatchi's anymore. She doesn't seem to work at all – not since our David was born." Having eaten the broccoli, Robert put down his knife and mashed the carrots and boiled potatoes into the gravy with his fork.

"I do wish you wouldn't do that," commented Christine. "It's not really good manners."

"Aye – so you say. But there's no one here but us. So it doesn't matter."

"You've done us a good stew this time, love," Christine commented.

They continued chatting and eating, going over the same old arguments which had been played many times over the years.

In London, even following three General Elections, the government was still grappling with the ramifications of leaving the European Union. In the early days following the Referendum, there had been a mood similar to 1940 after Dunkirk when, alone, Britain had faced the Nazi invasion of Western Europe. The spoken mood was of confidence, of blind belief that all would be well, that together we could and would come through. The unspoken mood, however, was very different. At the start, the city had defied all the odds and performed well, creating a false sense of optimism. With David Cameron and Theresa May gone, a brief flirtation with Boris Johnson and, subsequently, the Labour Party, the new Conservative prime minister and his cabinet had courted and gained the support of public opinion. Work was done to broker new economic deals to ensure that the fragile British economy might survive and even grow.

The extraordinary General Election in 2019 started much of that work, but subsequent elections had placed much of that work in jeopardy. With the passing of time and with a new government problems had inevitably arisen. The rise of a rather ungracious form of socialism initially had gained some favour with the younger voters. However, as the years passed, those supposedly left-wing students, who had been swayed by unsustainable promises of free education, graduated and entered the reality of work. Here they found a very different world where personal responsibilities outweighed political dogma.

After Boris Johnson, the Labour Party had formed a minority government, which very swiftly fell to a vote of no confidence. The Liberal Democrats were asked and refused to assist the Conservatives to set up another coalition. The Scots and the Welsh continued to court disaster with their agendas for independence and no one really knew what the Northern Irish wanted. The thorny issue of the hard border between Ulster and Southern Ireland was never really resolved but, despite that, relations with Europe at last started to improve. As the European economy continued to falter, the dream of a United Europe needed close allies if it was to succeed and as an increasing number of member states began to look more seriously at breaking away from Brussels, the hard line with Britain began to soften.

Although Britain's borders were now more secure, illegal immigration continued. Police numbers were again increasing in order to combat a growing degree of lawlessness. Seeing some of the criminal immigrants being deported, had originally created a mood of optimism, but slowly, inexorably, signs began to show that all was not well and that such optimism was misplaced. The golden age of continuing low unemployment was slowly coming to a close, demonstrated by the small but steady rise in those looking for work.

Investment in new public works, hospitals, airports, HS2 never seemed to happen and delivery from the NHS, local government and transport steadily worsened.

In the Cabinet Room of 10 Downing Street, the cabinet was holding its regular daily briefing.

"Prime Minister, you will have seen the latest unemployment figures, which will be published tomorrow. No sector of the economy is showing any improvement and, indeed, the growth of unemployment in the north east is now approaching 15%."

The Trade and Industry Minister broke down the national figures into the various parts of the United Kingdom. The picture was bleak in every area and the implications for the forthcoming General Election were very serious. The thought of another disastrous left wing government was the only real uniting matter for the Cabinet and each minister would sell his or her soul to avoid that. The Prime Minister had aged. Well, all his colleagues had aged. The responsibilities of running the country were taking their toll. Running the administration by relying on the Nationalists in Scotland and Wales and even those bloody Liberal Democrats who just would not lie down and die. The once elegantly dressed gentleman now looked old and his drive was considerably diminished.

"Colleagues." He looked round the cabinet table at the members of the cabinet. "The employment figures are not the only problems facing us at this time. Promises of increased exports to the Far East have not materialised. We continue to fall behind in our investment programmes. House building is a joke. The country's borrowing is far too high." His gaze finally fell on the Trade Secretary. "It is surprising to note that the only bright light in this unremitting gloom is the improvement in our relationship with the European Union."

"We have two years to pull this round. The days of relying on the press to give Labour a hard time have gone. The reality is that their left wing agenda continues to try to sell the public a set of policies that sound so good, but when the opportunity comes, Labour can deliver nothing except increased personal debt, increased unemployment, appalling trade figures and a worsening pound. I can still remember how the students cheered when Corbyn resigned.

"Today, our major threat comes from the consistent growth in popularity of the awful Liberal Democrats. Last year's council elections were disastrous and we now face the prospect of losing power yet again." He paused.

"We need a change of direction that will reconnect us with the voters. It must be a meaningful and long-lasting change of policy." Again, he paused and looked round once more. *Oh my Lord*, he thought, *they're going to leave it all to me.*

"So, by the end of next week, I want each Secretary of State to bring to Cabinet a proposal how their department will change direction, regain the initiative and demonstrate that the doomsters in the press are wrong. You will have seen the *Daily Mail*'s leader suggesting that leaving Europe was probably a wrong decision? Even the *Daily Mail*!" he added witheringly. He rose and he left his question hanging and the cabinet room.

At Richmond School, both David and John had finished their afternoon run and were showering.

"So, how long is this rain going to continue?" asked John.

"How do I know?" David looked at his pal expecting this to be the start of a leg pull.

But John was serious. "Well, you've been doing the research, so you must have some ideas."

"It's not an exact science, you know. Weather forecasting is a complicated business."

David explained in simple terms the movement of the mass of warm sea in the Pacific and how that movement was dependent on the direction of the trade winds.

"But does that make it rain here in England?" asked John.

"The weather systems created by El Nino move across the United States and Central America. The systems created by El Nino can cause tornados, hurricanes and massive rainfall. Mind you, the continued melting of the Thwaites Glacier in the Antarctic and the rise in sea levels is changing a whole load of systems. If a weather system from the Pacific gets sucked into the weather systems being created in the Caribbean, it can cross the Atlantic without too much difficulty."

John thought about this and then said, "I thought that hurricanes crossing the sea tended to decrease in severity."

"That's true to a degree, but the rain that's carried in the weather system will still come across and we've been having enough of that since last autumn."

"But why here this year?" persisted John.

"That's rather to do with the winds in the upper atmosphere and the weather systems over the Arctic. If they force the Atlantic systems to move southwards, then the western seaboard of Europe, including Great Britain, will catch the result. If, however, the Atlantic systems force the Arctic systems back, then the rain will often fall in the ocean or on the Scandinavian coastline. As I say, it's complicated."

Like two men in the saloon bar of a pub, they continued chatting about the weather, why some winters have frost and snow and others are just long, cold and wet.

Chapter 3
Wednesday – Eight Days to Go

The tornados in the Caribbean had caused massive disruption to shipping from Trinidad in the south, as far north as Jamaica. The wind speeds in Mexico and Texas had increased, but no structural damage had been caused. The rainfall in Galveston and Houston was intense and the weather systems were continuing to move to the east.

As he walked home, David's thoughts drifted back to the previous year when the long, warm spring had preceded a somewhat indifferent summer. He had been persuaded by his mother to join the local tennis club where he had been introduced to Jackie Bleasdale. She was pretty, with dark brown hair and brown, sparkling eyes. Standing about 5ft 3, with her head tilted slightly back, her shoulders were strong and squared and she had an exciting glint in her eye. David knew at once that she was not one to be messed about. She demonstrated an internal control which meant that she knew what she wanted and how to go about getting it. At the same time, she was fun, her conversation witty and her ideas outrageous. David fell for her in a big way and was now learning that having a girlfriend, playing rugby and doing his 'A's were an almost impossible, even a toxic mixture.

Almost every day, his thoughts would return to that moment when Jackie suggested that they explore the local woods on the weekend.

And so, in early May, David found himself cycling over to Jackie's home on the Sunday afternoon. He was met at the door by Jackie's mother and after some meaningless small talk on both sides, Jackie arrived, jumping down the stairs to the hall, dressed in denim jeans, a loose, white blouse, with her lustrous dark brown hair held back with a hair band.

"Come on," she instructed David, "If we don't get a move on, the sun will be setting."

"Do be careful, dear," intoned her mother. "And you as well, David," she added as an afterthought.

They almost fell through the front door, in their eagerness to get away. Grabbing their bikes, they cycled down the hill, over the small stone bridge and up a gentle incline to the track that led to the woods. There was a gate at the end of the track with some bushes on one side.

"We can leave our bikes here," said Jackie. "No one will see them because all the walkers come this way in the morning. It's too late in the afternoon for them now."

They passed through the kissing gate and, as they turned down the path on the right, Jackie took hold of David's hand. As their hands touched, David felt a tingle which started at his fingers, moved quickly up his arm and ended in his solar plexus.

"This way." Her voice sounded a little husky.

As they walked, the air felt warm under the trees and they moved closer together until it was easier for him to put his arm round her shoulders. She seemed to snuggle closer to him with her shoulder pressing into his armpit. He could smell the scented aroma of her hair and he felt his heart thudding with anticipation. He had never been as close as this to a girl before and he was completely consumed by the intensity of the moment.

The path went up a short rise and then dropped into a grassy clearing. Jackie led David across the grass to an enormous beech tree and pulled him behind it. They stepped into a small glade, seemingly cut off from the rest of the world. At the back, there was a large boulder, set into the hillside. To each side and above were small saplings and bushes. Between the boulder and the beech tree was a lawn of soft, new, green grass, with the shadows of the leaves dancing at their feet. It was like stepping into a private room.

"This is my secret place," she announced. "I have been coming here to be alone for as long as I can remember. You are the first person I've ever shown it to." She stood on her tiptoes and gently kissed his lips. "Let's sit down over here."

They sat down, side by side with their backs to the boulder. It was still warm from the sun. David pulled her to him and they kissed again. This wasn't the first kiss for David, but it was the first with a definite undercurrent of intent. She parted her lips and pushed her tongue between his lips and teeth. The feel of her tongue in his mouth was curiously exciting and he eagerly did the same. The intensity increased as she put her arms around his neck and pulled him to her. When they broke the kiss, they both gasped for air and grinned at each other. He reached for her again, but she pushed him away.

"Wait!" she whispered. "Kneel in front of me, like this."

She knelt on the ground and David knelt in front of her. The grass was soft and the earth was dry. She leant forward and kissed him lightly on the lips. With her left hand, she reached for David's right hand and placed it on her left breast. He gently squeezed it as, with her right hand, she undid the top two buttons of David's shirt before slipping her hand inside onto his chest. She lightly ran her index fingernail over his nipple, feeling it harden beneath her touch. David looked into her encouraging eyes, which seemed to dare him to follow suit.

As he undid the buttons of her blouse, he heard Jackie's intake of breath as she squared her shoulders, thrusting her small, pert breasts towards him. The collar of the blouse fell from her neck and the sleeves slipped down the tops of her arms. Jackie, in the meantime, was tugging David's shirt from his jeans and undoing the rest of his buttons. As she leant forward to pull his shirt down his arms, he smelled her hair and her skin. He noticed the downy hair on her forearms. His shirt dropped to his elbows and, letting go of her blouse, he straightened his arms and the shirt fell to the ground. She did the same, with exactly the same result. She grinned again and he gulped as he looked expectantly at the vision of beauty before him. He was beginning to feel uncomfortably restricted inside his jeans.

Jackie reached out with her left hand and hooked her middle finger into his waistband and pulled. David knelt upright and put his arms around her shoulders to the back of her brassiere where he fumbled with the catch. He hadn't realised that it was made of two hooks and eyes but after a short moment of confusion, he got the trick of it and the garment fell apart. Jackie pushed her shoulders forward and the straps fell to her elbows, revealing two small, pert but perfect breasts, each with its hardening nipple. Taking her hands from his waistband, she allowed her bra to fall to the ground, then started to undo his belt.

"This is really hard," she whispered. "Can you help me?"

20

David pulled the buckle free and the leather belt loosened. Jackie immediately undid the top button of his jeans and started to pull down the zip. Not to be left out, David reached out to Jackie's waistband, slipped two fingers of his right hand inside and, with his left, undid the button. He pulled down the zip, revealing a pair of pink Marks and Spencer knickers. He eased the jeans over her bottom, as she put her hand into his pants and gently freed his erection.

"Do you really want to do this?" he asked.

"Oh yes!" she replied. "I've dreamed of this moment since I first saw you at the club."

Gently, she pulled his jeans and underpants down his thighs and, as she leant over, she quickly popped a kiss onto the tip of his manhood. David could feel the throbbing so intently that he thought he would pass out. Jackie stood up and leaning on the boulder, pulled off her jeans. Standing there in just her pink knickers, David thought that she was the most beautiful thing he had ever seen. He stood up and started to pull off his trousers, but Jackie stopped him. She knelt down in front of him, to help him. She pulled off his shoes, socks and pants as well, leaving him as naked as Adam in the Garden of Paradise. This time, holding it gently in her hand, she kissed his erection more firmly and sucked the end into her mouth. He could feel the swirling of her tongue around his glans. He had never felt so tense, so electric. She pushed the tip of her tongue into the slit of his penis and the electricity shocked up the shaft and into the pit of his stomach.

"Would you like to do that to me?" she asked as she released his penis and got back to her feet.

"Well, I've never done anything like this," David stammered, not really sure what she meant.

"Neither have I," she replied. "But I'm sure you'll find the right way."

He knelt down, his face level with her flat stomach. Again, he found himself wondering about the downy hair on her torso. He reached up to the back of her knickers and gently pulled the waistband down over her buttocks. Slowly, a trimmed bush of curly, dark pubic hair emerged, together with a rich aroma of, well – of a woman. He could feel his erection throbbing as he pulled her knickers down her thighs, her legs. Daintily, she lifted first one foot and then the other, as he removed them altogether. He pressed his face to the bushy mound, breathing in the intoxicating scent of her sex. She stood above him with her legs apart and her hands on his head. Tentatively, he pressed his face to her mound, but her sex was too far, hidden between the tops of her thighs.

"I think it'd be better if you lie down," he suggested.

"OK." Jackie lay down with her head resting on the beech tree's base. She raised one knee, giving him a glimpse of the ultimate prize.

"Thanks," he replied in a voice husky with anticipation.

He knelt down in front of her and, with his chest on the grass, he placed his hand on her hair. She jumped slightly, when his finger began to explore her lips. She moaned. He gently opened them, so that he could kiss the moist, warm area within. She opened her legs wider, bending both her knees. To his surprise, a small nodule appeared, in a small penis-like sheath. He licked it and she gasped with the pleasure of it. When he took his tongue away, it retracted, so he tried, with his fingers, to keep it in view longer. She arched her back, thrusting herself at his mouth.

"Try to bite it gently with your teeth." He did as he was bidden and she was squirming with delight beneath him. He realised that her moistness had increased. The taste was like nothing on earth. He pushed in his tongue and was rewarded with a moan of unbridled delight.

"Oh God!" she cried. "I'm going to come." With complete awe and wonderment, David watched as she suddenly went completely tense with her back arched. She straightened her legs beneath him and brought her knees sharply together, at the same time holding the hair on the back of his head and pulling him to her. She shook all over and lay still.

He knew she wasn't dead because she was still pulling his hair and he could hear her breathing. Beneath him and crushed into the soft new grass, his erection was slowly deflating, but his desire was still strong. He looked more closely at her breasts rising and falling as she breathed in and out. There was a fine, very soft covering of downy hair, just like on her arms. Her chest and neck were red and there were small beads of perspiration on her forehead, caused by the intensity of her orgasm. She moaned gently and her eyelids flickered.

"Wow!" she gasped. "I've never felt anything like that before."

"Have you done this before?" he asked incredulously.

"Only in my dreams, using my fingers," she replied candidly.

"Oh! I see," David replied, feeling a bit silly.

"Well, I know you boys play with yourselves. I expect you've come before." Jackie smiled at him. "And I expect you want to now!" she added.

David rolled off her legs and onto his back. To his surprise, his erection had completely disappeared, but the intensity in his stomach and solar plexus was still there. Both he and Jackie watched as his stiffness quickly reformed. She took it in her hand, feeling the glans and the shaft.

"It's silky smooth," she said as she moved her fingers up and down the shaft. The head was full of blood and David was sure she could feel it throbbing. She gently drew her fingernail over the glans, causing his erection to jerk in her hand. David could feel a familiar intensity concentrating in his groin. He breathed in sharply.

"Are you OK?" she asked.

"Please don't stop." David was going bright red as Jackie's hand moved up and down the shaft faster and faster. Suddenly, he ejaculated and she laughed with delight.

"That was fantastic." He looked at her and, to his surprise, she bent over him to kiss his erection and suck the rest of his ejaculate into her mouth. She then kissed him on the lips, opening her mouth so that he could share his taste. After a brief moment of revulsion, he enthusiastically returned her kiss, putting his arms round her and holding her tightly to him, as if he would never let her go.

They sat, side by side, talking about inconsequentialities, as the sun was slowly setting in the west. As the air cooled, they dressed in companionable silence, each deeply moved by the other's intensity, before walking back to the bicycles.

Chapter 4
Thursday – Seven Days to Go

The rainfall over Texas, Louisiana, Mississippi, Alabama and Florida was now accompanied by record speed hurricanes causing millions of dollars in damage. There were states of emergency in Baton Rouge, Louisiana and Birmingham, Alabama. The National Guard was organising the evacuation of Atlanta, Georgia.

Further north, on the border of Canada and the Great Lake states, the snowfall was the deepest in living memory and as soon as the snow stopped falling, the temperature dropped to record lows. Power cuts were causing serious disruption in Chicago and Detroit. Niagara Falls had frozen solid and illegal immigrants were taking advantage of the frozen river to cross over into the USA from Canada. Because of the cold, many were dying in the attempt, as were many older people in the poorly appointed condominiums in the cities. All air travel had been suspended, temporarily.

In the southern islands of the Caribbean, a new system had formed which, after moving north had swung to the west through the Lesser Antilles and was now moving north east into the Atlantic.

The weather forecast followed the news on Thursday evening. The news was not particularly good because the economy was stalled, unemployment remained high and the problems in the Middle East appeared to be just as unsolvable now as they had been 2000 years before at the time of Christ, when the Jews had rebelled about being a part of the Roman Empire.

Nothing changes, thought Michael Varley. *You'd think, after all this time, that we might have learned by now how to live with each other*.

As so often appears to be the case, the weather forecast was also pretty grim. The storms in North America had featured on the news, but with widespread blackouts, there were few pictures. David had watched the tracking of the weather systems and concluded that this was all caused by the El Nino Effect, bringing the warm mass of sea water to the west coast of Southern America, although no comment of that was made by the newscaster. Nor was there any comment about the rising sea levels caused by the melting of the Thwaites Glacier.

"I sincerely hope we don't get that snowfall over here," Michael commented. "If it's causing that degree of disruption in the USA, then Britain would simply fall apart."

"I told you that my science teacher, Mr Smith, has asked me to do some research into how the El Nino effect might affect our weather systems over here." David responded.

"Yes, I remember saying that I hope it won't be diverting your attention away from your 'A' levels."

"It's supposed to form part of the General Studies paper," David reminded his father glibly. "The awful snows in Canada have been caused by a particularly intense La Nina last autumn."

"When I was a boy, it was accepted as common knowledge that the weather in America would be followed by similar weather over here, only a couple of weeks later."

"It's not really as simple as that," David replied. "It depends on the velocity and direction of the jet streams in the upper atmosphere and how low the temperature is over the North Pole. People don't seem to realise how important the wind is as far as the future weather is concerned.

"Anyway, I'd better get to my room and do some more revision."

David got up and quickly left the room. He did have some revision, but when the subject matter is rather dull, it doesn't come easy. He wanted to look more closely at the weather systems in the USA and to see what effect they might have on Europe.

He switched on his computer and waited for it to warm up. He entered his password and opened up the internet. He clicked on 'current weather map USA' and was rewarded with a number of maps showing the cyclones and the anticyclones, the winds, the temperature, the rainfall and even how these systems were tracking during the day. He moved onto the Caribbean, to see what was brewing. There appeared to be a warm front tracking northwest, between the mainland of South America and the Greater Antilles.

I wonder how many people realise that the Greater Antilles is a general term for Cuba, Jamaica and Haiti, he thought. *That weather front appears to be deepening. It might cause some concern if it links up with the latest weather coming in from the Pacific.*

He checked to the west and saw a front tracking up the west coast of Mexico, up the Gulf of California and into the western seaboard states. This was following the same track as the front which had veered to the East and caused so much damage over the past few days in Texas and Louisiana and, indeed, the snow in Canada.

Gosh! he thought, *This new front looks even more intense that the last one. I wonder where the old one's got to.*

He moved his mouse and found that the area of low pressure was now leaving the Eastern USA, just to the south of the St Lawrence and Labrador. It was being predicted to pass over the Atlantic just to the south of Iceland and the North of Scotland, finally moving into Scandinavia.

That'll bring heavy snowfall to Scotland, I expect, he thought. *Probably in a couple of days. Mm! And more rain for us. I suppose.*

Oh well, I'd better get some revision done. He texted John to check which subjects he was supposed to be doing and then sent a text to Jackie. She had also been busy revising so, recently, there had been very few opportunities to get together. David really hoped that their relationship wasn't drifting apart. After that intense afternoon in the woods, way back in May, for one reason or another, there had only been a few opportunities to be alone together. Being educated at different schools didn't help, of course, and the weather through the summer and autumn had been plainly awful. They had kept in touch through texting, but Jackie lived just a bit too far away to allow them to meet easily.

His thoughts continued to drift away from his studies. *It's going to be difficult if I get a place at Sheffield and Jackie gets her place at Bristol*, he thought. *I just wonder what she wants from me. It seems such a long time since we were last together.*

Across London, in his small house in Poplar, Fred Shemming was getting ready to go to his evening shift at the Poplar Fire Station on the East India Dock Road. He was a big man, six foot five, with broad shoulders, black hair and an easy manner. Popular with his colleagues and reliable in his work, he had been promoted to station commander at the early age of 28. Now 35 and married to his pretty West Indian wife, Dinah, he had two children aged 6 and 4, Fred was content in his work and with his life. He kept fit playing football and coaching the youngsters. An enthusiastic Christian, he was a church warden at his local Pentecostal Church. In his spare time, he was studying through the Open University for a degree in Business Studies.

It had been a quiet winter to date. The most serious incident had been a kitchen fire, when a pan of oil had been forgotten and caught fire. He had led Blue Watch that evening and the fire had been extinguished with no loss of life and surprisingly little damage to the property. Even more surprising was the reception he had received when he visited the property after it had been renovated. He was invited in by Mr and Mrs Khan, introduced to their children and offered tea. After discussing the reason for his visit and passing over the advice and leaflets concerning fire prevention, he suggested that the eldest boy, Adnan, a rangy lad of 8, might join the local football club.

But it had been a difficult season with the continual rain throughout the autumn, making the pitches unplayable on too many occasions. Adnan had fitted in well to the team and was becoming a reliable central defender. He had that uncanny ability to read a game and what he lost in speed he fully made up in anticipation. Fred was of the opinion that if Adnan could get his speed up, then he might even become a real prospect for the senior team, even the youth team at West Ham.

Out to the east, near Hadleigh in Essex, Thatched Barn Farm was a well-run and well-organised business. Predominantly arable, Martin Havers, the owner, had recently introduced a small herd of 25 Herefords. He had become increasingly concerned at the amount of chemicals that he sprayed onto the land each year. The soil had become as hard as concrete in the summer and thick mud in the winter. His yields were being driven down because of a lack of worms, to nourish and aerate the soil and he thought that some natural cow dung might redress the situation. His land stretched from the main road, down the slope and over the railway line, as far as Hadleigh Bay. The southern boundary gave way to the sea wall and, on the other side, the tidal mud flats.

When he discussed the suggestion of cattle with his wife, she was enthusiastically in favour. He explained that the quality of the soil was deteriorating and this was forcing him to spend far too much on fertilisers.

"I've been saying that for some years," replied Jennifer. Jennifer was a typical farmer's wife, rosy of cheek, bright of eye and becoming just a little plump. She did the books for the business, leaving Martin to get on with the ploughing, seeding and harvesting. Now that the children were grown up, the workload naturally increased, of course, as the available, free labour disappeared. Charlie, the eldest, worked in the city as a lawyer. Megan was dating the local blacksmith and happily pursuing her love of horses. The youngest, James, had joined the army and had recently been commissioned.

"I haven't calculated how much we might save on fertiliser, but natural dung will have the added benefit of encouraging worms back into the soil."

"I don't expect we will see any real, financial benefits for some time," said Jennifer. "And there will be additional costs for housing and feeding them over winter."

The experiment was reasonably successful and the cattle had thrived. After only five years, there had been a noticeable improvement in the land. The expenditure on chemical fertilisers was now contained and Martin was looking forward to seeing it reduce over the next few years.

Frustratingly, over the current autumn and winter, the weather forced him into a seemingly idle existence. He needed to get his land ploughed, but he couldn't get onto it. He had done all the necessary maintenance on his farm equipment, even spending time cleaning the plough and the harrow. All his spring seed was ready for planting. His elder son, James, was coming home for a fortnight's leave towards the end of February. He just hoped that the weather would relent sufficiently to get the fields ploughed.

The weather was good for Andy. Working as a cabbie in the city and the West End, the rain was creating a never-ending supply of fares. With the economy visibly stagnating, while the succession of weak Governments each appeared incapable of presenting a sensible manifesto for improvement, there was a general degree of depression throughout the country as everyone waited for the politicians to act. And to add to the misery, the weather had been so wet that an increasing number of people were ignoring the Underground and using cabs to get from the office to their stations. He had toyed with joining Uber but had found that there were no real benefits while he remained successful in picking up his fares on the street so, to date, his decision had been a good one.

He lived on his own in Kennington. He had previously been married for five years, but his wife had died in childbirth. Two days later, the baby had also died leaving him with no children and, having come to terms with his joint loss, he now preferred living on his own, appreciating the freedom. His wife's life insurance policy had paid off the mortgage, with a tidy sum left over. His income allowed him sufficient lassitude to get involved in his passion, photography. He specialised in panoramic scenes, especially sunrises and sunsets. Mind you, there had been precious few of either to write home about, over the past few months. He also dreamed of building a reputation as a fashion photographer and, somewhat to his surprise, he had been able to persuade a number of his fares to model for him.

He was parked on the London Wall rank, when a customer leaned into the cab and asked to be taken to Waterloo Station. It was raining again and Andy waited for the young lady to settle herself before setting off. She was soaking wet and her blonde hair was hanging down like rat tails, dripping with the rain.

"I see you got caught in the shower," he commented.

"Yeah," she replied. "It never seems to stop raining these days and my office is too far from the tube to walk easily."

"You seem to have a lot of stuff." Andy looked through his mirror as she settled her handbag, her shoulder work bag, her computer and her umbrella. "It can't be easy carrying that lot around."

"It isn't." She looked up and smiled. Her whole face lit up, the tiredness sloughing from her eyes. Andy turned onto Queen Victoria Street before crossing the Thames via Blackfriars Bridge for the short run to Waterloo.

"You a secretary, then?" he asked.

"Not really. I work for a couple of blokes who deal in finance and I have to keep track of all the contracts they do. It's all on the computer, of course, but with interest rates different all over the world, I have to make sure all the documentation is done to reflect the exact costs at the time of the deals. It's a bloody nightmare when the computers go down, because then everything has to be recorded by hand. They went down again, today. They say it's the weather, but I reckon it's because they're trying to do everything on the cheap."

As she chattered on, Andy watched her face and wondered whether she might be interested in doing some modelling work with him. She was quite tall, with an elegant neck and shoulders. Her face was slightly drawn with pale blue eyes. She looked tired, as though she alone carried all the responsibilities of her employers on her shoulders.

26

"You seem to be catching it all ends up," he commented. "Doesn't sound like 'job satisfaction' to me."

"It isn't, really," she agreed. "When the electrics go down, I have to take home all the paper trades and re-enter them into the systems to make sure that all the appropriate paper trails are up to date. It's really boring work. I was hoping, when we voted to come out of Europe, that the company I work for might relocate somewhere more exciting in Europe. But the exit negotiations took so long, everyone seems get used to doing business electronically. And," she added, "no one now seems to be moving abroad. So we're just stuck here in wet and miserable London, with barely enough to live on."

Just as Andy was exiting the roundabout outside the station, he wondered again whether she might be interested in earning a bit extra cash in hand.

"Do have enough time in your day to fit in another job?"

"Not really."

"Well, in my spare time, I do some photographic work. I'm always looking for new talent."

"Get out of here!" She laughed. "Me? Don't be silly! My face looks like a washed-out pair of jogging pants. But thanks for the laugh!"

He pulled up at the front of the station as she gathered her bags together. She paid the fare through the sliding window and he released the door. As she got out, he said, "Listen, here's my card anyway. Have a think about it. If you want to, give us a ring and we can take it further. It's up to you."

"Cheers." She put the card into her purse along with the change and walked into the station.

Andy watched her, tall, assured with her coat flapping around her legs, as she disappeared into the station. *Don't suppose I'll ever hear from her*, he thought.

The young lady walked into the station and looked for the trains to Richmond. She had about twenty minutes to wait and went to the newsagents to buy a magazine and a bar of chocolate for her short journey.

That was a strange suggestion, she thought. *I wonder what he sees in me. I suppose I look a bit vulnerable since Michael seems to have stopped seeing me. Mind you, I knew that would never last, but he has been a bastard, taking everything for granted and then just spitting me out. Will I ever learn?*

I wonder what sort of photos he wants of me. And I wonder how much he pays. I expect he will pay, but it'll never be enough and I suppose he'll just use me and then spit me out as well.

Turning over all these thoughts, she got out at Richmond and walked through the rain to her ground-floor apartment.

Chapter 5
Friday – Six Days to Go

Over in America, the new weather system had now moved out into the Atlantic. Although the winds had been strong and the rainfall heavy, it hadn't added significantly to the damage of previous week in the other states. It was now tracking eastwards at a rather leisurely pace towards the Azores.

The previous system was combatting a large anticyclone centred over Greenland. This was having the effect of slowing down its passage across the Atlantic and at the same time making it deeper and more vicious. It was currently to the south east of Labrador.

The clear up in the southern states had begun and interstate travel had been resumed.

In the United Kingdom, after all the rain of the previous week, the sun had made an appearance, although there was no warmth in it and the wind stayed cold. The temperature had dropped, but everyone was hopeful that a full football programme would be played over the coming weekend.

In the city, Andy was taking the day very steadily. He knew, now that the rain had gone, that his workload would be light. He wondered whether it might be worth while taking the day off.

David went to school with the promise of a school match on the Saturday morning, should the pitches be playable.

If the wind stays, it'll keep any possibility of frost off the pitch, he thought. *It'll also help to dry it out. Then we just might get a match at last.* He sent a text to his gran up in Yorkshire, telling her that he might be playing a school match the next day.

Up in Yorkshire, the sun had also made a surprising appearance.

"Well, love," said Robert. "I didn't expect to see the sun today. But it's still welcome."

"I wouldn't hold your breath." Christine answered him in her normal, pragmatic manner. "There's no warmth in it."

"I reckon! The wind's dropping as well."

"Then we're going to have frost, aren't we?"

"After all that rain, if the temperature gets low enough, then that could cause some damage. It won't do the roads any good and we'll only get more potholes."

"I don't know about you, but all those promises given by the Brexit people, you'd think that some of the saved money could have been spent on our roads."

"Anyway," continued Christine, "I've had a text from our David this morning. He reckons they'll be playing their school match tomorrow, if the frost holds off."

"Well, it should do, down in that there soft southern Jessie country!"

The appearance of a thin, wintery sun in Essex had made precious little difference to Martin's day. The land was still too sodden to work, but he hoped that the wind would start the process of drying the topsoil.

We'll need at least three weeks of this, he thought. *And that'll still not be enough. Could do with a week of hard frost as well, to break up the soil.*

He walked towards the cowshed, just to check that all was well. His cattle had all been under cover since the beginning of October and the cost of winter feed was beginning to hit Martin's pocket. He wondered whether the cost of the feed was less than the cost of fertiliser for the land.

Down in the East End, Fred Shemming was coming off the night shift. It had been another long night of inactivity. His log showed no incidents, not even a false alarm.

Well, at least I've had the opportunity to look at the importance of the city to the British economy, he thought to himself.

As he walked home, he popped into Rajinder's to buy the *Daily Express*. For weeks, the editorial had been slating the government for its apparent lassitude over most aspects of British life. Week by week, comments were growing ever more harsh, as though the paper was shifting its political stance to the left.

"Morning, Raj!" he greeted the diminutive owner. "Any good news at all?"

"Nothing, mate." Raj replied in the cockney twang demonstrating his third-generation status. "It says this sunshine, if that's what it is, will only last a day or two and then we'll be back to more bleedin' rain."

"Do you reckon we'll get a match tomorrow?"

"Depends whether the pitches have dried out enough and if the rain holds off. You have any trouble last night?"

"Nope! Like a graveyard. Not a cat stirred; not a dog stirred!"

Fred paid for his paper and sauntered off to his home. Dinah was waiting for him in her nightie and dressing gown, with his full English already cooked and just needing two eggs to be fried.

"Hi, sweetheart," he murmured as he nuzzled her neck. "Have you done all this for me?" He looked at his plate piled with bacon, sausage, tomatoes, baked beans and fried bread. "You certainly know the way to this man's heart."

"Don't you be putting on any airs and graces with me," Dinah answered, as she cooked the eggs. "You say the same every morning!"

He stood behind her and slipped his arms round her waist, opening her dressing gown. He cupped her breasts, one in each hand. As he walked home, he knew that she wouldn't be dressed yet, although very soon their two boys would burst through the door.

"And you can stop your silly antics as well, while I'm cooking," she chided, gently slapping at his hands. But he knew, as he felt her nipples hardening, that she was happy to be fondled. He turned her round, bent down and kissed her hard on the lips. She put both her arms round his neck, which raised her nightie to reveal her shapely brown thighs. He stood up straight, lifting her off the floor as though she was a toy. "Stop it," she giggled. "The boys will walk in."

"That makes it all the more exciting, but I suppose you're right," he grumbled as he put her down. "Sunny side up please." Pretending that he wasn't disappointed, he sat down and started to read his paper.

"Raj says that we might get a game tomorrow," he commented. "If the rain holds off. There's more rain forecast for later, but no one seems to know when."

"It'll only make for more washing, when they come back all dirty."

"You know you love it when they have a good time and win."

She put the eggs onto the plate and then placed the plate in front of him. "Now, eat up and keep yourself strong, because I've got plans for you." She whispered into his ear, allowing her breasts to rub invitingly against the back of his neck. She went to the door and called to the boys that breakfast was ready and that they mustn't be late for school.

At school later that morning, David had a word before the physics lesson with Mr Smith.

"I was looking at the weather systems in America, last night, sir." He hesitated.

"Go on," replied his teacher.

"Well, it just seems to me that we could be in for a bit of bad weather towards the middle of next week."

"Why?" Mr Smith was well aware of David's intelligence, but was also cautious as he didn't want David to get cocky with this new fad.

"You remember I researched the effect of El Nino on weather systems in the United States? And you then asked whether the same effect was felt over here?" David looked up at Mr Smith.

"Go on," he repeated.

"Well, it seems that it does. The weather front that created so much rain in the southern United States and all that snow up on the Canadian border – well, you'll have seen the enormous amount of damage, power lines destroyed, all flights in the US cancelled."

"Go on." Once again, he repeated.

"That weather front is now over Labrador and it's continuing to deepen. There seems to be some form of anti-cyclone over northern Greenland, which is holding up its progress a bit. But if it deepens anymore and then continues across the Atlantic to Scandinavia, we'll probably see a repeat of those winds and the rain over the north of England and Scotland. There's another big anti-cyclone over Finland and Northern Russia, which could also slow its progress."

"Surely, there's nothing unusual in all this. It sounds like pretty normal winter weather to me."

"But that's not all. There's a second depression which has just left the West Indies and seems to be moving quite fast along a more southerly trajectory. I've estimated that both of these depressions will arrive in European waters at much the same time. Both are deepening and the attendant winds are very strong."

"What are you actually saying, David?" Mr Smith wasn't really patronising the boy, rather he was encouraging him to present a case however far-fetched it might be.

"Look, sir! Putting it simply, the winds from a depression off the Scandinavian coast will blow southwards, forcing sea water down the North Sea towards the Thames estuary. A depression over southern England will have a similar effect, but that'll force seawater eastwards up the English Channel. There could be widespread flooding in Holland and Belgium, also northern France, but the worst problems could well be in London."

"That does sound a bit dramatic to me, David. After all the Thames Barrier was built to combat just such an event. Anyway, it's time to start your Physics revision."

David felt as though he had been brushed off, rather like an irritating wasp at a picnic. Somewhat disgruntled, he took his place next to John Dickinson and opened his physics textbook and checked his notes. But rather than concentrating on the lesson, his mind was drifting. He wondered whether the storms would reach Britain early enough to affect the Saturday match. Probably not, he concluded, but his thoughts then drifted to how bad the storm might be. Outside the classroom window, the sun was struggling to make an impression through a layer of low, thin cloud.

His thoughts also drifted to Jackie Bleasdale. They often did as they now seemed to be reduced to keeping in touch only by email and Facebook. They hadn't seen each other for weeks. There had been a plan to go to a couple of parties over Christmas, but Jackie had gone down with a bout of flu and then her family had gone away for a few days. It just didn't seem to be working anymore. Jackie had promised to come over for a school match, but there hadn't been any since the New Year. *Until tomorrow*, he thought excitedly. *I must send her a text!*

Surreptitiously, he reached into his pocket and took out his iPhone. Under the desk, he silently switched it on. The screen appeared with the familiar time and date. He swiped his thumb across the screen from left to right and entered his code. All his icons appeared and he selected text. He tapped the icon for writing a message and entered Jackie's name.

"Hi Jackie," he wrote. *"Been 2 long since we met. Got a match 2mrow. Any chance you cd get here for 2.30. Playing Streatham Comp. Should be a good game bcuz no sport so far this term? We'll both be wanting to knock 7 bells out of each other!! Hope you can. Let me know. Love David xxx"*

He pressed 'SEND' and put his phone away.

Just over 10 miles away, Jackie was supposedly revising history, when she heard her phone vibrate. She reached down, got it out of her bag and looked at the message.

Now, that is surprising, she thought. *Not a peep since New Year and, suddenly, he wants me to drag over to Richmond tomorrow.*

Over the autumn, Jackie had tried to concentrate on her revision, at the same time seeking more independence from her parents. It was true that her thoughts of David receded a little as she pushed her own boundaries, but her memories of their meeting back in May, still remained strong. She hoped that they would be able to see each other more often, but the disappointing weather reduced any opportunities to repeat that experience. They were together on a number of occasions, but the chance to get really close just hadn't happened and that was very frustrating. She still reminisced over the intensity of their first meeting, but other normal distractions for a teenage girl had helped her thoughts of David to drift.

Mind you, I'm not doing anything tomorrow so it might be fun to catch up again.

She texted her reply, saying that she would be at Richmond School at 2.15. As she pressed SEND, she felt her heart miss a beat and her stomach muscles contracted causing a pleasurable flutter down to her very essence.

Chapter 6
Saturday – Five Days to Go

The northern depression had moved from Labrador to Greenland, where it deepened in intensity and the local temperature dropped. The winds in the Atlantic, to the south of Greenland had previously slackened, but now, encouraged by the lessening of the anti-cyclone, they were increasing again to storm force.

The southern depression, although warmer, was also deepening as it moved to the southwest of the Azores. The wind speeds were gale force, but that was not unusual.

Both weather fronts were approaching the area of high pressure over the European land mass and, between the two, there was an area of calm, dry weather.

When David woke on Saturday morning, he jumped enthusiastically out of bed and went to the window. His bedroom overlooked the back garden, facing east. Their neighbour's back garden was beyond the bottom hedge and that house was a mirror image of the Varley's house. Although there were trees at the bottom of the garden, David knew that Mrs Potterton, if she were looking, would be able to see him, standing at the window, quite naked. He liked Mrs Potterton, even though she was older than his mum and dad. She was a widow and had done some babysitting for David, when he was very young. Still attractive, she intrigued David, especially as she was in the habit of hanging out her washing while still wearing her dressing gown. Although he wasn't completely sure, it appeared to David that, like him, she was quite at home sleeping in the raw, but he had never been able to confirm this. Mind you, it had given him the opportunity to speculate on many evenings, just before dropping off to sleep.

David hadn't seen Mrs Potterton since October, because the weather had been so awful, so it was a bit of a surprise to see her that Saturday morning. As she reached up to peg out a blouse, she must have seen him standing at the window. She reached a bit further along the washing line, allowing her dressing gown to gape open, giving David more than a glance of her thigh. He felt a stirring as he watched, mesmerised. Facing her neighbour's windows, Mrs Potterton bent down to the basket. The top of her dressing gown fell open, somewhat invitingly David thought, giving him a perfect view of the swell of her breasts and her cleavage. He couldn't see her nipples, of course, but as she stood up, she gave him a half wave and a smile. He waved back!

What a great start to the day, he thought, as he wrapped his towel round his waist and wandered to the bathroom for his shower. His half erection was already diminishing and he knew that he had a maximum of ten minutes before his father would want to shower. His grandfather, during a family holiday in Yorkshire a few years before, had described his son-in-law's daily ablutions as a shit, shower and a shave. Ever afterwards, Michael's time in the bathroom each morning was known as the three 'shushes'.

Whistling to himself, he dressed and ran down the stairs to the kitchen where his mother was preparing breakfast.

"That smells really good," he said appreciating the aroma of bacon and eggs.

"Well, you've got a match today and it might be the only match you get this term, so I thought you'd better be as prepared as possible."

"Cheers, Mum!"

David sat down and drank a glass of orange juice, before eating his cooked breakfast. He glanced at the paper but saw no news of the impending storm.

Perhaps they don't realise, he thought. *I don't think I've got this wrong, but Mr Smith was pretty dismissive. I don't suppose he's really interested in the weather.*

He was finished before his father made an appearance. "Looks like you'll be lucky today," he remarked as he retrieved the *Daily Telegraph* from his son. "You should get the whole match played."

"Jackie has told me that she might come and watch," said David. His mother's ears pricked.

"We haven't heard that name recently," she commented.

"Well, we've both been pretty busy with revision stuff and the weather's been too bad to be cycling over to her house. It'll be better when I've passed my Driving Test and can borrow the car."

"What?" David's father sat up straight. "I'm not so sure about that."

"Perhaps I could have an old banger, instead," David suggested.

"No!" said Sarah. "If you're going to have a car, then it'll have to be in good condition."

Michael felt that this conversation was getting out of control, so he sought to regain the parental authority. "If you get decent grades in your exams and win your place at Sheffield University, then I'll look into getting you a car. If not, then you'll have to get into the workplace, earn sufficient money and buy your own." He picked up the paper, wondering what the response would be.

"Thanks, Dad," said David, trying not to smirk. "That seems a fair deal to me."

He got down from the table, collected his rugby bag and humming a quiet tune, he forced himself to saunter out of the house. As soon as he was on the pavement, he punched the air as though he had scored the winning goal in a cup final.

It only took him twenty minutes to walk to the school. He knew he would be early, but he had previously arranged to meet up with John and the team coach to discuss in detail the tactics they would use.

In Hadleigh, at Thatched Barn Farm, Martin Havers announced at breakfast, that he would try to plough the top paddock. "I can't really do any harm," he suggested to Jennifer, "Because it's the field that drains the quickest and, so far, it's had the least attention from the cattle. The ground should be firm enough to take the tractor and the plough."

"Just you be careful," said his wife. "I know you! You'll find it OK to start with and then you'll just press on, even if it starts to become impossible. The bottom corner always stays wet longer than the rest. So, if you find it getting difficult, come home."

"I know. I'll be careful. But this sunshine and on a second day is just too good to miss." And with that, he went through the door into the yard.

Walking towards the barn, he was glad of the time taken over the autumn and winter to service all his vehicles. It would be a matter of mere moments to hitch the plough to his trusty Massey Ferguson. The sun had lifted his spirits and he felt that, at last, spring might be on the way. As a countryman, he should have known better.

The tractor started first time and he manoeuvred it towards the plough. He reversed into the appropriate position and put on the handbrake. Getting down, he went to the back and hitched the plough to the tractor, ensuring that the bolt was firmly in place. He half lifted the plough, so that he could drive through the barn door and then lifted the plough fully upright for the short journey to the top paddock. After passing through the gate, Martin again got down to look more closely at the state of the ground.

We might just get away with this, he thought. *But I'll have to start at the top and plough back and forth, rather than up and down.*

With that, he turned his mobile phone to his chosen music, 'hits of the 1960s', put in his earplugs and set off to the top of the field. At the top right-hand corner, he turned parallel with the hedge that was the northern boundary, dropped the plough and set off westwards leaving a furrow of clean soil, still shiny with moisture, but not sticky like mud.

At the far end, he lifted the plough and swung the tractor round to face the opposite way. With the big rear tractor wheel running in the new furrow, he turned the plough over and dropped it ready for the second run. The second run was always more difficult than the first, because the line had to be kept. This meant that Martin had to keep swivelling in his seat, ensuring that the tractor's direction was correct and that the rear wheel was in the furrow and not on the newly turned earth. Despite more than thirty years' experience, Martin was always surprised that it took two or three furrows before his standard reached a satisfactory level.

With luck, I'll get this done by lunchtime, if it's not too wet lower down.

After breakfast, Fred Shemming was getting ready to meet his youth team. The previous evening, he had telephoned a pal who was involved with a team of similar age and ability based in Canning Town. He worked for the Parks Department of the London Borough of Newham and knew that there was a football pitch available up to midday on the Canning Town Recreation Ground, just off Newham Way. Through the Fire Service, Fred was able to borrow a minibus and he had already contacted all his team, instructing them to be ready at the Poplar Recreation Ground near to the Fire Station at nine o'clock. He now drove to the meeting place and was pleased to see all the boys, including Adnan, were gathered there, waiting for him. He stopped the van and got out.

"Morning, boys! Come on, let's get going." He opened the side and rear doors. All the bags were dumped in the back and the boys got in the side. Adnan got in the front passenger seat and put on his seat belt.

"You ready for this, Adnan?"

"Yes, Coach. We were just saying that it's been ages since we last played and we're all going to be a bit rusty."

"The boys at Canning Town are a good bunch and they're well coached so they'll give you a good run. You'll have to concentrate hard on your positioning because they've got a pretty nippy striker. Mind you, they'll be just as rusty."

They chatted together as Fred drove down the East India Dock road, over the flyover and onto Newham Way. It wasn't a long journey and very soon they were parked at the Canning Town rec, debussed and ready for action.

Jackie Bleasdale decided to get the bus from Wimbledon to Richmond. She had got out of bed a little later than planned and knew that she would be late. She would miss the kick off by a good twenty minutes, she estimated.

After grabbing a slice of toast, she put on a coat and scarf and set off, walking to the bus stop. She had decided to wear her dark jeans and boots, with a warm T-shirt under a long woolly jumper.

As she got on the bus, she began to feel more excited at seeing David again. Although she had been busy with her revision and her local friends, she now realised how much she had missed him. She had regularly replayed their time together in her mind, especially in bed before going to sleep. As she settled at the front of the bus, upstairs so she could see the road ahead, she felt a tingle of anticipation begin to build in her lower stomach.

At Richmond School, David, John and their coach had been talking tactics. They all knew that the team wasn't match fit and that it was bound to be a tight game, filled with errors. At midday, a minibus drove into the carpark next to the pitch and the opposition began to disembark. David, John and their games teacher went to meet the opposition.

Andy invariably started work late on a Saturday. He usually used the time to tidy up his house and do his weekly shopping. He also spent some time with his photos that he kept in date order on his computer. This Saturday was no different. After a quick breakfast of cereal and tea, he had driven to the big Sainsbury's on Brixton Hill.

He was in the tinned vegetables aisle when his mobile started to ring. "Hi! Andy here," he answered.

"Oh! Hello," said a lady's voice, somewhat hesitantly. "I don't expect you'll remember me, but I was a customer in your cab on Thursday. You took me to Waterloo Station…" Her voice trailed off.

"Yeah, of course I remember," he replied, wondering who on earth this lady might be. "How can I help?"

"Well, you mentioned that you might be able to get me some extra work. We didn't have time to discuss any details, but you gave me your card."

Andy was rather surprised that someone should have called him. It was usually the other way around, with him getting the contact mobile number and following it up. He only used the business card to demonstrate that he was pukka and to put people at ease.

"Yeah. I might have something for you." Thinking quickly, he added, "Perhaps we could meet to discuss what you're looking for and whether I might be able to help."

"I don't know. Perhaps this isn't a very good idea."

"No, no. Hang on. If we meet for a coffee, you'll be able to see what's what and if you don't like it, then you can walk away. There's not much point in calling and then doing nothing about it."

"Well, I suppose that's fair," she answered. "Where would be a good place to meet?"

"Well, I drive a cab, so I can get to most places without much difficulty. Where are you?"

"Richmond," she replied.

"If you tell me where we can get a decent coffee, I can meet you there."

"There's a Costa Coffee on the Quadrant."

"Yeah. I know it. That's OK. When's good for you?" he asked. Then he added, "I could be there at about half past two this afternoon."

"All right"

"By the way, what's your name?"

"Alice."

The game in Canning Town followed the usual pattern for an under 10s soccer match. Twenty boys, plus two goalkeepers and one referee, chasing about a field, following a white leather ball. From above, the twenty boys looked, for all the world, like a school of fish or a flock of birds, twisting and turning without any seeming purpose.

On the ground, however, it was rather different. Fred had been trying to teach his team that position and passing will always be superior to the collective chasing after the ball. Adnan completely understood this and, using his ability to read a game, he stood out from the crowd. Suddenly, the ball came to his feet and, looking up, he saw that his right wing was slightly detached from the crowd. He kicked the ball to a point between the wing and the touchline. More by luck than judgement, the pass was exquisitely weighted and completely wrong footed the defence. The wing chased after it, taking it deep into the opposition half. He only had the goalie to beat, as he entered the box. Instead of advancing to make the shot more difficult, the goalkeeper appeared rooted to the spot and the winger slotted the ball between him and the upright. Goal!

When the game was over and the boys were back in the minibus, before setting off, Fred talked to them, congratulating Bill, the winger, on his goal. He carefully explained that Bill's opportunity had come as the result of Adnan's pass, which was exactly what he had been trying to teach them during their midweek training sessions. Adnan and Bill glowed with pride and the others began to think it through on the short journey back to Poplar.

At eleven o'clock, as Martin reached the end of yet another furrow, he stopped. Turning off the engine, he took out his coffee flask. *Mm,* he thought, *I've done about a quarter and it looks OK. This field has drained better than I thought and the plough has done its job well.*

He sat back and stretched his back, listening to the music in his headphones. He looked up to the pale blue sky and then back over his furrows. A few seagulls had gathered and were feeding on the worms that had been disturbed.

There really aren't many birds, he muttered to himself. *I must keep this field as open pasture after the next harvest and put the cattle on it. Then it will need some decent muck worked into the soil to improve it. Mind you, it's going to take some time to get the quality up all over the farm.*

He looked to the west, towards Tilbury and London and then to the east towards Southend. He could see no indication of a change in the weather. The sun was shining and the rest of the field was waiting his attention. He threw out the dregs from his coffee mug, put away the flask, started the tractor's engine and set off once more.

Over in Richmond, David and John with the rest of the team had run onto the pitch to be confronted by the opposition from Streatham Comprehensive.

"They don't seem too big," David muttered to John. "We should be OK here."

"Depends on how well they've been organised and coached," John replied.

"At least they'll be no more match fit than we are."

"Maybe." John looked at David. "We've got to keep possession as much as possible. No kicking it away," he instructed.

David kept looking towards the touchline, to see whether Jackie had arrived. There was no sign of her when the referee called the captains together for the toss. John lost and the opposition chose to kick off.

The game followed an expected pattern of over-enthusiasm, tempered by a growing tally of penalty kicks. Without an opportunity to play for most of the term, both teams had realised that it would take a little while for the players to settle into any rhythm and reduce the knock ons and off sides. The referee, fully understanding this, tried to play as much advantage as possible, even though this benefitted the Streatham fly half who, scooping up a loose ball, passed sweetly to his left. His inside centre caught the pass and kicked over David's head. He was aiming for a deep touch, but slightly sliced his punt and the ball went towards the try line instead. The Streatham left wing was fast and ran inside the Richmond fullback, took the ball on a lucky bounce and went over to score in the corner. The try was not converted and the score was still 5-0 at half time.

Looking towards the entrance to the playing fields, David had noticed Jackie's late arrival, just before the Streatham winger scored. His heart jumped and he immediately lost all coordination in his hands.

While he was sucking his half-time quarter orange, he waved to Jackie and felt quite giddy when she waved back. She was smiling and looked so attractive in her tight jeans and sweater. She had allowed her sheepskin coat to fall open in what was a quite normal manner but to David it appeared to be extraordinarily provocative.

The teams changed ends and Richmond kicked off. As fly half, this responsibility fell to David. He kicked high, but too long and the ball went straight into touch.

"Come on, David," said John. "I know Jackie's here, but you must concentrate on your game, not her."

"Right," David muttered. He put Jackie into the back of his mind, while John marshalled his scrum. Streatham put the ball in on the halfway line, but Richmond produced a sudden, concentrated push which completely surprised the Streatham scrum. The ball popped out on the Richmond side and the scrum half took it forward 10 metres before being brought down. Curling round the ball, he presented it to his flanker who passed it to David. David was lying slightly deeper than normal, as he had also been momentarily surprised by the Richmond shove. He took the ball on the burst, did an immediate sidestep completely wrong footing the opposing fly half and sprinted towards the right-hand corner flag. He only had the fullback to beat, who had been lying deep all game and was now swiftly cutting off David's line of attack.

He took a quick glance to his left and saw a Richmond shirt on his shoulder. He drew the Streatham fullback closer before passing the ball to his outside centre, giving him an open opportunity to simply catch the ball and score under the posts. David retrieved the ball, placed it and converted the try.

"Let's do that again." John encouraged his team as the Streatham side was lining up for the kick off. The fly half drop kicked the ball to the Richmond twenty-five metre line. The ball was caught cleanly by the scrum and a maul formed. Slowly, the Richmond team advanced up the field, lost possession which then allowed the Streatham team to move forward. This was the pattern for the rest of the half, neither side being able to break the deadlock and create an advantage. It sapped the strength of the boys and they began to make more and more silly mistakes that even the referee was unable to ignore. Scrappy, tiring and totally unspectacular, everyone breathed a sigh of relief when the final whistle was blown and the referee said, "No side."

The Streatham team lined up on the touchline, creating a passage through which the Richmond boys passed. There was some backslapping and a few words of congratulation. In their turn, the Richmond boys also lined up allowing the Streatham boys to pass through in the time-honoured manner at the end of all rugby matches. As David turned away, he heard his name called. It was Jackie. The boys were already disappearing into the club house, so he walked over, all thoughts of the match receding rapidly from his mind.

"Hello!" He looked at her and wondered why they hadn't found much more time together over the past six months. "How are you?"

"I'm great," she replied, moving closer to him. "Did you win?"

"Er, well, yes. I think we did." David had forgotten all about the match as he drank in the vision standing in front of him. He breathed in her warm, welcoming scent. Her coat was still open and David could see the beguiling swell of her small, pert breasts under the sweater. She leant closer to him and kissed him on the cheek.

"To the victor the spoils," she whispered into his ear, pulling him towards the side of the club house. Despite feeling so tired after such a gruelling game, David could feel his lower stomach stirring. She pulled him into a passage, between the clubhouse and a storage shed. He started to put his arms round her, but she stopped him by opening her coat so that he could slip his arms round her inviting body, under the coat. As the coat fell back around them, he felt the warmth of her and he kissed her hard on the lips. She opened her mouth and gently pushed her tongue into his. It was like an electric shock and had an immediate effect on him.

"I'll have to get my shower," he muttered. "I'm all muddy."

"Well, you can't go in like this," she giggled, squeezing his erection.

She pulled him further back between the club house and the shed, where it was darker.

He moaned as she took hold of his hand and slipped it under her sweater and T-shirt. David needed no further invitation and felt her nakedness up from her stomach to her ribs and her breasts.

"Bloody hell!" he exclaimed. "You're not wearing a bra!"

He looked round, guiltily, but they were quite alone. She pulled urgently at the cord of his shorts and slipped her hand inside. She could feel his manhood standing hard as iron as her finger moved down its length. Her knees felt weak as David's left hand moved up her spine, rucking up her jumper. As he held her close with his left arm, she allowed his right hand to find and fondle her left breast. Her nipple hardened and ached with exquisite pleasure as he kissed her hard on the mouth, their tongues entwined like two baby eels. She undid the button at the top of his shorts and the second button, allowing them to slip over his buttocks. He undid the top button of her jeans and pulled down the zip. He put his hand inside the waistband.

Crikey, he thought, *no knickers, either. What am I getting into?*

He pushed his fingers gently between the lips of her sex, hearing her moan with pleasure as he found her clitoris, already extended. She was moist and warm as she drew his erection closer to her. Urgently, she pushed down her jeans below her knees and then, opening her knees, she pulled his penis between her legs. David pushed gently and, as Jackie arched her back with her jeans slowly slipping down to her ankles, he felt the glans suddenly move inside her secret warmth. He put both his hands behind her, holding her buttocks one in each hand, and lifted her completely off the ground. As he held her tighter, he felt her compliant body move closer to his. She bent her legs until her boots were pressing against the shed wall. She opened her knees wider, which allowed her to accommodate his complete length. As she arched her back, her head moved away from his and, with her bottom supported by his hands, she lifted up her sweater, exposing both her pert breasts with their rock-hard nipples.

"Push harder," she murmured. And then, as he complied, "Oh God, that's wonderful! I'm going to come."

Locked inside her, David felt the same, feeling her body convulsively contract around him. He pulled out, wondering if he would burst, as Jackie threw her arms around his neck and held him tight to her. His penis erupted over her lower stomach and feeling the sudden warmth, she straightened her legs until her feet were on the ground, then she let go of his neck, squatted in front of him and sucked out the rest of his ejaculate. Standing up, she pulled up her jeans, did up the button and the zip, and rubbed the rest of his ejaculate off her tummy with her T-shirt, before pulling her sheepskin coat tighter around her.

"Now, was that worth waiting for?" she murmured with a small smile, her eyes dancing with excitement.

"Oh, yes!" David replied, doing up his shorts. "But I will have to get inside for my shower. People will be wondering where I am."

"Always the practical one," she teased.

"When can I see you again? There is so much I want to know about you."

Somewhat coquettishly, she replied, "I'll send you a text when I'm free. I've got to revise all next week for the exams, but I might be free next Saturday."

"That sounds good. Can you wait now until I've had my shower and we could go out this evening, perhaps...?" he trailed off.

"Sorry, no." She wrinkled her nose and looked at her watch. "I'm going to have to dash to catch my bus."

She started to walk away, but he caught her arm and stopped her. They kissed again.

"Must go," she said. "I'll text you." She walked away down the drive to the main road.

For a moment, he stood stock still and watched her go, before turning to go into the club house. At the gate, Jackie hesitated and turned back, but all she saw was the closing door.

During the afternoon, after his break for sandwiches and the rest of the coffee from his flask, Martin Havers had continued to plough the top paddock. As usual, his wife was right, because the ground had become increasingly wet as he had slowly worked his way down the field. When he stopped for his lunch break at about 1pm, Martin noticed that he had ploughed just over half the field, although he was expecting to have completed at least two thirds.

It's getting stickier now, he thought. *I must be careful, especially in that bottom corner. Anyway, at this rate, I won't get there before dark.*

He munched his cheese and homemade pickle sandwiches and drank the rest of his coffee, listening to Classic FM on his headphones.

Just lower down the field, Martin studied a slight dip in the land, mentally noting that he should swing the tractor round with more care at that point, especially as the ground was getting wetter. He packed away his plastic box and thermos, restarted the engine, dropped the plough and set off once more.

When the tractor crossed the width of the field towards the west, Martin noticed that the plough was getting easier, but as he ploughed back towards the east, the ground became wetter and stickier. On approaching the dip, he had noticed earlier, instead of turning in a loop to the left while switching the plough, Martin decided to do a three-point turn. He lifted the plough, turned to face down the hill and stopped. Putting the tractor in reverse, he realised that the dip was steeper than he had realised and as the tractor reversed up the slope, the big, ribbed rear wheels had to bite deeply into the earth in order to retain traction.

Still facing downhill, he reversed the plough and gently turned to his right in order to set the plough for the next furrow. He was soon back on firmer ground and, looking back, Martin noted that the next five or six turns would all have to be done with greater care. He stopped to look at the lie of the land and how the field sloped more steeply just at that point. He decided that he would complete the next twelve furrows, taking great care while turning in the dip, before calling it a day, because by then he would be losing the sun and the field would be getting increasingly difficult.

Alice got off her bus in Richmond and walked slowly towards the Costa Coffee at the Quadrant. When she arrived, she saw that Andy was already there, sipping an Americano, while watching the door. As he waved to her, she realised that he had seen her, losing any opportunity there might have been for her to change her mind and quietly disappear. She lifted her hand in acknowledgement and joined the queue.

"Yes, love," said the man behind the counter.

"Oh, just a medium cappuccino please," she replied.

The man turned to the machine and set the drip going, while he squirted the steam into the metal milk jug. When it was completely frothy, he banged it twice on the counter, before wiping the steam nozzle. He poured the hot milk into the coffee and, with a teaspoon, put the froth on top. Alice was mesmerised by the process, although she had seen it all too often before.

"Chocolate on top?" The barista enquired.

"Er, I don't know…" she tailed off.

"Course she does," said Andy over her shoulder. "And I'll pay for that."

After handing over the cash, Andy picked up the cup and took it to his table, Alice following just behind. He put it down and pulled out a chair for her to sit. He noticed that she sat on the edge of her chair, with her knees firmly together. She was leaning forward, with her hands clasped together in her lap and her shoulders slightly hunched. Altogether, it was a pose of concern, personal protection and timidity.

"Well, here you are," said Andy, wondering how to overcome her discomfiture. He leaned back and looked at her. She did not return his look and stared fixedly at her coffee. "Come on, Alice, I'm not going to bite." He laughed quietly, trying to put her at her ease.

Without moving her head, she looked up at him, striking a pose of concern mixed with curiosity.

"I nearly didn't come," she said. "In fact, if you hadn't seen me, I would have gone. I was ready to run, but I saw you waving and I thought to myself that I shouldn't be that pathetic." She babbled on, all the while looking at him through her eyelashes, slightly rocking to and fro.

"But you did and now you're letting your coffee go cold."

She stopped her gentle rocking and reached out her hand to take hold of the handle of the cup. He noticed a slight tremor in her fingers and, to overcome it, she held the cup in two hands, feeling its warmth. She took a small sip, leaving a beguiling deposit of chocolate on her top lip. Andy saw that Alice had a very fine covering of blond hair on her upper lip and wondered if it was the same on her arms. Seeing him looking at her mouth, Alice quickly licked her lip with the tip of her tongue.

"Is the coffee OK?" he asked.

"It's fine. Lovely," she replied

"Would you like a piece of cake or a biscuit as well?"

"Oh no. I've got my figure to think about."

"Well, yeah," Andy murmured, "That's what we're here for."

"I suppose so."

"Do you want to know what I do?"

"Yes, please. I mean, it's not seedy or anything, is it?"

"Certainly not!" Andy retorted. "Basically, the process is to create a photographic portfolio and when we've selected the best pictures, I then place the portfolio in front of various agencies. This could be the start of a modelling career, flying all over the world for photoshoots in the most exotic of places and for any number of products – clothes, shoes, jewellery, food, cosmetics. Anything and everything."

"But I'm just an ordinary person," Alice protested.

"And so you will remain, unless you grab this opportunity with both hands. Just like you're holding your coffee!" He laughed again and this time, realising that she was still holding the cup in both hands, she also smiled. She put the cup down, sat back in her chair and looked directly at him.

"How much do you pay me for my pictures?" she asked.

"Well, at the start, some girls come to me and actually pay me to create a portfolio for them. They can pay anything between £500 and £1000. But, as I have suggested doing this for you, I am willing to take a chance with your face and take some shots and to start building your portfolio for nothing."

"Don't I get anything from this?"

"Course you do. But at this stage, right at the start, you have to look at it as an investment. If all goes well, you could be earning thousands, even hundreds of thousands each year. Look at Naomi Campbell and Kate Moss."

"But I'm not like them," said Alice. "They're beautiful and everyone knows it. I'm just plain old me."

"But they still started at the very bottom," said Andy. "And, anyway, if you don't try, how are you ever going to know?"

"What do I have to do?"

At last! Andy thought. *She's on board and will soon be putty in my hands.*

"I've got this little studio in Battersea," he said. "It's not much, but it's at the top of a building and has fantastic views over the river. You can see right up the Thames from Chelsea to the city. I don't actually live there. My gaff's in Kennington. But it's all set up for a photo session right now, if you want to have a go. My cab's just round the corner and we could be there in less than half an hour. Couple of hours taking photos and I'll have you back in Richmond in time for tea."

"Oh! I didn't realise that it would be so quick. I've not put on my best clothes or anything."

"That doesn't matter," Andy explained. "It's your face that I want to capture. You have the most fantastic eyes, especially when you look at me through your eyelashes. I'm sure that there are several makeup companies that can use your eyes, especially if I can capture that specific look."

"Oh! OK then." Alice felt her heartbeat pick up as they left the Costa Coffee and walked around the corner to where the cab was parked. He opened the door for her, saw that she was settled in the nearside seat and then got into the driver's cab. He checked his mirror, opened the glass panel and asked if she was OK, before driving away.

In the middle of Saturday afternoon, Sebastian Fortescue Brown returned from a pleasant lunch. He walked through the swing doors of the Gloucester Palace Hotel, which, following the death of his father, he now owned outright. Seb was 50 years old, tall with a military bearing and always well turned out in a three-piece suit, lace up leather shoes, white shirt and club tie. He often wore a flower in his lapel and invariably carried a rolled-up umbrella. He looked to the very inch a man of property and financial independence.

The reality, however, was rather different. He did indeed own the hotel, but when he had inherited it, there had been a disappointing level of debt. He had never actually seen military service, but he had spent three years at a minor public school in the Home Counties, before leaving at age 16 with a few very indifferent 'O' level results. But, while at school, he had observed how the upper middle classes behaved and he had learnt how to copy them. His father had enrolled him in a sixth form college in the West End, from which he had played truant on a consistent and regular basis. But he wasn't bunking off to waste his life. Instead, he had started to earn a living, firstly stocking shelves in a supermarket on the Edgware Road, but his real education began when he started to work in Soho.

Today, his knowledge of the seedier parts of Soho was second to none. He was acquainted with pimps, prostitutes, managers and owners of sex shops and strip clubs, Chinese restaurants, Indian takeaways, for many of whom he had either worked or done favours. He also knew most of the girls who had worked in and left Soho over the years. He had been married, for a short while, to a working girl called Maisie and this had prompted a massive fallout with his father. The marriage didn't last.

As the years passed by, Sebastian had earned a reputation as a fixer, often sailing very close to the wind, but always remaining on the right side of the law. However, he had never built up any real capital, always believing that his luck was about to change and that his day was about to dawn.

When his father died, eighteen months before, being the only son, Sebastian inherited the hotel, along with an ageing Bentley. After the accounts were finalised, his father's accountant presented them to him and explained that the hotel, although in credit, was not producing sufficient profit. It was suggested that he might consider selling up in order to realise the capital. Real estate in central London would, of course, produce a sum beyond his wildest dreams. Tempting though the proposal was, Sebastian finally turned it down.

Instead, he looked more closely at his new assets. He sold the Bentley and considered how best he could utilise the hotel. It had a pillared central entrance, set up five stone steps from the pavement, with two Georgian windows on either side of the double front door and two bay windows beyond that. Built over five floors, the kitchen and laundry facilities were in the basement. The ground floor was taken up with the dining room, two lounges, the reception area and the hotel offices in the rear. Each of the next four floors accommodated five double bedrooms, all en suite, with an old-fashioned lift connecting each floor, from the basement to the fifth floor. The fifth floor was the accommodation area for the staff. There were eight smaller rooms, with skylights, plus a common bathroom to the rear.

It had been built during the reign of Queen Victoria, as living accommodation for 'gentle folk', who no longer lived in their big country houses, or had returned in retirement from the colonies. Its greatest asset was a large parking area to the rear of the building, with enough room for 20 vehicles.

In the First World War, the hotel had been used as officers' quarters and after the Armistice, Seb's grandfather had taken back the building, sprucing it up with a lick of paint and installing a billiard room in the second lounge. How it survived through the 1930s' recession had always been shrouded in mystery, but the Second World War witnessed a further revival. Sebastian's grandfather was able to pass a good, solid business over to his son in the 1960s. In his turn, Sebastian's father had maintained its profitability through the millennium, before bequeathing it to Sebastian himself.

With all his connections in the underworld, Sebastian began to realise that this was an opportunity sent by his fairy godmother to make a lot of cash.

After all, he thought, *what a hotel will always have is a regular supply of different people, paying for accommodation, often in cash and what many of his contacts had was cash that needed to be brought back into circulation.* Firstly, he made rooms available to people who needed to 'disappear' for a short while, but when he began to consider that if any of his new 'guests' were followed to the hotel, the finger of suspicion would too easily be pointed at him.

42

So he had set up a proper scam where he made the hotel rooms available for 'names', who didn't actually exist. They would be listed in the hotel register and, indeed, they would only ever pay in cash. The cash thus generated was put through the books in the normal way. All the appropriate taxes were meticulously paid. For those guests that were introduced by his underworld contacts he received an additional, separate payment as his personal fee. He banked the hotel takings on a daily basis, in accordance with the register that was carefully maintained.

The added benefit to this process was that he was able to dispense with the bulk of the staff. When he had inherited the hotel, there were five kitchen staff, three people working on reception and eight chambermaids, one of whom helped in the laundry. There was also a maintenance man. This enabled the hotel to function on a split shift basis. Of the original seventeen employees, only two now remained in reality. These were people he had known from childhood, the cook Betty and her common law husband, the maintenance man, Fred. However, he had retained a number of other names 'on the books', even to the extent of paying their tax and National Insurance. At least three of these 'names' and their details had been supplied, for a fee of course, by his Soho chums for certain individuals who had, in fact, disappeared.

The number of real guests was very few and they were carefully selected and vetted. A room could be made available for private assignations and there was a small but growing number of acquaintances taking full advantage of this facility.

However, this didn't mean that the other rooms were not used. There was a steady need for accommodation for a better class of working girl, who would be seeking a rather more luxurious workplace for her clients. Of the hotel's 20 bedrooms, 10 were currently occupied. The girls were allowed to decorate their rooms as they liked and, if they wished, were able to meet their clients in the lounge of the hotel, where there was a small, but well stocked bar. The rules stipulated that the girls had to be properly dressed at all times and that there would be no unseemly behaviour. For this, they paid a fee direct to Sebastian. These fees were put into the books as 'Accommodation for Business Meetings'.

Of the other ten bedrooms, eight could still be used for guests, but more frequently and, for an agreed fee, they were made available for a small but select number of regular customers. With the correct introductions and connections, Seb was building up a list of people that he felt were discreet enough to make use of this service. The last two bedrooms had become bedsits, one for himself and the other for Betty and Fred. They were retained solely and specifically to make up any rooms that might have been used and to deal with any maintenance matters. Betty and Fred had worked with Sebastian's family for over forty years and were regarded as part of the family. Although unmarried, they had been in a relationship for as many years as they had worked at the Gloucester Palace Hotel.

Because there was no longer any need for the staff quarters on the fifth floor, Sebastian made these rooms available for storage. For a cash deposit and a monthly fee, the lessee was given a key and, very quickly, there was a wide variety of articles being stored on behalf of an equally wide variety of individuals. There is no doubt that the Police, had they known, would have harboured a particular interest in the Gloucester Palace Hotel.

Sebastian had enjoyed his lunch with a friend from the Chinese community who was looking to store a quantity of 'herbs' for a short while. There were still three rooms available on the top floor and, having been advised that the value of the goods was between £100,000 and £150,000, he had suggested a deposit of £5,000 and a monthly rental of the same, payable in advance. He knew that this would encourage Mr Ying, not only to move his goods quickly, but also to come back at some time in the future. The cash was deposited in the private safe that Seb kept hidden under the floor of his office. Together with the other illegitimate money, it would slowly be fed into the bank's cash flow in accordance with the number of 'residents' staying overnight.

It is not surprising that the cash flow of the hotel had dramatically improved, making its financial future secure. Sebastian was already building a nest egg of some proportion. But his ship of state had slipped across the wind and was now potentially vulnerable, should the authorities become suspicious in any way.

And all in the space of 18 months, he thought.

Chapter 7
Sunday – Four Days to Go

Saturday evening was still and cold. While there were two storms building to the west in the Atlantic, the big anti-cyclone over Russia was also expanding, bringing freezing temperatures to northern and Western Europe. Northern France saw the thermometers drop to minus-10 and while the wind stayed calm over the British Isles, the forecast was for icy roads with the possibility of freezing fog in some rural areas. The week's forecast indicated that the cold weather would be short-lived with a strong southwesterly breeze on Tuesday, building to gale force in southern counties on Wednesday.

In London, Sunday morning was bright and frosty. The temperature was lower than expected and there was ice over the local ponds. The roads had been salted by the local councils, but drivers were still being surprised by the conditions and there was a rise in minor road traffic accidents.

Out in the Atlantic, the movement of the southern depression had slowed, but was continuing to deepen. It was now some 400 miles to the south of the Azores. The northern depression had moved southeast from Greenland towards Iceland, increased in intensity and was now just beginning to bring increased rain and snow to the northern Atlantic. Wind speeds were also increasing.

David woke, after exceedingly pleasant dreams where he had been playing mixed rugby with his Richmond school team and girls from Jackie's college. Everyone was naked and there seemed to be a need for a lot of scrums. However pleasurable the dream had been, it faded rapidly as David got out of bed, to go to the bathroom. He could hear his father gently snoring in his parent's bedroom. He checked the time – quarter past seven and decided to go for a run.

Quickly dressing in a track suit and trainers, he quietly let himself out of the house and ran towards the local park. His breath came out as vapour just like the steam trains of old. The sun was already bright in the east, making the frost glitter like twinkling Christmas lights. It was a beautiful morning, albeit a little slippery under foot.

There was no one about, not even any cars on the local roads. David felt that he was the only person left in the world, following some form of international disaster. He ran into Richmond Park via Richmond Gate and decided to do two circuits of the northern half, above Sawyers Hill. When he reached Sheen Lane, where he would normally turn right, he decided to see whether Adam's Pond was frozen. He carried on down the bridal track, back to Sawyers Hill and so back to Richmond Gate. As he started the second circuit, there were a few more people in the park, a couple walking their dogs and he saw several cars and a couple of buses. London was slowly coming to life, the sun was higher and the frost on the trees was beginning to melt creating a dappled effect on the ground. He ran on, relishing the stiffness leaving his legs following the match. It was good to be alive, fit and young.

On returning home, his mother was in the kitchen making a cup of tea. She had explained, when David was very young, that no Yorkshire family can start a day properly except with a cup of tea. And, of course, it had to be Yorkshire Tea from Harrogate, although she always maintained that it never tasted as good unless made with Yorkshire Water! London water was a constant disappointment to her.

"There's a cup of tea for you," she said, as David came through the door. "Have you been on a run?"

"Cheers, Mum," he replied, thinking that she was stating the bleeding obvious. He flopped onto a kitchen chair.

The tea was hot and reviving. He held the mug in both hands, watching the steam rise, as his fingers thawed out.

"I've got a meeting this morning with the Save Heathrow Group," said Sarah. "I suggest you get into the bathroom now, before your Dad gets up."

"OK," David replied. "I'll go up straightaway. Anyway, I've got a ton of revising to do. I thought a run would shift the stiffness from my legs after the match, as well as clearing the brain."

He went upstairs, wondering what Jackie was doing.

Alice was awakened as the sun shone brightly into her bedroom. Her thoughts immediately went to the small room to which Andy had taken her. He had driven her to Battersea, to one of the streets just off the Albert Bridge Road. The flat was at the top of the building, set into the roof, where a skylight with windows on three sides was built into the roof. This made the room seem bigger and it was definitely lighter. It was, in fact, a bedsit that belonged to one of his lady friends, currently working overseas in Bahrain. Andy had been given the keys, basically to keep an eye on the flat and to keep the place clean and tidy.

After getting out of the cab, Andy had led the way into the building, mentioning that the room was on the top floor and that he was sorry that there wasn't a lift. He indicated that she should go first, saying that there were four flights of stairs and the door was at the end of the landing. He followed behind, carrying a holdall with his equipment and looking at the fall of her coat and her trousers. He was thinking how much of a shame it was that she wasn't wearing the skirt and blouse like she had the day before.

At the top, she turned to her left and stopped. Andy produced the key for a Yale lock and opened the door. Inside, because the room was chilly, Andy turned on the electric fire and both electric heaters. He opened the curtains, lighting up the room. There was only a little sunlight, of course, because the window faced north east and it was already well into the afternoon.

"If you look out of the window, you can see up the river towards the city," he remarked.

She walked across the room to join him and started to pick out the famous landmarks in the distance – Battersea Park and, just beyond, the old power station, the London Eye and away in the distance the Shard. Through the left-hand side, she could see Battersea and Albert Bridges and the Telephone Tower on the northern skyline.

"The view from here is really fantastic," she turned to look at him, but Andy was busy in the little kitchenette. He was putting on the kettle to make a drink.

"I can't run to real coffee, but I do have Douwe Egberts" he said. "And there's fresh milk in the fridge." He thanked his lucky stars that he had stopped by and put a fresh carton of milk in the fridge, before driving to Richmond. "You don't take sugar, do you?"

"No, thanks," she replied. She looked round the room, which was surprisingly spacious. There was a double bed, a small settee with two single armchairs and a table with two chairs. The kitchenette was to the left of the door and set towards the rear of the building. Beyond it, there was another door, which she presumed would lead to a small bathroom.

"This is a very nice flat" she remarked. "But you told me that you live in Kennington, so how are you able to use it?"

"It belongs to a friend of mine. She's working overseas on a six month contract," he answered. "She asked me to look in from time to time to make sure that everything's OK. She also lets me use if for my photographic stuff as well."

"Do you do a lot of that?" Alice realised she was chatting to put off the moment when Andy would want to start the session.

"I used to do a lot, but I pick and choose who I want to work with these days."

He opened the bag and took out a rolled-up umbrella. He then produced an extension and fitted the umbrella into it. It was now long enough to concentrate the light behind the subject. Next, he brought out four spotlights and plugged them into a 4-gang extension. He placed one spot on the top of the wardrobe and one on the chest of drawers. He then moved the table to one side, leaving just one armchair in place. He placed the third spotlight on the table. There was a screen already in place behind the chair.

"Can you sit here, please?" he asked.

She sat, still in her coat, as indicated and, once again, her hands were clasped tightly in her lap with her shoulders slightly hunched with her body leaning forward. She stared at the floor, wondering what was going to happen. Andy produced a lightweight tripod and a digital camera from the bag. He fixed the camera and checked the settings. He looked at the screen, centring on Alice's image and took a shot. The flash made Alice jump.

"Oh!" she exclaimed. "I wasn't ready for that."

"That's OK. I was just setting everything up and wanted to make sure that the light and the angles were right. Here, look. This is the picture."

He carried the camera to her and showed her the image. She blinked when she realised how lost and vulnerable she looked.

"I'm not sure I like that."

"Don't worry. That'll never be used. It was only a tester. Now, can you sit up a bit straighter, but with your head still bent forward, but with your eyes looking through your lashes at the camera?"

As he was talking, he placed the camera on the tripod. "That's good." He took two more shots. "Now, can you turn slightly to your right, but still keep your head bent forward and still looking into the camera?"

Slowly, Alice began to relax and as the heaters warmed the room, she also began to feel warm. "Can I take my coat off, please?" Andy looked at her and suggested that before taking it off, she might just open it. He took some more shots as the coat was opened, before she finally straightened her shoulders and allowed the coat to slip down her arms.

"Ah!" said Andy. "I didn't realise that you were wearing a cardigan."

"Well it was quite cold when I came out to meet you."

"Of course it was. I wonder if Jenny has any blouses you could wear. She's about your size." He slid open the wardrobe door and, there hanging on a rail, was a selection of blouses. "Go and choose one," he suggested

"Are you sure it'll be OK? I'm not sure that I'd like a stranger taking and wearing my clothes without my knowing."

"Oh yeah. It's fine." He reassured her. "Because Jenny is aware of what I do, she knows that sometimes I need to borrow some of her stuff. But she's a classy girl and I'm sure you'll find something you like."

Alice looked at the rail of blouses, cotton, silk, rayon, all in bright designs and all very well made. She chose a red, flowered pattern and disappeared towards to bathroom to change. Andy placed the fourth light on the windowsill and adjusted the angle. When she emerged, Alice had tucked the blouse into her jeans and although it fitted well over the shoulders, it was quite loose around her body.

"This is lovely," she remarked, as she made her way over to the chair.

"Can you stand to one side of the chair and put your hands on its back?" She did so.

"And lean forwards from the waist?" The light behind her now showed her body as a silhouette through the blouse. "Mmm," he added, "I'm not sure about this. Perhaps you could pull the blouse out of your jeans?"

The effect was startling. The blouse now hung properly and as Alice lifted up her head, the pose became extraordinarily erotic, as her breasts became more noticeable. But it was more the look of her eyes that seemed to promise the world and the small smile on her lips seemed to indicate that she knew just how to deliver on that promise.

"The jeans don't look right. Here, look at this." Alice went to the camera and looked at the shot. Although she didn't want to say so, she had to agree. "Did you see any skirts when you were rummaging in the wardrobe?"

"Hang on. I'll have a look."

She checked the rail below the blouses and there was a selection of skirts in wool, cotton, linen. Some were long, some short, some formal and others casual. She selected a plain white, pleated, rayon article, with a side button and a zip. She went to the bathroom to change into it and when she returned, her whole demeanour was different. She walked into the room with a new confidence and poise, head up and looking straight at Andy.

"That's a good fit." He looked approvingly at her. "But I'm not too sure about the blouse. Is there a white one to match?"

"I think so." Alice went back to the wardrobe and selected a white crepe blouse. With her back to Andy, she and took off the red flowered blouse, replacing it with the white crepe. As she was doing up the buttons, she turned back and realised that he had been taking photographs of her. She tossed her head to settle her hair, pulled shoulders back and sat down. She now realised where this photo session was leading and, much to her surprise, she felt comfortable with it.

And now, waking up the next morning, she wondered whether she had been a fool. *Not as much of a fool as sleeping with bloody Michael Varley. I'm going to knock all that on the head*, she thought to herself as she luxuriated in the memories of the day before.

Martin realised that Saturday night was going to be cold but when he woke on Sunday morning, he was surprised at the depth of the frost. *Mind you*, he thought. *It'll be having just the right effect on that ploughing I did yesterday. I wonder if the sun will be strong enough to let me get that top field finished.*

He walked out of the kitchen into the yard and through a gate into the middle paddock. He kicked the ground with his boot and found that the frosty crust wasn't too deep. Yes. It seems all right. I'll give it a go after breakfast.

He went back inside where Jennifer was up making the breakfast, grilling bacon and making toast. She had put on an ancient coffee percolator and the aroma was warm and inviting.

"Do you want any eggs?" she asked.

"Two please," he replied.

Milton Jackson worked shifts and Sunday was the last of his three days off. His shift pattern was three days on earlys, three days on lates, followed by three days off. As it was Sunday, he felt that he should meet with his family. Milton, just a few months off 50 years old, lived on his own after his wife, Joan, had left him, taking their three children with her. Joan was already in a new relationship with another man and planning to marry him. The three children were not overly happy with this change to their lives and they missed their dad. Milton knew this and was aware that they would be pleased to see him, even if it was inconvenient to Joan.

Working as a train driver on the London Underground was well paid and, although he had to find the money for the mortgage each month, now that Joan and the kids had left the marital home, he was just beginning to understand and appreciate the financial freedom this presented. The major downside in his life was that he missed his kids and that he often felt lonely.

I must get a girlfriend, he thought. *I wonder how Pamela would get on with the kids.*

He stretched in his bed, got up and went to the bathroom, before going downstairs to the kitchen to make a cup of tea.

Pamela was a colleague on the Underground who had flirted with him, but they had never pursued anything. She was blond, in her mid to late thirties and getting just a little thickened around the waist.

But she is pretty and I know she lives on her own. Mind you, she might not want to get involved with a West Indian. Perhaps I'll give her a call and leave the kids to next weekend.

Outside, he noticed that although there was frost on the ground. The cherry tree just beyond his kitchen window was already dripping as the frost melted in the early sunshine, indicating that the day was warming up.

It'll be good to go to the park and just wander around, he thought. *Yeah. I'll phone Pamela.*

He checked his watch and decided to shave and shower first.

In Yorkshire, the overnight frost had been more severe and there was a freezing fog that Sunday morning. Christine snuggled closer to Robert, who was already awake, but pretending still to be asleep. Finally, he threw back the duvet and stood up.

"Do you want a cuppa?" he asked.

"Yes and a digestive please," Christine replied.

Robert walked over to the window and looked through the curtains.

"It's foggy this morning and cold." After putting on his slippers and dressing gown, he went downstairs. As he passed the front door at the bottom of the stairs, he could feel cold air coming through a gap at the bottom of the door, reminding him that it was well overdue for being fixed. He knew Christine wouldn't be happy until it was done. They did have a draught excluder, but it wasn't very efficient and, really, they needed a new door.

He boiled the kettle, made the tea and put milk into the mugs, before pouring the tea. He took a couple of digestive biscuits out of the tin and put them in his pocket. Back upstairs, he put his own mug into the bathroom and took Christine's into the bedroom, taking the biscuits out of his pocket as he went through the door.

"Didn't you get a plate?" she grumbled

"Only creates more washing up," he replied, logically. "I'm going to shave."

A normal Sunday in Huddersfield was starting and the fog wouldn't stop the gentle chuntering between them.

By nightfall, however, the fog had gone and there was a distinct lift in the temperature, with a gentle westerly breeze blowing away the last of the mist and frost.

The same westerly breeze had arrived over west London around midday. Alice had arranged to meet Andy in the afternoon at the apartment in Battersea. She decided to dress rather more suitably in a knee length, flowing black skirt, which set off her long, shapely legs, with a white silk blouse and a thick Arran jumper. Just for devilment, she had also put on hold up stockings instead of tights and her prettiest underwear. Over the top, she wore her coat with a scarf. She had also brought a few extra clothes in a small holdall.

Arriving at the house, there was no sign of Andy's cab, so to kill some time, she walked round the corner and on to Battersea Bridge. She stood in the middle, looking down at the river Thames below. The tide was in and the river seemed very full. All the houseboats, moored on the far bank, were floating high and Alice couldn't remember when she had last seen the river so high. The gentle breeze moved her coat around her legs, reminding her that she was only wearing stockings. She decided to walk back and as she turned the corner, she saw the cab and Andy taking out some equipment.

"Hi!" she greeted him.

He jumped. "I didn't expect you to come from there," he replied. "Come on. I've already got the heaters on, to warm the place up."

He picked up the box and opened the front door for her. She went up the stairs first, giving him an opportunity to see her calves and the stockings. It was cool in the house, but the room was very warm, when Andy opened the door. Alice realised that the heaters had been on for a little while and she quickly slipped off her coat.

"Do you want to see the pictures I took yesterday?"

"Oh yes!"

"I've prepared a bit of a portfolio on this laptop." The computer was on the table and Alice sat down to look at the photos. "I haven't put them all on. Only the best." He explained.

"That's all right," she replied. "Hey! These look OK to me."

And indeed they did. Even though Andy had had no training, he obviously had a natural talent. He had caught her nervousness at the beginning, her caution and her shyness. He realised that Alice would now be much more comfortable with the camera and he looked forward, with a growing anticipation, to the rest of the afternoon.

Alice was delighted with the pictures, realising that she had grown in confidence during the session. As she had changed from one blouse to another and from one dress to another, she could detect the change in her demeanour. Her shoulders had relaxed, her head had come up and her back had straightened. She now knew what she wanted to do and how she wanted to capture it on film.

"Can you send these pictures to me?" she asked.

"Well, they are of you, but you must understand that, as the photographer, the copyright actually belongs to me." Andy explained briefly the peculiarities of the Law of Copyright before remarking that he didn't think it would do any harm to send her the file. "Shall we make a start?"

"OK."

"Perhaps you could slip off your jumper and sit in the armchair."

The chair was quite deep and as Alice sank into its comfortable seat, she felt her skirt riding up her thighs. Glancing down, she saw that the tops of her black stockings were just beginning to show. As she sunk further into the chair, she arched her back, pulling her shoulders back and pushing out her chest. Andy could see the pattern of her bra through the flimsy silk and remarked, from behind the camera "Really, you know, you don't need to wear a bra, do you?"

"Well I don't always." Alice replied. "And when I'm wearing a figure-hugging dress, I'll not wear knickers either!" She laughed quietly.

"Blimey! I'd never have thought that."

"Well, a girl has to look her best and a knicker line is so unattractive!"

Slowly the session continued with Andy asking Alice to undo this button, lift that hem, and show the stockings and so on. The bra came off quite early and, soon after, the whole ensemble was replaced with a mid-thigh tight dress from the bag that Alice had brought.

"Do you see what I mean about knicker line," she said, bending over and sticking out her bottom.

"Yes, I do. Perhaps you can wear the dress as you would want." He suggested. She turned away from him, bent over, reached up under her dress and hooked her thumbs into the legs of the knickers, before pulling them down. Behind the camera, Andy recorded each move deliberately. Daintily, she stepped out of one leg and then the other, before placing the garment in her holdall.

"Now, do you see what I mean?" she asked, repeating the previous manoeuvre.

The knicker line had gone and Alice's natural figure now graced the dress, making her look sexy and inviting. She sat down on the end of the right arm of the armchair, her long right leg stretching to the floor and her left arm draped along its back. Looking straight at the camera, with just the smallest indication of a smile, she lifted her left knee and put her foot onto the other arm. The dress naturally slipped up her thigh, exposing the tops of her stockings and more than a little of her thigh. Slowly, with her back arched and her shoulders pulled back, making her breasts stand proud and pert, she turned her body towards him, with her right foot on the floor almost as though she was riding a horse.

As she straightened her right leg, her shaven pussy almost came into view, but Alice demurely brought her bent left knee across to the other leg where she gently slipped the calf over her right knee, before placing the fingers of both hands onto the knee, all the time looking straight into the camera. She looked at her watch, realising that the time had been slipping away.

"I'm going to have to go now," she announced. "Perhaps we can arrange another session for next weekend."

"Wow!" He replied. "I do hope so. Anyway, you've got my email address on the card I gave you. If you send me a message, I'll send you the photos in a file." As he talked, he continued to take photographs.

Alice slipped off the dress, standing completely naked in front of him, apart from her black hold up stockings. She started to put on her other clothes, first her bra and next her skirt. As soon as her coat and scarf were on, she picked up the holdall and went to the door.

Andy was devastated. He realised that he had lost the upper hand and seriously considered preventing her from leaving. He now knew that Alice was in full control of their situation and that she was completely manipulating him.

Just over the river and up the hill in Kensington, Sebastian Fortescue Brown had spent a rather pleasant, if somewhat disconcerting afternoon, counting the money in the safe that was hidden from view, beneath the floorboards of his office. The hotel's old fashioned safe was in the same room, but in plain sight. Sebastian's thinking was that, if a thief broke into the office and stole the hotel safe, no further thought would be given to the real hoard under the carpet.

To his surprise, he had counted over £200,000. Most of the money was illegitimate, of course. Some could be attributed to the "residents and guests," some to the rental of the rooms on the top floor, but a large percentage was dirty cash from the underworld, that Sebastian was quietly but steadily laundering. Naturally he received a percentage for this activity, but even that income had to be dealt with. His "employees" all received wages and had their tax and National Insurance paid, although only two of them actually existed. It had been a time-consuming process to get all the names onto the books. They were a mixture of people who no longer lived in Britain, although their documents and passports had been retained by their erstwhile employers. Some were actually dead, but their deaths had never been registered. Sebastian knew all this, but quickly realised that keeping the name within the taxation system was a real boon.

The wages were paid into several separate bank accounts, all set up in the different names, but all in fact owned and controlled by Sebastian. He kept a record of all these illicit transactions, in a ledger that was never shown to anyone else.

The hotel's account books, which were scrupulously maintained, were audited regularly by his father's accountant, who was now his own financial adviser. Tim Watson was blithely unaware of the new arrangements at the Gloucester Palace Hotel and, had he had any inkling of the money-making schemes being actively pursued by Sebastian, he would have run a mile.

Sebastian had been aware for some time of the growing problem, under his floorboards, but only now began to appreciate its magnitude. Although, through the hotel's money laundering activities, he was already building up a sizable, "legitimate," investment fund in his own bank, there was too much illicit cash on the premises and the laundering processes were beginning to take too long for him to handle, on his own. He needed to put another scheme into operation where he could shift substantial amounts of money into other investments, even overseas. He needed a money broker.

He could start with his growing investment fund that had already been through the laundering process. This capital fund was already well over £50,000 and this was completely attributed to the profitability of the hotel. After all, he had very little outgoings of a personal nature and the hotel was, to all intents and purposes, performing very well. Most rooms were regularly let, the staff was efficient and well paid, and the income was all accounted for and properly taxed. There were no reasons why anyone or any authority should want to interfere.

Sebastian had even decided that the staff had all performed so well that he had paid them all a Christmas bonus – taxed, of course. However, this had only addressed a small part of his other growing problem.

He now needed to grasp the nettle and he decided to make an appointment, in the morning, to meet with an investment broker during the coming week. One of the girls had entertained a gentleman in her room, about two months before Christmas. The client had had given Seb his business card. Discovering that he could also discreetly entertain people, the gentleman had returned one Wednesday in early December, accompanied by his secretary. They had left the next morning, after an early breakfast.

After an early lunch, Martin took out the plough with the intention of finishing the top field. The sun was warm enough to have melted all the frost and the field had continued to dry out in the gentle westerly breeze. The furrows from the previous day stood out deep and solid, in long, straight rows. *Mm*, he thought. *That looks better than I expected.*

More than half of the field was complete and he had finished, the night before, several rows below the dip that was disconcerting him. He positioned the plough and set off. The plough dug deep and clean, without any hint of the increasing heaviness that was starting to cause the concern the day before.

The next hour's work continued without incident and, with well over two thirds of the field now complete, Martin stopped for a coffee. He was at the furthest westerly point of the field and, as he sat, listening to Classic FM he looked towards the east, mentally appraising the work he had completed. It was now half past two and he reckoned on a further hour's work. He turned in his seat and looked to the west. Way over London, he thought he could see a build-up of cloud way down on the horizon, although the sky remained completely clear overhead.

Better get on, he thought. *There'll be another frost this evening, I expect. The more I do now, the less I'll have to do later, especially if it rains.*

With that, he put away the flask and got on with the job.

When Milton finally found Pamela's number, there was no reply. He spent the next couple of hours cleaning up his flat, before calling her again.

"Hello," she answered.

"Hi there, Pamela." Milton's deep, Jamaican voice rumbled across the ether. "It's Milton here."

"Well, I did guess that," she responded. "What can I do you for?"

"I was just wondering, with it being a lovely day and such, whether we could grab a coffee in the park and, perhaps, a couple of beers later. That's if you're not too busy."

"Oh! No, no! That's fine. I'm not doing anything today." Pamela stammered, wondering how Milton had her number. "I was only planning to watch a couple of old movies, after doing my washing. Going to the park'll be lovely." She wondered why her heart had started to beat so strongly.

"That's great. Can I meet you at about two o'clock? I live in Lambeth. Where's a good place to meet you?"

"I'm over in Walworth," she replied. "Not so far really."

"Ok. That's easy, then. Elephant and Castle tube station, Bakerloo line, going north."

"I'll see you there at two," she replied, wondering what on earth she was going to wear. She settled for a newish pair of slacks with a cashmere, roll neck sweater and an overcoat. Smart, but not as though she had gone to too much trouble.

Over in Lambeth, Milton was having much the same thought. Now he had finally called her, he needed to strike the right balance. He finally decided on an open necked orange shirt with tan trousers, a thick, green, woollen jumper and his black bomber jacket. He decided against a hat.

He now felt excited, glad that he had finally taken the plunge, but was also filled with enormous angst as to whether it was a good idea or not.

Too late to back out now, he thought. *If I do, I'll be at the butt of everybody's jokes and teasing. Anyway,* he rationalised in his mind, *I've been meaning to do this for ages, so now's the time.*

And, with that, he left his home for the rendezvous.

For her part, Pamela, was also having thoughts. *This is what comes of flirting with him, I suppose. I mean, he's a nice guy and all that, but I don't really know him. I suppose it'll be an opportunity to find out. But what if he's really boring and only after one thing.*

Well. He won't be getting any of that! At least, not on the first date and definitely not if he's boring. If he is, he won't get a second chance, so that'll be all right.

She flashed her pass and went down the escalator to the Bakerloo line. As she reached the platform, she saw Milton studying the Underground map, as though he didn't know it by heart.

"Hello!" She touched him on the arm.

Milton turned, smiled broadly and took her hand in his. "Hi! You look nice."

Pamela smiled back and gently squeezed his hand. "You look good too," she replied. "Where are we going?"

"Thought we could go up to Oxford Circus and then walk down Oxford Street to Marble Arch. If we want to stop, we can. If we want to walk further, we can. Let's keep it easy."

They caught the next train going north and got out at Oxford Circus, travelling up the escalators to the swirling crowds at the top of the final flight of steps. They exited the tube station on the north eastern part of Oxford Circus and immediately crossed Regent Street, walking down the gentle slope in front of the John Lewis department store. Pamela put her left arm through Milton's right and, as they avoided the crowds of pedestrians walking towards them, they strolled contentedly towards Marble Arch. Just before they reached Selfridges, they stopped for a coffee and were surprised to find a table.

"I suppose the sales have basically finished," Pamela commented.

"And time is getting on, as well." Milton agreed.

With further companionable small talk, they resumed their walk, now up the gentle slope towards Park Lane and Hyde Park. They crossed the dual carriageway on the pedestrian lights and entered Hyde Park at Speakers' Corner. All the crowds from Oxford Street had now melted away. There were no longer any speakers, for they had long since finished haranguing the crowds. They stopped to look at Marble Arch, isolated from the park itself, on a traffic roundabout.

"It looks quite lonely over there," said Pamela. "Let's go over." They crossed Cumberland Gate and stood below the massive marble construction.

"It shouldn't really be here at all," remarked Milton.

"What do you mean?"

"It was built to be the state entrance to Buckingham Palace, way back in George the Fourth's reign. It was supposed to commemorate him, but he died before it was finished. Anyway, the palace wasn't being used for much in those days and when Queen Victoria was crowned, it was she who decided to make it her London home. As such, the building was thought to be too small and the required extensions meant that the arch had to be moved. So it came here. Many people say that it was put on the place where the Tyburn gallows had stood, but that isn't exactly true."

"How do you know?"

"I find history interesting. Tyburn was the place where public executions had taken place for hundreds of years. A massive triangle of beams had been built, supported on three massive upright poles. It could be used to hang as many as 24 at a time. But it wasn't here, where Marble Arch is now. Tyburn was just over the road to the north on that traffic island, there." He indicated another traffic island at the bottom of the Edgware Road. "It's not easy to get to it with all these vehicles.

"In the old days, prisoners would come from Newgate Prison, up to Oxford Street and then all the way here in open carts. With a couple of stops for a drink, it would take over two and a half hours. Tyburn would have been a small village on the outskirts of

London, in those days. The last hanging was in 1783. After that, public hangings took place outside Newgate prison.

"It's funny to think that only 54 years later, Queen Victoria was crowned."

Arm in arm, they started to stroll down Broad Walk towards Hyde Park Corner. The sun was now setting in the west and the air was becoming distinctly chillier. When they reached Hyde Park Corner, they took the underpass to Green Park and continued down Constitution Hill towards Buckingham Palace. They soon reached the big roundabout in front of the palace itself and Milton pointed out where Marble Arch had once stood. He explained how all the extensions of almost 200 years earlier had created the façade of the palace that is so well known around the world.

"Well, aren't you going to tell me about Green Park as well," commented Pamela, as they left Hyde Park Corner.

"There's not really much to tell. It was a swampy, grim place before Charles the Second bought it. It had been a part of the Poultney family estate. They subsequently became the Earls of Bath. Anyway, King Charles put a brick wall around the park and laid out the paths. He even had an ice house built. I suppose its greatest claim to fame is that Handel's Music for the Royal Fireworks was first played here.

"Today, I think it's a lovely, peaceful place to walk and chat with a friend. Mind you, it used to be a dreadful haunt for highwaymen and thieves, before London had spread out so far and became so large."

"I feel very safe with you," Pamela remarked as she held Milton's arm tighter. She looked closer at him, realising that he was quite the educated man with a real interest in life.

"We're just about to go into St James Park, which I think is far more interesting," he said, before they crossed over the Mall and followed the footpath on the north side of the lake to the Blue Bridge.

"This all used to belong to Eton College. God alone knows why. It was also swampy and near St James Hospital which, in those days, looked after lepers. London itself was based where the city is now and with the river Thames acting as the main sewer in the olden days, the whole place must have been pretty smelly.

"So, the rich and privileged began to buy land to the west, because the prevailing winds would take the stench away to the east. Henry the Eighth bought the land from Eton College. He also bought York Place from Cardinal Wolseley and then built York Palace, which later became Whitehall.

"Later, James the First had the land drained, which would have left the River Tyburn flowing through the middle. The river still runs, but it's now all enclosed and in culverts. It comes all the way from Hampstead, through Marble Arch, down to Green Park, under St James Park and then into the Thames. Today, it's all part of the sewage system that was built during Victoria's reign. This lake is supposed to have been a part of the river Tyburn.

"Anyway, Charles the Second made the park available to the public and it quickly obtained a pretty awful reputation for open acts of lechery. So the years roll by and nothing much really changes." Milton kissed her and they both laughed. They left the park, walked down Great George Street into Parliament Square and so to Westminster tube station.

Chapter 8
Monday – Three Days to Go

The big anti-cyclone over Russia and northern Europe was still holding up the progress of the depressions that had moved across the Atlantic. The first was almost stationery over Iceland and the second was between the Azores and the southwest coast of Ireland.

In London, the Meteorological Office was now watching the changes to these depressions, both of which were continuing to deepen, causing wind speeds to rise quite dramatically. Warnings were issued to shipping in all sea areas to the west of Ireland, ranging from Storm Force in Trafalgar to Severe Storm in South East Iceland and Bailey.

The weather over the United Kingdom remained still and cold, with patches of freezing fog over northern England and southern Scotland. Temperatures had dropped overnight to minus-5 degrees in many areas and out in the country there were even reports of minus-10 degrees

Martin Havers got out of bed as soon as the alarm went off. He walked to the window and looked through the curtains. *Bugger*, he thought. *There's too much frost out there to get much done today.*

Through the window, he could see the frost on the grass, the trees, the fence posts and his small pond was completely iced over. Over in the distance, he could just make out where he had been ploughing over the weekend. The furrows now looked just like neat rows of shallow snowdrifts.

He glanced to his right, looking at the cowshed, where his cattle were housed for the winter. *I'd better make sure they are all OK.*

And with that, ensuring that he didn't disturb his wife, he padded to the bathroom.

Alice was already dressed and just finishing her breakfast, as if a piece of toast and a cup of tea could be called that. She was rather looking forward to the day ahead. It was time to show Michael Varley that she was no push over and, indeed, was probably worth a decent pay rise.

After returning home the previous evening, she had had a long bath, using the Fenjal that her mother had given her for Christmas. Although the bath oil invariably made a mess of the plug chain, it did have remarkable restorative properties. She had woken feeling smooth and relaxed all over and when she applied her eyeliner, she thought that her eyes were sparkly and bright. Yes, she was looking forward to her day.

Michael Varley, on the other hand, was not feeling so bright. He knew that he had to prepare for a conference that was scheduled for Thursday morning, when he would make the opening speech of welcome. This would require his staying over in town on the Wednesday evening, as his colleagues and guests would be arriving throughout Wednesday afternoon and would be wining and dining all that evening. He wondered whether Alice might stay over as well. They had created a bit of a relationship when he had taken her to the Gloucester Palace Hotel just before Christmas, but he didn't understand why, since then, she had been a bit distant. He had put it down to employer/employee relationships. *Perhaps I should give her a rise*, he thought.

He left home, leaving David to make his own way to school, and caught the train to Waterloo before taking the Waterloo and city link to Bank. Emerging on the north side he walked briskly to his office on London Wall. As he emerged from the lift on the fifth floor, he found the lights already on. Alice was in the little kitchenette brewing up coffee. She had also bought a couple of chocolate croissants.

"Morning, Alice," Michael called out as he came through the door into the small lobby. His mouth began to water as he could smell the croissants and the coffee.

Instead of turning to his left, towards his office, Michael turned to his right, dumping his brief case and coat on a chair by the reception desk. He walked down the corridor listening to the coffee percolating. He saw Alice, squatting down on her heels in front of the small fridge, putting away the milk. She was wearing a wraparound dress which had split open and was exposing more of her thighs than he might have expected. She also had on a cardigan and had obviously spent more than a little time with her make up that morning. Her eyes were subtly enhanced by eyeliner and eye shadow, bringing out their deep blue colour and sparkle. She had also taken great care with her eye lashes, which were long and inviting. Her dark blonde hair was lustrous, falling onto her shoulders.

"Did you have a good weekend?" Michael asked ingenuously.

"Surprisingly, it turned out really well," she replied, as she stood up. The dress hung just above the knee, with a tie in a bow on the left-hand side, just on her hip. She was also wearing skin-colour stockings which, with their natural musculature, made her long legs look magnificent. "Are we expecting Trevor today?" she asked guilelessly.

"No. He's still in Paris and is scheduled to come back on Wednesday. In time for the conference on Thursday," he added.

Trevor Le Grove was Michael's partner. He had set up Le Grove Investments back in the 1980s when Margaret Thatcher's Conservatives were in power and the Stock Market had rocketed forward. Unlike many similar companies, however, he had survived the later difficulties of Gordon Brown's Labour administration at the turn of the century, because his portfolios were not singularly linked to stocks and shares and he had moved much of the investments into cash at the right time. Michael had joined him, just as Gordon Brown was taking over from Tony Blair at Number 10. He had helped to steer the firm through that rocky period, when so many banks fell foul of the subprime lending fiasco. Too small to attract serious investigation, large enough to be attractive as a bolt hole for a number of wealthy clients and sensible enough to keep those clients fully appraised of the changing market place, Le Grove Investments had built up an enviable reputation for solid rather than spectacular returns, for safety rather than speculation.

With this in mind, Michael had continued to build the client listing and, with the Brexit vote in 2016 having initially revitalised the city, somewhat to the surprise of the Bank of England and the Government, he was able to further enhance the bank's reputation, even maintaining a reasonable profit level over the turbulent years that had followed. He was now keen to take the bank even further. Like Trevor, albeit some twenty years younger, Michael had created a reputation of fairness and caution, which was now playing well for his own plans.

"I'll bring in the coffee in a couple of minutes," Alice announced. She didn't really like Michael coming into the kitchenette, believing that it was her domain. "Oh, and by the way, there was a telephone message left yesterday from a Sebastian Fortescue Brown. I've typed up the details and put it on your desk."

"Right. I'll go and deal with it." And with that, he turned on his heel and strode up to his office at the other end of the corridor, collecting his briefcase and coat on the way.

Sitting behind his large traditional desk, he picked up the message.

Hello. My name is Sebastian Fortescue Brown and I am the owner of the Gloucester Palace Hotel in Kensington. This message is for Mr Michael Varley. We met a couple of months ago, when you booked a room at the hotel and we had an opportunity to speak for a few minutes, during your stay. I understood that you are a money broker and I was wondering whether you might be interested in investing some capital on my behalf. The hotel is generating good profits now that I have introduced new marketing ideas and up to date accounting facilities.

I will telephone on Monday morning in order to arrange a meeting with you.

That sounds interesting, thought Michael. *I remember that's the hotel where I took Alice back in December. They were very discreet and looked after us very well. Maybe we should try to stay there again on Wednesday night before the conference.*

He looked at the message again and saw that there was both an email address and a telephone number. Glancing at his watch, he noticed that it was already past nine o'clock, so he decided to call. Before he could pick up the phone, there was a gentle knock on the door and Alice came in with the coffee and croissant on a tray. She placed the tray on a well-polished sideboard.

"This looks quite interesting," Michael remarked holding up the message. "I was just about to call him."

"Isn't that the hotel where you took me in December?" asked Alice, as she poured Michael's coffee.

"Yes, I believe it is."

Alice picked up the cup and saucer, together with a small jug of milk and came round Michael's desk to put them just to the right of his leather-bound blotter. As she put the cup down, Michael put his hand on her waist.

"As you know, I have to make the welcome speech to the bloody conference first thing on Thursday morning," he remarked. "And I was wondering if you would help me finish the final draft on Wednesday evening. We could have dinner and then stay at the Gloucester Palace again." His hand moved down from her waist, over her hip, to the top of her thigh. She didn't flinch or move away. She turned and looked at him.

"It's something to think about. I'll have to check to see that I'm free on Wednesday," she murmured. "Do you want me to contact Mr Fortescue Brown to make the appointment? Would you prefer it here or in Kensington?" She stepped back, breaking the contact with him.

"Ah, yes!" he replied. "I think it would be better if you did that. And, on balance, it may well be better to meet here." He handed her the message.

Alice looked down at him with a half-smile, gave him the briefest of nods, turned and left his office.

She went back to her own desk. She had her own office behind the reception area, with a direct view of the door. She put down the message and made the call.

At the hotel, Sebastian was mildly surprised to hear his telephone ring quite so early on a Monday morning. Arrangements were quickly made for him to attend Le Grove Investments at 11.00 am that morning. He did a quick mental check of his assets, put some papers on one side, ready to be placed into his briefcase and decided that he would travel by taxi.

He called Andy Greene, to book the ride. Fortunately, Andy was free and said he would arrive at 10.15. This left Sebastian with a clear half hour to get his thoughts in order.

Alice put her head round Michael's door to tell him that Mr Fortescue Brown would be arriving at 11.15 am. *That'll put him in a fix,* she thought as she walked back to her desk. *I'll go back into his office at quarter to eleven to find out exactly what he wants me to do on Wednesday.* The thought of setting him up made her heart pump faster.

David had walked to school, fully expecting his day to be filled with revision for his various exams. As he entered the school grounds, he bumped into his science teacher.

"Good morning, Mr Smith."

"Good morning to you, Varley," Mr Smith replied. "What's the latest on the weather front?"

"Well, sir, last night, I checked the passage of the two depressions in the Atlantic. They both appear to be stalled at the moment, probably because the anti-cyclone over northern Europe and Russia is so strong. That's actually causing all the cold weather and the frost. I guess we were lucky to get the match played on Saturday afternoon.

"Anyway, the two depressions are rather like the fists of a boxer, waiting to deliver the old 'one two', as soon as the time is right." David would have continued, but Mr Smith held up his hand.

"What do you think is going to happen?" he asked.

"Weather forecasting is notoriously difficult," David replied. "But instead of reducing the intensity of the depressions, this anti cyclone appears to be making them deeper. The wind speeds have increased and the forecasts for all the fishing areas to the west of the British Isles are pretty grim. So, if they start to move eastwards again, they will both bring some pretty severe weather right across the country."

"Will that mean snow, or just high winds?" Mr Smith persisted.

"Well, I don't really know, but I would expect the weather to change by tomorrow evening and because this cold from Russia has been so severe, then any moisture driven into the country will first fall as snow. Actually, thinking about it, there should be heavy snowfall at first, with drifting in the high wind, but this will quickly change to rain as the temperature rises. That could lead to localised flooding as the snow melts on the hills and, of course, with the water table still so high from all the rain we had in the autumn, any floods might be quite severe."

"There's one other matter you might want to look at," remarked Mr Smith. "When are the next spring tides due?"

"I'm sorry, sir. What are they?" asked David.

"The passage of the moon around the earth has an effect on the height of the tides and particularly in the spring and the autumn. The moon has the tendency to pull and push the sea, especially when it's closest to the earth. This can have a dramatic effect on the ebb and flow of the tides.

"So, if the water table is high, making the rivers run in speight and if the tides are high as well, there might be nowhere for the water to flow into the sea. I can see you think this is a bit far-fetched, so I suggest you research Canvey Island in 1953."

David was a little sceptical at this notion, but decided that, as soon as he returned home that afternoon, he would look into it, just to check whether there was any credence in Mr Smith's comments.

Martin Havers was at a loose end. He had all but finished ploughing the top field on Sunday afternoon. There was only a small patch right at the bottom, where the ground had still been too wet. The frost had again put paid to any thoughts of ploughing anywhere else on the farm. He had already walked through the cowsheds and checked over the cattle. It was warm in the shed and smelled of hay, making Martin reluctant to leave. The cows seemed content, having had their first feed. Several were pregnant and everyone was looking forward to seeing the new additions to the herd, come the spring.

He walked into the workshop. There was his old tractor, in bits, at the far end of the shed, waiting for some love and affection. It had been a good workhorse and, really, he should have had it sold for scrap years ago, but like most farmers, he was loath to do so on the basis that it might be useful one day. In the corner, behind the old tractor, was a neat pile of corrugated iron, which had come from an old barn that had been demolished some twenty years before.

This place needs a real clear out, thought Martin. *I'll get onto it, as soon as the weather improves.*

He walked out of the shed and stood, looking over his land, sweeping down towards the Thames. The sky was clear and pale blue, with the sun making everything sparkle, but there was no warmth in it. He looked towards London but couldn't make out the clouds that he had seen on the horizon the day before. There was a keen wind blowing in from the east.

All the way from the Urals, I expect, he thought. He turned and made his way back into the warmth of the kitchen.

Milton was on an early start on that Monday morning. He was up at 5 am and on his way to work by 6 am. This was the first of three days of early starts. That never put him in the best frame of mind. Today, however, it wasn't so bad because Pamela was very much on his mind. He now considered that it was a stroke of genius to make contact, because the time they spent together was so easy and relaxing. He had forgotten how good it can be, just to share time with another person.

After walking to Westminster station, they travelled together back to Waterloo, where they decided to eat in a local curry house, before walking back to Pamela's home. At the door, he thanked her for such a wonderful day and asked whether they might be able to do it again sometime soon. She readily agreed and, after giving him a quick peck on the cheek, she disappeared behind her front door. Milton turned away with his heart singing and walked back to his own home, happy and content.

For her part, Pamela wondered whether he was wanting to come into her home, ostensibly for coffee. She was surprised and, she admitted to herself later, rather disappointed that he let her peck him on the cheek at the door, before she closed it. She was very content at the way the afternoon had developed. It could have been like a tourist trip round the parks of London, but she didn't feel like that. Milton made it all sound so interesting, so much so that she was looking forward to seeing him again. She decided to send him a text.

Thanks for a great afternoon, Milton, she wrote. *I had a super time. Look forward to seeing you again soon. Pamela x.*

When the message pinged on his mobile, Milton jumped. In his rush to answer it, he nearly dropped the phone onto the kitchen floor. He wondered how best he should respond.

Red Watch, at Poplar Fire Station, was also on earlies. Fred Shemming took over at eight o'clock, after an early breakfast at home. He bought a paper from Rajinder on his way to the Fire Station and was now settling down to read it. There were no incidents in the night and everything was calm. At about ten o'clock, a Fire Service van arrived, carrying the internal mail. There was a personal letter for Fred from Human Resources, inviting him to consider studying for a potential promotion to Watch Officer. This had happened before and when Fred had followed it up, it soon became apparent that the Service was wanting him to consider moving to North London. That wasn't in his plans at all. He and Dinah were really happy in Poplar and the boys were doing well in school, so a move would not have been welcome.

I'd better see what this is about, he muttered to himself, picking up the phone.

After a good conversation with the head of HR, Fred now understood that both Watch Officers at Poplar were about to be promoted and moved to other parts of London. This would mean that two replacements were a necessity and, to cover in the short term, two temporary Watch Officers would be appointed.

However, it was well known and appreciated that Fred knew his area and its residents better than any other Fire Officer in the London Fire and Rescue Service. Because of this, the head of Human Resources had made it absolutely plain that, should he pass the exams and gain the necessary promotion, he would be first in line for one of the two posts. And this would, of course, attract a reasonable increase in salary.

Fred stood there, wondering if he should discuss this with Dinah first. She was always able to read between the lines and to understand whether there were any other, possibly detrimental, agendas. But, to him, it all seemed pretty straightforward. He wouldn't have to move; he would get a promotion; and he would get more money. He went to the computer and typed an email, accepting the proposal.

At quarter to eleven, Alice took a fresh pot of coffee through to Michael. His chair was pushed back from the desk and he was reading a financial journal. She collected the dirty cup and saucer and the milk jug from his desk.

"Mmm, thanks!" he murmured, looking up at her. "Have you given any thought to my suggestion?"

"Actually, I have," Alice replied.

She poured coffee into a fresh cup at the sideboard and then took it, together with a small jug of milk, to his desk. As she bent over to place it on the place mat, he put an appreciative hand on her right buttock. She remained quite still as his hand travelled down the outside of her leg to the hem of her dress. He put his hand onto her stockinged leg and began to run it up, inside the dress. She leant gently to her right, allowing her to move her left foot slightly to the left. When his hand reached the top of her stocking, he continued upwards to her buttock and her hip. To his surprise, he encountered no knickers and, as if to prove it to himself, he ran his hand over her bare buttocks and up towards the small of her back. She turned, using her left foot as a pivot, to face him and with the same half smile giving her features a look of calm control, she bent her right knee before lifting her right leg over his knees. If any confirmation of the state of her underwear was needed, Michael was no longer in any doubt.

Sitting on the edge of the desk, with her legs either side of his, Alice looked into his eyes and began to undo the belt on his trousers. She followed this by loosening the trousers themselves, pulling the zip right down. She could already feel Michael hardening under her touch, as she pulled up his shirt and began to caress him through his underpants. He started to undo the bow at the side of her dress, but she stopped him. Instead, still looking him firmly in the eyes she raised both her hands to her shoulders and, with her thumbs, she slowly drew back the silken fabric to the tops of her arms, letting the sleeves drop to her elbows. This allowed the garment to gape at the front, exposing both her small, but perfectly formed breasts.

She pulled the front of the elasticated band of his underpants down to release his erection. She then hooked the waistband beneath his scrotum and held his erection in her right hand. Opening her legs just a little more, she moved forward and allowed his glans to touch her vaginal lips. Her sex was moist and warm.

"And what exactly is it that you want me to do on Wednesday evening?" she whispered into his ear.

"Well…" Somewhat at a loss for words, he stammered. "There will be the final draft of the speech to finish," he tailed off lamely.

She leant forward with her hands on his shoulders so her nipples were brushing against his chest and whispered in his ear, "Is that all?" She could feel him trying to push his penis into her, but by slightly straightening her legs, she was able to deny him that pleasure.

"Well, we could … that is we might … or maybe …" Again, he tailed off.

"Will you want to do some of this?" she asked, sitting back a little so that she allowed him to ease his glans part way into her vagina.

"Of course I will," Michael replied, trying to reassert his authority.

Straightening her legs again, so that he was once more disengaged, she said, "All I want, Michael, is a 25% pay rise. I really think I am worth more than that, but I'm not 'greedy'. Is that a reasonable increase, for the extra work I do for you?"

She was now standing, her legs on either side of his, her feet in her high heels, her hands on her hips, her dress off her shoulders with both her breasts proudly exposed, looking straight into his eyes. He looked away and muttered, "I can hardly refuse, can I?"

At that point, the carriage clock on his desk discreetly chimed eleven times, immediately followed by the doorbell. *Bloody hell*, thought Michael, *he's early.*

Alice reversed her previous manoeuvre, lifting her right leg over both of his. She stood up straight, not a hair out of place and her make up immaculate. She raised her arms allowing her dress to slip back onto her shoulders. She pulled it straight at her waist so that it lay correctly between her breasts, before smoothing it down over her thighs. She turned to walk to the door, where she hesitated and looked back at him, seeing him deflated and dishevelled.

"I'll give you five minutes before I bring him in," she announced. "With some fresh coffee."

With that she opened the door, closed it behind her and walked down the corridor to the front door, where she admitted Mr Sebastian Fortescue Brown. She could hardly believe what she had just done, but she knew it was true because she could feel the slippiness between her legs as she walked down the corridor.

She took his overcoat and umbrella and asked whether he would prefer black coffee or white. Advising him that Mr Varley was not quite ready, she suggested that he should sit down in the reception area for a couple of minutes. Very soon, there was a buzz on the intercom and she left her desk, went over to his chair and invited him to follow her to Mr Varley's office.

Returning to her desk, she typed up a letter from Michael Varley to herself, confirming the salary increase, based on the special skills and benefits that she was now bringing to the firm. She did a second copy for the accountant and a third for the bookkeeper, to ensure that Michael Varley would be unable to renege on his decision. She then placed them into the signature book ready to be signed as soon as Mr Fortescue Brown had left.

Feeling pleased with herself, she made the coffee and took it into Michael's office, where he was listening intently to Mr Fortescue Brown's proposition. They were sitting in two low armchairs, with an elegant coffee table between them. She placed the tray on the table and poured the first cup for the visitor, bending low at the waist allowing her dress to gape discreetly but invitingly at the front. He took absolutely no notice. She poured Michael's drink and, with her back to Mr Fortescue Brown, she repeated the action, but with her right leg slightly forward so that as she bent forward the dress was pulled up her back causing it to split, exposing some of her stocking top and thigh. Michael did notice!

That morning, Councillor Christine Sykes attended a charity coffee morning for the local library appeal. In the years following Gordon Brown's Labour Administration, there had been several years of severe cutbacks to Local Government, resulting in the closure of many local libraries across the country. In some areas, however, groups of well-meaning and rather enterprising people formed Library Action Groups. When first set up, local councils were happy to assist, seeing these groups as a possible method of keeping libraries open to the public.

At the same time, because the reduction of Government Grant to local authorities was so severe, councils were forced to sell off many of their public buildings. This was the death knell for many libraries, because such a large number used to be housed in municipal buildings. There were a few, however, that survived these culls but they were now invariably private organisations, hanging on by their fingernails, often in virtually impossible financial situations.

Christine was a member of one such local committee, but no one else knew that her daughter was married to a city money broker. Not that Christine had been reticent in letting Sarah know of the financial difficulties facing the local Colne Valley library. Sarah had, one evening in the previous autumn, mentioned this to Michael, but he had very quickly diverted the conversation away from what he felt was an attempt to extract money from his own wallet.

The coffee morning raised over £300, which was a drop in the ocean compared with the money that was needed. Set in its own building, the committee had been able to arrange an 'Asset Transfer' whereby the Library Committee had taken over the financial responsibility for the building itself. For over ten years they had been able to keep the organisation in the black with certain agreed payments from the council. These had now ceased and the overall financial reality was dawning on them that the building, far from being an asset itself, was in fact a heavy liability, needing considerable and regular funding for its upkeep.

Representing a Liberal Democrat ward in a marginal Labour/Conservative constituency, Christine realised that she had no real opportunity to obtain the Member of Parliament's assistance. *After all*, she thought, *it was the Tories that brought about these cuts. Far too deep and the austerity went on for far too long.* She had tried to gain the interest of the new Labour MP, following the snap General Election way back in 2017, but she had been far too busy nursing her fragile majority to pay too much attention.

Basically, Christine was looking for a minor miracle.

Christine's daughter, Sarah, spent the morning at a charity coffee morning. As Chairperson of the Richmond Music Society, the committee was discussing an agenda to raise funds for the coming year's concerts. In ordinary years, the society generally raised sufficient funds from its subscribers to afford the fees of the various pianists, quartets and other performers. But the following year was to be the celebration of the 125th anniversary of the birth of the founder and the boat was being pushed out. Frederick Simpson had been born during the First World War and had almost immediately become an orphan because within weeks his father had been killed on the Western Front. Two years later his mother succumbed to the influenza epidemic which had swept through Britain soon after the Armistice.

Frederick's early life was consequently unsettled, until his paternal grandparents finally took responsibility for his upbringing, after the death of his mother. His grandfather was a haberdasher in Kingston on Thames and, with the growth of the town, his business had flourished. Indeed, he had become an alderman at the turn of the centenary and a Justice of the Peace in 1910. A pillar of respectability, he had not been pleased when his only son, Joseph George, had taken up with the pretty daughter of the local hostelry, the King's Arms. Indeed, he had cut Frederick's father out of the family will, whereupon Joseph had started to work in the pub for his father-in-law.

It was not long, however, that the young couple realised that they wanted their own independence. They left the pub and bought a small terraced house before Joseph joined the army in 1913, just before the outbreak of the Great War. Following a period of leave in 1916, Frederick himself was born. Despite the obvious financial difficulties, Frederick's mother and father had created a loving home. His mother, who all too soon had become a widow, struggled to bring up her son on her own and when she died, Frederick was taken by her parents into the pub.

His paternal grandfather, Alderman Joseph George Simpson JP, was not happy with this arrangement, despite having disowned his son several years earlier. Now, he had a war hero as a son, albeit deceased, and an orphan grandson. To the Alderman it was obvious that he had to take over the financial responsibility for his grandson's upbringing, particularly as he carried the Simpson name. As it happened, although he didn't comment at the time, the landlord of the King's Arms was pleased with this turn of events, as all the necessary costs related to the responsibility for Frederick's upbringing would pass to the Alderman.

When Frederick was eight, in 1925, he joined the local Preparatory School, with a view to being sent to boarding school at age thirteen. His schooling included music and, almost immediately, he demonstrated a remarkable talent. This was nurtured and developed. The Alderman was encouraged to put Frederick forward for a bursary at the Westminster Abbey Choir School. This life of privilege was severely dented in 1930, when he was expected to join Westminster school, where music was and still remains an integral part of the school's curriculum. The haberdashery store in Kingston, which had given the Simpson family such a stable lifestyle, was now under severe financial strain when the Alderman suffered an unexpected stroke. No longer able to maintain his close control of the business, he became reliant, firstly on a manager, who was incapable of combatting the effects of the Depression, and later on his wife. The store was taken into receivership in 1938, when Frederick was 21.

Because of his exceptional musical talent, Westminster School had covered all the necessary fees for his education and, indeed, his time at Oxford University. Frederick had little knowledge, at that time, of the generosity being extended towards him, but soon after his graduation, he was advised by his grandmother of the debt he now owed to his old school. His grandfather never recovered from the stroke and died soon after the store finally closed its doors. Feeling a deep sense of gratitude, Frederick returned to Westminster School and joined the staff as a music teacher. Here he was able to let his talent develop, to start composing and performing, creating a second, lucrative career in parallel with the school.

He was both talented and lucky. Performing in the 1930s was not easy. However, the new fangled BBC offered an outlet for his talent and he soon learned that investment in records, record players and artistes had great potential. He set up in business, firstly owning a shop for musical instruments, gramophones and records, but later as an agent. He was far more successful than his grandfather had ever been, even though these activities were severely curtailed by the Second World War. His own war service was uneventful and he was able to maintain his agency work. Upon his discharge, he opened a small chain of record shops and increased his involvement in the careers of various entertainers.

He founded the Richmond Music Society in 1951 as a means to offer newly qualified classical musicians an opportunity to develop and demonstrate their skills in public. It was an immediate success and, happy to remain in the background, the society had given him much pleasure over the years that followed, until his death in 1997. He never married and left the bulk of his rather substantial estate to Westminster School, to assist other boys whose families were struggling to pay the fees.

Sarah Varley was well aware of the weight of history on her shoulders. When Frederick died, aged 80, he left a reasonable bequest to the society with the comment that he hoped it would flourish for many years to come. Sarah felt that the society had been loyal to his wishes and it remained reasonably successful. Some years before, one of the lecturers at the West London University arranged for concerts to be given in one of the university halls for a peppercorn rent. The only proviso was that one concert each year would be set aside to allow the students an opportunity to display their talents. The lecturer was now the vice chancellor and the arrangement continued to the benefit of both the society and the university.

In order to celebrate the 125th anniversary of the birth of their benefactor Frederick Simpson, however, it was agreed that the society should invite a number of past performers, whose careers had later blossomed, to give a series of concerts. *All very well in principle, of course*, Sarah thought, *but not so easy in practise.* To cover the costs of newly qualified musicians was one thing but the finances of established performers was indeed something else. The budget immediately doubled and although ticket sales were proving to be strong, it was obvious that the additional costs would not easily be met. It would be necessary to raise further funds by sponsorship. This had never been done before and some committee members were dogmatically opposed. They viewed the whole matter of discussing money as unseemly and somewhat tawdry, until Sarah, with her blunt Yorkshire approach to life, pointed out that these established musicians would have to be paid and, instead of raising the money elsewhere, perhaps these committee members could write the necessary cheques to support the Anniversary Celebrations? This proposal was met with a stony silence, followed by a grudging acceptance of the sponsorship programme.

So it became Sarah's job to raise the various funds prior to the commencement of the school year in September, when a series of eight concerts was planned to be presented on a monthly basis. Being a Yorkshire lass, she was canny enough to keep her cards close to her chest. She knew that the subscriptions would raise around half the overall financial requirements. She also knew that there were certain funds held in reserve, but she still set the committee a target of raising the other half by sponsorship, advertising and fund-raising events. What she basically needed was a list of 10 benefactors, each donating £1,000. Naturally, all this was mentioned to her husband, in the hope that he might become one of the sponsors. Needless to say, although the proposition was firmly lodged in his mind, it had not become a priority.

There were seven months in which to raise the money and support was already secured from one local business. An application was made to the Lottery Fund and this was now being assessed. The local council simply turned her down without any real discussion. She seriously considered an approach to Westminster School, but was uncertain as to the possible outcome. Rotary and the Lions both listened with interest but, to date, had produced no concrete support. It was all rather depressing.

After lunch and with an hour so spare, David went into the school's computer library, supposedly to revise for his exams, but actually to look up 'Spring Tides'. He now appreciated how much an effect the moon had on the earth and as he read further, he began to understand the importance of those moments when the sun and the moon were both influencing the movement of the tides at the same time.

Without the tides, of course, some towns and ports would have no involvement with the sea. In the olden days, the flowing tide would allow the seamen to bring their ships far up the beach and when the tide ebbed, their keels and bottoms could be cleaned of weed and barnacles. He supposed this was still done with small boats, but large liners and ships would be brought into dry dock. Even then, a strong spring tide would assist in bringing a vessel into dock, before the gates were shut and all the seawater pumped out.

This regular movement of the tides was controlled by the movement of the moon. He knew that the moon didn't have a circular axis round the earth, but was egg shaped, or elliptical. When the moon was closer to the earth, then its gravitational pull was stronger.

As David read on, he learned that the tides in the English Channel could be large. This meant that a considerable mass of water moved up and down the Channel twice each day. He also learned that because the Channel was so narrow between Dover and Calais, the flow of the water could be very strong. He also read that the North Sea was relatively shallow between East Anglia and Holland. This also had the effect of making the flow of seawater an important factor to coastal shipping.

He then remembered what Mr Smith said that morning. "There might be nowhere for the water to flow into the sea." But, if the tide was so high, would the rivers stop flowing altogether? David began to wonder what might happen if the wind was so strong that the wind and the tides combined. *That would be pretty disastrous,* he thought.

As he walked home after school, he wanted to know whether the two depressions in the Atlantic were moving at all; also, whether they were deepening and what level of wind speeds were being generated. He now knew that the spring tides were expected at the end of the week and he felt as if he was completely alone in watching a natural calamity unfold. It was still cold, with a stiff easterly breeze, coming off the north European landmass. After eating his evening meal, he went to his room to check the shipping forecast.

The southern depression was starting to move north east, towards the southern tip of Ireland. It was still deepening and the wind speeds were increasing. The northern depression was slowly moving east and was currently at a point some 200 miles off the north coast of Scotland. The warm, moist air had met the cold dry air of the continental anti cyclone and along the northern weather front wind speeds were also increasing. It was snowing in Scotland, with heavy drifts being forecast. It was even snowing in north Cornwall.

Chapter 9
Tuesday – Two Days to Go

"Here is the fishing forecast for Tuesday. The depression between the Azores and the Bay of Biscay has moved north east towards Ireland. It has deepened and the wind speeds have increased to 60 knots and are expected to rise further. The rainfall is intense and visibility is extremely limited. All shipping is advised to avoid all sea areas from the Azores northwards and eastwards to the African coastline and Europe.

"The depression over Iceland has also deepened and is slowly moving in an easterly direction towards Norway. Wind speeds have increased to storm force, reaching speeds of 55 knots. Snow is falling along the whole of the weather front, making visibility virtually nil. All shipping is advised to avoid all sea areas to the north and east of Great Britain."

The presenter then began to read through the various sea areas and it soon became apparent that the weather fronts were bringing a vast amount of high wind and rain.

As David went into the kitchen on Tuesday morning, he heard the 7.30 am brief weather report. Somewhat laconically the presenter announced that snow was expected along the west coast from Cornwall, through Wales, northern England and Scotland. In Ireland, the forecast was for rain. There was no specific mention of the wind increasing.

"It seems we're back to the same old weather," his father remarked. "More rain on the way."

"It's a bit unusual to have snow in Cornwall," David commented.

"By the way, Michael," his mother cut across their conversation to address David's father. "Did you get any chance to see whether Le Grove Investments could assist the Richmond Music Society?"

"I had a potential new client in only yesterday," Michael replied. "He needs to find a home for some cash, but he will be looking for some form of return. I'm talking further with him today and will be starting to map out a programme for him."

"I'm only looking for about £1,000."

"Yes, I know." Michael put down his paper. "Mind you, your mother might want an investor for her blessed library, as well." And with that, he carefully folded the Daily Telegraph, put it into his briefcase and shrugged on his overcoat. He was ready to leave for the day.

"Come on, David! Or you might be late for school."

"It's not even eight o'clock yet, Dad. You seem to be keen to get away this morning! I don't need to be in until 9.30, so I'll walk."

Michael gave Sarah a perfunctory kiss on the cheek and turned to the door. David went back upstairs to check the movement of the weather fronts. They were both moving inexorably towards the east. In the south, the warm, wet air coming off the Atlantic was hitting the cold anti cyclone, which was making it snow, but in the north the temperatures were also plummeting, along with snow and high winds.

It won't last long, David thought. *Not in the south west. Different matter in Scotland, though.*

He saw that in the north Atlantic the depression after passing the north of Scotland was now moving slowly towards the Norwegian coastline. It was sucking down an increased amount of cold air from the Arctic and that was creating the exceptional snowfall. As yet, however, the wind over Scotland was only approaching gale force. David decided to text Jackie, advising her to take a coat as the weather was changing rapidly.

"Hi Jackie. You OK? Seems ages since Sat. When RU next free? Can do 2mrw. Let me know. BTW, take a coat today. Wthr changing. Rain coming. Talk soon. XXXX"

He sat at his computer desk wondering what she really thought of him. *She certainly gets me going*, he thought. *I hope I do the same for her.*

His phone pinged. Crikey, that was quick. Her text was short and to the point.

"Can meet tomoz at 6 for abt hour. Got to be home for just after 7."

"How about Costa in Richmond?"

"Gr8. CU there."

David picked up his books, put them in his bag and went downstairs. He called 'Bye' to his mother and went to school.

In the Gloucester Palace Hotel, three people were taking breakfast. Sebastian sat in the dining room, watching the couple at the table near the door. The man was a partial acquaintance, having been introduced several months ago, but there was no specific contact with him. He was recommended by a friend in Soho. In his mid-forties, he was well dressed in a Savile Row suit, with a white shirt and club tie. His black shoes were highly polished. Despite the turnout, however, everything appeared to be slightly used and that, thought Seb, is because he's wearing yesterday's clothes.

It was the same with his companion, a pretty lady, young enough to be his daughter, but old enough to be independent. She was wearing a short black skirt, together with a white, almost transparent, blouse. Her black bra was deep cut, showing a considerable amount of cleavage. She was smiling a lot, obviously in his thrall and enjoying her 'morning after'. They were sitting side by side and his left hand was idly stroking her right thigh. As she sat down, her skirt rode up, giving Sebastian a rather unnecessary view of her thighs, especially when her companion's hand pushed the hem of her skirt up even further.

Their shenanigans were rather putting Sebastian off his food. Betty invariably cooked a decent breakfast of bacon, eggs, sausage and tomatoes with toast and tea. Real coffee was also available plus orange juice, as required. He was trying to formulate in his mind the amount of money that he could start to 'invest' with Le Grove Investments. His meeting with Michael Varley had been interesting but, as yet, unproductive. He knew that Michael sailed close to the wind in certain respects. He had, after all, stayed at the Gloucester Palace twice. The first time was back in the summer, when one of the girls brought him back. And then in November he stayed the night with his secretary.

Their discussions had focussed solely on the money that Sebastian was now ready to invest. In addition, he was wondering whether Michael would be able to shift any of the illicit funds that were getting out of control under his office floor. He also wondered whether Michael might be persuaded, perhaps even blackmailed.

His mind was again distracted as he watched the man put his hand under the tablecloth once more and onto the young lady's thigh. She opened her legs slightly and he slid his hand up further. She opened her legs even more and her skirt rode up so far that the tops of her hold ups were completely exposed. She glanced across the room and saw Sebastian watching them. Instead of pushing her friend's hand away, she opened her legs even wider. Her skirt was now but a circle of cloth around her waist and, because she had no knickers, she was displaying a cleanly shaven pussy. She smiled at Sebastian, put her own hand into her lap and with her middle finger, she gently ran it up her slit, before putting the finger into her mouth. Sebastian watched. He didn't react. He didn't even acknowledge her smile.

As her companion now put his middle finger into her, she whispered into his ear and reached under the table with her own hand. She put it on his trousers, feeling his erection and began to pull down his zip. Having seen enough, Sebastian rose from his table, picked up his paper and walked slowly out of the dining room, leaving the couple to enjoy whatever breakfast they desired.

He sat down in his office and began to make a few calculations. He was trying to work out how quickly he could shift the stash of dirty money hidden under his floor. Of course, some of it belonged to clients and his percentage would need to be taken into account. There were only so many so-called employees on his books that he was able to utilise, but it would be stupid to pay them more than the going rate and bonuses could only really be given at Christmas. He soon reached the conclusion that, on the basis he didn't receive any further cash, it would take over two years to move it all. And, of course, with more cash coming in all the time, that time lag was going to shorten and become an increasing problem.

As he sat there, thinking about his situation, he realised that the safe under the floor was itself too small and that he may well have to construct a secret strong room in the cellar. He wondered whether Fred would be up to the task and decided to go down to look at the cellar rooms that morning. What he needed was a false wall, with a secret door, behind which he could store all manner of illicit goods. It would need suitable space with good shelving, but above all a foolproof access.

He stood up and left his office, walking to the stairwell of the building. The stairs themselves passed around the old-fashioned lift with access onto each floor through a sliding door. The inside walls of the stairs encased the lift itself. On the left of the lift shaft, there was a door which opened onto the stairs that led down to the cellar. On the right, there was a similar door, which opened onto the stairs leading up to the first floor, at the top of which was another door. On each floor of the hotel, therefore, the doors not only offered fire safety, but also acted as excellent draught proofing.

From the cellar, on the lower level, there was access to the carpark at the rear of the building. The lift, which had a single split/sliding and automatic door, operated on each floor.

Sebastian went down the stairs through the left-hand door to the cellar, where the layout of the rooms was very similar to the ground floor. He passed through the door at the bottom. There was a passage on his left, which led past the kitchen and the laundry, to the rear of the building. In front of him, there was a large space between the lift and the front of the building. This was immediately below the reception area on the ground floor. On his right there was a storage cellar.

He turned left and walked down the passage past the kitchen and the laundry to the rear of the building. At the back, there was a pair of doors, leading to a small loading bay outside, allowing access for delivery trucks. There was also a separate door which opened onto a small landing before leading down a few steps, giving pedestrian access. Beyond these doors was another storage cellar, which appeared to offer Sebastian some potential.

Both cellars could also be accessed from the front and the rear as there was a connecting door between them.

The whole building was supported by the central lift shaft and stairwell, but Sebastian immediately noticed that the kitchen was larger than the equivalent room on the other side of the building, which made the laundry somewhat smaller. With a growing sense of excitement and realisation, he concluded that he might be able to construct a new, separate room, which would be under the lounge and games room. The water supply and soil pipes for the building were at the back behind the laundry, so they would cause no problems. The electricity, telephones and gas supply came in through the front of the building, straight from the street, into the cellar where the fuse boxes and gas meter were conveniently situated. Again, these would not be in the way.

Returning once more to the open space, he stood facing the lift door. He realised that there was potential space, under the stairs, from which he might access a newly constructed hideaway between both the storage rooms. The wall to the left of the lift was bricked up, as far as he could see. He considered that the wall could be removed and the space behind turned into a walk-in cupboard. The left-hand wall of this cupboard might then conceal the entrance to his secret room. He went back up the stairs to his office on the ground floor and decided to telephone Le Grove Investments in order to pursue the urgent need to invest his ill-gotten gains.

After putting all the photographs onto his laptop, Andy downloaded a large selection onto a removable file and was now trying to make contact with the world of advertising, to see whether he could live up to the promises he had made to Alice. He was finding it far more difficult than he had imagined. He quickly realised that he needed a go between, a person who could not only see the potential of the portfolio but would also know those people behind the doors that were currently closed to him.

The photographs were sorted into three specific categories, each of which were filed separately. First, there was a file of basically fashion shots of the many outfits Alice had worn, taken from different angles and showing off her long, shapely legs, her beguiling face and her upright, somewhat arrogant carriage. They were good photos, but not especially different from a million others.

The second file was definitely more pornographic. Although now rather dated, he knew there was still a market for topless girls, naked girls and girls in various erotic poses. The file was actually much smaller than he had expected, but he hoped that, if this was the line to be pursued, then he would be able to take many, many more. But even as he indulged himself in that thought, there was a creeping realisation that it was Alice who was now in control and that it was she who would dictate the future.

In the past, Andy was always able to dupe the various girls that he had photographed with his major purpose of getting them into bed. When that happened, it was invariably a deep anti-climax for him, as the girls had invariably been far too easy and had shown no class whatsoever. Alice was definitely different. Her whole demeanour demonstrated class and control.

Andy's third file was a very personal one and made up of the best from the other two files. It only had eight photographs in it, but Andy had stared at each one for minutes at a time. They showed the change that came over Alice from the reticent, rather concerned woman, whom he had met in the Costa Coffee, right through to the sophisticated lady who had cut short the session on the Sunday afternoon, leaving him frustrated, intrigued and concerned that he might have lost her.

He was considering his options when he had received the call on the Monday morning to take Sebastian Fortescue Brown from the Gloucester Palace Hotel to Le

Grove Investments in the city. He didn't know Mr Fortescue Brown at all well, although he had driven him on a number of occasions, albeit infrequently, over the past year. Andy realised that his client knew people all over Soho, but there wasn't a real opportunity to open up the subject of his dilemma during the journey either to the city or back to Kensington.

His thoughts were interrupted as his mobile chirruped in his shirt pocket.

"Andy?"

"Speaking."

"This is Sebastian Fortescue Brown from the Gloucester Palace Hotel. Are you free this morning?"

"Yes, sir," replied Andy. "Where do you want to go?"

"I need to be back in the city by 11.30 am. Can you do that for me?"

"Certainly can! I can be at the hotel in about 25 minutes. That'll leave forty minutes to get you to the city. Will it be the same address as yesterday?" he asked.

"Yes. I'll be waiting outside."

Andy put the files and his laptop into a holdall and, picking up his car keys, he left his house and walked quickly to where the cab was parked. He would have to push it to get from Kennington, over the river and up to Kensington, but with good use of the bus lanes, he was over Vauxhall Bridge in no time and speeding along Grosvenor Road and the Chelsea Embankment. Turning up Beaufort Street and Drayton Gardens, he avoided all the potential congestion at Victoria, Sloane Square and South Kensington. He arrived outside the hotel just as Sebastian exited through the front door.

They set off to the city along Cromwell Road, cutting down Hans Road and onto Belgrave Square. He then drove down Grosvenor Place and up Buckingham Gate to Birdcage Walk, past the Houses of Parliament and up the Victoria Embankment and so to the city. They arrived at Le Grove Investments at 11.20 am.

Although Andy wanted to seek advice from Sebastian, he felt that he should wait until the return journey, when his passenger would hopefully be more relaxed. He knew he would have to park up for some time.

As soon as Sebastian finished ordering the cab, he immediately called Le Grove Investments. Alice answered the phone and dealt with the request for an immediate meeting. As Michael Varley was already beginning to fret about his speech, she felt a meeting would be a welcome diversion. She would also have an opportunity to type up his notes and amendments, putting the whole presentation into a satisfactory format. She was in a very relaxed frame of mind, because Michael, the evening before, signed the letters concerning her salary increase, without so much as a murmur.

Upon his arrival, Sebastian was ushered into Michael's office. Alice made coffee as the two men were exchanging pleasantries. After taking the tray into Michael's office, she then left them to their meeting.

"I'm a little surprised to see you back so quickly," Michael remarked. "New clients normally take a week or so to mull over the necessary details."

"The proposals you've outlined are not so difficult to understand, especially while interest rates remain so feeble," replied Sebastian. "Anyway, it's not just the immediate investment that's on my mind. Yesterday, you encouraged me to speak openly, to give you as full a personal financial position as I could. This I did and, very quickly, we reached a conclusion as to the format of investment that would be both tax efficient and might also offer a reasonable return. You also indicated that there were further possible opportunities, including property investment.

"As it happens, I have other matters I wish to raise with you and I wonder whether it might be possible to do this in a more relaxed atmosphere over a spot of lunch."

"Of course," Michael replied. "I'll just ask Alice to arrange a table. It shouldn't be too difficult in the middle of February. Have you ever eaten at the Sauterelle?"

"Oh! I've heard of that. It's at the Royal Exchange."

"That's right. And quite convenient for us here at Le Grove Investments."

Alice was able to secure a table immediately and both men left for lunch. Sebastian felt rather nervous as he turned over in his mind the words he might use in broaching the question of his growing capital. He completely forgot to tell Andy that he would be at least a couple of hours.

As he walked into the Grieg's sandwich shop at Victoria Station, Milton was really surprised to see Pamela already sitting at a table in the far corner with two other Transport for London staff members. She saw Milton come through the door and waved to him. The two men with her turned to see a handsome, well-built West Indian coming into the shop.

"Who's he?" asked one of the men.

"He's a good friend," replied Pamela. "Don't start any trouble, because I reckon he could make mincemeat of you both."

She knew that both men were members of the National Front, although they tried to keep their membership well concealed whilst at work. One of them was keen on Pamela and was trying to persuade her to go out with him. He was becoming a bit of a pest. He now started to seethe as he realised that she was already quite friendly with Milton and happy to have a West Indian for a friend.

For her part, although she had enjoyed her Sunday afternoon with Milton, she did wonder whether Milton would pursue the friendship or whether it might just disappear like early morning mist on a warm summer's day. His text had given her hope that it wouldn't.

"Hi, Milton." She stood up to greet him. "These are two friends from way back, Carl and Les. Why don't you join us?"

Hardly able to contain his rage and disgust, Carl got up and muttered that he was due on shift and, turning their backs on both Pamela and Milton, they both hurriedly left the café.

"Who were they?" asked Milton. "I recognised Les. Isn't he the guy who had a bit of a problem a few months back with the police? I can't remember the details, but I seem to recall that he was suspended for a while."

"Yeah," Pamela was a bit discomfited by this, but she looked straight at him and decided to give a brief but factual account. "He had been at an anti-immigration rally and was arrested for throwing a bottle. As it happens, it wasn't Les who threw the bottle, but it hit a man on the head and he had to have hospital treatment. Les was reported, because he was wearing his work uniform and he was subjected to a formal investigation. Fortunately, the whole incident was caught on CCTV and this showed that Les was not the guy who had thrown the bottle."

"How come he knows you?"

"Actually, it's Carl who knows me. He's been trying to get me to go out with him for months now. Les is just his mate. But Carl isn't my type at all. He's hard and demanding – and he's married. He doesn't know that I know that so he continues to pester me."

"Hang on," said Milton. "I'll get a sandwich and a coffee. Do you want another drink?"

"No thanks. I'm fine."

When he returned to the table, Pamela seemed to have relaxed. Milton put his sandwich and coffee on the table and sat down next to her.

"Thanks for the text." He looked at her. "It felt really good to get it."

"That's OK." She looked at him and felt her stomach melt. She was falling for this man so deeply and very quickly.

"It was the kiss at the end that made it so good."

Pamela felt her face flush slightly and she briefly glanced down at the table. Milton reached for her right hand and gently held it in his. She felt the contact quiver up her arm and settle, floating on her liquid stomach. She could think of nothing sensible to say so, instead, she smiled at him with both her mouth and her eyes.

Milton saw her eyes change to become glittery and bright. *She looks so beautiful,* he thought. He looked at her hand, held in his, comfortable and relaxed.

"Most girls I've met since my divorce have said that I talk too much. That my interest in history and the stuff that I've discovered makes it hard for people to talk to me. I suppose I do hide behind my knowledge and I hope I didn't bore you on Sunday afternoon."

"No, not at all," she stammered a reply. "As a matter of fact, I thought it was all rather fascinating. Actually, I wish that I knew more."

"Well, I know that it's not everybody's cup of tea and I have been told that I can rabbit on a bit, when given the chance. You were a bit of a captive audience!"

As they chatted and enjoyed each other's company, they were both surprised how comfortable they had become with each other and how relaxed they were. Milton finished his sandwich, still holding Pamela's hand and then drank his coffee. He looked at his watch.

"I've got to go," he announced. "I've still got a couple of hours before the end of my shift."

"I finish at five today," Pamela replied. "Perhaps we could meet later and I could cook you some tea?"

"I would really like that." Milton stood up, still holding Pamela's hand. "Shall I wait here for you at five?"

"Good idea. By the way, can I have my hand back please?" She laughed, as Milton looked at her enquiringly, then realised the reason for her question. He bent down and kissed her gently on the cheek.

"See you later."

"Bye."

As he left the cafe, Milton saw Les and Carl near the steps to his platform. They had obviously been hanging about outside, waiting for him. As Milton turned to go down to the underground, they followed and as they walked round a sharp corner, Les punched Milton in the left kidney.

"Oy! If you know what's good for you, you'll leave my girl alone." Les pulled Milton's shoulder so they were facing each other, leaving Carl behind him. The breath had been knocked out of him, but Milton was recovering quickly.

"She isn't your girl and never will be," he replied. He saw in the reflection of an advertisement on the wall, that Carl was about to punch him, so he quickly moved to his left and the right arm jab completely missed. At the same time, he raised the heel of his right hand into Les' face, aiming for his nose. The punch wasn't hard enough and Les was able to ride it. Carl grabbed Milton from behind and pinned his arms. Les drew back his right fist and punched Milton hard in the face. Again, he was able move just enough to deflect the full force of the blow, but it damaged his left ear.

Realising that he had to resolve this attack quickly and with as little damage as possible to himself, Milton, after moving to his right to avoid the punch, now moved back, catching Carl off guard. He raised his right leg and brought his foot down hard on Carl's instep and ankle. There was a crack and, immediately, Carl shouted painfully and let go. Now free to move, Milton moved swiftly onto his left and with his right foot kicked Les fully and hard in the testicles. He doubled over in pain. Milton looked back at Carl, who was sitting with his back to the tunnel wall, nursing what looked like a sprained ankle.

"Try that again, you pieces of shit and you will both end up in hospital." Milton stood up and walked away.

Crumpled against the wall, Les felt the pain spread through his stomach, as though he was being burnt with acid. His eyes were watering, but his mind was already planning his revenge. He crawled over to Carl.

"You OK?" he asked.

"I think that black bastard has broken my ankle." Carl looked down at his foot which was certainly at an odd angle.

"Let's have a look." Through bouts of nausea, Les picked up Carl's right foot and tried to move it back to a normal position. "Does that hurt?"

"Yes, it bloody does!" Carl shouted with the pain.

"We've got to get you up to the surface. Can you stand on the other foot?"

Slowly, the pain was receding from Les' groin and he helped Carl to stand on the uninjured foot. With Carl's left arm over his shoulder and with his right arm around Carl's waist, Carl was able to lift his right leg and hop painfully on his left. They made slow progress back to the surface where a member of the public called an ambulance.

After lunch, Sebastian called Andy and the cab was waiting at Le Grove Investments, as he and Michael Varley returned from the restaurant. Sebastian considered that their meeting had been fruitful as Michael had agreed to accelerate the movement of illicit cash through his systems by including both investment proposals for the library in Yorkshire and the Centenary Concerts in Richmond. At first, Sebastian was a little unsure of these ideas as neither appeared to return the capital in a reasonable time, but Michael explained that both should be regarded as long term investments, which would provide an annual income, albeit rather small. In this way, there would be a legitimate annual income for as long as was necessary.

Michael was thinking that he would have to keep all these transactions well organised within the financial books of Le Grove Investments. So long as there was a paper trail demonstrating capital received, capital invested, interest accrued and distributed, commission paid and capital repaid, then no one would need to look too deeply at anything else. Michael's initial reluctance was based on his thoughts that Sebastian's money might be somewhat grubby, but when Sebastian reminded Michael of his visits to the hotel before Christmas, everything began to fall into place.

They parted company at the door to Le Grove Investments and Sebastian got into Andy's cab feeling rather satisfied with the lunch time discussions. The only potential downside was the size of the commission Michael had requested. It was somewhat larger than Sebastian expected. But even that would be worth paying when it became obvious that greater amounts of money could be moved and laundered and that this would make Sebastian even more beneficial to his underworld contacts.

As he settled into his seat for the return journey to the Gloucester Palace Hotel, he realised that Andy was talking to him.

"I wonder if I can ask your advice, Mr Fortescue Brown."

"Advice about what?"

"Well, I do a bit of photography work and I've met a lady who could really make it big."

"Big in what? Pornography?" Sebastian asked.

"Not necessarily. It's more her eyes than her body." Andy struggled to explain that Alice could have a great career as a model, even an actress.

"I've created this portfolio," he said. "Basically, it's of the girl modelling different clothes. Actually, she's more of a lady than a girl. She must be in her mid-20s. I was wondering whether you had any contacts in the advertising industry, where I could try to get some interest in her."

"My contacts would probably be more down the pornographic channel," Sebastian replied. "But I do know couple of people who sometimes place models. I'll have a word and if anything comes of it, we'll split any commission 50/50."

Andy nearly drove into a Keep Left bollard when he heard that, but he said nothing. As they drove into the carpark at the back of the hotel, Sebastian asked Andy whether he had the portfolio with him. Andy said he had and Sebastian invited him into the office to look at it and to assess the contents.

He sat down at his desk and switched on his computer. Andy passed over the computer stick which Sebastian plugged in. An array of pictures covered the screen. Sebastian clicked on the first picture of Alice looking somewhat discomfited, shoulders hunched, head down. He immediately recognised her but said nothing. As he scanned through the selected pictures, Sebastian quickly realised that Alice had turned the tables on poor old Andy and by the time he reached the end of the portfolio, it was quite obvious that Alice was now fully in control of her own destiny. Now she was only using Andy, who had lost all hope of ever regaining his superiority over her.

"When did you take these?"

"Over Saturday and Sunday."

"How many have you rejected?"

"About half, I guess."

"Do you have any others that you've kept back for your own purposes?"

"Just a few. About a dozen."

"I presume they are rather more..." Sebastian hesitated. "Interesting?"

Andy grinned. "Well, yes, I suppose they are."

"Do you have them here?"

"No."

"Have you shown these to..." again Sebastian hesitated, "the young lady?"

"Not all of them. I've explained that I am the copyright owner of the pictures and she seemed to understand that. She's already got a copy of the selected pictures from our first session on Saturday."

"How did you meet her?"

"She used my cab on the bloody awful day last Thursday when it was raining like hell. We chatted on the way to Waterloo and I gave her my card. I was really surprised when she phoned me on Saturday morning."

I bet you were, thought Sebastian. He looked again at the pictures on the computer. Without telling Andy he had saved the whole portfolio to his Pictures file before closing down the computer. He gave the stick back to Andy.

"I'll make a couple of enquiries for you, but I'm making no promises."

"That's really good of you," Andy replied. "Anyway, I'd better get going." He walked to the door. "So, I'll be hearing from you, soon?" Sebastian just nodded.

And with that, Andy left Sebastian's office, went down the staircase to the basement and the back door.

In the city, Michael called his mother-in-law in Huddersfield.

"I think I might have a proposition which could be a resolution to your financial problem with the library," he said after they had exchanged the usual pleasantries. "I have a client who is wanting to invest in property over, maybe, a 20-year period. You will retain ownership of the building, but he will become a financial partner. Although you will both have responsibilities for maintenance and upkeep, he will expect you to deal with all that. You will pay him an agreed monthly amount, until the capital has been fully repaid."

"Will there be any interest to pay?" Christine wondered what she had done to get such news which seemed like a miracle from heaven.

"Of course there will," Michael replied. "I'll draw up a schedule which will show you what the monthly payments will be. Everything will now depend on the amount you need, how much you can afford to repay and how long you want the arrangement to last."

"Well, you've rather taken by breath away, Michael. How soon do you want your answers?"

"I do realise that this may well have come as a bit of a shock, but I rather feel that my client will want everything resolved by the end of next week."

"Initially, we'll be looking for about £50,000. Is that too much?"

"No. That should be absolutely fine."

After further conversation about the family, Michael put down the phone and called for Alice to come in. He dictated to her the broad outline of the contract and asked that it should be ready to be sent to Mr Fortescue Brown the following day.

Michael now phoned his wife, Sarah.

"Hi, Sarah."

"Hello, Michael. What do you want?"

"I seem to recall that you were telling me that you were having difficulties in raising the necessary funds for the centenary concerts."

"That's right. We are."

"How much are you needing to raise and how much have you got so far?"

"We'll need £10,000 and we already been promised £2,500. I know it's only small beer compared to the amounts you normally talk about, but it's vital for us."

"If I was able to inject £5,000 straightaway, would that help at all?"

"Enormously. But can you do that?"

"I've got a new client who is looking to put some money towards 'Good Causes' and I immediately thought of you."

"What will he want in return?"

"Can you give him some sort of prominence for a concert? Maybe, he could be named as a sponsor? Something like that."

"That would be easy and we could throw in four complimentary tickets as well."

"OK. I'll sort all that out with him. By the way, don't forget, I'll be staying up in town tomorrow night. Before the meeting and my speech on Thursday morning."

"Yes. I remember."

After school, David firstly went home where he changed out of his school uniform into denims, T shirt and sweater and his new pair of trainers. Making sure he had enough money, he set off for Richmond town centre to meet Jackie. He reached the café at half past five, fully realising that he was early by at least half an hour.

As it happens, Jackie had skipped her last lesson and was home early enough to get ready and arrive in Richmond town centre by five o'clock. She had spent the extra time looking at the shops and boutiques, generally wasting time but actually buying nothing. She made her way to the Costa Coffee where she arrived at just after six o'clock. As she went through the door, she didn't see David, who was sitting at the back of the café.

He had seen her come through the door, dressed in a mini kilt, knee length socks, a tight low-cut top and her sheepskin coat. Her long dark wavy hair was slightly damp from the drizzly rain and, as she scanned the café menu more carefully, she placed a loose lock of hair behind her right ear. She saw David with his hand raised in greeting. He was walking towards the counter.

"Hi." He put his hand on her arm. "What can I get you?" She kissed him quickly on the cheek and looked up at the board behind the counter. "Can I have a de caff skinny latte, please?" she asked.

The barista, having heard the request, started its preparation, as Jackie went to David's table and sat down. After paying, David followed with her drink and a second cappuccino for himself.

"Thanks for coming." All of a sudden, he felt quite tongue tied.

"That's OK." Jackie slipped off her coat, letting it hang over the back of her chair. As she eased it over her shoulders, she pointed both arms towards the floor, leant slightly forward, arching her lower back. It was quite obvious that she had, once again, come out without her bra.

"You look fabulous!" David murmured, entranced with the vision before him.

"Thanks." She looked at him through her long eye lashes, seeing a good-looking young man with broad shoulders, smiling eyes and an honest, trustworthy face. "You're not so bad yourself."

He started to chuckle. She looked at him quizzically. "What's so funny?"

"Well, I was just thinking that the last time we met, we were like two very old friends and now, we are stuttering over our conversation, as though we've never met before."

She giggled. "You're right." And with the ice broken they both started talking at once, happy and comfortable together. There were only a few customers in the café and David had selected a very discreet table, away from prying eyes.

"I didn't realise that you had decided to come to the rugby last Saturday just to fuck me," he said.

"I thought I'd give you a nice surprise."

"It certainly was. But with all my jizz on your T shirt, weren't you cold on the way home?"

"Not really. My sheepskin is really warm and the jumper is too. Anyway, as soon as I got home, I had a really hot bath and lazed about all afternoon. After dinner, I watched telly with my mum."

"So you didn't have to dash off straight afterwards?" David felt mildly put out.

"Well, I could hardly hang around the clubhouse with your cum all over my clothes, could I?" She laughed. "I had no idea how long you would be with your mates and I just thought it would be more sensible. Anyway, I'm here now, aren't I?"

She leant over to him and kissed him on the lips. To stop her chair over balancing, she put her hand on his thigh. As she expected, he responded and as she opened her lips, she felt his tongue pushing between her teeth. She slid her hand further up his thigh to his crutch and was rewarded with a growing bulge.

"Someone might see us." David felt a little concerned.

"Not at this table. And I know exactly why you chose this one." She giggled again. Looking into his eyes, she took his hand and placed it on her own thigh. "I wonder what you might be able to do with that."

Her mini kilt was so short that none of it was actually on the chair. He stroked her thigh up to her own crutch and was surprised and a little disappointed to feel a pair of knickers. The look of fleeting disappointment on his face had obviously given him away.

"Were you hoping for a repeat of Saturday?" she whispered.

"Not really… Well, yes, actually!" he stammered.

"That can always be arranged." She got up from the table and disappeared into the Ladies loo. When she reappeared, her black socks were now over her knees. As she sat down, she seemed to flick her bottom so the hem on the mini kilt avoided all contact with the chair. "Have another go," she suggested.

David put his hand on her thigh once more. When he reached her pubic mound, he found it devoid of knickers and hair. She opened her legs a little and he could feel her dampness. He moved his fingers against each thigh in turn, opening her legs just a little further and then a little further still, until he was rewarded with an access to her opening labia and her clitoris. As he gently rubbed it, she moaned quietly and invitingly. He stopped.

"Oh God!" she said, pleading with him. "Don't stop now. It feels so good and I know how much you enjoy doing it to me."

He returned to his task with a gentle enthusiasm and, suddenly, she arched her back and squeaked. He felt a flood of liquid on his fingers and reached for a paper napkin.

"Thanks." She took it from him and put it between her thighs, mopping up the liquid on her chair.

"Did I make you pee?" he asked, somewhat concerned.

"No. Sometimes when I cum it's so powerful that I squirt this liquid. I don't know why, but it feels really intense. I know it's unusual, because the girls at school don't react like that. At least they don't say that they do.

"I don't suppose you noticed, but I squirted on Saturday as well. When I was with you."

She looked at her watch. It was ten past six. She got up, put on her coat and with her back to the rest of the café, she put on her knickers.

"I've got to go. I promised I would be home for dinner and I've got to get ready. Let's meet again soon. Are you busy tomorrow? Let's go to the cinema."

"No. I mean, yes. It'll be great to see you again and I'm sure I can be free tomorrow."

And with that she was gone, leaving David frustrated, exhausted as though he had just run a marathon and with his thoughts all jumbled in his head.

With the return of the rain in Essex, even though it wasn't very heavy, Martin still felt that the ground was too wet to plough and, because of that, all his frustrations were back. *Who would be a farmer?* he thought. *The weather is always difficult. Too wet, too dry and too windy.*

The phone rang and as he was in the office, trying to stave off his depression, he was able to answer it straightaway.

"Hello! Martin Havers speaking."

"Hi, Dad. It's me, Charlie. I thought I'd ring because, with all this rain, I realise that you'll be going up the wall with frustration."

"Hello Charlie. You are absolutely right. We had a couple of decent days over the weekend and I was able to get the top field ploughed, but everything else is waiting for this damn' rain to stop."

"Thought so. I was wondering if Paula and I could come and stay for a few days. I've got to get some holiday in before the end of March and it would be great to see you and Mum."

"'Course you can. You know that you are both welcome at any time. When do you expect to get here?"

"Tomorrow evening, if that's OK? We can then help you with some odd jobs on the farm over the rest of the week and the weekend."

"I'm sure that'll be fine, but apart from the ploughing, I'm pretty much up to date. But that doesn't matter because it'll be great to have a chance to catch up and put the world to rights. We could do that over a couple of pints."

"Sure will, Dad. And thanks. I've got to go. Give our love to Mum."

"Will do. See you tomorrow."

And with that, Charlie was gone, leaving Martin holding the phone in his hand and wondering what the real reason was for a visit at such short notice. Charlie had been an excellent pupil through his school career, but he ducked out of university in order to go 'travelling'. Surprisingly, his subsequent career wasn't affected by this. Tall, good looking with broad shoulders and invariably well dressed, Charlie had never been without a pretty girl on his arm.

Since returning to the United Kingdom, he worked in the Information Technology industry selling all sorts of technical matters that basically floated well above Martin's head. He always seemed to be doing well, judging by the cars he drove and the holidays he took. On one occasion, he flew all the way to Australia for a long weekend simply to attend a friend's wedding. Some might have thought this somewhat extravagant, but Charlie just considered it to be the norm.

Now in his mid-thirties, he was settling down somewhat, with a delightful girl, Paula. To his family, it was rather a surprise that Charlie chose to marry a more down to earth lady, compared with the string of vacant, trophy-like photographic models. Paula was intelligent, good looking and practical. She maintained a firm grip on Charlie's lifestyle and Martin suspected that she was also trying to organise his career. No longer pretending to be part of the jet set, Charlie seemed to be more interested in walking his chocolate Labradors and helping out at the local cricket club.

I wonder why they want to come and stay. Martin's thoughts drifted through all the negative reasons, until he decided that it would just be better to wait until they arrived. He wandered through to the kitchen, where Jennifer was preparing their evening meal.

"Who was on the phone?" she asked, as he opened the kitchen door.

"Charlie."

"That's strange," she replied. "I forgot to tell you. James phoned earlier today and asked if he and Megan could come and stay for a few days."

"I wonder what's going on," Martin muttered, quietly and then said, out loud. "That's exactly what Charlie said. He and Paula are coming tomorrow evening and staying until the end of the weekend."

"That is strange," repeated Jennifer. "I wonder if we should now be expecting a call from Helen."

"I doubt it. The last we heard, at the end of January, she was in New Zealand. I might send her an email, to see if she knows anything."

They sat down to their evening meal, as the wind started to pick up from the west.

Chapter 10
Wednesday – One Day to Go (Day)

The high pressure over northern Europe had spread to the west over France and Great Britain but was now receding in the face of the two deepening depressions, the first in the north Atlantic moving towards Norway and the second just to the south of Ireland. The winds were increasing and all along the extended cold front, there was heavy rain or snow.

The northern front was now dragging freezing temperatures from the northern Polar Regions, causing unprecedented blizzard conditions. The wind was blowing at force 9 southwards across the northern Atlantic and the snowfall over both the western and eastern Scottish coasts was causing havoc. Fort William in the west was already cut off, as were Inverness, Aberdeen and Dundee in the east. The National Grid was struggling with the increase of electricity usage as the public turned up their thermostats and this was worsened because of the weight of snow on the power lines, coupled with the vicious wind, causing a multitude of breakages. Telephone lines and telegraph poles were damaged in an increasing number of locations and all bridges and motorways were closed to high sided traffic.

In the south of the British Isles, the wind was now blowing straight up the English Channel at over 60 knots, this being "violent storm" force on the Beaufort scale. The wind was causing exceptionally high waves, with much increased airborne spray being added to the heavy rainfall. Visibility was reduced to nothing. Trees had been blown down over Cornwall and Devon, but the snowfall of the previous day had disappeared in the face of the exceptional rainfall. Flash flooding was forecast and, as in Scotland, there were many blackouts as the National Grid struggled to maintain a power supply.

The Meteorological Office had sent an urgent note to the Cabinet Office in Downing Street, urging concern that these weather fronts were likely to cause widespread damage, local flooding and structural damage.

The Prime Minister looked round the Cabinet Table and asked for comment. The Home Secretary asked if there were any specific forecasts for certain areas.

"Apparently not, as yet," answered the Prime Minister. "I am advised that the weather conditions in Scotland are exceptionally appalling, with many interruptions to the power supply. No doubt the First Minister will have her finger on the pulse." He looked at the First Secretary for Scotland.

"I have had no word from Holyrood," he replied. "And based on our last exchange of words, I don't really expect any."

The Home Secretary continued. "You may recall, Prime Minister, that considerable coastal flooding was forecast in East Anglia a couple of years ago. We advised local people to evacuate and seek refuge on higher ground." The Home Secretary didn't add that because the flooding hadn't actually happened, the evacuees were not happy with the over-cautious attitude promoted by the Environment Agency. She looked over at the Secretary of State for the Environment.

"The Environment Agency has advised that the country is likely to suffer from two weather fronts, one in the south and the other in Scotland. I have also been reminded that the Spring Tides are likely to reach their maximum tomorrow. I feel that we would be wise to heed the advice of the Agency, to put all the emergency services on alert, including the Armed Forces."

The Prime Minister looked at the Defence Minister. "As always," he responded, "We will work closely with the Police and the Fire and Rescue Services wherever possible. I feel that the most important matter is to ensure that the public are kept fully informed with a series of hourly bulletins."

The cabinet meeting moved onto other agenda items before breaking up. A statement was drafted for the media, especially radio and television. In a further attempt to bring the appropriate information to as many people as possible, the same messages were sent out on social media.

On his way to the station, Michael Varley reckoned that the wind was so strong that there were likely to be delays throughout the rail network. He was carrying both his briefcase and a small overnight bag. His mind was full of conflicting thoughts. His speech, due to be delivered first thing tomorrow morning, was uppermost in his mind, but this was overlayed with the anticipation of being with Alice overnight.

As it happened, there was no delay to his train and he was able to reach his office by half past eight. As always, Alice was there before him and the coffee was already made. In addition, there was a small, warm croissant on a plate with a pat of butter and a small amount of raspberry jam.

On entering the office that morning, Alice put her own overnight bag into a cupboard, ready for the coming evening. She considered that, even with her increasing hold over Michael, she was not yet ready to stand her ground against his advances completely. After all, having just extracted a pay rise, it might be better to demonstrate her thanks rather than to be detached and distant. She took in his coffee and croissant and was rather surprised that, when she put the breakfast tray on his desk, he did not put his hand on her waist. Indeed, he ignored her completely.

Perhaps his manners are improving, she thought.

As she left his office, to return to her own desk, she saw that the post had arrived. She carried it through to her office and started to open it.

After breakfast, it suddenly dawned on Martin that, this coming weekend, he and Jennifer had been married for forty years. *That's why the boys have been in touch,* he thought. *I must nip into town and get her a present and a card. Every year, I forget and every year, Jennifer has a go at me. Well, not this year, because I've remembered!*

He lifted his head to see Jennifer looking at him quizzically. "Are you all right?" she enquired, wondering why he was grinning like a Cheshire cat.

"I'm absolutely fine. Why do you ask?"

"When you sat down, you appeared to have all the troubles of the world on your shoulders. I realise that you must be very frustrated with the weather and I can't blame you for that. But suddenly, your face changed. You started to smile, as though you had just received some exciting news."

Martin shook his head. "No, not really." He said. "I was only thinking that it'll be good to see Charlie and James tonight. We haven't had a houseful for such a long time."

"Yes and I'll have to get down to the shops to buy enough food for them all, so I won't be lingering here this morning. What have you got planned?"

"The weather is even worse today," Martin replied. "Have you heard this announcement from the Government that the weather over the next two days is going to be pretty awful with local flooding, interrupted power supplies, gale force winds. I thought I would walk down to the river, to make sure everything is OK down there."

"You be careful. I know what you're like. If you see something that needs to be fixed, you'll get on with it with no thought whether you need two or three other people to help you. If you do find something wrong, please wait until Charlie or James get here." And with those instructions, Jennifer put on her coat and left through the kitchen door. Martin watched her get into the old Astra and drive out of the yard.

I'll give her five minutes, he thought. He tidied away the breakfast things, put on his coat and muffler, before closing and locking the kitchen door behind him. He got into his somewhat smarter BMW series 3 and drove out of the yard towards Brentwood. Some years before, he was delighted to discover an excellent jeweller on the High Street. Since then, for several Christmases and Birthdays, he had become quite a regular customer.

As he entered the door, he realised that he was dressed more for working on the farm, than for purchasing some jewellery. He felt rather unkempt and dishevelled but was immediately put at ease by the proprietor.

"Good morning, Mr Havers."

"Good morning. I do apologise for coming in dressed like this."

"Not at all. As always, you're most welcome. What can we do for you on this rather blustery day?"

"Forty years married and I almost completely forgot." Martin found himself explaining about Charlie's odd telephone call and then being told that, earlier the same day James had been talking with his mum. "So, it seems that I'm to be the butt of an elaborate family joke, because it's a well-known fact that I regularly forget birthdays and anniversaries."

"Has the date been and gone?"

"That's the thing. It hasn't. Not yet. The actual day will be on Saturday."

"And did you say forty years?" enquired the jeweller.

"Yes. I suppose there's a specific stone for forty years and I expect that will cost me a fortune!"

The jeweller looked closely at Martin and replied, "Not necessarily."

Some twenty-five years before, the jeweller moved his business from Hatton Garden in London to Brentwood. He did not regret the calmer atmosphere away from the city. He shrugged, opened his arms slightly and gently grimaced. "Traditionally, forty years is celebrated with rubies." The grimace was replaced by a smile.

"Bloody hell!" Martin exclaimed. "Rubies. I suppose it's some sort of a reward for putting up with the husband for so long. I mean forty years is two life sentences and more. Come on, let's see what you've got."

"Have you any idea what you have in mind?"

"Not really. A pair of earrings and a necklace, I suppose."

"I won't be a moment." The proprietor disappeared through a door at the rear. When he returned, he was carrying two trays and several boxes.

"These are rather nice," he murmured. Opening the first box, he produced a pair of ruby earrings, set in silver. "I can do those for £200."

"Each or for the pair?" Martin laughed nervously.

"Oh, the pair, of course." He chuckled.

The jeweller opened the second box. The ruby earrings sparkled up at Martin. The stones were slightly larger and the setting dangled a little lower than the first pair. "I think you will find these will match this necklace rather well." He jeweller murmured, encouragingly.

The necklace was a sliver chain which spread slightly over the chest to accommodate three rubies, one larger than the other two. They were set in a similar design to the earrings. Martin noticed the price in the corner of the tray was £400. *This is going to be one expensive day*, he thought.

"I can only agree with you. They do match – really well," he commented. "I can see the price of the necklace, but what about the earrings."

"Ah yes. The earrings. They are priced at £350."

"Blimey, that's a bit steep," Martin reacted. "Can we negotiate a discount for buying the set and for me being a regular customer?"

"Of course, of course," replied the proprietor. "Putting the two together, maybe I could reduce the overall cost by, say, ten percent."

"I think we had better look at the other boxes and the other necklace." Martin now looked at the second necklace, but it only had the one stone and the setting was definitely less attractive. "Do the earrings in the other boxes match this?" He asked, noticing that the price tag was for only £150.

"Indeed, they do."

The jeweller opened both boxes to display two sets of earrings, with smaller stones and inferior settings. The better pair was priced at £120 and the lesser pair at £95.

"That seems more my price level." Martin wondered whether he now had a bargaining edge.

"I'm sure your wife will more than appreciate the other stones."

"I'm sure she will, but my bank manager won't." They both laughed.

"Maybe, if I suggested twenty percent?" The jeweller looked rather deprecatingly at Martin.

"If you make it £400 for the set, I might be able to stretch to that."

"Perhaps if you offered £500?"

"I'll offer £425 and not a penny more."

"Then I feel that we have reached a most reasonable compromise," the jeweller announced. "Would you like me to gift wrap your purchases?"

"Yes please."

After paying for the necklace and earrings and feeling rather pleased with himself for obtaining such a discount, Martin left the shop. Before returning to the car, he slipped into a card shop and bought a wedding anniversary card. He then drove home. He parked his car in the yard near the kitchen door, took his purchases into his office and placed them in the bottom drawer of his desk. He put on his boots, went out and walked down the hill, under the railway line, to the sea wall at the bottom of his land.

Glancing out of the classroom window, David saw that, for a brief moment, it had actually stopped raining, but the clouds were still scudding across a grey, leaden sky. The wind was really strong, even gale force. As he watched, he saw a fully mature beech tree on the far side of the rugby pitches bending to the might of the storm. Suddenly it slowly keeled over, leaving a large hole at its base.

"Gosh, that was impressive!" he exclaimed out loud.

"What's the problem?" asked the teacher.

"I've just seen the wind blow over a tree, sir, over there." David pointed through the window. All the other pupils strained to see.

"This is an important study period leading up to your A levels, Varley. You should have your nose in your book, not staring through the window." The teacher looked at the rest of the boys. "Back to your desks and back to work," he instructed.

Fortunately, there was only a further five minutes before the mid-morning break and, as soon as the bell rang, David picked up his bag and left the room. He knew that Mr Smith would be hurrying to get his mid-morning coffee. David jog trotted towards the staff room in order to intercept him.

"Excuse me, sir." He greeted Mr Smith in the corridor outside the staff room.

"Hello, Varley. What can I do for you?"

"About ten minutes ago, I just happened to glance through the window and I saw a tree actually get blown down."

"Well, I don't suppose this is the time to discuss the merits of revision as opposed to idly looking through windows." Mr Smith looked at the boy in front of him. *David has really filled out and is now ready for life, rather than the petty restrictions of school*, he thought. "The wind is very strong," he continued. "Have you checked what level on the Beaufort scale it would be, in order to blow down a tree?"

"I was going to do that during break. I can't remember exactly, but I think we must be getting gusts of over 75 miles per hour."

"And the rest," replied Mr Smith. "What do you think is happening in the English Channel?"

"Why?"

"You told me last week that you had checked the tides. I suggest you now check the direction of the wind in the Channel and what the tides are doing."

"Yes sir. I did do that and if I remember correctly, High Tide today in Dover will be at 14.10 hours. Then, the next High Tide will be about two o'clock in the morning."

"Did you also check when the spring tides are likely to peak?"

"Yes. Tomorrow in the middle of the day. At lunchtime."

"Do you have the same information for London?"

"London High Water is roughly two and a half hours after Dover."

"That sounds about right. And have you any idea how long this wind is likely to persist?"

"No, sir!"

"Then I suggest you might try to find out."

Mr Smith turned and entered the staff room. David took out his iPhone to search for the answers. He noticed that he had received a text from Jackie.

"Hi. Can you come out this evening? Good film in West End?? XX"

He texted back. *"Gr8. Where 2 meet? XX"*

He then checked Google and found that, to blow down a tree, the Beaufort scale suggests that the wind speed would actually be about 60 mph, being Storm Force. He walked outside where the wind was buffeting around the school buildings. As he looked across towards the school gates and the buildings over the main road, he saw a couple of slates dislodged from an old church and go flying down the road. *This is getting more serious*, he thought, as a thin, wintry sun broke through the cloud cover.

All along the south coast, High Water had been some two feet higher than expected. With the gales being so strong, there was no coastal shipping at all and the sea was bringing local flooding to some estuaries. The waves had been heightened by the wind to over 30 ft. and as these crashed onto rocky shorelines, the spray burst was impressive.

The storm seemed to be abating somewhat and the wind speed had dropped to Strong Gale. All cross channel ferries had been cancelled through the morning, but in the afternoon, it was decided that the wind had dropped sufficiently for normal service to be resumed, albeit some eight hours late.

In the north, the snow was still falling, as far south as the Midlands. It had been particularly heavy in Yorkshire and the M62 motorway was closed at first light, with little prospect of it re-opening very soon. The Highways Agency was struggling to deploy snow ploughs and snow blowers in either direction because the wind was creating massive snowdrifts across all six carriageways. As soon as one lane was opened, the snow drifted back in and ruined all the work. One plough even suffered the indignity of being towed out of the snow backwards.

Whenever the M62 was closed, there was always an increase of traffic along the old trunk road, the A62, from Manchester to Leeds, but even that was struggling. Lorries and cars had been abandoned haphazardly from Huddersfield out to the county boundary with Greater Manchester. And to make matters worse, a high sided vehicle had been blown onto its side in the Standedge gap. No one actually knew about this accident, because the snow had drifted and completely covered the lorry. The driver had been knocked unconscious as he slid down into the passenger seat. When he came to, he was cold, disoriented and completely blocked in.

Cllr Christine Sykes had already been on the phone to the local Highways Department. No one there was really in a position to give her any specific information or advice, other than to stay inside and keep warm. The news bulletins were advising that no one should leave their homes, except in the direst emergencies. Christine's phone was red hot with her constituents asking for information about gritters. It was all she could do to remain patient and polite.

Along the East coast, there had been some flooding and as the tide ebbed and flowed, the local people decided that matters were not really as bad as the media was leading them to expect. Even so, the snow was worse than many could remember, but in the afternoon, the wind dropped slightly, it stopped snowing and the world was suddenly presented like a Christmas card.

Schools had been cancelled throughout the north of England and the children were now playing in the snow, sledging, building snowmen and having snow fights. The Authorities were slowly re opening the road network, firstly along the main roads and, wherever possible, the motorways. The M62 remained a specific challenge with drifts of 10 feet or more over both carriageways between Saddleworth and Huddersfield. Driving had become so hazardous that the number of vehicles stopped on all lanes grew steadily by the hour. The wind was still drifting the snow, making any progress virtually impossible. The Police and the Ambulance Service called in all their resources and, working behind the snow ploughs, they started to drag out all the vehicles. Very few had actually been abandoned, but the death toll inexorably started to rise. The statistics slowly filtered to the news media and the bulletins became increasingly depressing throughout the afternoon.

Hearing of the blockages on the motorways in the north on the lunch time bulletin, Sarah Varley immediately phoned her mother.

"Hi, Mum! Are conditions really so bad up there?"

"They're bloody awful. And made so much worse by all the stupid people who keep driving far longer than they should. Manchester Road looks like a bomb site with cars abandoned everywhere. The snow ploughs can't get through. The M62 is closed and there's a rumour that Standedge is blocked."

"How much snow is there?"

"We've got about eighteen inches in the back garden. That's bad enough, but the wind is whipping the snow into drifts and as soon as one road get cleared, new drifts are forming. I reckon the best thing to do is to get in front of the telly and watch some old Star Trek movies."

"Obviously, there's no problem with the power supply then," commented Sarah. "Up in Scotland, many of the power lines have been blown down and there are power cuts everywhere."

"No. We're still OK here, but that's no guarantee it'll stay so. How are things down in the south?"

"It's been very windy and we've had a lot of rain with localised flooding. The rivers are pretty full anyway after all the appalling weather leading up to Christmas. But everything seems to be functioning pretty well so far. Michael's away tonight. He has a conference tomorrow and he's giving the first presentation in the morning. He left early this morning but, as always, I haven't heard if he's arrived in the city in one piece. David sent me a text to say that he got to school OK."

"Michael phoned me yesterday to tell me that he has secured funding for our library building. I'm not too sure how it's going to work, but apparently he has a new client who is interested in putting up the money."

"That's fantastic news," Sarah said. "Apparently, this new client has also been able to offer a grant to the Music Society so we can now plan in detail for the centenary season."

"Hang on," Christine said, "I can hear your father coming in. I'd better get his dinner ready because he'll want to get out again to make sure our road is clear."

"OK, Mum. Give him my love. Talk soon."

Despite the awful gales and rain, the Underground was working virtually without any hitches. There were one or two holdups out towards Epping on the Central Line with a fallen tree. Trains were halted at Woodford, which allowed the service over the rest of the network to continue without disruption. It was a similar story on the District Line south of the river Thames in Putney but, again, the disruption was minor and caused little inconvenience.

Milton completed his shift without any complications and emerged at Victoria to meet Pamela. Having been in the draughty station most of the morning, she was looking rather wind-blown. Her blond hair was in need of a comb and her face was flushed with the cold.

"Hi, Milton. Has everything been OK?"

"Sure. No problems at all."

"What's that mark on your cheek?" She reached up and touched him on his left cheek where Les had hit him the day before.

"Oh. I'd forgotten about that. After I left you yesterday, your two pals were waiting for me. One held my arms and the other hit me."

"Oh my God!" Pamela exclaimed. "What did you do?"

"I sorted it. I think one ended up with a broken ankle and the other won't be spending any time with a girl for a few days." Milton chuckled quietly. "They weren't to know that I had been in the Army and had trained for the Services boxing championships. I don't think they'll be bothering either of us anymore."

"Did you report it?"

"There was nothing to report. No witnesses. It was all over in a few seconds."

"Oh God! I'm so sorry!" Pamela's eyes began to fill with tears. "Anyway, they're not my friends. Never have been."

"Hey! Come on. I know that." Milton put his arms round Pamela and pulled her close to him. "I'm only teasing. And, really, I am OK." She put her arms round his neck and kissed his lips.

"Gosh, you feel cold," he said. "Let's go and get something to eat in the warm." Hand in hand, they started to walk towards the café. As they approached, they saw that the windows were steamed up and as they opened the door a warm, damp, friendly atmosphere greeted them.

A colleague shouted across the room, "Oy! Put the wood in the 'ole. It's bloody draughty with that door open."

"OK!" Milton ushered Pamela into the café and firmly shut the door. He looked across to see another West Indian laughing at them and gesturing for them to join him. They made their way across and sat down.

"Hi, Scott. You all right?" Milton greeted his friend. "This here is Pamela. She's a good friend of mine. Be nice!" he instructed.

"I'm always nice to your pals," responded Scott. "'Specially the good-looking ones."

"Careful," Milton warned, laughing. "Anyway, what's new?"

"Nothing. Absolutely nothing at all. I thought with all this wind and rain that we would have a difficult day, but it's been fine so far. Anyway, I've finished now and I'm going across to Poplar after me dinner to see a mate who runs a youth football team."

"Who's that then?" asked Milton.

"He's a bloke in the Fire Service called Fred Shemming. He's married to my cousin Dinah."

"Blimey, I remember her. She was stunning as a teenager." Pamela nudged him. "No, she was," Milton continued. "I've often wondered what happened to her."

"She trained to become a teacher and started work at a school in Stepney. Anyway, some years ago there was a fire nearby and the firemen had to evacuate the school. She met Fred that day and they started going steady after that and then they got married. Got two kids now. Both boys and they both play in this team."

"So, you keep in contact?"

"Well I've got to make sure that Fred's looking after them all, haven't I?" He looked at his watch. "In fact, I'd better be on my way."

And with that, Scott got up and left the café, allowing a sudden draught of cold air to blow through the door.

"Good afternoon, Prime Minister."

The Prime Minister walked into 10 Downing Street to meet with colleagues to be briefed on the developing weather situation. He entered the Cabinet Room and took his accustomed place at the centre of the table.

"Please bring me up to date," he asked.

"The southern depression appears to have centred itself over the Irish Sea. It is causing Storm Force winds in the Channel and all shipping has been advised to stay in port. Because the wind speeds have dropped temporarily during the morning, Channel crossings were restarted, but these will again be stopped as soon as all vessels have reached their destination. High tide has passed and the tide is now ebbing all along the south coast. More rain is expected across all the southern counties from Cornwall to Kent, together with strong westerly winds.

"In the north and in Scotland, matters are far worse. From Derby northwards, many roads have been closed because of drifting snow. The M62 remains closed and the gale force winds are making any early re-opening highly unlikely. There are drifts of ten feet and higher closing both carriageways and there are hundreds, possibly thousands of vehicles haphazardly stopped all over both carriageways all the way from Milnrow in Rochdale to Huddersfield in West Yorkshire. The death toll on the M62 is rising and has already passed thirty.

"The other main roads, which would normally take the motorway traffic, are also blocked by a combination of the snow and trapped vehicles. So far, power has been sustained and the radio stations plus the Television Services are broadcasting advice to the general public not to leave their homes. All cross Pennine rail services have been suspended. Effectively the west side of the country is cut off from the east side.

"The same situation prevails for the M6 in Lancashire and the A1 in Yorkshire, although there have been no deaths reported to date.

"In Scotland, the position is in some respects worse. The depression is now centred in the North Atlantic some 200 miles off the west coast of Norway near Stavanger. A combination of snow and storm force winds has brought down the power lines in a number of places. Indeed, it is already being reported that the disruption to power has never been as bad. Engineers are fighting to restore power as quickly as possible, but in some places it will the best part of a week before anything like normal service can be expected.

"The roads are a nightmare. All motorways are closed to all traffic. Many 'A' roads have been severed by both drifting snow and local flooding. All bridges on the main roads network are closed to all traffic. There has been some flooding in local areas, but the major problems are the heavy snowfall and the high winds which are combining to create drifting of considerable and unprecedented proportions. Because of the wind, it has not been possible to overfly the country and, in many respects, we are dependent on mobile phone reports because the landlines have been severed in so many places. Effectively, Scotland is now cut off from the rest of the United Kingdom and, indeed, its major cities are also basically isolated from each other."

The civil servant drew his remarks to a close. The Prime Minister looked at his colleagues, but no comments were forthcoming.

"What's the situation in East Anglia? Is the tide receding without any flooding?" he asked.

"There have been no reports of flooding anywhere on the east coast."

"When is the next High Tide?"

"At Dover, it will be at 2.00 am tomorrow. In London, it'll be at 4.30 am, so in East Anglia it will be about 7 in the morning."

"Has the advice to evacuate been taken up?"

"No, Prime Minister. The Environment Agency has advised my department that no one was evacuated at all and, further, that their advice has been downgraded following the passing of the High Tide."

"I sincerely hope that's a sensible conclusion. What are the forecasters suggesting?"

"That the depression off Ireland will move slowly to the east across southern England; that the depression over the north Atlantic will also move slowly east towards Stavanger; that they will both deepen, causing further high winds, with rain."

The Home Secretary looked up from her tablet. "Excuse me, Prime Minister, but I'm getting reports of flooding in Northern France. In relatively isolated places between Dunkirk and the Belgian border."

"Please keep an eye on all this and inform me immediately of any specific changes."

"Yes, Prime Minister."

As soon as he left the school premises, David hurried home to get ready for his evening with Jackie. They had planned to meet at the railway station and get the train into Waterloo. To give sufficient time to travel up the Northern Line to Piccadilly, they wanted to leave Richmond by 5.30 pm. As she lived further away from Richmond, it was more of a rush for Jackie, but she was already at the station when David arrived.

As he turned into the station, the wind seemed to be increasing once again, but there was no rain. It felt cold and David was glad that he had put on a warm woollen jumper over his shirt. Jackie was wearing her sheepskin coat, which was unbuttoned, showing off her mini, figure hugging dress underneath. It was a pale sea green colour and, with a pair of suede leather boots, her legs were shown off to perfection. David was entranced as he rushed forward to embrace her.

"Come on!" She pulled his arm. "There's no time for any of that. The next train leaves in exactly three minutes. I've already got your ticket."

And with that, they ran to the platform and boarded the train. Twenty-five minutes later, they were in Waterloo, descending the escalator to the Northern Line. They walked along the passage, hand in hand, chatting about everything and nothing, just happy to be with each other. In no time at all, they reached Leicester Square and travelled up the escalators to the surface. Emerging from the dusty warmth of the Underground, the air felt cool and fresh. The bright lights were enticing and the crowds of people, swirling around them, were both exhilarating and irritating. The noise was surprisingly loud, but this meant nothing to Jackie and David whose senses were attuned only to each other.

"The film starts at half past eight," Jackie announced. "It's on at the Odeon, so shall we get something to eat first?"

"All I want to do is to eat you," David replied somewhat crudely. Jackie playfully punched his arm.

"If you behave, perhaps you will," she laughed, her whole face lighting up.

They found a small, Italian restaurant close by the cinema, surprisingly with a free table. Sitting down side by side, after taking off their coats, David could feel a comforting and welcoming warmth coming from Jackie. They were sitting close to each other with their backs to the wall. Her thigh was pressed hard against his and as she made an amusing, or even a meaningful remark, she would lean sideways closer to him so that her upper arm and her shoulder seemed to nudge him. Her eyes were sparkling with fun, her hair seemed to be slightly scented and she was wearing a permanent half smile, which often broke into a full grin, revealing her perfect teeth.

After ordering two Peronis, they both decided to have a Pomodoro pizza to start. Jackie then ordered Italian meatballs and spaghetti for them both. David had never eaten meatballs and was reluctant, but after some mild suggestive teasing from Jackie, he agreed.

As he cut into the first one, Jackie said, "Do that very carefully, or it'll hurt."

"What do you mean?" David looked up at her, to see her laughing quietly. In answer, she placed her hand on his jeans and, giggling, gently squeezed. David nodded twice and his face went a little red. *She's so much more sophisticated than me,* he thought, as he started to cut his spaghetti.

"No! Not like that," she said. "Try it like this."

She put her fork into four or five strands of the pasta and started to twist it round, making a reasonable mouthful. Delicately, she lifted the fork, allowing the unwanted spaghetti to fall back onto her plate, before twisting it just once more and then, slightly leaning forward, she placed it in her mouth. She saw David watching her.

"Don't you have spaghetti at home?" she asked.

"No. Not really. Mum makes a good lasagne, but Dad says spaghetti is messy. He does what you've just done, but he uses a spoon, rather than the side of the plate."

"Yes. I've seen people do that. But only ever in England! In Italy, they will put a napkin into their collars and lean right forward. Well," she giggled, "Not the girls, of course. They are always much more elegant. Try it."

David picked up his fork and stuck it into his pile of spaghetti. He twisted it and got far too much. He let the tangled mess fall off the fork and started again. Jackie nudged him.

"Look over there," she whispered. On the other side of the restaurant, a middle-aged man was eating his spaghetti, just like Jackie had said. Serviette in his shirt collar at his neck, he was leaning forward and whenever his forkful was too large, he bit the strands, allowing them to fall back onto his plate. "That's the Italian way," Jackie whispered again.

"Do you want me to do it like that?" asked David, disingenuously.

"No," she replied. "That's just the other end of the scale." She laughed. "Don't stare at him. He'll get self-conscious."

"It is rather fascinating." David continued to watch the man, as he tackled his own meal.

He quickly got the hang of it, vowing to himself that he would never use a spoon to eat spaghetti.

After coffee, they ran hand in hand through the rain up to the cinema. David noticed that the wind seemed stronger and was whipping the trees in the square. It was also noticeably colder. It was almost half past eight as they went in and, to his surprise, Jackie produced the tickets from her bag.

"I can't let you buy my ticket," he protested.

"Why not?" she responded. "You bought the dinner."

"That was because you'd got the train tickets."

"Look. It really doesn't matter. I'm with you and you're with me and that's all there is to it, really."

They entered the darkened auditorium. Their seats were on the back row, next to the left-hand wall. It was warm and the seats were very comfortable. Jackie stood up to take off her coat. As she did, David couldn't help but notice how the hem of her dress rose enticingly up her legs.

She sat down again and whispered, "Did you enjoy the view?"

Quietly, he replied, "I certainly did. You've got the most beautiful legs in the world."

He would have been really surprised to know, at roughly the same moment, his father was saying almost exactly the same thing to Alice.

Chapter 11
Wednesday – One Day to Go (Evening)

As the evening progressed, the wind speeds increased all along the south coast. High Tide had come and gone in London just after four o'clock in the afternoon. As the tide had flowed along the south coast, there had been some local flooding in the river estuaries, but no more than might have been expected. The Environment Agency had issued alerts, but there had been no specific damage and no loss of life. The press had taken photographs of the spray from the breakers surging over rocks at Lyme Regis and crashing against the harbour wall at Dover. The next High Tide in London would be due at half past four in the morning. No one seemed to notice that, as Low Tide approached at midnight, the sea levels were still much higher than normal in Falmouth, Portsmouth and Dover.

As the wind continues to increase, the rain started to fall once more. The intensity of the downpour looked like a continuous shower billowing down the streets. Windows were buffeted as the wind moaned around the corners of buildings and amongst the rooftops. Right across the south of England, more trees were uprooted and, as the evening progressed, the reports of structural damage began to rise.

Michael Varley and Alice had enjoyed an early, excellent meal in a local restaurant. He had decided not to join his banking fraternity, giving, as his excuse, the need to work further on his welcoming speech for the morning. In fact, working together, they had finalised his address, quite quickly! It was almost half past eight when they finally struggled back to the Gloucester Palace Hotel through the wind and the rain. Michael's raincoat had been next to useless and the jacket of his suit had been soaked. Alice had fared little better. As soon as they entered their room, Alice announced that she was going to have a bath and that she would hang her clothes over the bedroom radiator where they could dry. Michael mixed her a rum and Coke. He made himself a whisky and soda.

As she went into the bathroom, Alice left the door ajar. She ran the bath and after taking off her wet dress, she re-entered the bedroom with it to hang over a radiator.

"You have the most beautiful legs in the world," he remarked. She slipped off her bra, stepped out of her knickers and picked up her drink.

"It'd be a shame to waste all that hot water," Alice said. "Shall I leave it for you when I've finished?"

"Good idea. I always find a bath most relaxing."

Holding her drink, she went back into the bathroom, once again leaving the door ajar. She squeezed out the full tube of bath oil and got into the bath. It was hot and relaxing as lay back luxuriating in the relaxing aroma. Through the open door she heard Michael switch on the television. Very soon the nine o'clock news came on and, amongst other snippets of reported storm damage, she heard the announcer report that fallen trees were blocking several railway lines, including between Waterloo and Richmond. There was further news of severe weather in the north, especially in Scotland where considerable damage was causing widespread disruption to power supplies. All football matches for that evening were cancelled and the cross-channel ferries were once again confined to port. There were some reports of widespread flooding in northern France and Belgium.

Michael pushed open the bathroom door. "Are you going to be long?" He looked at Alice in the bath, pink, relaxed with her hair tied up and her knees resting on either side. *God she looks so beautiful*, he thought.

Through half closed eyed, she looked at him and wondered why on earth she was even here. "I think I must have drifted off for a moment," she murmured. "I'll be about ten minutes or so. I'll give you a call when I'm ready."

Michael returned to the bedroom and took off his trousers. He carefully hung them inside the trouser press and turned it on.

After being told about the attack on Milton, Pamela felt she should keep a close eye on her texts and phone messages, as she was now worried that Carl and Les might arrange for someone else to 'have a go'. She and Milton left the station together and went back to his home, where Milton prepared a meal for them both. It was the first time she had eaten authentic West Indian food. The previous evening Milton had pre-prepared the goat's meat over a low simmer in the hope that he might persuade Pamela to come to eat with him.

He added ginger, garlic, thyme, onions and hot peppers to the meat. He could remember his mother saying that the garlic should never be crushed, rather it should be sliced and the onions should be skinned, cut in half and then in quarters, to retain the flavour. As his own preference, he chopped up a generous amount of ginger and added the hot peppers after removing all the seeds. Lastly, he added curry powder to the pan and after simmering for around three hours the previous evening, he had left it all to cool. Now they were home, it was only necessary to heat it up and add the potatoes. He also cooked rice and peas, to make it an authentic Jamaican dish.

They sat at Milton's kitchen table to eat, each with a glass of water.

"What do you think?" he asked.

"It's fantastic. It tastes so exotic and the meat is so tender. What is it?"

"It's goat's meat."

"Really? I don't think I've ever eaten goat's meat before."

"I'm not surprised. Because so much is halal these days, white folks won't buy it. As it happens, this isn't halal, but prepared by a West Indian butcher, who's a friend of mine. Not many people know that goat's meat is eaten by more people around the world than any other meat."

"Well, I think it tastes divine," announced Pamela. "And the rice and peas set it off so well. But it is rather hot!"

She could feel herself warming from the inside and knew that her face beginning to glow. Milton watched, fascinated with the change. He could see that the spices were making her eyes sparkle and there was a sheen on her forehead. She drank some water and ate a little more rice. Although he knew that West Indians liked their curried goat stew hot and spicy, he was also aware that the English palate sometimes tends to struggle with the spiciness. Pamela, however, was making good progress, after her initial surprise.

"I've always liked curry." She explained that, when she was a child, her mother had lived in a bedsit over a Bengali restaurant for a few years. Naturally, they both became quite used to hot curries and spicy food. Even so, she found it necessary to remove her pullover and continued the meal dressed in her work blouse and skirt.

92

After the curried goat stew, Milton provided an ice cream made with pineapple, mango and coconut. It certainly cooled down Pamela's mouth and she felt well fed and relaxed. It was quite some time since she had felt so comfortable in the home of another man and she really couldn't remember when a man had ever actually cooked her a meal. She felt very lucky to have found Milton. *Or did he find me?* she thought.

"I don't want to be forward or anything," Milton commented, "But I have a late start tomorrow. I'm not back on duty until lunch time. If you have to get back…" He trailed off.

"Actually, I'm in no real hurry because it's my day off tomorrow. So I don't have to get back home any time soon."

"That's OK," Milton smiled. "Let's forget the weather outside and take some coffee into the front room." They could hear the wind howling round the side of the house and the rain spattering on the windows. "It's not a good night for being out there."

He made the coffee and they went through to the other room. It seemed quite small although very well appointed and comfortable. There was a screen in the corner with a music centre and Skybox in a custom-made cupboard underneath. A coffee table was in the centre of the floor with two black leather settees set at right angles to each other. Milton put the tray of cups and saucers and the coffee onto the table before dimming the lights.

"Is that OK for you?" he asked. "I'll switch on the TV, it you want."

"No thanks. I'd rather just chat with you and find out more about you." Pamela looked at him, as he busied himself with the coffee. *He's completely in control of his life and his environment*, she thought. "Have you always lived in London?"

"My granddad came over to the UK on the Empire Windrush in 1948. He always said that he and the other Jamaicans had been promised that England would be like the Promised Land but, of course, it didn't really turn out like that."

"I've never heard of the Empire Windrush." Pamela looked at Milton, enquiringly. "What was that?"

"I'm really surprised, after the scandal that emerged in 2018. Don't you remember when the Home Office was caught in the act of deporting a number of West Indians who came to Britain as children, even babies? Their parents were here to help the so-called Mother Country reconstruct after the war. All their lives they had received education, worked, paid their taxes and National Insurance, only to find that the single specific document proving their arrival had been destroyed by the authorities."

"I do remember something about that," Pamela replied. "Wasn't it something to do with their landing cards?"

"That's right. And what made it so scandalous was the uncaring, ignorant attitude of the people working in the Home Office.

"It must be remembered that, after the war, the Government was concerned that the returning soldiers would no longer want to work in mundane jobs like public transport, the new National Health Service and Local Government. So they invited people living in the colonies to come over to England, to help with the re-construction. There was a vast amount of bomb damage everywhere and such a massive amount of work to do. In all the large cities, work was easy to find, but the lifestyle was very different from home. It was cold, wet and it always seemed to be raining.

"There was a chronic shortage of housing and, much to the Government's surprise, almost straightaway there was a rise in racism and discrimination. It was quite normal for people looking for temporary accommodation to be greeted by signs saying 'No Dogs, No Blacks and No Irish' hanging in the front windows.

"The amount of exploitation was massive. Some people got very rich owning houses that were cold, damp and dangerous. Many still had outdoor sanitation and yet the rents were high because there was very little choice. So many West Indians, who came over on what they believed was a promise of a better life with better wages and an improved standard of living, well, they felt trapped in an alien world, with no hope of salvation.

"There were nearly 500 Jamaicans on the first boat that came across and more followed. They spread right over the country and they became the backbone of the Health Service, nurses, ancillary workers, porters. The nurses did well because they were paid better than the rest. The men drifted into public transport and labouring, if they could find work at all. My Grandad and my father both worked for London Transport, so I'm third generation Jamaican working on the Underground.

"But the history isn't a proud one from anyone's perspective. It's really not surprising that the deprivation finally resulted in the race riots back in the 1960s. None of us have been good at integrating into normal British society. Yeah, it's true that we were kept at arm's length by the white folks for far too long, but sport had become a possible route to a better life. So had music. Others, of course, turned to crime and the black gangs on this side of the river seriously started to unsettle the grip that the white gang leaders enjoyed for so many years.

"I guess it's true that Scotland Yard used to turn a bit of a blind eye to gangs like the Krays and the Richardsons because, in the main, while they were in control, there was some sort of peace on the streets. With the new black gangs muscling in, however, street warfare broke out and, suddenly, Scotland Yard woke up. It was a simple, political decision to introduce laws like 'Stop and Search', even though there was little fairness or any Human Rights behind them. After all, the public were looking for a scapegoat and the immigrant West Indian community more than fitted the bill.

"And the politicians didn't help. I don't think they really understood. Strangely, Enoch Powell did understand, but too many people regarded him as a maverick. The black folks hated him, not because of what he said, but how his comments were reported in the press. It was all so depressing that very few of my friends and neighbours saw any sense in getting educated because the opportunities for a decent career for a black man just didn't exist. My old mum, however, made sure that I went to school and I now realise that my abilities are far better than I could ever have believed when I was a boy.

"But, all of a sudden, things changed. Some people worked all their lives and paid into their valuable pension schemes. They were now reaching retirement and their pension lump sums from the Health Service or Local Government allowed them to get rid of all their debts and their mortgages and still have a decent amount of money in their pockets. And, of course, new waves of immigrants were arriving. First the Pakistanis and Indians, then the refugees from Africa and the Middle East and even later the Eastern Europeans. All of a sudden, the West Indians were seen as having magically integrated into British society. We were no longer the bad guys. We were scoring goals for the England football team and taking wickets in Test Matches. It wasn't very surprising that the press and other commentators began to look for other, newer scapegoats for all the ills of society."

As he was talking, Milton realised that he was looking at his hands, at the wall, at the coffee table, anywhere but at Pamela. As he fell silent, he felt somewhat surprised at his outpouring and he looked up at Pamela. She was staring at him spell bound.

"I never realised that there was so much discrimination in England." Her face looked crestfallen, as though she was about to cry.

"Sadly, it's everywhere. It even exists in my own community, where some West Indians believe that we are better people than African migrants. I've even heard some

Jamaicans say that they are better than other West Indians. Of course, people try to paper over these differences by calling us Afro Caribbeans, but I always think that sounds more like a type of haircut!"

"How on earth do you cope with idiots like Carl and Les?"

"It's easier if you try to understand why they are like that. Remember, their way of life has been completely turned upside down. The days are now long gone when they would have simply walked out of one job and into another without any qualifications. In the old days, there would have been contacts right across the city and through such networks, legal or illegal, it was always possible to find work. It's not like that now. Wave after wave of immigrants have swept away that old order, but a new order hasn't yet been established. I suppose the last great statement by the die-hard British was to vote to come out of Europe.

"So I try to understand them and where they are coming from. In that way, I can stand up to them and, if possible, argue the rights and wrongs. Of course, Carl and Les are not really the debating types, so that's when it is sometimes necessary to fall back onto my more basic instincts."

Pamela reached across and took hold of his hand. "I'm so glad that I've met you," she said. She leant over further and kissed him on the cheek. Milton responded and put his arm round her and gently pulled her to him. They sat quietly for a while, before Pamela nudged him and suggested that they should clear up the pots in the kitchen.

In the middle of the evening, out at Thatched Barn Farm, Charlie and his wife Paula arrived. As they drove into a rain swept yard, Martin and Jennifer came out of the kitchen door to greet them. They quickly collected their suitcases and bags, before rushing into the house, to get out of the wind and rain. In the kitchen, the greetings and pleasantries had hardly been completed when there was toot of a car horn as James and Megan arrived.

Once again, everyone rushed out of the kitchen door to get all the baggage inside as quickly as possible. Martin suddenly stopped, when he realised that three adults had got out of the car. *It can't be*, he thought. "It is," he shouted. "Helen!" Jennifer looked across and saw her daughter struggling to get what looked like a trunk out of the car. All thoughts of the weather were banished as they hugged and kissed each other.

"Come on, quickly, or you'll catch your death," called Jennifer, clucking around them like a mother hen around its brood. "Anyway, why aren't you in New Zealand, Helen?"

"Well, I couldn't let the boys take over everything while I was away, could I?"

"What on earth do you mean?" asked Martin, as he shut the kitchen door behind them.

"You know. My inheritance and my position as the favourite child." She laughed.

"The favourite what?" asked Charlie. "You're only the favourite daughter. James and I compete as the favourite son, but I don't think we have any chance against a daughter."

The children disappeared upstairs with their luggage while Jennifer put on the kettle to make a cup of tea.

As they came out of the cinema, it was almost eleven o'clock. The wind and rain were so bad that there were hardly any pedestrians left on the streets. Leicester Square was virtually deserted.

"It's not going to be easy to get back home," said David, as they stood in the entrance on the cinema. He looked at Jackie. "Are you OK?"

Having put on her coat, Jackie was pulling him towards the Underground. "Come on!" she said. "We'd better get a move on."

She ran down the stairs with David following. On the platform the indicator board said the next southbound train was in two minutes. *At least the Underground is working,* David thought. They could hear the train in the tunnel and the stale, dusty air on the platform began to move as the train emerged into the station. It squealed to a halt and the doors opened. The carriage was almost empty and no one emerged. Jackie sat on one side of the carriage, facing David on the opposite side. In the rush from the cinema to the station, she hadn't had time to do up her coat and it now fell open. The hem of her dress had, once again, ridden up her shapely thighs. David watched, quite fixated, as the movement of the train gently shook her knees.

Fully aware of his complete attention, Jackie slightly opened her knees and forced her shoulder blades into the back of the seat. This made her bottom slide towards the edge of the seat, pulling the hem of her dress even further up her thighs. The train was slowing down as it entered Charing Cross station. Jackie put her knees together and leant forward, balancing on the edge of her seat, to talk to David.

"I like you, David Varley," she announced. "And I want to know so much more about you."

"I like you too, Jackie Bleasdale," he replied, as the train, once again, squealed to a halt.

The doors opened and closed, but there were no new passengers. With a couple of exaggerated jerks, the train set off towards Embankment. Jackie leant back again and parted her knees. David could see her black, sheer knickers, so sheer that nothing at all was left to his imagination. He tried to lean forward but found that the bulge in his trousers was too restricting. The train was now slowing as it came into Embankment. Once again, Jackie leant forward, closing her knees. As David looked through the window, he noticed that there were no passengers on the platform. The train stopped and the only other passenger in their carriage got up and left. As the train left, Jackie stood up and quickly took off her knickers. As she sat down again, she said, "Lick me!" She commanded.

David knelt in front of her, as she opened her knees and put her heels onto the seats either side. David could smell the now familiar, musky aroma as he pressed his face between her legs. He pushed his tongue into her and tasted her sweetness, as her flower opened revealing her bud. He gently nibbled at it with his teeth and was rewarded as he heard her sharp intake of breath, followed by a gentle moan. Her knees closed, tightly holding his head in place.

Suddenly, he felt the train brake and the intensity between them was broken. She released him and, as he stood up, the train lurched causing him to lose balance and fall onto her. She put her arms tightly round him and kissed him, feverishly. Releasing him, she stood up and deftly put on her knickers.

The train now entered Waterloo station and they got out. They hurried up to the surface to check on the trains to Richmond. A notice board announced, "All trains to Richmond are cancelled." David looked round and saw a guard at the barrier.

"What's happened on the Richmond Line?" he asked.

"Tree down, mate," the guard replied. "Won't be opening until at least tomorrow afternoon."

"How do we get back to Richmond?"

"Suggest you get a bus."

"Do you know the number?"

"Yeah. Hang on a sec." The guard called to another employee. "What's the number for buses to Richmond?"

"You have to get a 211 to Hammersmith. Change there and get a 419 to Richmond," he called back.

"Did you get that?"

"Yes thanks," said David.

They left the station, to catch the bus for Hammersmith. They were lucky as they didn't have to wait too long, before a big, red double decker came into view, displaying 211 on the front. They bought their tickets and climbed to the upper deck. No one else was there and they chose to sit at the front. As they went over the river, David noticed that the water seemed unusually high. He realised that the tide was coming in, but High Water wouldn't be for another five hours or so.

"Look at the river," he remarked. "There seems to be a lot of water."

"What's the problem?" replied Jackie.

"I realise that the tide's coming in," David muttered. "When I was talking to Mr Smith, he said something about the Spring tides. That's right!" He remembered. "High tide will be at about half past four in the morning, so it'll just be past Low Tide at the moment. That means there should be plenty of mud banks, but there aren't."

As the bus reached the halfway point, the wind buffeted it quite severely and Jackie caught hold of David's arm.

"Let's go down," she suggested.

"Hang on a sec. There's too much water in the river for it to be Low Tide. The tide will be coming in quite fast now. This must be the result of all the rain we've had yesterday and today. And I expect they'll have closed the Thames Barrier."

"What are you going on about?" she asked.

"The river. Look!" He pointed at the water just as the bus turned left into Parliament Square.

"I can't see anything. These buildings are in the way. Anyway, what did you mean?"

"It's the weather," he replied. "This storm is far more severe than normal and it's come at just the wrong time."

"Why? What do you mean?"

"Every spring and autumn, we get really high tides, called Spring Tides. The moon's gravity makes the tides higher than normal. But we've also got really high winds in the English Channel. They push the sea in front of it. This means that there is more water than normal at Dover and upwards into the North Sea. Plus, we've had so much rain that the countryside is saturated and the rainwater is draining straight into the rivers. There's far more water in them than normal. That's probably why the river is so high just now."

"But it'll just flow away to the sea, won't it?"

"Yes. But if the tide is higher than normal, then the Thames Barrier will be closed to stop the tide rising too high in London. Like here. And if it is closed, then the river will continue to fill up with all the rainwater coming off the land up beyond Oxford and out to the west. I expect it's always a tricky decision when to close the barrier. If it's still open, they'll want as much river water as possible to flow out."

"But, doesn't this happen every year?"

"Not to this intensity. I forgot to tell you that there's another storm causing all the snow in Scotland. It's also blowing the sea down the North Sea southwards towards the Thames estuary. I think we're going to be in for a very difficult few days."

Chapter 12
Thursday Morning

With the depression now centred over Oxford and still deepening, the winds in the English Channel increased to Hurricane Force. The sea had become so dangerous that all shipping was confined to port. There had been sporadic flooding as High Tide slowly moved eastwards along the south coast. The effect of the fierce winds on the Spring Tide was to increase the height of the tide to record levels and the towering waves had caused some local damage to the coastline infrastructure.

The depression centred between the Shetland Islands and Stavanger in southern Norway was having a similar effect on the height of the tides. There had been flooding in the Firth of Forth and along the north eastern coastline of England. The wind speed had remained at Storm level and this had been exacerbated by the driving snow. All shipping was confined to port.

At midnight, David and Jackie reached Richmond and as their bus crossed the Thames once more, David again remarked at the water level.

"Look, Jackie," he said, pointing at the river. "The level of the water is incredibly high. That's been caused by all the rain we've had over the past couple of days."

"Yes, and it's still raining now," Jackie replied. "I'm not too sure how I'm going to get home. I really didn't expect to be as late as this."

"Well, we can't be blamed for a tree being blown down on the railway line. You can always come and stay with us, if that's OK?"

"Oh! Are you sure? Thanks. I'm sure that'll be fine. I'll just send a text to my mum, to let her know," she replied, getting out her phone. "I can get a cab back home in the morning."

They got off the bus and scurried to David's home as quickly as possible, through the gales and the blustering rain. When they crashed through the front door, Sarah went into the hall to check on the commotion, only to be confronted by two soaking wet, but exhilarated teenagers.

"You look like a pair of drowned rats." She ushered them into the kitchen. "Hello," she said, looking at the bedraggled girl in front of her. "You must be Jackie." She turned to David. "I was expecting you home earlier than this."

"Oh yes!" Jackie stammered a reply. "I mean 'Hi'. Yes, I'm Jackie."

"Mum, please listen." David started to explain. "We've had a great evening, but the journey home has been really difficult because of this storm. All the trains from Waterloo to Richmond have been cancelled because of a tree being blown down onto the line near Barnes, so we've been forced to come back by bus and that takes forever. We didn't get into Richmond until after midnight and we've rushed back as quickly as possible.

"The rain is really heavy and the wind feels like it's getting stronger," Jackie added.

"So I suggested to Jackie that she should stay with us over night." David looked keenly at his mother. "She's texted her mum and that all seems to be OK. But I do think she should have a shower very soon because we're both soaking wet."

"Yes. You're right." Sarah looked at them both. "I'll get you some night clothes, Jackie, but get upstairs quickly. And leave your dress out for me to wash and dry. I'll get the spare room ready for you. Go on! Quickly! Upstairs!"

"Thanks, Mrs Varley. I'm sorry to cause all this fuss."

"Yes! That's fine. Go on, before you catch your death." She shooed Jackie out of the kitchen. "You'll find a bath towel in the bathroom cupboard. Leave your dress outside the door over the bannisters."

Jackie shrugged out of her coat. David took it from her and hung it over a radiator. He took off his own coat and did the same. He looked at his mother, who had an enigmatic look on her face, as though she was trying not to smile. They heard the water heater in the kitchen fire up and Sarah said that she must get Jackie's dress sorted. David looked at her, wondering why her accent had become rather more Yorkshire.

Sarah nodded at David and said, "You'd better get yourself upstairs as well and leave your clothes for me to deal with." And with that, she ushered him through the door and up the stairs. Once upstairs, David stripped off his shirt and trousers, handing them to his mother, who had already picked up the dress. She went back downstairs to the utility room, where she started a short wash programme. She heard the shower stop and knew that David would be in the bathroom with the girl. *And precious little I can do about that,* she thought.

She went back upstairs to find a nightie for Jackie. It would be too big, but it would do. She knocked on the bathroom door.

"Jackie, love. Are you there?"

"No. I'm here," Jackie replied, coming out of the spare bedroom with the bath towel wrapped round her body and another like a turban for her hair. She looked warm and content, with a red face and her wet hair tied up in another towel. She smiled at Sarah. "You are so kind. Thank you for taking me in."

"I expect you'll want a hot drink before you get to sleep. Do you like Drinking Chocolate or would you prefer Horlicks?"

"Oh. That's a good idea. Actually, I'd just like a hot cup of tea, if that's not too much trouble."

"I've got a nightie for you," Sarah said, handing over the garment.

Jackie giggled. "Thanks, but I don't normally wear anything in bed!"

"Well, that's up to you. But I think it might be an idea to slip it on while you come downstairs for your tea!" Sarah smiled. In the bathroom, they both heard the shower had stopped and suddenly, David appeared wearing another towel round his waist. He looked from Jackie to his mother.

"What's going on?" he asked.

"I'm going to make a pot of tea. I expect you'll have one, David? Jackie's coming down in my old nightie. The washing will be about done. I'll have your dress ironed before I get to bed."

With that, she smiled at Jackie and David and went downstairs.

"You appear to have made a good impression on Mum," David remarked.

"I only went and told her that I don't sleep in a nightie!" Jackie replied.

"Good," said David. "Neither do I. Well, not in pyjamas, anyway!" He put his arms round her and pulled her to him. "Come on! We'd better not keep her waiting!"

"She's been so kind and welcoming." David undid the towel at her neck, letting it fall to the floor. She quickly put the nightie over her head and as quick as the vision of her loveliness had been displayed, it was once again hidden from his view. Quickly they went downstairs for the promised cuppa.

Finally, Michael Varley fell asleep. He was troubled that Alice appeared to be so much in control. She emerged from the bathroom, reminding him that she had left the water in the bath. She said that she would press his suit trousers. He told her that he had already put them into the trouser press, realising that they were a bit bedraggled after returning to the hotel in the appalling weather. He decided to get into the bath, but he was disappointed because he was hoping to take the bath with Alice and now she was back in the bedroom quicker than expected.

As he disappeared into the bathroom, Alice quickly checked that the trousers were correctly placed in the press. She retrieved them just in time to save them from the dreaded 'tram lines'. She ensured that the creases would now be razor edge sharp and that his jacket would be dry. The radiators in the room were very warm and her dress already appeared to be dry. She made good use of the ironing board and it was soon ready for the morning. She put on her shorty nightgown and got into bed. It was almost midnight when Michael emerged, pink and bathed, with a towel round his waist.

"Already in bed? That's what I like!" he said, feigning a jocular mood. Alice smiled and looked up from her magazine.

"You must be feeling tired after all that effort getting your speech ready for tomorrow."

"Not really. Thanks for sorting out my suit."

"You're welcome." He pulled back the sheet on his side, dropped the towel on the floor and got into the bed. Alice put down the magazine and turned off her bedside light. She turned back towards Michael, feeling for his leg. He was lying on his back and felt warm and still slightly damp. As she ran her fingers up his leg, as he put his arm round her shoulders. But there was no reaction down below. She took hold of his soft penis, feeling no reaction at all. *I wonder if it's me,* she thought.

"Are you feeling concerned about tomorrow?" she asked. "I mean, this is rather surprising." She gently squeezed him.

"Actually, it's a bit embarrassing," he replied. "It's happened once or twice before, but never with you."

"Do you want me to see if I can give you a little encouragement?" she asked, as she slipped further down the bed. She rolled over his leg and turned onto her stomach. She was now lying between both his legs, with her elbows outside his thighs. She held his penis in both hands, pulled back his foreskin and gently licked the top. The base of his stomach contracted as she drew him into her mouth, her tongue gently rubbing against the shaft. She was rewarded with a slight stiffening, which encouraged her to suck more enthusiastically, running her tongue around his glans.

"Perhaps if I turned round, you could also lick me," she suggested. "That might help."

As she knelt upright, she gently closed his legs so that she could place both her knees on either side of him. She swiftly took off her nightdress, while he shuffled further down the bed, between her legs. She then turned round and moved back towards the headboard, until his head was between her knees. She placed both elbows on either side of his hips. As she leant forward to suck his penis again, she could feel his fingers gently opening the lips of her pussy and his tongue penetrating her. Despite the inadequacy of his erection, she felt herself becoming aroused, especially when her clitoris began to expand. As he sucked and nuzzled her, his penis hardened a little and she started to masturbate it.

100

But this was obviously not going to be a night of erotic activity. After that initial reaction, his partial erection diminished and, finally, she returned to her side of the bed.

"I'm sorry," he said.

"I think you should get yourself to a doctor. Erectile dysfunction can be a sign of all sorts of medical situations, but I expect you are just worried about tomorrow. Perhaps you'll feel better after a good night's sleep."

With that, Alice turned over and closed her eyes, leaving Michael to doze fitfully before falling asleep in the early hours.

Outside, the storm continued unabated. The intensity increased with the rain lashing down and the wind becoming even fiercer. High Water came, in central London, at 4.30 am, but no one really noticed at such an early time of the morning. By six o'clock, the early risers were beginning, with some difficulty, to make their way to work.

In Poplar, Fred should have been starting three days of late shifts but, because one of his colleagues was scheduled to have a doctor's appointment, he agreed to work one extra early. He slipped out of bed at six. He looked out of the bedroom window, more to check the state of the weather than anything else. He could just see the river between two tower blocks.

That looks a bit full. I'm sure High Water must have already passed, he thought.

Twenty minutes later, he was on his way to the fire station and, as usual, he stopped by the newsagents to purchase a morning paper from Rajinder.

The Thames Barrier was closed on the previous evening to counter the effect of the expected spring tide. However, the extraordinary level of rainfall right across southern England, falling on top of the already saturated land, was now draining into the Thames and all its various tributaries. Already the floodwater upstream was causing localised flooding near Oxford and the overall effect on the river itself was to raise its level throughout the whole of its course.

What Fred couldn't see, because the Thames Barrier was obscured by the river bending around the O2 Arena, was the level of water at Woolwich. Two hours and more after High Tide, no water seemed to have ebbed at all. Although concerning, there were no alarm bells ringing as yet, because there were still well over three hours to Low Water and still sufficient time for the tide to ebb.

He walked on to the fire station and clocked on at 6.30 am. Once again, the night shift had been quiet. Fred quickly received the report before taking over control from his colleague and settling down to another normal day.

Further down river, beyond Canvey Island, Martin had woken early. He intended to look once again at the river defences bordering the southern reaches of his land. When walking along the sea wall the day before, he was considerably surprised at the height of the water. He left the house by the kitchen door, just as night was reluctantly giving way to daylight. The sky was full of heavy rain clouds and the wind was extremely strong. It was raining heavily and Martin was glad that he had put a muffler round his neck, as well as a really thick Arran jumper to keep him warm.

He was halfway across the yard, when the door opened again, behind him. James was standing there, in his stockinged feet, but otherwise dressed as a carbon copy of Martin.

"Hang on a minute, Dad," he called. "I'll come with you." With that, the door shut for a moment, only to reopen with James wearing boots, obviously ready for whatever the weather might throw at him.

They walked in companionable silence down the track alongside the edge of the field. It was very muddy and, because of the ferocity of the wind, their progress was slow. In the distance they could see that the river was still very high and they wondered whether the sea wall would be strong enough to stop it flooding. Beyond the field was the London to Southend railway line, which had been built on a raised embankment. They passed under the lines, through a small bridge, and continued walking along the edge of a muddy field bordering the railway line before turning towards the river.

"This wind is really vicious," remarked Martin, as they approached the bottom of the field. In front of them was a barbed wire fence and the dyke running basically east west, acting as the sea wall which now hid the view of the river itself. Inside the sea wall was a ditch which, when the tide was out, emptied through a large concrete pipe under the sea wall with the aid of an automatic sluice. As the tide came in, the water would cause the iron door to shut, keeping the sea water off the fields. "Come on, the gate's just over there."

They passed through the gate, crossed over the ditch using a bridge made from old reinforced concrete joists and climbed up some muddy steps cut into the slope of the dyke. At the top, they looked out over the river. Although High Water had passed almost three hours before, the rough waves were still lapping more than halfway up the far side of the sea wall. They knew that the north shore of Canvey Island was immediately in front of them but, with the wind being so strong, it was almost impossible to keep their balance and, with the rain being so intense, the opposite shoreline was virtually obscured.

"I don't like the look of this," muttered Martin.

"How do you mean?" replied his son.

"Look how full the river is. It should be Low Water at half past ten. This lot will never ebb before then. Look over there." He pointed towards the east where Two Tree Island was just visible through the rain. "The water should already have receded, but you can still see a massive pool near the golf range."

"Yeah! I see what you mean. What'll happen when the tide turns and starts to come back in?"

"That doesn't bear thinking about. I remember stories of the 1953 flood of Canvey Island. Mind you all the sea defences have been heightened and strengthened since then. This dyke is now part of the sea wall defences from the Thames all the way north to the Wash. The Environment Agency is supposed to keep it all in good order."

They turned to face the west and started to stagger into the wind as they attempted to walk in the direction of South Benfleet along the pathway on the top of the sea wall.

"I want to check if there's any damage to the wall in those two places where it bends round the mud flats over there. Come on!"

They trudged for about half a mile with their backs bent almost double because of the ferocity of the wind. The sea wall curved away to their right and then sharply back to the left, creating a small bay. Over the years the wall had sunk slightly forming a natural dip. The wind whipped waves were still washing over the top the wall, leaving a lethal muddy surface on the path. On the landward side, a large pool had formed, draining into the ditch, which was absorbing most of the excess water. The ditch stretched as far west as Benfleet and as far east as Leigh on Sea. At regular intervals there were branches which ran north towards the railway line. Although the sea had reached the top of the wall at this point, the height of the tide had obviously not been that much greater than it was at present.

"Look at that, James!" exclaimed Martin to his son. "That natural dip in the wall is where it was been built over an old stream. The stream now acts as another sluice, but that could be why it's sunk a little over the years. I have advised the Environment Agency, but they have shown little concern to date."

"Is that all sea water, then?" James pointed to the pools of water on the landward side of the wall.

"Yes. But what's far more worrying is that the sea is still slopping onto the top of the wall and High Tide would have been well over three hours ago. The tide can't have been much higher than the water is now, otherwise there would be far more water on the landward side."

He went on, "And that must mean that the wind in the English Channel is so strong that it's stopping the natural ebb of the tide."

"What do you mean?"

"With the water so high now, when the tide starts to flow in again, in two or three hours' time, this part of the wall may well be breached. And if the sea comes over with enough force, it could wash away the wall itself. This is actually very worrying, because there are quite a number of places, on both sides of the river, where there are natural dips in the sea wall, all the way upriver towards Tilbury and Rainham. Maybe even towards London."

Sarah Varley woke at half past six every morning. She was always first in the bathroom, to ensure that she could get her husband and her son up and off to work and to school on time. On Thursday morning, when she woke, she immediately remembered that Michael was away in London in order to be present at the conference this morning. She then suddenly remembered that David came home very late the previous evening, with his girlfriend, Jackie.

I'll have to get then both up as early as possible, so that I can run Jackie back home in time to get ready for college, she thought.

She got out of bed, put on her dressing gown and went to the bathroom. As soon as she finished her shower, she quickly dressed and went onto the landing. She tapped on the spare bedroom door. There was no response. Quietly, she opened the door. The bed was still made and was obviously unused. *Little monkeys*, she thought. She tapped on David's door.

Before going to bed, Jackie and David went to the kitchen to have a quick cup of tea, before returning upstairs. As they reached the spare bedroom door, David indicated to Jackie that she should come into his bedroom. Without a second thought, as though it was the most normal thing in the world, she walked in, shrugged off the nightie and got into David's bed. Quick as a flash, he followed, where they snuggled up to each other and, exhausted with the hour and their recent adventures, they fell asleep in each other's arms.

During the night, David had stirred twice, first to slip his arm from under Jackie's head and later to move slightly to give her more room in the bed. As they settled to sleep, Jackie turned over, bent her legs and arched her back. She felt completely relaxed with his knees behind hers, his stomach warming her lower back, one of his arms over her waist with his hand cupping one of her breasts, while his other arm was under her neck and head. Contentedly, she had squirmed her body against his feeling his half erect penis against her bottom.

When she heard the tapping at the door, she jumped. She felt David get out of the bed and, turning over, watched him slip on his dressing gown. As he opened the door, the landing light lit up Jackie's face with hair splayed out over the pillow.

"Oh! Hi, Mum." He looked directly at his mother, expecting some immediate reprimand and was somewhat taken aback when she simply asked, "Did you both sleep all right? I expect you found that bed rather small for the two of you!"

"It was fine," Jackie replied. "We must have been really tired because I went out like a light."

"Me too," added David quickly.

Keeping her face straight, Sarah told them that it was now almost seven o'clock and that she thought it would be best for her to drive Jackie back home, so that she could get ready for college. "I sent your mother a text last night before I went to bed. I got a reply almost instantly, so I expect she was still waiting up for to hear from you. She thanked me for letting her know the situation. I'll phone her as soon as you've started your breakfast. Don't take too long."

As she went downstairs, David shut the bedroom door and turned on the light. Jackie sat up in the bed, with the duvet across her waist and legs. She stretched, raising both elbows level with her shoulders, clasping her hands behind her head and, arching her back, she pushed her head and shoulders back as far as they would go. The effect on David was startling, as he watched her breasts being pushed forward and her stomach tightening.

"There's no time for that," exclaimed Jackie with a giggle, seeing the effect she was having on him. "Come on! Let's get a shower." She slipped out of bed, walked quickly to the door, opened it and went to the bathroom. "Come on!" she repeated, as David just watched her, mouth agape.

Alice woke before Michael. She raised herself up on one elbow, listening to the rain beating against the window and looked at the displayed time on her iPhone. It was twenty past six. She slipped carefully out of the bed, not wanting to disturb Michael, who was sleeping deeply in the foetal position. It was warm in the room and, naked, she padded across the floor to the bathroom, where she cleaned her teeth and showered.

Emerging once more from the bedroom, she had a towel round her hair and a second around her body. She crossed the floor to the window and peeked through the curtains. It was still dark outside and rain was streaming down the windowpane. She watched the wind blowing through the tree on the other side of the road. *That's really strong*, she thought. Letting the curtain fall back into place, she sat at the dressing table and began to apply her makeup.

We need to be in the city at nine o'clock, she thought. *If I wake Michael at seven, we should be at breakfast by half past and ready to leave by quarter past eight. With this weather, we'll have to get a cab. I know that Michael uses someone, so I'll get the number and phone him while Michael's shaving. Everything else is ready.*

She blow-dried her hair and slipped into her dress. She had transformed it from the bedraggled article that was soaked the evening before. It was now crisp, dry and figure enhancing. She applied a little perfume just below her ears on her neck and checked her watch. It was five to seven. She went to the bed and, leaning over Michael, she gently shook his shoulder. Michael grunted, opened his eyes and looked up. Seeing Alice already dressed and ready for the day, he panicked.

"What time is it?" he gasped.

"It's OK," she answered, calming him. "It's just coming up to seven o'clock. There's plenty of time for you to shave and shower. Yours clothes are all dried and pressed. I'm just nipping downstairs to make sure that breakfast will be ready at half past. I need to phone for a cab. You have the number of a specific chap, don't you?"

"What? Oh yes! Thank you, Alice. You seem to have everything sorted out." Michael got out of bed and started to walk to the bathroom.

"I need that telephone number." Alice gently reminded him.

"Oh! Right. Hang on a sec." Michael went to his briefcase and opened it. He saw his speech neatly prepared and realised that his heart was already starting to race. Andy Greene's card was in a pocket in the lid. He took it out and handed it to Alice.

"I'm sorry about last night," he murmured, with his eyes averted from hers.

"That's OK. Don't think about it," she replied.

"But it's just not like me." He looked at her, pleading silently for understanding and comfort.

"It really is OK," she repeated. She put her hand on his arm. "These things happen and I do appreciate that you'll be under some stress just now. Now, hurry up and get shaved. I'm going downstairs to sort out breakfast." She turned away from him and left the room.

Downstairs, it was still quiet. Alice looked into the dining room, but there was no one there. She opened the door to the basement to go down to the kitchen. As she emerged from the stairway, she could hear noises coming from the kitchen. She opened the door and saw Betty, who was boiling a kettle.

"Can I help you, dear?"

"Yes, please. Mr Varley, from room 1, has to be away promptly at quarter past eight. Will it be possible to have our breakfast ready for half past seven please?"

"That'll be no problem, love," Betty replied. "Do you know what you want for breakfast?"

"We'll both have bacon and eggs please."

"Do you want any grilled tomatoes and mushrooms? Or baked beans, perhaps?"

"Oh, thanks. We'll both have grilled tomatoes as well, please."

"As soon as you go into the dining room, just press the bell inside the doorway. I'll then start your eggs. Do you want tea or coffee? And brown or white toast?"

"Tea for me and coffee for Mr Varley, please. And we'll have a mixture of toast. Thanks."

"That's fine, dear," Betty said. "Everything will be ready for you."

Alice left the kitchen and returned to the reception area by the stairs. She looked at the card Michael had given her. *Gracious*, she thought. *That's Andy. He's going to get a surprise!* She switched on her iPhone and dialled the number. It rang seemingly for ages before a somewhat sleepy voice muttered "Hello. Who's that?"

"Good morning, Andy," Alice spoke briskly. "This is Alice, from Le Grove Investments. I have a job for you. Can you drive Mr Varley and me into the city this morning? We are staying at the Gloucester Palace Hotel and we need to leave at quarter past eight. That's just about an hour from now. Can you do that?"

"Hang on a sec." Alice could hear Andy moving around. "It'll be tight but, yes, I can be there in an hour. What are you doing there?" he continued, his curiosity getting the better of him.

Alice cut him off. "I don't think you've got time to chatter. I suggest you get organised and get over to Kensington as soon as possible."

"Right," he replied and realised that the phone was dead. Alice had already rung off.

She returned to the room, where Michael was already dressed and just putting on his shoes.

"Breakfast will be ready as planned," Alice announced. "The taxi will be here at quarter past eight. We'd better go down."

She gave him back his card and held the door for him.

105

Rising regularly each day at six o'clock, Sebastian Fortescue Brown was already in the dining room when Michael Varley entered with Alice just behind. *Mm*, he thought. *A gentleman would hold the door for a lady.* Alice pressed the bell push. They went to a table near the window.

He nodded politely to Michael, before returning to his copy of the Daily Telegraph. Michael acknowledged him and sat down.

"Isn't that Mr Sebastian Fortescue Brown?" Alice asked Michael.

"Yes," he replied.

"I knew I had seen him before," Alice commented, as Betty entered the room. "I didn't make the connection when he came to the office, but it's all dropped into place now."

Betty went to a dumb waiter and took out a tray with the tea, coffee and toast. She placed these on their table and returned to the dumb waiter, where there were two breakfasts of two fried eggs, bacon, with a grilled tomato each presented on a separate plate.

"Be careful!" she cautioned them. "The plates are very hot. If there's anything else you need, just press the bell."

"Thank you," Alice replied. "And thanks for getting it all done on time." She smiled at Betty.

Breakfast was finished by eight o'clock and they returned to the bedroom, where they collected their bags and put on their coats. Outside the weather remained just as bad, with dark skies, high winds and driving rain.

Slowly, the tide receded and Low Water was reached in the middle of the morning. The river level above the Thames Barrier hardly dropped at all and below, the sea level only reluctantly receded. By Low Water, at 10.45 hrs, it was almost as though the tide hadn't really ebbed at all and the wind was creating really large breakers that were crashing into the sea wall.

The CEO of the Environment Agency had briefed his Chairman, who felt that the situation was so grave that it was necessary to request an urgent meeting with the Prime Minister. This had been arranged for ten o'clock, when the Home Secretary, the Defence Secretary, the Environment Secretary and the Chancellor would all be present.

As soon as David left to go to school, Sarah Varley drove Jackie to her home on the other side of Richmond Park near Wimbledon, where she quickly ran inside to get changed ready for college. Jackie's mother, Annabel Bleasedale, invited Sarah inside for a cup of coffee.

"Thank you so much for looking after Jackie last night."

"Well, they both arrived home looking like drowned scarecrows," replied Sarah. "They both needed a shower straightaway, if only to warm up, so it would have been well after two o'clock by the time I could have driven her home."

"It made a lot of sense to me as well!"

Chatting away like two old friends, Annabel took Sarah into the kitchen and put on the kettle. Upstairs, they could hear Jackie as she changed into suitable clothes for college. It wasn't long before their conversation turned to the weather.

"As we came down Petersham Road, we could see that the river was very high."

"This rain won't have been helping. My husband was telling me that the Environment Agency is so concerned that all leave has been cancelled."

"What does he do?"

"He's a Chief Superintendent with the Police based at Scotland Yard. I'm not too sure exactly what he does. He keeps all that away from the family. Jackie tells me that your Michael is something in the city."

"Yes. He works for a small investment bank called Le Grove Investments. He's at a conference this morning, making the welcoming speech for all the other delegates." She looked at her watch. "It's half past nine, so I expect he'll just about be starting."

"Is it? Already? I must get Jackie off to college." She went to the kitchen door and called up the stairs. "Are you ready?"

"Just coming."

Sarah said, "If it's any help, I can drop Jackie off on my way back home. We passed her college on the way here."

"Are you sure? That's really kind." Just at that moment, Jackie appeared in the doorway in jeans, sweater and coat, with her bag over her shoulder.

"Do you want some breakfast?" her mother enquired.

"I'll get some at college."

"Come on," said Sarah. "You need to be there for ten, don't you?"

They got back into Sarah's car and drove off in the direction of Kingston on Thames.

The impromptu cabinet meeting had not gone well. The Prime Minister and his ministers were firstly brought up to date with the weather situation. The low pressure, centred over Oxford, had deepened further and was causing hurricane force winds in the English Channel. There had been some local flooding along the south coast, but the wind damage had been much more severe in northern France and Belgium.

The snow in Scotland was continuing to fall and the wind was creating unprecedented drifting. In northern England, the M62 was closed and unlikely to open for at least another 24 hours. The river Ouse was swollen and York was under Flood Alert. There was also some flooding along the east coast but High Tide had passed with no reports of significant damage.

"That's basically where we are, Prime Minister."

"A rather comprehensive report of the current situation," he replied. "But what of the next 24 hours?"

"My worry, Prime Minister, is that the hurricane blowing eastwards up the Channel has denied the natural ebbing of the tide. Whereas the water should have fallen around 10 metres, it has only fallen an estimated 4 metres. This means that there is already too much water in the Thames estuary, with the tide beginning to flow once again. This will put the estuary and possibly even London under severe threat."

"The Agency advised us of a potential flood threat in the east of the country. Did this materialise?"

"No, Prime Minister, although the whole situation in Scotland and the east of England is still under careful observation. My concern in the east is that we have issued severe flood warnings on previous occasions, following which no significant flooding occurred. This only serves to compromise the effect of issuing such warnings again."

"You mean, the local people will not take your advice and won't evacuate."

"Exactly, Prime Minister. Although the situation in the north east appears less severe than the Channel, Kent and the Thames estuary.

"I must also add that the depression just off the Norwegian coast is also causing concern, because it appears still to be deepening. This is making the wind rise in a southerly direction. This, in turn, is forcing the sea to surge in a southerly direction."

The Prime Minister looked quizzically at his colleagues. The Environment Minister raised his head and asked, "What is the effect of the closing of the Thames Barrier? When

I came in this morning, the river seemed to be extraordinarily high. Is the barrier retaining too much water?"

"As soon as the tide had receded sufficiently, the barrier was lifted and the river level has started to reduce. It isn't going down fast enough, of course, because the outflow is restricted with the amount of seawater downstream in the estuary. The barrier will have to be closed again sometime between 13.00 and 14.00 hours and the concern is that, above the barrier, with the river taking in so much flood water upstream, there could well be localised flooding of varying severity."

"What does that mean?" asked the Home Secretary. "'Of varying severity'?"

"Well, we don't know where nor by how much. Of course, we do know where the likely flood areas are. These have been mapped and well publicised for many years. It's more a question of what we should do because it is impractical to evacuate all these areas. That would mean the movement of millions of people, most of whom will be away from home anyway, because it's an ordinary working day.

"I can only advise, Prime Minister." The Chairman of the Environment Agency continued, as he looked round the Cabinet table and commented, "If it were down to me, I would advise people to make their way home immediately and then to sit out the storm at home. I don't know how impractical that might be, but I can imagine it will place an intolerable strain on public transport. On the other hand, to reduce panic and to be able to monitor the situation as it unfolds, it might be better to make no comment at all, other than to raise the issue of potential flooding in London and the south east."

"I agree," said the Prime Minister. "Without access to specific facts, there is no other way forward. Please issue a media statement, worded specifically to alert but not alarm."

The sight of the river as he walked to work, was nagging away at Fred all morning. He considered whether it was a trick of the light and the rain. By nine o'clock, with all his paperwork complete, he was about to buckle down to some serious studying connected with his impending promotion. The thought of the river, however, kept creeping back into his mind, so he decided to climb the training tower to take another look. As he emerged onto the viewing platform, he felt the full force of the wind. Although the rain had lessened a little, the sky was still dark and menacing.

From the top, when he looked to the east, he could see the river after passing the Isle of Dogs, down towards the Thames Barrier. To the south, however, much of his view of Millwall was obscured by the Canary Wharf tower blocks, but he had a good view to the west towards the city of London. Between the rain squalls he saw that the Barrier was still open, but that the water on the far side seemed as though it was still High Tide.

I was right, he thought. *The water is still very high and it hardly seems to be moving. High Tide was at half past four, so it should almost be Low Water now. This is really strange.*

He now realised that the pair of binoculars, kept in his office, would be more than useful and decided to fetch them. When he reached the ground, he crossed the training area and entered the main building. He put his head into the canteen and was seen by his crew.

"Hi, boss. We've just boiled the kettle. You want some coffee?"

"Yeah! Great." Fred went in and sat down.

"Blimey, Boss, you're all wet! Where've you been in all this weather?"

"I've just been to the top of the tower."

"Needed the exercise? Bit of middle age spread?" His crew joined in the good-natured banter.

"Listen, guys," Fred responded, looking round at them all. "I'm a bit worried, because the river is still so high."

"Well, it should be after all this rain."

"I suppose so, but we're only an hour from Low Water and the river still seems pretty high to me. I checked the Barrier and it's open, but there doesn't appear to be much flow. I came down to collect the binoculars to take a closer look.

"I'm going to call the Environment Agency for an update. They'll have their hands full, I expect, but I know a guy that works there. I'll call him on his mobile. As soon as I'm fully briefed, I'll get back to you all." He stood up, picked up the mug of coffee and went to his office.

It took some time before his friend picked up. "Hi, Fred. You on duty, today?"

"Yeah! Look, I'm worried about the height of the Thames. We're an hour from Low Water, the Barrier is open, but there seems to be no outflow."

"You're absolutely right," agreed his friend. "Look, Fred, we've got a situation building up here. The gales in the Channel have stopped the tide from ebbing properly. There's been an enormous amount of flooding on the continent. It's still raining heavily right across the country from the Chilterns to London. Several rivers have already gone over. Our Governor decided to brief the Cabinet direct and is at Downing Street right now. The tide will turn in about 40 minutes and we'll be closing the Barrier again. I reckon you can expect some flooding in London with this lot."

"Are you serious?" asked Fred.

"Can't put it plainer, mate."

"Cheers, Jim. Appreciate the info. Let's get a pint together soon."

He put down the phone and sat there for a couple of minutes, mentally analysing the information and planning how best to organise the station's resources to respond to the situation. He grabbed the binoculars and went back up the tower. As he emerged at the top for the second time, the rain was still drifting past in heavy squalls, as though a giant hand was opening and closing enormous net curtains. Once again, he turned to the east and, as he stared at the Thames Barrier, he saw the massive gates being hydraulically lifted into position. *They must be more concerned with the sea than the river flood water,* he thought.

Nature, of course, when she is so minded, can make mankind look pathetic and particularly feebleminded. Sensible plans and strategies, when calculated on paper, can fall apart like tissue paper lanterns in the rain. A wrong word here and a locked door there can have massive implications that are completely out of balance with the norm.

The media statement was written and issued to all the appropriate channels.

The Environment Agency, on behalf of the Government, advises that the current weather conditions are likely to prevail for the next 24 hours. The heavy rainfall has already caused local flooding throughout the Thames Basin and there is every likelihood of further flooding both in the London area and throughout the south east. The emergency services are already dealing with a number of fallen trees. However, all major roads and railway routes remain open.

You are advised to keep to your normal travel arrangements. If there are any changes, please follow the instructions.

Please keep calm at all times.

Travel arrangements for commuters into London will inevitably include the Tube, the buses and the railways. Because the vast majority of commuters work on the north side of the river, all those people arriving and leaving London from Victoria, Charing

Cross, Waterloo, London Bridge and Cannon Street stations have to cross the river one way or another. Both Grosvenor Bridge, which carries the rail tracks to Victoria, and Hungerford Bridge, which does the same for Charing Cross, therefore become strategic river crossings.

Most commuters utilise automatic travel facilities. Oyster cards give immediate access to the systems, but if the computer systems fail, then the cards will not work and that will leave hundreds of thousands of people all wanting to have their specific query answered – and immediately.

But the commuters into and out of London are both resigned and more than a little resourceful. Having encountered many transport disruptions, both man made and natural, over the years, the commuter has become hardened to the vagaries of travel and will stoically put up with most interruptions. On that Thursday, however, it was the inclusion of the last sentence – *Please keep calm at all times* – that made all the difference. And, of course, it only takes one or two to create a change from normality.

Ashika, a cleaner at a bank in the city, was drinking coffee in the Nespresso Café on Cheapside with her friend Ruksana. Their morning's work was already done. A small television was playing at the back of the coffee shop. Neither was taking any notice of the show because Ashika was relating a long story to Ruksana about a recent family wedding in the Punjab. Ruksana was trying very hard to listen and to concentrate on the story, but she was extremely tired and really only wanted to get home. Her eyes were drooping as she glanced round the coffee shop when, suddenly, she noticed that the television programme had been interrupted. The announcer's face was replaced by another person and, although she couldn't really hear what was being said, she could read the moving strap line at the bottom of the screen. She jumped slightly when she read the words '*Please keep calm at all times*'.

Ruksana nudged Ashika and said, "Look at that!"

"Look at what? I'm telling you about what Rahman said at the wedding."

"I know. I'm sorry, but there's an announcement on the TV about the weather."

"The weather has been bad, but I wouldn't have thought it needed a TV announcement." Ashika laughed.

"No, look!" Ruksana persisted. "It says to keep calm at all times. Why does it say that? It must be really bad and something terrible is going to happen."

Ashika turned in her chair and looked at the screen. "Oh my God," she blasphemed. "I've got to get home." She jumped up, knocking over her stool. The noise made the other customers look up and others saw the message on the screen. Ashika, with Ruksana in close pursuit, made for the door and started to walk rapidly through the wind and rain to St. Paul's tube station. Other customers followed close behind. The last one out knocked into a passer-by who was on his mobile.

"Hey! Watch it!" he remonstrated.

"You'd better get moving, mate. London's going to be flooded."

"You what?" He caught hold of the customer with his free hand. "What did you say?"

"I've just seen it on the telly, pal. This weather is causing flooding everywhere and London's going to get it."

A disembodied voice down the phone called, "What's going on? What did you say?" but the pedestrian discontinued the call to send a text to his office saying, "I'm not coming back in. Just seen a message that London is going to be flooded and I'm off home."

That message was received by several of his work colleagues, who forwarded it to their friends. Someone put up a message on Facebook and another on Twitter with the hashtag *'Please keep calm at all times'*. And so, the best laid plans of the Environment Agency were superseded.

Office workers began to stream out of the high-rise buildings in an attempt to get to the tube stations as quickly as possible. With them, all logic and rational thought disappeared at much the same rate.

As Ashika and Ruksana reached St. Paul's tube station they quickly descended to the platform for trains to Liverpool Street. They were lucky as a train arrived soon after they reached the north bound platform. The doors opened and they were able to find space, just before a small crowd emerged from the escalator. The doors shut and the train departed. It rattled its way to Bank, where there was a growing mass of people on the platform. Again, the doors opened and, after a little difficulty, closed again.

The train set off for Liverpool Street. It stopped twice in the tunnel, jerked several times and finally reached Liverpool Street station. Most of the passengers emerged onto the platform. They travelled up the escalators until they reached the main station. Outside, it was still raining.

Back in the city, the few who left immediately were soon overtaken by increasing numbers of people who very quickly clogged the entrances to all the tube stations. Where there were designated 'Entry' and 'Exit' systems, this flood of humanity simply ignored the notices and poured into the underground system. It was impossible for anyone to move against this tide, which was so dense that several people were carried down the stairwells without touching the stairs at all.

On the platforms, people were pushing and elbowing until, inevitably, someone fell onto the tracks. The safety systems immediately cut off the power and all trains came to a halt. The Central Line was the first to stop working but was quickly followed by the Northern Line and then Circle and Bakerloo Lines.

With the entrances to the Underground now blocked, people sought other routes out of the London. Many had to travel south and west to get home and were desperate to cross the river. They began to run down King William Street and Gracechurch Street towards Monument and London Bridge. Others, further west, were aiming for Southwark Bridge, Blackfriars Bridge and Waterloo Bridge.

By one o'clock the streets were filled with fleeing and panicked humanity.

Chapter 13
Thursday Afternoon

The depression centred over Oxford slowly started to drift to the east and fill. The effect was for the hurricane in the Channel to reduce to severe storm. The rain continued across all the south of England, with many rivers bursting their banks, causing considerable localised flooding.

Despite the slight reduction in the force of the wind, the concentration of the sea at the eastern end of the Channel remained very high and now the tide was flowing. There was widespread flooding in northern France and Belgium.

The northern depression to the west of Stavanger had deepened and the wind had increased to severe storm, bringing down power lines in Scotland and northern England. The wind which remained from the north, was still accompanied by heavy, drifting snow and, because the North Sea is relatively shallow, it was pushing the sea water southwards towards Holland and Denmark. The two concentrations of sea water met just before midday with the effect of creating a six-foot surge, travelling southeast at about 200 miles per hour. As it approached the land, the continental shelf created an undertow, which increased the height and power of the surge, but slowed its speed. Just after 1.00 pm, it surged over the protective dykes of the Zuider Zee, washing away all the vehicles on the A 7 motorway.

The effect of the surge, when its southern end reached the Thames estuary was to batter the land below Margate, before forming a swell of water which, rather like a river bore, moved westwards up the river towards London. Just before 2.00 pm, there was considerable flooding, as the sea walls were breached along the Essex coastline. The rivers Blackwater, Crouch and Roach were all overwhelmed with seawater flooding over the sea walls and onto the local arable farmland. In Kent, the surge inundated the river Medway and the Isle of Grain, whilst the Isle of Sheppey was completely cut off from the mainland when the bridge supports, carrying the A249, were undermined and collapsed.

The Thames narrows significantly between Sheerness in the south and Shoeburyness in the north. To the west of Shoeburyness lies Southend on Sea and beyond that Hadleigh. At 2.00 pm, the sea surged up Hadleigh Ray, pouring over the sea defences into Canvey Island.

The narrowing of the Thames had the effect of heightening the surge wave to about forty feet and increasing its power, but as the depth of the Thames also reduced, the speed of the surge wave slowed to about 20 miles per hour. It poured up Holehaven creek, flooding and damaging the refineries at Coryton, before sweeping over the stored and stacked containers at Thames Haven. Many containers were swept upriver before being dumped on the riverbank just north of Coalhouse Fort. The big southern bend in the river should have negated the speed and strength of the surge, but it was so high that it inundated all the southern bank up to Cliffe, leaving only Cliffe Fort as a small island in a mass of swirling, dirty, oily water.

On reaching Tilbury, the surge quickly overflowed into the sewage works and flooded over Tilbury dock, where the lock gates were irreparably damaged. Containers, already floating in the river, were rolling into the piers and gantries that line both banks, smashing them like matchsticks and sluicing them away. The water flooded into Tilbury town as far north as the Gateway Academy.

More containers from Tilbury dock were washed into the main river, as the tidal wave continued to flow upriver. On the south side, it forced its way up Robins creek before overwhelming Ebbsfleet United Football Club and flowing into the railway tunnel under the river that carries the Eurostar to France. The water funnelled along the tracks and into the tunnel at such speed and with such force, that it emerged like a geyser at the northern end in the Thurrock Trade Park just before the main tidal wave crashed into the oil storage depot. Much of West Thurrock was demolished and the northern approach road to the Queen Elizabeth II Bridge received a severe pounding from the floating containers.

After devastating the Manorway Business Park, the surge destroyed all the housing estates at Greenhithe north of London Road, before sweeping away all the vehicles at the storage depot, inundating the Campanile Hotel, smashing its way along Crossways Boulevard under the southern approach to the bridge and into the southern approach road to the Dartford Tunnels.

Because of the high winds, the bridge had been closed to all vehicular traffic, which meant that the M25 orbital road could only cross the Thames through the Dartford Tunnels. Both tunnels were completely full of traffic. After breaching the flimsy fence at the side of the road, the water forced its way into the tunnels. Its force was so great that the vehicles near the entrances were simply crushed and, as the water flowed into the tunnels, it created a concertina of crushed and ruined vehicles, deep under the river. Near the surface, the drivers were killed by being crushed but, lower down, they were simply drowned. There were no survivors.

At the northern end, the same disaster unfolded after the water had surged through the oil storage depot. It smashed its way along the new Eurostar railway, under the old local railway line, under the bridge approach road before bursting onto the approach roads to the tunnels. As the water forced its way into the tunnels, fountains spurted from the air vents on both sides of the river like the geysers in Yellowstone Park.

Leaving Tilbury and Gravesend devastated in its wake, the tidal wave quickly inundated the Rainham Marshes as far north as the A13. On the south side, Thamesmead and Abbey Wood were completely destroyed, leaving Gallions Hill standing proudly in a sea of devastation. The tidal wave of destruction was now about 30 feet high and moving up river at approximately 20 miles per hour.

Michael Varley's speech of welcome at the Mansion House started at just after half past nine. It was supposed to take forty minutes, but in the event he spoke for close to an hour. As he left the top table and sat down, next to Alice, he breathed a heartfelt sigh of relief. The speech went well. His audience already appreciated the difficulties facing the city, with such uncertainty facing the country since leaving the European Union. The delegates also picked up on his mildly jocular passages, although these were few and far between.

As Michael had a reputation for his plain speaking, together with his cautious nature as a banker, he was well respected amongst his colleagues. They knew that it was inevitable that he would cover topics the Government would rather ignore. The monthly industrial output figures were still in decline; unemployment continued to rise; inflation was also rising and the Bank of England had had no choice but to increase interest rates.

After a short break for coffee, the Chancellor of the Exchequer, addressed the conference. With a dry manner and a lack of common touch, there were many in the audience who were surprised that he had remained in office for so long. The feeling in the city was that he was now playing for high stakes but his hand was very poor, as though the deck was loaded against him as well as the rest of Great Britain. Britain, nowadays, seemed to have so few allies.

The small triumphs of various trade deals with the old Commonwealth countries never lived up to the political promises. Trade with Europe was increasingly difficult with the ever-increasing regulations. All the Presidents even including President Trump spoke warmly about the 'special deal' but, on practical terms, America continued to become more isolationist, demonstrating no real love of Britain. Britain was endeavouring to build an economic future based on its illustrious past, but the rest of the world remained totally indifferent.

The Chancellor was scheduled to speak until midday. As soon as he finished, many of the guests would depart with a chosen few invited to remain to take lunch with him, the Governor of the Bank of England and several other senior city and political figures. Michael and Alice were able to slip away and return to Le Grove Investments on London Wall. They made their way, bending into the wind, trying to avoid the rain as much as possible. As soon as they had entered the door, Michael went to his office and turned on his computer to check the prices' movements. Alice went into the small kitchen to make a decent pot of coffee, wondering why catering companies never seemed to provide satisfactory coffee. It was a mystery to her why those drinking it never seemed to complain.

As she opened the door to Michael's office, she could hear noises outside their front door. She took the tray to the sideboard, poured Michael a cup of coffee and took it over to him. As she bent over to put it on the desk, he put his hand on her waist.

"I like that dress," he remarked. "It suits you really well."

"Thank you." She moved away, back to the sideboard. "Can you hear a funny noise?"

"Funny peculiar or funny ha-ha?" asked Michael.

"It sounds like people running and shouting, but a long way away," she explained.

Michael got up from his chair and went to the window. "Look at that!" he exclaimed. Alice joined him. Looking down five floors to the street below, they saw hundreds of people running along London Wall towards the Underground stations. Most had no coats and were already drenched from the rain.

"What the hell's going on?"

"I don't know. Maybe there's something on the news." Alice moved to the television, which suddenly flashed into life. The first thing they saw was the announcer's grave face and a strap line spelling out the Government's warning. Alice gasped when she read the line *'Please keep calm at all times'*.

"No one's taking much notice of that," she said, moving towards the door.

"Where are you going?" Michael looked at her enquiringly. "There's absolutely no point in joining that lot out there. Where will you go? What will you do? Look!" He pointed out of the window towards the big road junction with Moorgate. "The crowd is just getting bigger and bigger. I reckon no one can get into the station." His voice began to rise with concern.

Alice's moment of panic had subsided to be replaced by an icy calm. "There's obviously something much greater going on. I don't know what, but it can't be a bomb. If it's to do with the weather, then it might be better to stay here."

"Stay here?" Michael interrupted. "What's here?"

"At the moment, we have power, light and warmth. I suggest we charge up our phones and tablets. I'll boil some hot water and fill our thermos flasks."

"Fill our thermos flasks?" Michael shouted at her. "We're not going on a picnic."

"No," she replied. "But we don't know how long we'll be here, nor how long we'll have power. So it's better to be prepared." With that she left him staring out of the window and went to the kitchen, wondering where her resolve had come from.

Since arriving at school, David was unable to concentrate on anything other than the weather. There was no time to check his computer to see what the two depressions were doing and whether they were starting to move. He concluded correctly that the southern weather front was filling slowly and beginning to move to the east. He was so concerned that he felt it necessary to send a text to Jackie. He knew that his mother would have left her at college, but he couldn't help feeling that events were only just beginning to unfold and he wanted to be there to see what would happen.

At eleven o'clock, the BBC app on his iPhone announced the media release concerning the problems facing London. He knew that his father was in the city giving a speech and he presumed that Jackie's father would also be at work. He texted Jackie again, suggesting that it would be really interesting to be in London rather than revising. They began to make arrangements for cutting school so that they could get up into the capital. They arranged to meet at midday at the railway station. He knew that the line was open again and that normal services were running.

He walked out from school at half past eleven. Jackie left college at much the same time and they met on time at Richmond station. Jackie was wearing an old pair of jeans, a cotton blouse and thick jumper plus ankle boots and her sheepskin coat. The train left only a few minutes later and they were in Waterloo before half past twelve.

The station was very busy and it was considerably hard work pushing to get through the crowds. They abandoned all thoughts of using the Underground when they saw the numbers of people emerging up the stairs at the entrance. Instead, they decided to cross the river on foot and left the station.

At lunch, Martin said that he and James would take the Land Rover down to the sea wall as soon as they finished eating. Charlie decided to join them, if only to satisfy his own curiosity of the level of the river. The wind was still strong and the rain was still falling heavily. Having experienced the conditions earlier in the morning, all were suitably dressed with warm jumpers, denims and boots plus wax jackets and heavy mufflers. They left the farmyard at ten minutes to two and drove down the track at the side of the first field. When James got out to open the gate, he could hear a strange, muffled roar. As Martin drove through, James knocked on the passenger window and shouted, "Dad! Get out here, quickly."

Martin put on the handbrake and got out of the vehicle, followed by Charlie. They immediately heard the same odd noise, coming from their left. They peered through the rain squalls and saw, in the direction of Southend on Sea, what appeared to be a mountain of water moving up the river towards them.

"Good God!" he exclaimed. "Just look at that!" He pointed at the enormous wave, which was now passing in front of them. They watched it race up Hadleigh Ray, spilling over the sea defences as though they were not there and completely inundating all the land between the seawall and the railway line. The railway was built on a low embankment but, along its length, there were a number of bridges to allow access to the lower fields. There was also a series of ditches between the railway and the seawall. The sea burst through these bridges, weakening and eroding the brick structures.

115

As the wave surged on towards Benfleet, it washed away parts of the embankment, leaving the track bent and buckled.

Martin and his boys were standing next to Hadleigh Castle, an old monument left as a ruin from the days of Edward III. The water continued to rise up the hill towards them. Martin suddenly felt an extraordinary build-up of rage inside him.

"God knows how much work I've put into that land and now look at it." He pointed to the fields below the ruined railway line. They were completely covered in sullen, dark and sinister water. "The ground will be poisoned with salt and God knows what else."

As they continued to stare at the flood, the rain eased a little and, before them, they could see a single expanse of water, right across Canvey Island as far as the Isle of Grain on the north Kent coast. Although the water continued to rise up the slope towards them, Martin refused to move. Rather like a latter day King Canute, he remained stock still three paces in front of his sons, almost as though he was daring the sea to flush him away as well.

"Come on, Dad," muttered James. "There's nothing we can do here."

"There'll be plenty to do as soon as the tide turns. The sea wall will be completely buggered and probably washed away, especially where we were looking at it this morning." He pointed in the general direction, but the wall was completely under water.

"I can hardly believe that we were walking on it less than seven hours ago."

"What?" Charlie exclaimed. "You were both down there?"

Martin turned to look at him. "What of it? The tide was out and it was important that we checked the state of the sea wall."

"But that – that wave thing might have come and swept you away. You were both being exceptionally reckless."

"Don't be stupid." James came to his father's defence. "That tidal surge will have been caused be a freak weather situation. And it came now, not at low tide."

As they were bickering, the water was continuing to rise up the slope in front of them. Martin took two further paces towards the water. He pointed at it and muttered, "Fuck off, you bastard!" He then looked up at the sky and shouted at the top of his voice, "Fuck off, you bastard!" As though in response to his command, the water seemed to stop rising.

After climbing up the training tower twice, Fred decided to telephone the Chief Fire Officer to see if there was any up to date information and to request any specific instructions.

He spent the next hour or so, talking with colleagues and formulating plans, should there be any change in the river and the weather. When the Environment Agency's warning came on the television, his colleagues called him into the common room. *Why, oh why did they have to add that last sentence?* he thought. *If anything, official advice like that seemed designed to create panic, not to save lives.*

"Listen guys! I've got a feeling we're in for a bad one here." He looked round at his friends. "As you know, I spoke to my pal at the Environment Agency, earlier. I've now been onto HQ and the message is the same. Bad weather conditions in the Channel are affecting the tides and flooding is expected in the London area. But no one can specify where or how badly." He paused and looked round at them all.

"Most of you have families nearby. I suggest you contact them now and get them here as quickly as possible. I just feel that we have a disaster unfolding and our major purpose is to protect lives. I'm going to call Dinah, to tell her to go to the school and get it evacuated and bring all the kids here. When this fire station was built, they included features for it to withstand flooding. Come on, let's get to it."

As soon as he was sure that Dinah understood exactly what she was to do, he telephoned the school, explaining that his wife would arrive very soon to assist with the evacuation of all the children and the staff to the fire station. The head teacher had already seen the Environment Agency's message and appreciated the urgency. She assured Fred that all the staff and children would be ready to leave within thirty minutes. By midday, they all arrived at the fire station, together with a number of parents, including Rajinder and his wife. Before locking his shop, he had packed up a large number of bags with food and water.

Fred also telephoned the manager at the Queen Victoria Seaman's Rest on the other side of the East India Dock Road and the Salvation Army Citadel on Kerbey Street. To each in turn, he explained the message from the Environment Agency and the added information from the London Fire and Rescue Service. He suggested that the Seaman's Rest and the Citadel should act as a temporary refuges, should the flooding in London get really bad.

At half past one, Fred again climbed the tower. This time, he remembered to bring the binoculars. He was thankful that the rain seemed to be easing. The river, from this height, looked sluggish and dark. It was very full but, as far as he could see, there was no local flooding. He looked upriver where, beyond the King Edward VII Memorial Park, he could see Tower Bridge and the iconic skyscrapers of the city of London, the Shard, the Gherkin and others, as well as St Paul's Cathedral and beyond them, even the top of the London Eye.

He turned to look southwards down past the east side of the high-rise office buildings of Canary Wharf, towards the O2 Arena and the Blackwall Tunnel southern approach. There seemed to be no movement of the sullen, dirty brown water. The wind was no longer as strong and there was a sudden burst of sunshine on the southern bank of the river. He looked up at the sky. The clouds were reluctantly lifting and the day was noticeably lighter, but the feeling of foreboding remained heavy on his shoulders.

As he turned towards the east and the Thames Barrier, he glanced at his watch. It was just after half past two. Behind him, he thought he could hear an odd, unusual mumbling sound. Cocking his ear, he turned back to face the west. This time he looked over Limehouse Basin towards Whitechapel. A movement caught his eye on the main road. He lifted the binoculars and could see people running and shouting on the Commercial Road.

I wonder why they are running this way, he thought. *If there's going to be some flooding, they would be safer in the city because the land slopes quite steeply up from the river.*

"That's right," responded Dinah. Fred jumped. He hadn't heard her coming up the tower, nor realised that he was talking out loud.

"Blimey! You gave me quite a turn." He pointed to the west. "Look there. Why are all those people running down the Commercial Road?"

"I don't know." Dinah turned and looked to the east. "But what's that noise, over there?" She pointed past his shoulders, towards the east.

Fred looked through the binoculars towards the Thames Barrier. Now that the rain had virtually stopped, the view was remarkably clear. Just beyond the Barrier, he could see the London City Airport and, further down river, the uprights of the Queen Elizabeth II Bridge. As he looked, he saw two fountains of water erupt on the Dartford side, immediately followed by two on the Thurrock side. *What the hell?* he thought.

And suddenly he saw the tidal surge, a wall of dirty black water sweeping up river towards him. Inexorably, purposefully and indiscriminately, it moved with a terrifying majesty, scouring all before it. The Rainham Marshes disappeared before his eyes, one moment an expanse of grass and muddy creeks, the next a sheet of dirty, oily water dotted with sea containers. A few moments later, on the southern side, Thamesmead and Abbey Wood were overwhelmed.

They watched, aghast, as jetties and gantries simply disappeared under the water. They could see that there were large, sea containers being washed upstream, tumbling over and over on the crest of that awesome wave. As one tumbled into the oil depot at Barking Reach, it must have snagged a power cable. There was a flash and the whump of an explosion as spilled fuel caught fire. He put his arm round Dinah and protectively drew her to him.

They watched, as if turned to stone, as the wave obliterated the piers of the Woolwich ferry before it swept over the Royal Docks pumping station and, aided by this access to the Gallions Point Marina, it flowed into and over the airport. Several aircraft standing on the tarmac were simply washed away, while others were swept into buildings and crushed, releasing hundreds of gallons of high-octane fuel.

They watched, as the wave battered its way through the shopping parks at the southern end of the Barrier and through the blocks of flats at the northern end, sweeping over the man-made Thames Barrier Park. The Barrier itself now acted as a weir with the contaminated seawater surging over the top, together with containers, cars, trucks, broken derricks and general detritus plus a growing number of drowned bodies. The gates stood firm against the increasing pressure of the water and the continual barrage of the heavy containers, but major and disastrous damage was inflicted to both riverbanks, where the floating containers were destroying much of the riverside infrastructure. With most of the riverside protection now being too low, the water had immediate access to the land on both sides of the river, with such devastating effect. It swirled around both the north and south ends of the barrier, eroding the land and undermining the buildings overlooking the river.

They watched, as Fred put his arm protectively round Dinah and pulled her closer to him, the water surging over Olympia Way and across the North Greenwich peninsula with the O2 Arena at its tip. The water poured into the Blackwall tunnels, both of which were heavy with traffic. He turned to look at the northern end of the tunnels, but the wave, after surging up the river Lea as far as Bromley Hall, had already overwhelmed them.

They watched, as the tower blocks at Blackwall proudly withstood the onslaught. They had been built with deep foundations and strong steel frameworks. Despite this, however, the continual battering from the heavy containers in the filthy, contaminated water finally overcame the glass work at ground level. As soon as the first crack appeared, the windows shattered and water poured into the lower floors. The tower blocks effectively slowed the progress of the surge at its northern end. Just to the south of the tower blocks, however, there was no riverside barrier to stop the water spilling into and inundating South Dock. The Blue Bridge was swept away before the wave was squeezed between the tower blocks of Canary Wharf and the hotel blocks at Marsh Quay. This had the effect of increasing the power of the wave, which swept away both the South Quay footbridge and the South Docklands Railway Bridge, before re-entering the river itself at the Marsh Wall roundabout.

They watched, with their hearts hammering in their chests, as the wave inundated and destroyed Cubitt Town, Millwall and the southern end of the Isle of Dogs, leaving only the tower blocks standing proudly, isolated and surrounded by the swirling, dirty water, their lower windows broken and their lower floors flooded.

Suddenly, Fred turned to focus on Commercial Road. The people had stopped running and were transfixed, staring towards the river, as the wave spread over the northern riverbank towards them. The wave simply overwhelmed all those who had already passed Limehouse station and were now on the East India Dock road. It tossed some into the air, while sucking others under the surface. Either way, they drowned.

They watched, as cars and vans were washed into the streets surrounding the fire station and deposited on the ground with total abandon. They watched, as the wave passed them by, moving with a frightening and unstoppable purpose, ever further to the west.

After witnessing the people on Commercial Road being overwhelmed and swept away, Fred focussed the binoculars onto Tower Bridge. The south side of the Rotherhithe Tunnel was already flooded, as the wave moved on to inundate Bermondsey. All the old warehouses, lining the south bank, were swept away by the heavy containers and vehicles in the water, as the mountain of water inexorably flowed on towards Tower Bridge.

Fred finally looked to the north. All the streets beyond the fire station, as far as the Limehouse Cut were flooded. Realising that his work was just about to start, Fred led Dinah downstairs. Together they had witnessed a devastation of the east end of London that was totally unprecedented. Even the German Luftwaffe, during the Second World War, had been incapable of inflicting so much damage in so short a time.

David and Jackie made slow progress against the crowds. They emerged from Waterloo station and forced their way onto Waterloo Road leading to the bridge. They watched spellbound as the screaming mass of people running towards them spread all over the road, with complete disregard for the traffic and their own safety.

"I just don't understand why they are all wanting to get to Waterloo. If there's going to be a flood, it will be on the south side," he muttered more to himself than Jackie.

"Why?"

"Well, look at the land on both sides – try to ignore the buildings – you'll see that the banking on the north side is much steeper."

Jackie looked and immediately realised that the south side of the Thames is actually very flat and low lying. She also noticed that the water level in the river was extraordinarily high. She was thankful to be on a high bridge. David took hold of her hand and pulled her towards him.

"Come on," he urged her. "I want to get onto the other side."

"Why?" she repeated.

"I think it'll be much safer over there."

"Then why are all these people running south."

"I don't know. They don't seem to be acting rationally. Come on!" he said again as he pulled her hand and started to walk to the north. "I want to get higher up, if that's possible."

"Why?" Jackie asked again, as she allowed him to pull her across the bridge, surprised at his dogmatic attitude.

"Two reasons. I want to see what's going on and the higher we are, the safer we'll be."

They started moving north again. It was no longer raining as they crossed over the river. First Blackfriars Bridge came into view followed by the twin towers of Tower Bridge. They saw Somerset House on the northern side.

"Do you know what that is?" David asked.

"No." Jackie looked at the imposing stone building. "It looks like a fortress."

"We'll try to get in there."

As they reached the north end of the bridge it was just after two o'clock. The wind was lessening and the clouds were lifting. The sun was trying to come out. They walked along the right-hand side of Lancaster Gate, before turning onto Riverside Terrace. David saw the arched entrance on his left and they both ran towards it. No one was around and they were able to walk into the building. They headed for the stairs and then walked down a short corridor. David tried a number of doors before one opened. They went in and crossed the room to a window overlooking the river. Below them was Riverside Terrace and, further down, Victoria Embankment. To their left, they could see three ships, riding high on the swollen river – one of the tourist boats, HQS Wellington and HMS President.

David looked further down river and saw that Blackfriars Bridge was as crowded with people as Waterloo Bridge. Even the Blackfriars railway bridge, which carries the trains to Blackfriars Station, was crowded with people. He nudged Jackie and together, further down river past the Millennium footbridge, they could see Southwark Bridge and, beyond that, London Bridge. After looking at the river for about thirty minutes, they were about to leave. The room they were in was as silent as the grave. Suddenly, beyond the window, they could hear a growling sound rather like a distant artillery barrage.

Jackie turned to David. "Can you hear that odd noise?"

"Yes. It seems to be coming from down river. And it's getting louder."

They looked down the river and then eastwards towards the noise. In the very far distance, they could see the twin towers of Tower Bridge, just to the south of the Tower of London itself.

As they watched, through the raised roadways of Tower Bridge, they saw the river reared up like a mountain. It suddenly burst out of the Upper Pool, through the iconic towers of the bridge and past the Tower of London itself.

They watched as the water flooded over Bermondsey, engulfing the land around the Shard and London Bridge Station, past London Bridge and Southwark Cathedral and into the housing estates of Southwark itself. As the wave reached HMS Belfast, it ripped the ship's moorings out of the ground and the vessel began to drift upstream, until it struck London Bridge with such force that its bow became stuck fast under the central arch. Masonry was dislodged, causing many people to fall into the water and onto the deck of the old vessel.

Horror-struck, they continued to watch the water relentlessly surge past Southwark Bridge, Tate Modern and Blackfriars Bridge. Although the height of the wave was now reduced to about twenty feet, this remained sufficient for the detritus in the water, the empty containers, vehicles and an increasing number of dead bodies, to be deposited considerable distances from the river itself. The mere concentration of the buildings, with so many narrow streets between them, seemed to be slowing down the surge, but its power was so great that it cut a swathe of appalling destruction.

The water surged into the Bakerloo line at Lambeth North tube station. The flood doors had half closed before power to the line was cut. The force of the water was so great that it tore the safety doors off their mountings, before sluicing down the access tunnels to the platforms. The whole station was completely filled with dirty, oily water, pushing all the waiting passengers onto the tracks and into the tunnels where they drowned. The water carried the bodies under the Thames to Embankment, Charing Cross and even Piccadilly stations. When it reached Piccadilly, its force was only sufficient to fill the track bed and the waiting passengers on the platforms watched in disgust as, at first, dead mice and rats floated past, before the full horror struck them as drowned people began to emerge from the tunnel.

To the south of Piccadilly, a train on the southbound track was halted by the lack of power. This obstruction in the tunnel effectively stopped the numbers of drowned people floating past. Instead, they piled up, in front of the driver's cab, effectively creating a barrage. This made the situation far worse at Charing Cross, as the rats and mice followed by a large number of drowned people, were washed onto the platforms, amongst the waiting crowds who were unable to move back because of the force of the more people coming down the stairs. The loss of power had created dark, claustrophobic conditions, as the people began to claw at each other in an attempt to get out. Many slipped and fell. Some lost their footing at the platform edge where they slipped and fell into the water before they themselves drowned alongside the bodies who had been carried in by the flood water. Slowly the water rose up the walls and into the connecting tunnels, until it finally reached the roof of the tunnels. Everyone left on the platforms and in the connecting tunnels was finally drowned.

On the north bank, except for Katherine Dock, most of the land by the city remained relatively unscathed. The natural steepness of the riverbank and the land behind it formed a barrier high enough to restrict the flooding. Even so, for the first time in centuries, the dry moat around the Tower of London was filled with water. Traitor's Gate was completely ruined when it was struck a glancing blow by a bus floating in the flooded river.

As the surge passed them, David and Jackie watched it sweep inland at Charing Cross over the wall of the Victoria Embankment and into Horse Guards Avenue. They watched the wave pick up a double decker bus on the Embankment, before being hit a glancing blow by one of the tourist boats that had been ripped from its mooring. The surge flowed past all the famous offices of state and into St James Park, leaving the Houses of Parliament and Big Ben in its wake looking somewhat like a cruise ship moored in a marina.

The death toll was growing rapidly, particularly underground. The carnage in all the road tunnels had been immense, made worse by so many vehicles being crushed, but this was massively exceeded by numbers of dead in the Underground system. The sheer volume of people that tried to escape from the city and from Westminster via the Underground, caused people to slip and fall in the tunnels and on the stairs. They literally had no chance of survival and were simply trampled to death. In the panic to get away, there was little demonstration of human generosity and care. It was simply a question of 'Survival of the fittest and the devil catch the hindmost'.

The London Underground has been developed over the last one hundred and fifty years and is an exceptional transport system. Built next to a tidal river, it has flood safety systems, but these are powered by electricity. Should the power supply be interrupted, then there are emergency systems primed to take over. In the event of an incident where the power is cut, the safety process has a short delay before the emergency system kicks in. Each Underground line theoretically has its own power supply, but the passenger tunnels and escalators interlink with the whole system. Being the most recent lines that cross beneath the river Thames, the new Victoria and Jubilee lines are the best protected and their flood systems shut down quickly and efficiently, even in the interconnecting passenger tunnels. It was, however, a very different story on the Northern and Bakerloo networks.

At the same time as the water inundated London Bridge and Borough stations, the crowds on the platforms at both Monument and Embankment stations were so dense that people were simply pushed off the edge of the platforms and onto the electrified lines. There they were electrocuted causing an immediate shutdown of the power. Trains stopped mid tunnel and all the lights went out. The escalators stopped and the lifts shuddered to a halt. The emergency systems did not kick in before the water was able to enter the tunnels and to flow down the stairways and the lift shafts towards the platforms. The pressure of the water was so great that the cables carrying the lifts simply snapped.

The lift cabins dropped down the lift shafts, hitting the bottom with such force that the passengers suffered a multitude of broken legs, pelvises and spines. But they had no time to consider their fate, nor even to react to the pain, as all were immediately drowned when the water overwhelmed them.

The big steel flood doors stayed open and the water, unimpeded, flowed deep into the underground network, sweeping drowned people at the front, until it reached the platforms themselves. Here it simply pushed the mass of humanity onto the lines and into the tunnels, before flowing northwards under the river towards Monument and southwards past the Elephant and Castle towards Kennington. Here the lines branch both to the north as well as the south. The water, therefore, was able to flood both northwards to Charing Cross and further to the southeast beyond Oval.

Above ground, Jackie and David watched as the horrific disaster unfolded before them, the mountainous wall of water sweeping westwards across Waterloo, over the Jubilee Gardens, knocking down the London Eye before crashing into Westminster where it swiftly inundated Westminster Station. The containers and vehicles in the water reduced Westminster Pier to matchwood, before sweeping into and across Parliament Square, up Great George Street and into St James Park. Many trees were uprooted by the progress of the heavy containers, although their weight, coupled with the gentle upward incline of the land now had the effect of reducing the power of the surge and slowing it. Several cars were swept into the park with one finally coming to rest wedged against the gates leading into the marooned Buckingham Palace.

The modern buildings of Westminster, seemingly so substantial with their stone facades and brick fascias, are predominantly of a steel framework construction. Most were capable of withstanding such a water borne barrage. Older buildings particularly on the south bank and without the benefit of deep foundations, were not so fortunate and many succumbed to the unceasing battering of the detritus in the water. Those people trapped inside the collapsed buildings were either crushed or drowned and as the walls fell down, broken gas pipes and electric cables were exposed. Before the power was cut all over London, several heavy containers cut through these cables causing them to short and arc which, in turn, ignited the escaping gas. Explosions could be heard across the city with increasing regularity.

Jackie looked at David, her face ashen and frightened, and asked, "What are we going to do now?"

David shook his head. His heart was full of despair, but his immediate thought was of his father, stuck somewhere in the city.

"That was awful," he replied somewhat lamely. "I wonder where my dad is."

"And mine!" replied Jackie.

"Of course." David protectively put his arm round his girlfriend. "He'll be at Scotland Yard, won't he?"

"I suppose so." She looked up at him before saying, "Well, we could go there and see if he can help us."

In the cabinet room at No 10 Downing Street, the Prime Minister was presiding over an urgent meeting with the Home Secretary and the Minister for the Environment.

"Can you give me any up to date information?" he asked. "I'm due to make a statement in the House this afternoon and it seems that we are constantly being overtaken by events." He looked at the Home Secretary. "I understand that there has been a considerable movement of people from their offices in the city to the Underground."

"Yes, Prime Minister. No one really understands why. Basically, it appears that the city has downed tools and run."

"But, why? Surely everyone knows that the city is built on higher ground and with the most sophisticated construction techniques. It must be one of the safest environments in the world."

"It would appear that the message put out by the Environment Agency did not have the desired effect. The movement of all those people has clogged the transport system and the Underground is struggling to cope."

"What is the situation with the weather?" The Prime Minister turned to his Environment Minister.

"The weather fronts have caused a swell in the North Sea," he replied. "I am advised by the Environment Agency that it has moved south east down the North Sea and made landfall in Holland at just after one o'clock this afternoon."

"Did it cause any damage?"

"Yes, Prime Minister. I am led to understand that, at its commencement, the swell was some six feet high, but when it reached the continental shelf, the speed of the swell slowed from almost 200 miles per hour, down to about 20 miles per hour. This caused it to act like a mini though concentrated tsunami, reaching an estimated height of 25 feet. The tide was already flowing and the sea was already high."

"For pity's sake, man," the Prime Minister interrupted. "Did it cause any damage?"

"Yes, Prime Minister. The sea surge was so great it inundated the Zuider Zee and has caused considerable damage to northern Holland, even as far south as Amsterdam." He stopped and looked up at the Prime Minister. "There has been much loss of life and structural damage. Unfortunately, communications have been lost as we believe that power production in Holland has been interrupted."

"And this was at one o'clock, Greenwich Mean Time?"

"Yes, Prime Minister."

"Is this sea surge still moving?"

"Yes, Prime Minister."

"Where is it now?"

"I was advised at ten to two, just as I was arriving here in Downing Street, that it has entered the Thames Estuary. That was almost an hour ago. Information remains sketchy, but we are aware that its speed has reduced significantly."

"Will this make it grow in height as in Holland?" The Prime Minister turned white as he asked the question.

"I am advised that it will. However, I am also advised that it is not expected to surge beyond the Thames Barrier."

"What happens if it does?"

The question remained unanswered. Outside, they could hear a rumbling and the building was shaking. The Prime Minister stood up and walked to a window which overlooks the rose garden at the back of Downing Street. Below him dirty, oily water was flooding round the corners of the building. He looked more closely and saw two floating corpses.

"If your sea surge has reached Westminster, the Thames Barrier must already have been breached. God be with all those in the Underground. They must be beyond all help." He strode to the door and opened it. "Summon COBRA with immediate effect," he instructed.

David and Jackie continued to stare at the unfolding scene of devastation below them. The wave had passed in front of them from left to right and finally disappeared up river towards Pimlico. In its wake, it had left enormous destruction. Buildings had been annihilated, power lines exposed, gas pipes unearthed, bridges destroyed, railway lines

123

buckled and broken. Empty containers had rolled with incredible force through housing estates, crushing the houses, indiscriminately killing the occupants, before the water swept the rubble away. Cars, vans and trucks, swept upriver from as far away as Gravesend, were now deposited in roads, gardens, hospital forecourts and office building entrances. The more modern tower blocks remained firm. The strength of their construction and their deep foundations gave them a solidity. Even where the ground floors windows were broken allowing the water to surge up the stairwells, the upper floors were basically unscathed, although in every case power was interrupted.

It was onto this scene that Jackie and David stared, having witnessed a sight of biblical devastation. They were completely unaware that the wave of destruction was continuing remorselessly up river, flooding over the riverbank into Battersea Park, smashing into pulpwood all the houseboats moored off World's End, flooding into Chelsea and Fulham as far north as the Hammersmith flyover, inundating Chiswick and even flowing into Kew Gardens. The height of the surge continued to diminish because of the twists and turns of the river itself and as it passed Craven Cottage, it was now only about six feet. Because the river was already so high with flood water, this was still sufficient to flow over the river bank into the London Wetland Centre and completely contaminate the waterpark, before crossing the rest of the Barnes peninsula, flooding houses, finally re-joining the river at the Leg o' Mutton.

The height and strength of the wave was no longer capable of washing the big containers over the riverbanks. Some still floated in the middle of the river where they continued to damage and destroy whatever was in their path. The western side of Isleworth Eyot was completely blocked with this detritus; Richmond Lock and its footbridge were both destroyed, but by the time the surge reached Twickenham Road Bridge, the only visible signs of the devastation down river, were the floating bodies and the oily scum on the surface of the water.

Because of the incessant rainfall, the river was already dangerously high and as the surge passed by, it slopped over the riverbanks onto the riverside paths and roads. There was already localised flooding from Eel Pie Island up river towards Teddington Lock, but not with any particular structural damage. Now, the surge simply made the swollen river overflow, contaminating the water treatment works at Hampton, Molesey and Walton and causing damage to the boathouses of the riverside properties as far west as Shepperton.

On that Thursday morning, Sebastian decided to take a practical look at his plans to construct a hideaway for his illicit money. He knocked on Jack and Betty's apartment door soon after breakfast. Betty was already working in the kitchen and Jack was on his own, reading the morning paper.

"Sorry to intrude, Jack." Seb walked into the living room. "I was wondering if I could discuss a project with you." He started walking slowly up and down the room.

"What's that then?"

"Do you have any idea what is under the stairs as you go down into the basement?" Seb paused, hoping that his next words would not cause the breakup of a long relationship. "I need to create a space, hidden away from prying eyes, where I can keep some documents and other objects."

"Oh! That shouldn't be too difficult Mr F B." Jack's candid response rather took the wind out of Seb's sails. He stopped walking and looked directly at him.

"How do you mean?" Seb sat down on the edge of an armchair.

"My old dad told me that there used to be a further cellar below the basement. It was blocked up before the outbreak of the Second World War. I wasn't around then, of course, but I gather that your dad was already in discussion with the Ministry of War, with regard to giving the hotel over to the military, should it be needed."

"How can it be accessed?"

"Simple enough, Mr F B," replied Jack. "What you think is a blank wall next to the lift shaft is, in fact, a false wall at the top of another flight of steps leading further down."

"Bloody hell!" exclaimed Seb. "That'll save a vast amount of effort."

"What do you mean? Do you want to open it up? That'll be a bit beyond me these days, what with my arthritis."

"Yes! I know. But your advice and your memory will be invaluable. I can provide all the necessary labour from other contacts." Seb stopped and began to consider the possibilities. "But I will still want to disguise the entrance. I don't want to advertise that there's more space lower down."

"That won't be easy," remarked Jack.

"No, it won't. I can call on one of my business contacts to discuss how best it can be done." He stood up. "First, however, I want to look behind that wall. Can you bring a drill and a hammer and chisel down to the basement?" Seb left the room and went to his own apartment, where he changed into overalls.

Ten minutes later both he and Jack were in the basement, looking at the blank wall next to the lift doors. It had been plastered flush as though there was nothing behind it at all. Seb knocked on the plaster and was rewarded with a distinctive hollow sound. He knocked in an organised pattern all over the wall. It all seemed to be hollow. He gently pushed the wall and the plaster moved slightly under the pressure.

"This might be easier that I thought," he murmured. He drilled a hole through the plaster. Other than the plaster itself, there was no resistance at all. He tried another few holes and finally completed a full circle before putting down the drill. He picked up the hammer and chisel and began to knock out the plaster. He found that the wall was simply double thickness plaster board, nailed onto a simple three by two wooden frame. When all the plasterboard was removed, they realised that the frame had been placed six inches in front of a door, which was just like all the other doors in the stairwell of the hotel, at the back of the top step. Fred produced a heavy-duty bin bag for all the broken plasterboard and rubbish.

Seb contemplated the door for a few moments. Someone, a long time ago, had removed the door handle, no doubt to assist in constructing the false wall. There was also a large keyhole. He pushed the door, but it was firmly closed.

"Have you got an old door handle that'll fit this?" He looked at Jack, enquiringly.

"As a matter of fact, I have. And I've got a big key that'll fit that lock. They are both in my spares' cupboard. Dad told me never to throw them out and I've often wondered what they were for. I'll nip upstairs and get them."

While he was away, Seb picked up a sweeping brush and cleaned away all the dust and cobwebs behind the false wall that had accumulated over the past eighty odd years. There was nothing remarkable about the door. It needed a lick of paint, perhaps, but beyond that it was just the same as all the other doors.

Jack soon returned with the door handle and the key. He also brought a tin of WD 40. Seb checked to ensure that the door handle was solidly fixed to the spindle, before inserting it into the lock. He twisted the handle and, to his surprise, it turned without too much effort. It was stiff from a lack of use, but even when turned fully the door remained shut.

"It must be locked."

"Let me see," said Jack. He put the red attachment tube onto the nozzle of the can and sprayed some of the oil into the keyhole. They waited a few moments while the oil penetrated the lock itself, before Seb inserted the key. It slipped easily into the lock and he was able to turn it without difficulty. He twisted the door handle again and firmly pushed the door. It opened, to reveal stone steps descending into a darkened stairwell. Just like on every other floor in the building, eight steps down, there was a part landing. Seb realised that there would be a further four steps, followed by a part landing and then a further eight steps. At the bottom, there should be another door.

He looked to his left but could see no light switch. He could make out an old gas mantle halfway down the wall. He walked down a few steps, reached up and twisted the gas tap to check the supply. There was no hiss of escaping gas.

"This cellar must have been closed off well before the time the hotel was converted from gas to electricity. That would have been in the 1930s. The lift must have been installed at the same time, because there is no access to it from below. The actual hoist machinery is all on the top floor."

"My dad told me that he remembered when the lift was put in." Jack commented. "It was after the abdication of Edward VIII, but before the start of the second war. So around 1937, I guess."

"A bit late for a hotel at the top of its game, but exceptionally good timing for the war. It seems that the gas supply has been cut, so we'll need a torch."

"I thought we might. I've brought one with me." Jack produced a small pocket torch with a very bright beam. He led the way down the stairs.

At the bottom, they found that the door had been left open. Seb shone the torch to his right where they saw a solid brick wall. To his left, just as on the floor above, they found a passage running to the rear of the building. Halfway along, there was a door on the right. Seb was somewhat surprised that it opened easily when he turned the handle. Beyond the door, there was a cellar immediately beneath the kitchen. A few boxes had been left haphazardly on the floor.

A second door was at the end of the passage and it opened into a large cellar situated under the laundry and the entrance dock from the car park. There were old wine racks on the walls and a large table in the middle of the floor. The far left hand wall was brick. It was obvious that the whole cellar was constructed under only two thirds of the building.

"I've seen enough," Seb announced. He turned round and returned to the basement with Fred following behind. When they reached the top of the cellar stairs, Seb locked the door and removed the door handle and the spindle.

"Put these back into your spares cupboard. And keep them safe because I'll want them again very soon."

He walked up the stairs to his office, where he sat down behind his father's desk. Glancing at the desk clock, he realised that they had been down in the basement for over three hours. It was now almost one o'clock. He had a small television in the corner of the office and he turned it on. The first thing he saw was the statement from the Environment Agency concerning the immediate weather situation. Seb listened with little concentration, as his thoughts were more focussed on the morning's discovery. He jumped when he realised that the presenter had advised everyone to 'Stay Calm'.

I need to get to Soho, he thought, reaching for the telephone. He dialled Andy's number.

"Hello. This is Sebastian Fortescue Brown. Are you free?"

"Yeah. I'm over in Battersea," Andy replied. "How can I help?"

"I need to get to Soho as soon as possible."

"I can be with you in twenty-five minutes tops."

"I'll be waiting outside."

Seb made another two calls, before slipping off his overalls and re-dressing in his suit. He left the hotel at twenty past one.

Andy was rather surprised to receive Sebastian's call. He was at his friend's flat in Battersea, getting it ready for a further photo session with Alice on the coming weekend. Having convinced himself that she could be a potential star he now knew that he would have to treat her with complete respect. Finding out that she worked for Michael Varley was a big surprise. The fact that she had completely ignored him was a further confirmation that Alice was not to be treated with disdain, nor to be patronised but rather she was to be looked after with total courtesy and consideration. That was why he was at the flat, making sure it was clean and welcoming. All the surfaces were now dusted and the floors vacuumed. The fridge was cleaned and restocked. The bathroom was clean and there was even a vase of flowers on the table.

Seb's call had come just as Andy was putting away the Dyson. He was ready to leave, so he locked up and went downstairs to his taxi. It was only a short journey, over Battersea Bridge and through Kensington, to get to the Gloucester Palace Hotel. Just as he was parking the cab, Seb came through the front door.

"Where to, guv?"

"Carlisle Street in Soho. You know the way. We've been there before." Seb settled back into the seat by the nearside door.

"Be about twenty minutes. There seems to be quite a lot of traffic about."

But it wasn't the traffic that lengthened the time of the journey. It was the increasing number of people thronging the streets. Sebastian looked up from his paper, as the taxi stopped yet again.

"What's going on?" he asked.

"Apparently the Environment Agency has issued a flood warning for London," Andy replied. "I saw a brief snatch of the statement on the news. Hang on! I'll see if I can get it on the radio." He fiddled with the knobs and suddenly they both heard the latest announcement, ending with *'Please keep calm at all times'.*

"I can't understand why they broadcast messages like that," Seb commented. "It only causes panic. Just look at all these people on the streets."

"You're right. It's totally ridiculous." Andy agreed, as he drove out of Knightsbridge, round the top part of Hyde Park Corner and into Park Lane. It was just two o'clock, as he worked the taxi through the traffic at Marble Arch and into Portman Street. Suddenly all the people seemed to melt away and he had a clear run up Wigmore Street to Cavendish Place. He crossed Regent Street and quite soon turned right down Berniers Street. He crossed over Oxford Street and finally arrived at Carlisle Street.

"Please wait," instructed Seb. "I won't be more than half an hour." He got out of the cab and entered the building.

At the top of the stairs, he entered a comfortable, well-appointed waiting room. The young Eurasian woman behind the reception desk looked up and smiled.

"Good afternoon, Mr Fortescue Brown. I'm sorry, but Mr Chao is still engaged. I'm sure he won't be more than a few minutes."

Unseen by Seb, she pressed a bell push under her desk to alert Mr Chao. After speaking with Andy, one of Seb's two other calls had been to Mr Chao. As his arrival was at the agreed time, he was mildly irritated to be kept waiting. Very soon, however, the door to the left of the receptionist's desk opened and a tall Englishman emerged. He turned in the entrance, to say good bye to Mr Chao and to shake his hand. After a brief glance at Seb, he left the office.

Mr Chao came into the reception area to greet Seb. "Hello, Seb. It's been too long. I'm sorry to keep you waiting. Please come in." He ushered Seb into his office, followed by the receptionist.

"Would you care for coffee?" she asked.

"That would be very civil," Seb replied.

The two men sat down in two matching brown leather armchairs. There was a low coffee table between them. Mr Chao looked at Sebastian enquiringly, waiting for him to explain his visit.

For ten minutes or so, Seb followed the time-honoured ritual of discussing a number of unrelated topics, Mr Chao's health, the state of business, the current political situation, until finally, Seb decided it was an appropriate time to broach the real reason for his visit.

"Mr Chao," Seb started. "You've known me for over twenty-five years and I think, in that time, we have built a good relationship."

"Very true, Sebastian. I remember when you first assisted me in my supermarket. You were efficient and reliable. Indeed, even when I asked if you could assist with certain extra tasks, you did not shirk away. Yes." He nodded. "I agree. We have built a reasonable relationship."

"Thank you." Seb nodded and looked Mr Chao in the eyes. "I now need your assistance in a somewhat delicate matter which needs to be discreet, resolved quickly and just as quickly forgotten."

"That sounds rather intriguing." Mr Chao returned the look, as the receptionist re-entered the office, carrying a tray with a large cafetière and two cups and saucers. She poured the coffee and left them.

"When you say, 'just as quickly forgotten', I presume you are looking for some people who can assist you now, but who will soon be moving on elsewhere."

"Exactly!"

"The trouble with you English is that you always need to reach the point so quickly, without observing the common courtesies of conversation," Mr Chao observed.

"Indeed," replied Seb, wondering why Mr Chao had decided to revert to the opening gambits that he thought were already satisfied. "We still have so much to learn in this world from the older and wiser ways of life."

Mr Chao nodded and sat back in his chair. He was a handsome man, with a shock of white hair, carefully brushed back over his head. His black eyes were devoid of emotion and his face was unlined. Although of some age, he exuded knowledge and power, but strangely without being menacing. He and Seb had worked with each other over the years, generally when Seb could be of assistance to Mr Chao. In those early days, Mr Chao had come to rely on Seb's inherent knowledge of the British way of life, but now their relationship was built on mutual trust. Mr Chao appreciated that, recently, Seb had stepped up in the world, having inherited his father's hotel. He had changed and was more confident in himself. He was no longer drifting, but in control of his present and his future.

"How is the hotel business?" he asked.

"We're doing very well, indeed."

"I hear that you only have a skeleton staff there, these days."

"When I inherited the business, it was necessary to make some fundamental decisions in order to bolster up its profitability. There were a number of staff changes, but I feel we now have the balance just about right." Seb leant forward and picked up his coffee. Mr Chao continued to observe him. After taking a sip, Seb leant back in his chair, placing his hands on the arm rests.

"This is a most comfortable chair," he remarked.

"Thank you," Mr Chao replied. "My nephew built them to my specific design and instructions." He also leant back and crossed his legs. Seb immediately relaxed, realising that he had passed some hidden test.

"So, how may I help you specifically?"

"I am aware that you employ or have knowledge of certain workmen who could create a hidden doorway in my hotel."

"Yes," Mr Chao nodded slowly. "That is so."

"I want to construct a room, the entrance of which is known only to me, but which I can access without difficulty."

"Will you require such a door to be operated manually, or powered by electricity?"

"I've already thought about that," Sebastian replied. "The problem with electricity is that the power supply can be cut. On the other hand, it can assist with creating much greater security. I thought that an electrical system, which can be overridden manually, might be best. I don't really want to install a backup source of power."

"As with a separate generator?"

"Indeed." In his turn, Sebastian nodded.

"All of this can be done," Mr Chao announced. "There will be a price to pay, but I'm sure we know each other well enough not to be concerned too deeply with the need for paperwork and invoices. I will send my elder son to see you this evening. You already know Lee. He's proving to be an excellent administrator. I understand your need for discretion and we will employ no more than two workmen, both of whom are soon to leave London to work in the United States of America. We will need a discreet access, so the comings and goings are not observed by idle eyes."

"Thank you, Mr Chao. I was sure that I could rely on you for your knowledge and assistance. I look forward to meeting with Lee this evening. Shall we say at eight o'clock?"

"That will be excellent." They both stood and Mr Chao indicated for Seb to walk towards the door. Mr Chao opened the door and shook Seb's hand.

"Thank you so much for coming to see me. This has been an enlightening meeting."

"I'm grateful for your time, Mr Chao."

Sebastian nodded to the receptionist and went down the stairs to the waiting taxi. Just as he got in, all the lights in all the buildings went out. *Just what we need*, he thought. *A bloody power cut.*

Half an hour earlier, the gentleman who kept Seb waiting, after leaving the building, went back to his own car and his driver drove him to Scotland Yard. The roads were becoming increasingly packed with people. In conjunction with the Home Office, Chief Superintendent Kevin Bleasdale was heading up a police enquiry into missing immigrant workers. His meeting with Mr Chao was only one of an on-going series of meetings with prominent businessmen, whose enterprises were dependent on low paid, often immigrant workers. Mr Chao had many different interests and was a surprising source of information, but much of which, although accurate, would in the event turn out to be somewhat dated.

Chief Superintendent Bleasdale was pursuing a number of leads within businesses which were basically operating legitimately, although very close to the margin. Farmers in East Anglia and Lincolnshire, most of whom had voted to leave Europe, now found that their source of cheap labour from Eastern Europe continued to disappear like early morning mist on a warm summer's day. Kevin Bleasdale was not a political person but blessed with a high degree of common sense. He had voted to 'Remain' but only to ensure that his holiday trips to Europe would not become affected in the future. He had little sympathy with those farmers, whose profits were based on intensive labour – fruit picking, potato lifting and so on. Without thinking, they had voted for purely historical reasons to leave the European Union.

For decades, even before Britain's entry into what had then been called the Common Market, those farmers' livelihoods were based on the back-breaking work of immigrant labour. But now, a different form of labour was emerging. Peasants from Eastern Europe, North Africa and even the Middle East were being encouraged to come to Britain, often illegally, to be 'employed' in conditions of total servitude, some might even say slavery. They were held in dormitories, paid very low wages, most of which was later deducted as 'living costs'. The gang masters hired out their labour to local farmers, making a considerable profit on the deal.

But it was not only in agriculture; in all the low paid industries a similar pattern was emerging. Girls were imported for the sex trade, although ostensibly as domestic workers; boys too were brought in for the sex trade on the pretext they would be working in kitchens in the restaurant trade; there was even a market for domestic workers whose employment was often completely hidden from the authorities. And, of course, many of these workers would arrive in the UK when quite young, but after a few years of deprivation and unremitting hard work, their usefulness to their owners and employers had gone. Thus, an even newer industry was emerging, basically one of removal and disposal.

Although no one would officially admit any collusion, there was an understanding that the economy did, in some part, depend on these immigrant workers. Many of the vegetables in Britain's supermarkets were hand-picked, washed and sorted by immigrant labour. The farmers were invariably content to allow hiring contractors to supply the labour and, in the main, they asked no questions so long as the harvest was collected.

With the Brexit vote, the supply of au pairs reduced dramatically. Back in the '50s and '60s, young, western European girls answered advertisements to work in private homes for little more than board and lodging plus some spending money. The draw, of course, was the opportunity to learn English while living as a member of the family. After joining the Common Market there was a steady formalisation of this process but with the vote to leave, the availability of these young ladies was drastically and quickly reduced.

The previous ad hoc arrangements had been overtaken long ago and would never be reintroduced. Instead, seeing opportunities opening, new companies had been formed, acting as agencies to place young ladies, especially from Eastern Europe and possessing some Basic English, with good British households. Many girls saw this as an opportunity to exchange their drab existence and total lack of a future in their home environments into a life of excitement and travel. Many were duped into handing over their personal documents and many were brought into homes where they were treated no better than scullery maids and sex slaves. All their wages were used to pay off the 'loans' that had been created to pay the travel costs to the United Kingdom.

And in the major cities and larger towns, the restaurant industry was awash with so called students who were paid, not by the restaurateurs, but by the companies that brought them to Britain. Again, their documents were taken away, for 'security reasons', but in reality to ensure that the workers were unable to run away.

There were many different organisations dealing in this miserable human trafficking and all seemed to act independently from each other. In fact, there was a degree of collusion despite the intense competition between various organisations, most of which were unregistered. The heads of these illicit businesses were well known to each other, although they rarely met and communicated only when necessary and through third parties. Most had legitimate businesses which were used as a shield and, indeed, for money laundering purposes.

Mr Chao, whose family enterprise was created shortly after the Second World War, was well aware of all these matters and more. His family originated from Hong Kong and was involved in prostitution and drug dealing back in the '50s and '60s. Today his major interests were in property development and ownership. His dealings with the police stretched back to the days when he was moving the family business away from drugs. He was quite happy to create a good impression and build a close liaison with certain police officers, in return for a degree of protection. Mr Chao also retained an old-fashioned attitude to business. He had a total aversion to human trafficking, despite fully understanding the economics. He was aware of the importation of people through the container ports in London and his network of informants kept him fully updated of the movement of human cargoes.

His conversation with Chief Superintendent Bleasdale was generated by a rumour that there were a number of containers lying on the dockside in Tilbury that contained people, rather than the goods as specified on the bills of lading. The containers had been adapted to carry human beings and their final destination was already determined. Chief Inspector Bleasdale believed that Mr Chao was involved with this illicit trade. He was also aware of the appalling weather forecast. He had been to Mr Chao's office in a futile attempt to avert a potentially appalling disaster. As it transpired, the tidal surge hit Tilbury some twenty minutes after his departure from Soho. No one, except the importers of course, knew that certain containers destined for Lincolnshire were actually carrying people rather than machine parts. Even Mr Chao didn't know.

Milton and Pamela were having a lazy morning. They slept late, rose slowly and leisurely breakfasted together. Pamela came downstairs wearing Milton's dressing gown. It was quite short, falling just to her knees and of a wraparound design. Its tie around belt had long since disappeared and she held it together across her body in a display of feminine modesty. When she entered the kitchen, Milton was busy with the kettle. The kitchen was clean and tidy as, before going to bed, all the pots and pans from their evening meal were cleared away.

"Well, hello!" Milton turner round as he heard the door open. " I'm just making tea."

"Smashing. Thanks." Pamela looked at him thinking *What a lovely man. He really is so considerate.*

"Come on in and sit you down." Milton pulled out a chair for her.

"Why thank you, kind sir," she replied, continuing the game of antiquated courtesy.

"Would madam prefer cereal or toast?"

"Normally I just have a rushed cup of coffee and a slice of toast."

"Oh!" Milton stopped in his tracks. "Would you prefer coffee rather than tea?"

"Tea is perfect," she replied. She looked at him, wearing only his pyjama trousers, his torso black and muscular and, now, all hers. She sat down and watched him making the toast and setting the table for her. She tried to hold the gown together, but as she sat down, it opened at the knees. She needed both hands to pull her chair closer to the table and that allowed the garment to gape even more. Glancing at the window, she noticed that Milton was watching her in the reflection. He turned to look at her, with a big grin on his face.

"I rather feel, after last night, that the need for all this modesty has become a bit irrelevant."

"I suppose you're right!" Pamela replied, returning his smile. As he brought the butter and marmalade to her, he bent down and gently kissed her cheek. She reached up with her hand to pull his head closer to her. As her arm lifted, her shoulder pulled back and the gown slipped off even further, exposing her breast.

"Now, that's what I like for breakfast." Having put down the butter dish, he gently cupped her breast in his hand. With her other hand, she reached behind the chair, to find his expanding penis. She cupped his balls, as she felt his other hand opening the rest of the gown and then moving down to her stomach and beyond.

Milton broke the kiss and murmured into her ear, "You'd better eat your toast before it gets cold!" Reluctantly, she let him go and he proudly returned to the other side of the table.

"I should have asked," Milton continued. "Did you sleep well?"

"Oh, yes, thanks. I've had the best night's sleep in ages. Which is surprising, seeing as how you were so insistent on other activities!"

"Pamela, you are a lovely woman!" Milton looked at her, with a semi-serious expression on his face. "You are good company. You are good looking. Why the hell aren't you married and raising a family?"

"I tried it once. And with a lovely fella. But it just didn't work out. He had his friends, his career and his training schedules. I wanted togetherness, children and a home to look after. After a few years, we realised that we were poles apart mentally and called it a day. Since then, I suppose I've become more cautious and much more particular! I've been out with more than a few guys, even stayed the night with one or two, but no one has really sent shivers up my spine." She looked somewhat crestfallen, then continued, looking up at him. "At least, until I saw you."

"And how long ago was that?" Milton asked, disingenuously.

"Must be about six months now, when I first came to work at Waterloo." She daintily ate some of her toast. "You walked across the forecourt with an air of authority. Actually, it was almost … ownership. Some person, a lady, stopped you and asked a question. You carefully listened to her before giving her your reply. She thanked you and disappeared. You then smiled to yourself and walked away. It was just an ordinary thing, but you made that lady feel as though she was the only person important to you and I knew then that I wanted to know you better."

"I don't remember that," he replied, shaking his head. "It's something that happens all the time. Just one incident would hardly stick in the mind. But I do remember when I first saw you in the café. It was probably late in September. You were sitting at a table on your own and I remember wondering why someone like you should have no friends. I thought that you looked like a flower, but with no bees buzzing round. And I thought it rather sad, even a little strange."

They continued chatting, comfortable with each other, when Milton suddenly said that it was nearly eleven o'clock. He stood up and switched on the radio.

After the news, the Environment Agency's announcement was broadcast.

"That doesn't sound good," he remarked. "I think I'd better get up to Waterloo and see what's what."

"I know it's my day off, but I think I should come with you," she replied.

They both stood up and while Pamela went upstairs to get dressed, Milton washed up the breakfast dishes.

They were both ready by half past eleven and left Milton's house together, to walk the short distance to Waterloo station. This normally took around twenty-five minutes. When they arrived, just before midday, the station was full, but everything seemed to be functioning as expected. Milton glanced over to the entrance to the Northern Line. It was busy and more people than normal were emerging.

"We need to get higher. Come with me this way. Quickly."

He turned to Pamela, took hold of her hand and pulled her to a stairway which led up to the pedestrian bridge over Waterloo Road.

Waterloo Station is built at least two stories above ground level but can be accessed from both Station Approach and Waterloo Road. Station Approach was built around the station itself, to allow a separate access for vehicles, mainly taxis. It runs from the south end of the station, gently rising and passing the roundabout with Spur Road, the vehicular access from Waterloo Road itself. Station Approach then turns around the building to the west to run parallel with, but one storey higher than Mepham Street. At the far end, it slowly descends to ground level where it joins the big roundabout at York Road. Here the traffic accesses the big circulatory system which connects Waterloo Road, Waterloo Bridge, York Road and Stamford Street.

Just to the south of the roundabout, the site of the BMI/Imax cinema, is the pedestrian bridge, which gives access from the station to the Pleasuredrome and the Waterloo East Theatre.

Milton pulled Pamela up to the access for this bridge, fighting a pathway through a growing number of people, who were trying to get down to the trains. It took a surprising amount of time to force their way halfway across the pedestrian bridge where they stood to one side, allowing the thickening crowd to surge past. Milton checked his watch. It was already half past one.

"Why've we come here?" Pamela looked at Milton with concern written all over her face.

"That guy on the TV, when we were having breakfast, from the Environment Agency, said there was likely to be local flooding from the rain and the wind we've been having."

"Yes, I heard that, but…" Pamela's voice tailed off.

"At the end of the statement he said, *'Please keep calm at all times'*. I've no idea why he said that, but all these people trying to get into the station are obviously wanting to get out of London. For London to be seriously flooded, there has to be an inflow of water up the Thames of massive proportions. The Thames Barrier should hold off a surge from the sea, but if it doesn't, the consequences will be unimaginable."

Pamela clutched his arm tightly. "Will we be safe here?"

He shrugged. "I don't know. I'm not sure what's happening, but at least we can see from here."

Outside the wind was dropping and the rain had finally stopped. He took Pamela's arm and they retraced their steps back towards the station. Instead of going down the stairs with the rest of the people, Milton led Pamela through a door. Inside, there was a stairway which led upwards to the offices on the top floor. At the top, they could see the river Thames from Blackfriars Bridge all the way to London Bridge. Their view of Tower Bridge, however, was partially blocked by the Shard.

"Look at the river." Milton pointed to the north, towards the Victoria Embankment and the Strand.

"What do you mean?"

"It's hardly moving and it's really high."

"Could it be High Tide?"

"I'm not sure," he replied. "But if the tide is still coming in, it looks like it might come over the top."

"Well, over there the land rises quite steeply." Pamela pointed from Blackfriars all the way back to the top end of Waterloo Bridge.

"It's not like that on this side of the river," Milton replied. "Well, not here. It's all quite low lying right across to Southwark and Bermondsey."

They remained in that top corridor, looking out of the window to observe the growing crowds, the slow rise of the river and the improving weather. At ten past three, Milton and Pamela were looking down river towards Tower Bridge when they both saw the surge burst through the twin towers. The wave continued to the south of the bridge and, as it swept over Southwark, it seemed to be coming straight at them. At first, the railway line that runs from London Bridge to Charing Cross, seemed to hold the surge in check. It had been built on an embankment, but with any number of bridges giving access from south to north. The water quickly erupted through each and every opening, before being joined by the surge which had now crossed Tooley Street, Thomas Street and Long Lane. It swept round the tower blocks, with the destructive containers, rolling over and over at its crest, which were cutting a swathe through the smaller buildings, rather like a combine harvester in a wheat field.

They watched as it carved its way over Southwark, destroying almost everything in its path, leaving only tower blocks in its wake. Even some of these blocks of apartments succumbed to the constant battering and simply collapsed. Pamela and Milton could hear screaming, as people were overcome by the water and simply swept away. She grabbed Milton's arm as they remained frozen to the spot, stunned into inactivity.

The wave burst across Blackfriars Road, completely destroying the housing around the Ufford Street Recreation Ground and the Waterloo bus garage. The water surged around the tower blocks on the corner of Sandell Street, destroyed the Network Theatre and the Fire Station Restaurant, before hitting the pillars holding up Station Approach. Buses from the garage were swept into and along Waterloo Road, breaking the windows of the shops and cafes under Station Approach. Behind the buses came even more heavy containers, which had already been carried such a long distance up river from the freight terminals. They crashed into the pillars, some of which gave way, causing Station Approach itself to sag and this, because of the weight of the cast iron and glass, made the roof collapse in a shell burst of broken glass.

Above this destruction, Milton and Pamela could feel the vibrations of the collapsing Station Approach through their feet and they heard the bomb blast sound of glass breaking as the roof imploded. Behind the wave they could see a vista of dirty water, collapsing buildings, floating vehicles and, above all, bodies. There were drowned bodies everywhere, swirling around in the current, being carried hither and thither seemingly without purpose, just drifting, slowly and steadily towards the west, as the tide continued to flow into and across London.

In the Palace of Westminster there was a degree of confusion and panic. Already maintained in a state of readiness because of past terrorist attacks, the Members of Parliament and the Noble Lords were familiar with a restriction of movement, accompanied by interminable security checks. In reality, these only caused minor irritations. The greatest degree of intrusion came from the hide bound constrictions of parliamentary procedure, particularly as most members' offices were now located on the other side of Bridge Street in Portcullis House. The distance between Portcullis House and the Palace of Westminster is not far – indeed some have suggested it would have been better for the health of our elected members if it were farther! – But following the passing of the surge up the river, the ground floors of both buildings were flooded and all power had been cut.

Behind the surge, the tide continued to flow and the water continued to rise. The mayhem in the entrance to Westminster Underground station was worsened by a double decker London Transport bus being washed onto its side, onto the pavement and into the pillars by the Caffe Nero. As the ingress of water into the underground system flowed under the Thames, the pressure of the water caused pedestrians trying to get into the station to be sucked down the stairwell towards the platforms.

In Downing Street, after calling a meeting of COBRA, the Prime Minister attempted to contact the Conservative Chief Whip in the Commons. The telephone system had ceased to function and the mobile phone networks were increasingly unreliable. From the rear of the building, he could see through the trees towards Horse Guards Parade. It was already under water and the water level was still rising.

"Well, we're trapped here until the tide turns," he remarked. "Do we have any open communication with anyone?"

"There is still radio coverage, with the Army. I can probably raise the Chief of the General Staff, but this might take some time." The Chief Secretary to the Cabinet turned and left the room.

The Prime Minister returned to the Cabinet Room with the Home Secretary and the Minister for the Environment.

"We must assess the extent of the damage," he stated. "But without any form of communication, that is going to be difficult. When is the tide scheduled to turn?"

"I'm just looking at my notes, Prime Minister." The Environment Secretary carefully checked his file. "High Tide in the Pool of London is scheduled for 16.50 hours."

"That means the tide will continue to come in for a further ninety minutes." He sat down deep in thought. There was a gentle knock at the door and a senior civil servant in the Cabinet Office entered.

"Prime Minister, currently all communication by land line and the mobile phone networks has been interrupted by severe cuts to the electricity supply. Downing Street has switched to its old, diesel powered emergency generators. These will give us power internally for approximately six hours. We are now attempting to restore the old communications network that was installed during the Second World War. It hasn't been used or even tested for over sixty years, so we aren't particularly hopeful. The best option, at present, is radio and I expect to be advised within the next few minutes whether we have established a direct link with the Ministry of Defence."

"Thank you." The Prime Minister pulled a notepad towards him and started to write a list.

"We must first restore power. Get in touch with the Central Electricity Generating Board. While that is being done, we must assess the extent of flood damage. And we must look at the potential death toll. We need to have the Police and the Environment Agency involved as quickly as possible. Indeed, all the emergency services." He paused.

"We will need additional hospitals and medical assistance. I expect that some hospitals will be out of action because they will have been inundated themselves, so we must set up temporary hospitals as quickly as possible. We will need supplies of food, clean water, clean clothes and warm blankets.

"We must endeavour to reduce the sense of panic in the public. And that won't be easy. Mind you, if no one can travel, then they might be persuaded to return to their places of work. To tell them to return, we will need the police in boats with loud hailers."

"But I must have information. I need to know the current situation."

"Indeed, Prime Minister." The Environment Secretary looked at the Home Secretary. The Prime Minister continued. "Has any contact been made with Scotland Yard?"

"Not as yet."

"What about the river police?"

"I don't think so, Prime Minister."

Chapter 14
Thursday Evening – Before High Tide

The depression over Oxford was filling and slowly drifting eastwards towards the East Coast of England. By High Tide in London, it reached the coast and the wind speeds dropped dramatically to 30 miles per hour, designated 'Strong Breeze' on the Beaufort scale. The direction of the wind moved from West Sou'west to Sou' Sou'west. The rain stopped.

In the north, the depression to the west of Norway was also filling and drifting north west across the Scandinavian landmass towards the Gulf of Bothnia. At sea, the wind speeds reduced to 40 miles per hour, or 'Fresh Gale'. The northern reaches of the North Sea were still very rough, but the snow stopped falling in Scotland and Northern England. In addition, the wind direction shifted to Westerly and the temperature rose to 3 degrees centigrade.

Across the north of England, power supplies were intermittent, as the National Grid was overwhelmed, not only by the problems caused by power lines having been broken, but also by the effect of the power cuts in London. The whole grid was under pressure with the increased demands for supply and reduced levels of generation as, one by one, the nuclear power stations on the east coast, cut their output in order to ride out the storm.

In Scotland the power supply was even worse, as power lines were down in all regions. The Central Electricity Generating Board was slowly coming to terms with the immensity of the task to restore power in all regions. Senior staff were being called in to assess and tackle the breakages. All leave was cancelled. Communications were appalling following the failure of most landline telephones. The power needed to generate the mobile phone networks was also down.

As soon as the breakdown in communication occurred, the Army swiftly started work on restoring its old wartime radio communications and connections with the Ministry of Defence in Whitehall were soon up and running. The quality of the connection was not the best, but it was slowly improving. The necessary power was being provided by diesel generators.

The Local Authorities on both sides of the Pennines were working to cut through the enormous and unprecedented snow drifts that had completely closed the M62 motorway from Rochdale to Huddersfield. Other roads across the Pennines were also blocked; the A62 from Manchester to Leeds, the A65 from Kendal to Skipton and Leeds, the A66 from Carlisle to Newcastle were all subjected to massive snow drifts.

The M6 from Lancashire to Carlisle was also blocked, particularly where the motorway skirted the Lake District, as was the A1 from Yorkshire up through Durham and Northumbria. In effect, the Local Authorities in the North of England were forced into separate action with little or no cross border co-ordination.

In Scotland, the situation was catastrophic. Snow had fallen across the whole country, bringing down powerlines, blocking both rail and roads, isolating towns and villages. The Scots, however, are familiar with short term disruptions to their lives in the winter and, basically, buckled down to wait out the storm. The east side of the country was affected more than the west.

In Whitehall, somewhat to the Prime Minister's surprise, the old radio connection with the Ministry of Defence was re-connected and, finally, he was receiving reports of the extent of the devastation. Helicopters were airborne, on the initiative of the armed services, filming the inundated landscape, until there was insufficient daylight. The skies cleared and the moon was full. The wind continued to drop and, as the air became still, the temperature also dropped.

The tide began to ebb at about five in the afternoon. The water was now deeply contaminated with oil, sewage, all forms of detritus including dead animals, spilled cargoes and, above all, dead people. In the main river, there were buses, cars and containers floating often just below the surface, together with boats of all shapes and sizes that had been ripped from their moorings.

All along the edges of the flood, from Margate and Hadleigh in the east right through to Teddington in the west, people had congregated firstly from a morbid sense of curiosity, but after witnessing the enormity of the devastation, they started to set up teams to recover bodies and save people who were trapped. These early efforts lacked any co-ordination, were disjointed and often unsuccessful, but these paltry beginnings amply demonstrated the fortitude of the human spirit.

Fred Shemming surveyed the devastation from his observation post at the top of the training tower at the fire station. The station itself was surrounded by water, but he knew that part of the station's kit included three inflatable dinghies with outboard motors. It would be a bit of a task to get at them as they were probably under water, at ground level. All his firefighters, together with the school children and their teachers, were safe in the canteen on the first floor.

Looking at the tower blocks, standing stark and silent mostly without lights and, seemingly with no life within, he realised that the best advice that could be given would be for people to stay put. He knew that some of the buildings had self-generating facilities but wondered whether there would be the necessary personnel to man them. He looked to the north where he could see the extent of the flood.

He checked his watch. It was now half past three and the light was fading fast. The wave, that enormous wall of water had passed by the Isle of Dogs just over thirty minutes before. One of his crew had looked up the tides in his newspaper. High Tide was still an hour and a half away. He didn't know whether the water would continue to rise. He expected it would, but not in such a devastating manner.

He went down the tower and accessed the canteen across the bridge. Inside, everyone was sitting quietly. The children were being looked after by their teachers, while Dinah was helping to prepare sandwiches. There was no power and it had been decided that it would be better to consume Rajinder's provisions rather than risk them becoming contaminated.

Fred surveyed the scene and caught the eye of his deputy, Terry. He beckoned him over.

"It's a real bloody mess out there. The tide is still coming in and will for another hour or so. The wind's dropping and it's stopped raining, but the flood is covering everything except the skyscrapers. There's no power and I am presuming that there will be no re-connection for some time. Some of the tower blocks will have their own generators and they should kick in quite soon. It's beginning to get dark, so we'll be able to see which blocks have power and which don't. The sky is clearing and there will be a moon, but I've no idea how long we might be able to rely on that. There's no telephone nor mobile connections. So, we're basically on our own.

"As you know, we've got inflatables, but they're in the garage down below. The water will have flooded the garage, but the inflatables are stored quite high up and should be OK. We've got to get them. The water will be contaminated, but I'm going to have a go. I just hope that the main door isn't bolted."

"How are you going to get in, Gov?" Terry, his deputy, quizzed him.

"Over the roof and through the skylight."

"What? The same way those tow rags did a couple of years ago, you mean."

"Yeah!"

"But we put in additional security after that break in."

"I know. I'll just have to force my way through it." Fred thought a bit further. "Anyway, there won't be any alarm, because there's no power."

"You'll then have to open the doors. You'll have to do that without power, using the manual system."

"I know. And it'll be under water. So I will need a volunteer. We do need those boats."

"You can count on me, Gov."

"Thought so. Let's get to it."

The fire station was constructed in the form of three large boxes. On the left was the garage, which housed two pumps. It was two stories high. Next to it stood the administrative areas on the ground floor, above which were the canteen, the toilets and a couple of training rooms. There were also three small bedrooms. Finally, there was the training tower. The tower stood slightly apart from the other buildings and access was normally from the ground floor. There was a secondary access, however, over a short bridge from the canteen.

Fred decided that the easiest way to the garage was over the roof of the admin block. To get on the roof, he would need to go up one flight of the stairs in the tower, swing out of the window onto the roof of the short bridge. It would only be a short drop to the flat roof of the admin block. From there it would be a simple task of accessing the garage roof, as there would only be a low balustrade to cross. Lighting in the garage was supplemented by four large skylights. Following the recent break in, the glass had been replaced by toughened, burglar proof glass and the fittings had been improved. They were supposedly impregnable.

This won't be easy, he thought.

Fred and Terry found some rope, a couple of axes and a flashlight. They quickly explained the plan to the rest of the crew. Fred designated a crew member to be on watch at the top of the tower and to relay any relevant information as quickly as possible.

Fixing the rope inside the stairwell of the tower, Fred swung out and easily gained access to the roof of the short bridge. Terry followed. The rope was left attached to the tower. They hurried across the roof of the admin block to the balustrade.

"Listen, Gov," said Terry.

"What?"

"Can you hear a sort of low murmuring over there?" He pointed towards the west. "It sounds like an electrical hum."

"It's the sound of people running on the East India Dock Road. There must be quite a crowd at the George Tavern by now."

"How do you know?"

"I heard the same, when I was up top with Dinah. And everything between here and Limehouse is under water."

"Oh right." He looked up at his boss, "How are you going to break the glass?"

"I'm not!" Fred surprised Terry. "I'm going to chop out the skylight completely."

"That'll be hard work!"

"Come on then. We've no time to lose."

They ran to the nearest skylight and started to chop at the roof around it. The roof was made from interlacing metal struts, overlaid with timber. They were able to cut through the timber quite easily, until they had exposed the whole skylight, which was bolted to the metal frame. Fortunately, it had not been riveted and they were able to undo the bolts with their equipment. Soon the skylight was hanging by just two bolts. Fred removed one and the whole fitment slowly slipped into the roof space, bending the last bolt. They both pushed on it, to encourage gravity. At last there was enough space to pass through.

"Right!" said Fred. "If I remember correctly, pump No 2 should be underneath us. It's pretty dark in there. Have you got your flash lamp?"

"Yes, Gov. Hang on!" Terry turned on the torch and passed it over. Fred shone it into the garage. The cab of the pump was about seven feet below him. The water was much lower than he had expected, coming half way up the wheels on the second pump.

"This might be less tricky than we thought. I'm going to climb in, holding onto the roof. At full stretch, I should be standing on the roof of the cab."

"OK, Gov. Give us the torch and I'll light the way for you."

"Cheers!"

Fred sat down on the edge of the metal frame of the roof. He rolled onto his stomach and, with a firm grip on the frame, he lowered himself into the garage. At first, he kept his elbows and forearms on top of the metal frame, but as he descended, he realised that the drop was a little further than anticipated. Finally, he was hanging at full stretch from his gauntleted hands.

"Can you see how far I'm above the cab, Terry?"

Terry chuckled. "If you stretch your toes down, you should be able to touch it."

"This is no laughing matter, you know." Fred smiled back at his deputy but did as Terry suggested. To his relief, he made contact with the cab and let go. "That was interesting," he remarked looking back up at the sky. "Come on, Terry. I know you're a bit of a short arse but I can always catch you."

Terry quickly repeated the same method and in no time was hanging at full stretch from the hole in the roof. Fred grabbed him round the chest and Terry let go.

"Blimey, Gov, I never know you cared!" Terry looked round, flashing his light. "That's strange. Why's the water so low?"

"I thought the same. The doors must be holding back the water like lock gates in a canal. We won't be able to force them open on our own. The outside pressure will be too great.

"I estimate that the depth of the water outside is about six feet round the buildings. The other pump can drive through that."

"That's right! We won't get the doors open without the power of a pump."

"Right! Let's break out the inflatables. Must make sure we don't inflate them in here!" He pointed his torch to the key safe on the wall just inside the door. "The keys to both pumps are there. We'll put the inflatables over there, at the back of the garage. When we've got the outboards ready as well, we can start up the pump engines. I want you to use the ladder extension to push against the hinges of the left-hand door. We need to let more water in to lessen the outside pressure."

Terry was listening carefully. "Why not just try to drive through the doors?"

"The doors open outwards and the water pressure is forcing them shut. Even with the power of the pump, we won't be able to open them. I'm hoping that, by buggering the hinges, the pressure from outside will force the door and let more water in. As soon as there's a depth of about four feet, I reckon we'll be able to force the doors off their hinges with the other pump."

They manhandled the three inflatables from the storage area to the back of the garage and tethered them to the back of the second pump. They placed the outboards on top, well away from the water, together with additional cans of fuel. Collecting the keys for the pumps, they climbed into the cabs and started the engines. Terry aimed the extendable ladder at a point between the door and the wall of the garage. Revving the engine before engaging the gear, he drove straight at the wall. There as a crunching sound as he hit the designated spot with the top of the ladder, followed by a screech of metal. He reversed back to survey the damage and was rewarded with a small stream of water at the bottom of the door. He reversed back a little further and repeated his actions. *It's just like trying to break into a castle with a battering ram*, he thought. His second effort was more successful and the inflow of water became far more significant.

He shouted across to Fred, "I'll do it once more," lifting one finger. From the cab of the second pump, Fred responded with an upturned thumb and watched as Terry repeated the process for a third time. At last, the outside pressure forced the bottom of the door into the garage and the inflow of dirty, contaminated water doubled in strength. Terry pulled back once again and kept the engine ticking over.

When the rate of the inflow had eased, Fred positioned the second pump facing the central point of the doors. Slowly he drove forward, with specific purpose, into the doors. There was a sharp cracking sound as the bolts holding the doors secure were pulled from their mountings and slowly the doors began to open. Fred drove through the shattered doorway into the dark, flooded central forecourt of the fire station, towing the three inflatables behind. He braked, put the engine into neutral and climbed out of the cab. He slowly climbed down and, with the water up to his chest, he waded to the rear of the pump to the inflatables.

After making sure that the outboards and the cans of fuel were well out of the way, he untied the first and pulled the toggle. With a whoosh, the craft inflated. He attached one of the outboard motors and placed two cans of fuel into the craft.

After inflating the other two and attaching the outboards, he manoeuvred the first to the side of the pump where he was able, using the rear wheel as a step, to get into the boat. He was about to start the outboard when he heard the throbbing of the engine of the second pump splutter and die. He called across to Terry.

"Are you OK?"

"Yes, Gov. The engine's flooded, so this pump is now useless."

"Right. I'm coming in to get you."

Fred started the outboard and carefully re-entered the garage. Terry was waiting for him and without any fuss stepped out of the cab and into the inflatable.

"That's taken us the best part of an hour," Fred said to his deputy. "It's now dark and there are no street lights as far as I can tell. There are plenty of cars further to the north, so I think we had better start ferrying the kids out of the station up to the Salvation Army Citadel." He steered the boat round the garage to the back where he could see his team with flashlights waiting for him.

"Pete!" he shouted up at the faces looking down.

"Yes, Gov."

"Is the rope still secure?"

"Yes, Gov."

"Toss it to me."

Pete gathered up the loose end of the rope from the roof of the short bridge and threw it to Fred.

"Stay here, Terry." Fred caught hold of the rope. "I'm going back inside to explain what we're planning."

"Hang on, Gov," Terry replied. "You don't need to show off your climbing skills."

"What?"

"Well, if you take the boat round the back of the tower, there will be a window at about this level, won't there?"

"Bloody hell!" Fred muttered. "I'm losing it. Of course there is."

The tower was built as an enclosed staircase, around a central well. On each level there was a platform with a window, with the stairs climbing ever upwards, until they reached the observation platform four stories high.

"That took longer than I thought." He gathered his colleagues. "The hard stuff is about to start. First, we'll take all the children, teachers and parents to the Sally Army Citadel. That's not too far.

"Second, using the station as a base and staging post, we will start to search for survivors down West Ferry Road. We will concentrate on the housing estates because the tower blocks appear to have survived intact. I'll need two inflatables working the estates and the third ferrying survivors from here to the Citadel.

"Third, I'll control Boat 1, Terry will control Boat 2 and, Pete, and I want you to take control of Boat 3.

"Fourth, I need someone to stay here at the top of the tower and to relay any information and observations. Vic, you can carry on doing that, please, as you've already started. Have you anything to report to date?" Fred looked at the young recruit. Vic, short for Victoria, was the first woman who had worked at Poplar Fire Station and was very proud of her position. Although not tall, she was exceptionally wiry and had a dogged approach to everything she attempted. It was almost as though she had a point to prove, but she was no feminist. She only wanted to fit in and be part of the team.

"Yes, Gov. As soon as I got to the top, before it went dark, I could see both up river as far as Tower Bridge and down river as far as Queen Elizabeth Bridge. On the south bank, everything appears to be flooded between the Valley and Greenwich, as far inland as Woolwich Road. From Deptford to beyond Tower Bridge, everything is under water as far as Camberwell.

"When it went dark, it became pretty obvious that all the power in London has blacked out. The only lights you can see, apart from tower blocks that have independent generators, are from vehicles on roads and bridges high enough to have escaped the water and from a number of fires that have started, particularly near the oil storage depots.

"I've seen seven helicopters go across from west to east. It was too dark to make out their registrations, but I've only clocked one coming back.

"I used the binoculars to try to identify some of the things that were floating upstream. There were containers, buses, vans and cars. I could see people trapped inside some of the cars. There's a lot of other stuff swirling about, a lot of wooden beams and planking and, it took some time to identify that they are actually..." she paused and gulped. "A lot of bodies. Hundreds of bodies, just being swept upstream, obviously drowned." She stopped, realising the enormity of her report.

"Thanks, Vic." Fred went over to her and put his arms round her.

After a few seconds, she pushed him away. "I'm OK, Gov. It's just..." Again, her voice tailed off.

"So many of them?" Fred finished for her. She nodded. "Are you OK to carry on?"

"Yes, Gov. Gov? There is something else."

"Go on."

"Well, I wondered if it would be sensible to drop off a firefighter at a tower block so that advice can be given to the residents and survivors and, maybe, start the emergency generators. As each block is visited, the firefighter can be collected and taken to the next block."

"You're right! Thanks for that." Fred turned to his teams. "We'll drop off two, one per tower block. When you are satisfied that the residents can perform the necessary, you will flash us as we return and we'll divert to take you to the next block."

"OK. Let's get to it."

The designated teams immediately picked up the necessary equipment and dispersed to the inflatables.

Martin and his two sons stood watching the river for at least an hour after the wave passed in front of them. Strangely, even though the tide continued to come in, the water did not appear to creep further up the hill towards them.

Martin checked his watch. It was three o'clock. He didn't know when High Tide was scheduled, but he realised that the amount of water stretching from Hadleigh to the Isle of Grain would, in due course, ebb out to sea. He also appreciated that the freak wave would have caused massive damage not only to the trading estates that line the river all the way to London, but more so to the flood defences on both sides of the river Thames.

The southern boundary of his own land, alongside Hadleigh Ray, was a dyke which had been upgraded, years before, to a sea wall by the Environment Agency. He knew that it could well have been undermined by such an inflow of water. He needed to assess the damage, but that would have to wait until the tide ebbed and the water drained off his land. Already they could see that the railway line was totally unusable, with rails buckled, embankment walls damaged and the bridges undermined and probably unstable.

He would need timber and iron sheeting to close up any gaps in the wall and all such gaps would have to be closed quickly so that the next incoming tide didn't wash through to create even more damage. That would now be the major difficulty; closing the gaps and keeping the next tide out. It would be an immense task and would require careful and swift planning.

At last he turned to face his boys. "Got to get cracking," he announced. Charlie and James looked at him. "The tide will start to ebb and as soon as the water is off the land, we must assess the damage to the sea wall."

"Can't really do anything until the tide's gone out," said James, ever pragmatic.

"I realise that, but we can start to get together the stuff we'll need."

"Do you still have your digger?"

"Yes, but it's a bit old now. We'll have to see if we can get it to start."

They all climbed into the Land Rover and Martin drove them all back to the farm. James disappeared into the barn with the keys for the digger, while Charlie hooked up the tractor to a trailer. He was backing the trailer towards a neat pile of corrugated iron, when he heard a massive roar as the digger's engine suddenly fired, with an explosion of blue diesel smoke from its exhaust.

"You'll find an old generator in the other barn, as well as some outdoor cable and lights," Martin said. "Check that all the lights are OK."

"Right oh!" Charlie disappeared.

"James. Please carry on loading up the corrugated iron. I've got to see a neighbour to beg further equipment. My mobile's not working, so I'll have to go round. I'll pop my head into the kitchen to see if your mum and the girls can help you."

"OK. Dad, it's just coming up to five o'clock, now. I don't think there's going to be much we can do before dawn."

"No! You're wrong. We've got to assess as best we can, even if it's dark. Otherwise another tide will be coming in and that may well create even more damage." And with that he left James.

Soon James was joined by his mother, Jennifer and his wife Megan. As soon as they saw what he was doing, they both disappeared inside to change into more appropriate clothing.

Martin, meanwhile, had driven out of the yard to his nearest neighbour. Tom Spedding and his forebears had farmed in Hadleigh for over three hundred years. Locally, he was regarded almost as nobility and there was nothing that he didn't know. Unlike many people in similar circumstances, he was not standoffish, nor condescending. Very approachable, he was popular and his opinion was sought on all aspects of farming, from when to plant and when to put the bull to the cows. He was already in his yard when Martin drew up.

"How the hell did you know I was coming?" Martin greeted the older man.

"Actually, I 'bin expecting 'ee for two hours or more," Tom replied. "And afore you ask, I ain't never seen nothin' like this afore. Nor even heard tales of the like."

"Did you see the wave coming in from the sea?"

"Matter of fact, I did. I'd just bin upstairs for a call of nature, like. And I was looking out of the winder o'er the fields down to the sea. Must have 'bin about two o'clock."

"That's right. My boys and I were on our way down in the Land Rover, to check the wall. We were stopped at the gate near the castle. Luck, I suppose."

"Luck dun come into it, youngster. The Lord looks after the good uns."

"Well, I don't know about that." Martin looked at the old man. "We saw the sea just wash over the sea wall and flood all the lower fields. And now the power is down, so I can't get any information nationally or locally."

"No, you won't. And what I know of the guv'ment, it'll likely be some time afore you do! And then it's likely to be wrong!" Tom ushered Martin into his kitchen. "I expect you're worried about your wall."

"Yes, I am."

While Tom was making a cup of tea with the big aluminium kettle on the Aga, Martin told him that he and James had walked along the wall that morning and how they had seen the dip. He also told Tom how he and his boys had watched the sea inundate Canvey Island as well as all his lower fields, beyond the railway line.

Tom shook his head. "It's not good. I remember Canvey in '53. The whole population had to be evacuated. That was before the concrete sea walls were built, of course. An old fren' of mine was farming on the river Crouch, not far from Burnham. He had the longest sea wall breach from Norfolk all the way down to here. It took him two and a half days to close that breach, working round the clock."

"I've heard you talk of him before and that's why I'm here," said Martin, quietly. "I've already got some corrugated iron and some wooden stakes. Quite by chance all our children are at home. As soon as the tide's gone out far enough, we'll be down at the wall to survey the damage."

"What? In the dark?"

"Got to. Can't wait until tomorrow. There'll be another high tide in the early morning and I want to try to close any gaps before that comes in."

143

Tom nodded his head. "Reckon you be right, youngster! Is there any equipment you need?"

"The more I've got, the quicker we can get done," Martin replied.

"I dun do much m'self these days," Tom muttered. "But I'll roust out my lads and send 'em down to 'ee."

Martin finished his tea, thanked his neighbour and went back to his car. As he drove back to Thatched Barn Farm, he noticed that the wind had dropped and the clouds had parted. The moon was already up and shining brightly. *Perhaps it won't be too difficult to check the state of play*, he thought.

When he arrived home, he went straight into the barn where James had already loaded all the corrugated iron and metal sheets onto the trailer. He could hear the generator humming in the other barn. He went inside the house to check in the newspaper when low tide was expected and was pleased to note that it would be just before midnight.

"Listen boys," he called his sons to him. "I've spoken with Tom next door. He's going to send some of his lads across with some extra equipment. Low tide is expected just before midnight, so I expect we'll have a good seven or eight hours, starting when the water has drained off the land. I expect that will be around seven o'clock this evening. We'll have some difficulty getting under the railway line, because I'm assuming the bridges will be too dangerous and we might have to go right round near to Benfleet. With the state of the tracks, there'll be no trains, so we might be OK." He looked round.

"Basically, in the first hour, I want to assess if there are any breaches and how big they are. I've dug out an old Ordnance Survey map and, if necessary, we can log the damage on it, so we all know what we're supposed to be doing and where. If there are two breaches, we must try to repair both at the same time.

"Surely it would be better to get one done properly, before doing the next." Charlie interrupted his father.

"No, Charlie. If we leave one breach open, when the tide comes in, it will wash in and come round the back of the repair where it is likely to wash away all the work that we'll have done. We can't afford that to happen, because that'll simply undo all that work and take us back to square one. Actually, worse than square one, because the next tide is likely to widen the breach, so we'll be even further back."

He paused for a moment and then went on. "While we're waiting for the tide to go out, we're going to get a bite to eat because I expect we'll be hard at it right through the night. The next High Tide is due about quarter past five in the morning. If we can keep the water out, we will be able to keep on building up the wall. I will not rest until this is complete and solid."

Martin turned and looked at the trailer that James had filled. "Before we go in, I must check what you've got together."

There was an enormous pile of corrugated iron sheeting, stacked neatly in two piles. In a separate pile on the barn floor, the girls had brought together all the wooden stakes. There must have been between sixty and seventy. Martin nodded his approval and went into the other shed, where Charlie had finally got the reluctant diesel generator to start. It was now running smoothly.

"Have we got enough fuel?" Martin asked.

"The big tank is about half full, but I haven't had time to find any cans to carry supplies with us."

"You'll find a number of old army surplus jerry cans in that far corner. There must be at least six. Fill them all. What about the lights?"

"There were a few bulbs that had blown. I found new ones in the cupboard and have replaced all the duds. So the lights are OK."

"Good." Martin nodded once again. "And are you confident that the generator will start when we get down to the wall?"

"Yes, Dad," Charlie replied. "It was tough to get it going the first time, but I reckon it'll start OK now that it's been running for half an hour or so."

"Did you find the spot lights?"

"Yes. Helen has loaded them in the back of the Land Rover. There were six altogether and I've tested them all. There are also some brackets so I can attach them to the Land Rover's roof rack."

"Well done, Charlie." Martin took his older son to one side. "Just one other thing, Son. It's going to be really tough down there and I know that you will be looking for the easier way to do things. Please don't do that. If anything goes wrong, I will be taking the responsibility, so all I ask is that you do exactly what I tell you."

"Don't worry, Dad. Everything will be fine."

In Downing Street, the Prime Minister was feeling deeply frustrated. At last, after an interminable wait, some information was beginning to come through. The light faded fast and the country's capital was coming to terms with the immensity of a devastating blow. Even so, he still didn't know the full extent of the damage, the death toll, nor how soon power might be restored. Without such basic knowledge, he considered that he was unable to make any meaningful decisions. He also realised that now was the time to act, but how? Now was the time to lead, but how? He realised, despite the lack of meaningful information, that there were decisions to be made, even if they might ultimately be wrong. He couldn't sit in a state of suspended animation any longer. He left his office to find the Chief Secretary to the Cabinet. He was outside in the main office.

"We need to act."

"Yes, Prime Minister."

"Do we have any specific information as yet?"

"I understand that a film of the devastation has been made from a helicopter, before darkness fell. With all electrical power interrupted and the local streets flooded, we are restricted to delivering messages by hand, using a police launch." The civil servant looked harassed as he briefed the Prime Minister. "We also have a similar system of hand communication with the House."

"Where's the film?"

"It should be arriving any time now."

As he was speaking, a policeman ran up the stairs with a brown padded envelope. He stopped, saluted and handed the envelope to the Prime Minister.

"Is this the film?"

"Yes, sir."

"Right. Please come into the cabinet room. Let's have a look at it." He handed the CD to the civil servant, who inserted it into the DVD player, as the Home Secretary and the Environment Secretary, closely followed by the Chancellor of the Exchequer, entered the room.

The film had been taken from a helicopter flying down river from Heathrow. The helicopter had flown eastwards towards Richmond and the pilot had started filming as soon as he reached the river Thames. The time in the top left-hand corner of the screen was 15.10, as the river came into view. The quality was not good, because the light was already fading fast, but the rising moon gave the film a ghostly and rather terrifying aspect.

As the aircraft continued to fly down the centre of the river, nothing appeared to be out of place until, suddenly, they could make out the enormous wave coming from the east. The time showed 15.25 and the helicopter was over Chiswick Bridge. The pilot banked to allow the camera to focus further downstream towards Hammersmith, before hovering over the river as the wave passed below. Behind the surge, the river Thames seemed to take on a completely new aspect. Moonlight was being reflected off a vast wedge of flooded water. Because of the lack of light, it was really difficult to judge specifically the full gravity of the devastation. Having hovered, as the wave passed beneath the helicopter, the pilot finally began to fly further to the east, passing Hammersmith and on towards Chelsea.

Looking at the film, the Prime Minister could see that the flood water had inundated Chiswick and Fulham. Battersea, Vauxhall, Southwark and Bermondsey were all under water, as was much of Pimlico and Westminster. As the aircraft flew further down the Thames, the horrified viewers were able to catalogue mentally the famous suburbs that had apparently been swept away – Whitechapel, Limehouse and Poplar, the O2 Arena, Newham and Beckton, including the London City Airport and the Thames Barrier. Thamesmead, Rainham Marches and Purfleet were all flooded, as were Grays and Tilbury, Canvey Island and the Isle of Grain. Towards the end of the film, the helicopter hovered over the estuary between Southend-on-Sea and Sheerness, with the time on the screen showing as 16.50.

In the moonlight, the imagery remained indistinct, but the overall picture had become blindingly clear. London was facing a major catastrophe and this was compounded by the panic demonstrated by so many people trying to escape the capital before the wave arrived.

"My God," muttered the Home Secretary. "It looks as though the map of London has been redrawn."

"I need to get across to the House." The Prime Minister was beginning to appreciate the enormity of the devastation, shown by the film. "When the tide turns, there will be further damage as the water flows off the land. In any case, the Members need to be informed." He looked round. "How can I get there?" He noticed the policeman, still standing in the corner. "Did you come here by police launch?"

"Yes, sir."

"You can take me across to the House."

"I'm not sure about access."

"Well, no one will have been able to leave. If the place is inaccessible, we'll call it a fact-finding mission." And with that, he disappeared to collect his coat.

After the wave passed them, Pamela and Milton carefully looked out over the extent of the water around Waterloo station. As far as they could tell, the station was marooned. In the water, they could see the bodies of people and various animals. They were floating about aimlessly, turning this way and that, caught in small eddies. Daylight was already fading and the station was completely blacked out, making it impossible to see anything with any clarity. From their vantage point, they were able to make out the expanse of the floodwater stretching from the Victoria Embankment in the north, as far as Camberwell in the south and, except for the skyscrapers; in the diminishing daylight they were unable to see any other buildings of note. It was increasingly difficult to make out any specific landmarks because the whole of London appeared to be suffering the same power cut. Moonlight was reflecting off the water and beyond the flood, the lights of grid locked traffic formed a beacon of hope on both horizons.

Looking through a window at the back of the room, Milton realised that the London Eye had fallen and he could see, even in the gloom, that the Archbishop's apartments at Lambeth Palace were surrounded by water, as the park was completely flooded. The only sign of life was the traffic snarled on the bridges. On the north side of the river, Pamela could make out the Houses of Parliament, but it was quite obvious that all the streets around the Palace of Westminster were under water. As she watched, she saw the spotlights of a river police launch, carefully being steered over the river wall, past New Scotland Yard and towards Downing Street.

"We can't stay here." Milton gently took her by the arm and pulled her to him. "We'll be needed below."

"Milton. What can we do?" Pamela's voice was husky with emotion. "How on earth can we help?"

"There will be people who need to be looked after. This is a disaster that no one has predicted and it's up to us to try to cope."

Pamela nodded. "I suppose you're right."

They carefully made their way down the darkened stairs and into the corridor where the pedestrian bridge comes into the station. There were some people, just standing there, stunned into inaction with the awful sights in front of them. Milton made for the stairs.

"You can't get down there, mate." A burly man in shirtsleeves stopped him. "It's all flooded further down."

"What about the platforms?" Milton asked.

"Dunno, mate."

"They should be OK because they are higher up than ground level. It's only one flight down from here." Milton looked back at Pamela. "Come on, Pam. We'll go down and see what we can do."

"Right, then! I'll come as well," said the man.

One step at a time, they went down the next flight of stairs and pushed open the door into the station itself. There were crowds of people, but very little noise. It was almost as though the people had all been struck dumb by the enormity of the disaster. The floor of the station was dry but, reflected in the moonlight Milton could see water on the tracks. There were some trains just standing there, as though waiting to depart, but nothing was moving in the darkness of the station.

"Why's it so quiet?" asked Pamela.

"I don't know. It's really eerie," Milton replied.

He walked purposefully towards the barriers, where he expected to find other staff. There was no one. All the electric barriers were closed and this was preventing people from milling onto the platforms. There were plenty of people about, but they appeared cowed and literally overcome by what they had just witnessed. In the gloomy stillness, Milton thought he could hear a child crying.

"Can you hear that baby?"

"Yes. I think it's coming from platform 4."

"Come on. Let's have a look."

They jumped over the barrier and ran along the platform edge. As they drew closer to it, the noise of the crying baby increased, but they still couldn't see anything. Milton dug out his mobile and swiped up to get the torch icon. In the dark, the light seemed very bright. He flashed it down the platform, but still they saw nothing. He then pointed it over the lines, which were under water and was rewarded by a glimpse of white.

"What's that?" He pointed.

"It's the baby. I wonder where its mother is." Pamela used her iPhone torch to look more carefully down the track. She saw a dark shape about twenty yards away. "There!"

"I'll have to get down into the water." Milton put his phone onto the platform edge and sat down next to it. He slowly let his legs drop downwards and he then rolled his body so that his stomach was on the platform edge and his weight was taken by his arms.

He lowered himself further down and, at first, he could feel the water leaking into his trainers and then creeping up his legs. He dropped the last foot or so, with a bit of a splash. Reaching up, he was able to get his phone and he splashed across the tracks to the baby.

The little girl's face was puckered up with fright and her woollen clothes were completely soaked. Her eyes were tight shut, as though she was trying to keep out all the horrible sights around her. She was floating, but her shawl had snagged on something under the water. Milton picked her up and was rewarded with her eyes opening, immediately followed by her mouth from which came a high-pitched wailing. Milton cuddled her to his shoulder and waded back to the platform edge.

"Here, Pamela. Can you take this little one, please?"

Pamela was already kneeling at the edge and reached down to take the child, whose wailing was already diminishing into heartbroken sobs.

"I'll check out that other shape, over there."

He waded down the track, where he found a young woman in a dark overcoat, face down in the water. He felt for a pulse, but there was nothing. She was dead, but he knew he couldn't leave her there. He realised that it would be really hard to get her up to the platform. She was lying on her front, with her legs twisted beneath her. Milton lifted her into a sitting position and then knelt beside her. Leaning forward, he put her arms over his back behind his head and then knelt upright. The weight of her body was now spread across his shoulders, but her legs were still under the water. With a big effort, he lifted up one of his legs, so that its foot was firmly on the ground. He now leaned forward, taking the weight of her body onto that leg and braced his other leg against the rail track. He was now able to straighten the first leg and lift the body completely.

"You'll have to help me roll her onto the platform," he called to Pamela.

"I'm here." She had put the baby down and was already kneeling at the edge. As Milton came close enough, Pamela was able to grab hold of the belt of the woman's coat and pull her closer. With her other hand, she grabbed the coat's collar and, with Milton pushing from below, they were able to roll her onto the platform edge.

And that was the moment a miracle occurred, for as she was rolled onto the edge of the platform, the woman coughed, releasing a torrent of filthy water from her mouth. She inhaled raspingly, coughed again and opened her eyes.

"Where am I?"

"Waterloo Station."

"What? I can't be." She coughed again, hacking up water from the deepest recesses of her lungs. Pamela tried to roll her over, but the woman resisted. "I can't move my legs." She started to cry. "Where's my baby?" She desperately looked around.

"It's OK. We've got her here. She's safe and sound."

Milton called from the rail track. "Pam, I can't get up without a hand."

"Hang on! I'm here." Pamela put her hand onto the woman's shoulder. "I won't be a sec." She went to the platform edge. Milton's face was just visible in the light of her phone.

"Can you lie face down with your body at right angles to the edge? I'll then pull myself up using your jacket as a rope."

"Right. And hurry!" Pamela did as she was asked and Milton grabbed hold of the coat in the middle of her back. As he pulled himself up, he grabbed her waist band of her trousers. She put her arms round him, to stop him sliding back. He then grabbed her leg and, all of a sudden, he was up and lying, panting on the platform.

"The woman." Pamela gasped. "She's alive."

"What?"

148

"And she needs our help."

They crawled over to the woman, who hadn't moved. "Where's my baby?" She asked.

"She's just here." Pamela picked up the baby girl and brought her to her mother. "Why are you so surprised to be here in Waterloo station?"

"Tracy and me, we was just walking home, when I heard this noise. I got her out of her pushchair and the next thing I knew, we was caught up by this enormous wave of water. I've never been so frightened in all my life. I shut my eyes tight and held onto Tracy with all my strength. We was rolled over and over and then everything went black. I mean, like what's happening?"

Pamela sat next to the woman and put her arm round her, cradling her. "Shh! Your baby's safe and you're safe. That's what matters. Where do you live?"

"In one of the flats at Nelson Square. We'd only been to the Tesco Express on The Cut, when I heard that noise." The woman looked round. "Why's it all dark?"

"There's been a power cut." Ever practical, Milton then explained, "We were right up high, in the offices looking over Station Approach. We saw this enormous wall of water coming up the river from Tower Bridge, flooding everything in its path. I don't know what's caused it, but you're safe now and I reckon the lights will come back on before long. I think we should try to get you into the main station, where there will be other people able to look after you and your baby."

All over London and in many parts of the country, the weather literally overwhelmed the National Grid. With power supplies damaged throughout the capital, the distribution sub stations were unable to cope and simply closed down. Across northern England and throughout Scotland, the blizzards brought down power lines, cutting off vast areas of both countries.

To make matters worse, the loss of power set up a chain reaction, which closed down the landline telephone system. Mobile phone communications were similarly affected, because they are also dependent on electricity. Water flooded into many street boxes and underground cabling systems. Despite their claims that their communication facilities were quicker and more reliable, even the new fibre optic systems were struggling to cope because, ultimately, they too rely on electricity to convert normal communication into light pulses. Because it is inert and impervious to wear, fibre optic cabling is perfectly capable of working under water, but the loss of power at the exchanges now demonstrated a massive problem with this form of communication.

In Birmingham and across central England, however, most of these calamities were having little or no effect. There was some flickering of the lights and some interruption to the vast numbers of computers and laptops upon which modern business is so reliant. Even the mobile phones were working to a degree although connectivity was considerably reduced. From Nottingham, through the Midlands and down to the southwest, people's lives generally continued with little disruption. There was a natural concern, however, when the BBC stopped broadcasting in the mid-afternoon. All communication with the capital was also lost, but this concern was short lived as people continued with their lives and simply switched to other, more local news feeds.

In Aldershot and other army barracks throughout the south and southwest, the loss of any form of communication with London rang serious alarm bells. Senior officers swiftly established links with each other and with other local emergency services. It was quickly realised that London was facing an immense catastrophe and that immediate aid would be required. Night was already falling by the time the first relief columns were rolling along the M3 and M4 motorways, with back up facilities including field hospitals, boats, bridging equipment, lighting and power plants, but much more importantly, trained personnel.

As communications were re-established with the Ministry of Defence, information began to flow in both directions. The Ministry used its own initiative to transfer its knowledge to Downing Street and the Prime Minister's office. By the time the Prime Minister was being carried by boat to the House of Commons, he was much better informed. On arrival, he immediately sought out the Leader of the Her Majesty's Loyal Opposition, in his own office.

"Ah, James!" he greeted him. "There you are."

"And where else would you expect me to be, Prime Minister?"

"Yes! Yes! This is why I have come straight to you, to brief you on the sketchy details that I have received to date."

"I thank you for that, Prime Minister." He leant back in his chair interlaced his fingers and placed his hands under his chin, to await the news. Still standing, the Prime Minister looked down at him and, demonstrating a very brief moment of irritation, he very slightly shook his head. He took a deep breath.

"It would appear that the storms have created unprecedented conditions in the North Sea, creating a sea surge which travelled primarily in an east south east direction. It made landfall in Holland just after one o'clock GMT. The southern end of that surge entered the Thames estuary at about half past one and began to make its way up the river causing devastation on both banks. The surge was so strong that it created a wave some 40 feet high on top of the already high tide.

"This wave has flowed over sea walls in the Thames estuary, inundated Canvey Island, flowed over the top of the Thames Barrier and flooded many parts of London. Full details are not yet available because the loss of power has compromised communication, both electronic and landline. The Underground has been overwhelmed and there are rumours that some stations have been flooded.

"I have seen some video evidence of the damage caused. The video was taken from a helicopter, flying from west to east, as daylight was fading. It would appear that many of the modern tower blocks have survived, but older buildings and riverside housing estates have been devastated.

"Because of the loss of power, it has been difficult to confirm much of this information. Contact has been made with the National Grid and work is already underway to reconnect the electricity supply as quickly as possible.

"The situation in the north and in Scotland is complicating matters further because there have been excessive falls of snow coupled with considerable drifting. Power lines are down throughout Scotland and I am advised that it will be some days before a reasonable service is resumed.

"It is my intention, therefore, to declare a state of emergency and I hope that I will have both your support and your cooperation. James, this is not a time for petty politics. I have no doubt they will return in the not too distant future but, for now, I simply ask that we can come together to present a united face to the House. I am certain that, by such an action, you and I will help the people of this country to come to terms with this catastrophe."

The Prime Minister stopped talking, turned round and saw that an aide had provided a chair. He sat down and looked at the Leader of the Opposition. He lifted his head and regarded him, sitting straight backed in his chair, obviously waiting for some response.

"I agree," he replied shortly. "When are you intending to address the House?"

"I will be making the same statement as I have given to you, as soon as I leave here."

"I think it might be helpful, if we both enter the chamber together."

"Thank you. I am sure that will give the right message to all our colleagues."

When, some ten minutes later, the Prime Minister entered the chamber alongside the Leader of the Opposition, they were greeted with complete silence. Unusually, his statement to the House was also received in absolute silence from those members present. He then sought leave to attend the House of Lords and, breaking with all protocol and tradition, both he and the Leader of the Opposition were allowed to enter to address the upper chamber.

In Somerset House, David and Jackie watched the majestic wave roll past them, causing incredible damage to both riverbanks. As the day turned into dusk, they realised that they couldn't stay where they were and, very soon, they would have to try to get back home to Richmond. David put his arm round Jackie in an attempt to comfort her and she nestled closer, half hiding her face in his chest.

"What are we going to do?" she asked, her voice trembling.

"Well, we can't stay here. That's for sure."

"What was that?" she asked, slowly shaking her head from side to side.

"I don't know for sure, but you remember I said that the wind yesterday was causing a build-up of seawater in the channel?" he went on. "Well, I reckon that the depression in the North has done the same thing and created another massive build-up of water.

"This second build up will have crashed into the first and caused a sea surge and when that entered the Thames estuary, it will have reared up even higher, causing that wave."

"But it was so high."

"I know. To be that high here, it must have crashed over the top of the Thames Barrier. I mean, did you see those containers floating in the water?"

"Yes. Why hadn't they sunk?"

"I suppose they must be airtight, so when they are empty, they'll have some buoyancy. I expect that they will float a bit like icebergs, with much of the bulk under water. If they get to the front of the wave, they will start to roll and then the damage they cause could be devastating because they'll just mow down anything in front of them."

"But all those people…" Her voice broke off.

"I know." David glanced round. "Look! We can't stay here and, anyway, there will be a lot of people out there who will need our help."

"What can we do? Two kids against all …" She paused. "Against all that."

"I don't know, but if we don't go and see, we won't find out."

David turned to leave, with Jackie still snuggled into his chest. Finally, she pulled herself away and, hand in hand, they walked to the door. As they carefully went down the stairs in the darkened building, they could hear the hum of traffic over towards Covent Garden and the West End. However, as they came out of the building and looked towards the river and the embankment, there was complete darkness and a terrifying stillness. They emerged onto Riverside Terrace where, in the moonlight, they could see that the wave must have crashed over the Victoria Embankment wall, smashing the RNLI Lifeboat's facility next to Waterloo Bridge.

As he looked to his left, David saw that a boat had been washed half onto the road. Below them, almost under Waterloo Bridge, a bus had been hit and forced onto its side, before being washed further down the road. David ran down the steps and waded through the water to the bus to see whether there were any people trapped inside.

"We've got to get the emergency door open." He pulled at the back window, but the fitting was bent.

"You'll need a lever of some sort," Jackie said helpfully.

151

"Can you see if there's anything lying about?"

Jackie looked round and saw a broken metal fence next to the flooded pavement. It seemed that the bus had been washed into the fence that then swept further on towards the bridge. She pulled at an iron pole and, to her surprise, was able to extricate it quite easily.

"Here! Will this help?"

"Brilliant. Thanks."

David immediately noticed that one end of the pole was shaped like an old spear. He inserted the sharp end into the small space where the frame had buckled. He was able to push it in about an inch before he started to force open the window. With a reluctant screech and a sudden smashing of the toughened glass, the emergency window opened and David was able to push his head inside.

"Is there anyone injured?" he shouted. He was rewarded with a moan a little way further inside.

As he clambered inside, David realised that the right-hand side of the bus was now adjacent to the road surface and under the water. The left-hand side was above him. The passengers had been thrown across the bus and were now draped over the seats half in and half out of the water. The moaning got louder as he made his way over the right hand seats and inert bodies of men and women. He couldn't ascertain their condition but, because they didn't protest when he clambered over them, he presumed they were either unconscious or dead.

Suddenly, over his shoulder, there was a light. After following him inside, Jackie opened her phone. In the bright beam, David saw an arm raised a few feet in front of him, with its hand slowly waving at him. It was an old man. Although he was in a sitting position with his back to the roof of the bus, his legs were trapped under the water by two other female passengers. One of the women was wedged between the seats. She had fallen head first from her seat on the left-hand side of the bus onto the old man. Her head was under the water and her coat and dress had fallen open, leaving her legs bare and draped over his shoulder. The other woman had fallen on top of her. The man was cradling the second lady's head to him as best he could, but it was covered in blood and she wasn't moving.

"Thanks, lad." The old man looked up at David. "Just to let you know, since the bus went over and stopped here, the water has slowly been rising. I think this one's dead." He touched the waist of woman draped on his chest and shoulders. "She hasn't moved at all and her head is under the surface. This one's still breathing, but she's not moving at all."

"What about you, sir?"

"I'm OK, I think, but I can't move my legs because this one's holding me down." He indicated the lady on top of him.

"Right. Any idea how many were on the bus?"

"Not really. It wasn't full. Well, quite empty really. No idea how many are down below." Suddenly, David realised that he was on the top deck of the bus and that there would be more people on the lower deck.

Jackie moved past him and slowly made her way to the front. She couldn't see any more passengers and when she finally reached the stairway, she began to crawl downwards to the lower deck. This was rather difficult because the stairway was partly under water. As she emerged into the lower deck, she heard someone else moaning.

"Where are you?" she called.

"Over 'ere, luv." Jackie shone her phone towards the rear.

There were two men and a woman all in a huddle about halfway down. They all appeared to be OK, but none of them was moving.

"Are you OK?" Jackie asked.

"Not really, no," one of the men replied. "My foot is caught under the seat and I think my leg is broken. This lady here is unconscious and this other bloke has got a wrenched shoulder or a broken arm or something."

"We've got another guy upstairs with a potential broken leg, but we have managed to open the emergency exit. And there's another woman out cold," Jackie informed them. "Do you know where the driver is?"

"No idea, luv."

"Right!" Jackie said. "Look, I've got to check if he's still alive, because the water is still rising and his cab will be under the surface."

"That's OK. We're not going anywhere!"

Jackie made her way back past the luggage area and the stairs to the cab, clambering over safety glass. The driver was still sitting in his seat holding the steering wheel, but now, of course, he was on his side with his head resting on the window of the driver's door at a most peculiar angle. His neck appeared to be broken. As his head was under the surface, he would have drowned anyway. Jackie quickly looked away. She stood up on the inside cab safety window to see if could reach the door of the bus. She could only just touch it but was unable to exert any pressure to try and open it. She turned back to the three passengers.

"Are there any other passengers?" she asked.

"Dunno, luv!" the man replied. "I think there might be a couple of kids at the back. I was asleep when the bus went over and can't remember if they had got off."

"I'll have to have a look."

Jackie started making her way to the back of the bus, clambering over the seats. She passed three more male bodies, each one not moving, with their faces under the surface. Right at the back, on its left-hand side, the bus had received a severe blow. She could see that the windows above her were completely shattered. And there, in the corner, sitting quietly and clinging to each other, were two young people. Their eyes were wide open, as they watched Jackie slowly make her way towards them.

"Hi. Are you two OK?"

The boy slowly shook his head from side to side. The girl just clung to him more tightly. "Are either of you injured?" Again, the boy just shook his head.

"Well if you can move, I could really use some help." Jackie pointed upwards to the broken window. "I need to get up there, so that we can all climb out." She turned back to the front and shouted, "David, can you hear me?"

"Yes!" a disembodied voice replied.

"I've got a broken window down here. It's completely shattered and if I can get the people to move, we should be able to climb out quite easily. I've not assessed their injuries yet. You might have a broken window up there as well."

"Yeah. You're right. I can see it. Towards the back."

"I've got five people still alive down here that we need to get out."

"Right! It's the same up here. Second window along from the back. Hadn't noticed before. I'm coming to you. Won't be long."

David explained to the old man what he was about to do. He then returned to the emergency exit and clambered out. He noticed that the water had risen by perhaps a couple of inches. Now, using the opened emergency exit for footholds, he clambered up the outside of the bus until he was standing on its left-hand side. He could see a deep gouge from the roof to rear wheel, breaking both the ground floor and upper floor windows. It looked as though something had been washed out of the river and over the wall before hitting the bus a glancing blow, sufficient to knock it over onto its side.

Looking through the upper window, he could see Jackie's light inside.

"Jackie?" David knelt down on the side of the bus.

"I'm here!" she replied.

"Whatever else we do, we've got to get these people out. It won't be easy because they will have injuries that we can't assess. Do you have any uninjured people who can help?"

"There's a couple of young teenagers, but they appear to be badly traumatised."

"We really could do with their help. Are they nearby?" Jackie turned her phone and shone the light into the corner, where the girl was still clinging tightly to the boy.

"Can you give us a hand?" David asked him direct. The boy slowly nodded his head up and down. "Good. Just hang on there. I'll get back to you in a sec.

"Jackie, I've got two others alive on the top deck. One is an old guy and he seems to have a badly injured leg. The other is a woman and she's completely unconscious. I can't move the old guy until the unconscious woman has been moved. She's lying on top of another woman who appears to be dead and they're both pinning the old man down. What's your situation?"

"I have two men and a woman. She's unconscious and both men have injuries. A broken leg and a wrenched shoulder. The two kids appear to be OK physically."

"Right. I suggest we deal with mine first. We should be able to extricate them through the emergency window. Can you get out of your broken window onto the side of the bus?"

"Yes, I think so. I can use the seat to climb up."

And with that hopeful comment, she turned to the man who simply nodded and waved at her to get on with the plan. She then turned to the boy, who was whispering to his girlfriend. She was vigorously shaking her head and holding him in a vice like grip. Gently he prised open her fingers and slowly pulled away from her. She started to cry, quietly at first and then louder and louder, until her wailing was reverberating through the stricken bus. Suddenly, he slapped her across the face and the wailing abruptly stopped. "I'm sorry," he whispered. He turned and followed Jackie, climbing up the seat and out of the bus. He crawled to the upper deck broken window and looked inside. He could see Jackie and David struggling to move the body of the unconscious woman off the old man.

He dropped into the upper deck and went to help them. David gently lifted the shoulders of the unconscious woman and Jackie lifted her legs. Carefully and with the help of the teenage boy, they manoeuvred her across the seats to the emergency window at the back. David indicated that the lad should get out first, to ensure that the lady, when she came through the window, wouldn't be dropped or left with her face below the surface of the water. Slowly, but surely, the woman's body was pushed feet first through the window. The lad took the weight of the woman, but had to let her down into the water, because she was too heavy for him to hold. Quickly, David climbed out of the bus and picked up the body. He carried her up the steps, until he was well above the water line.

"Do you think your girlfriend could get out and help look after the passengers as we get them out?" David looked at the young lad.

"I will ask." He turned and climbed up onto the side of the bus and dropped through the lower deck window. Soon they both emerged and the boy smiled at David and nodded his head.

"Good. We'll concentrate on the old man now." He turned to go back through the emergency exit, where Jackie was waiting with the old man. He was still pinned down by the dead woman. When the bus toppled over, she had landed head first onto the window next to the man, knocking herself completely unconscious. As the bus settled on its right side, her head remained below the surface of the water and she quickly drowned. David and Jackie pulled at her, but she was stuck fast. In the gloom, it was the teenage boy who noticed that her coat was caught fast and that no amount of tugging and pulling was going to shift her. He realised that, if her coat could be taken off, then it would free the body and make the task much easier. He tapped David on the arm.

"Take coat off," he said in broken English. "It…solid."

"God, yes! You're right." Immediately, David understood.

They eased first one arm and then the next out of the sleeves of the coat. The three of them were then able to lift the body of the woman off the old man. They placed her with some dignity in the next-door seat space.

"David, his leg is caught under his seat. I think it might be broken."

"Yes, I thought so too." The old man looked up.

"Have you got her out OK?" he asked.

"Yes, she's fine. But we're going to concentrate on you now."

"Listen!" The old man caught David's sleeve. "I know my leg's fucked. Just get on and do what you've got to do."

"It's going to hurt like hell."

"Can't be helped, can it?"

"We're going to try to move your foot out first. It's under water, so I expect it'll be pretty numb because of the cold," David said hopefully.

He reached under the surface until he could feel the ankle and foot. *It's not so much the leg as the ankle,* he thought. "Jackie, can you try to bend his knee as I pull the ankle free?"

"OK." She leant over the man and took a firm grip on his knee.

"Ready?" asked David.

"Ready!" she replied.

She pulled the knee up, trying to make it bend, as David eased the foot free. Suddenly the knee bent completely and she fell onto the old man. He chuckled his thanks. As with the previous passenger, they now had to make their way over the seats to the rear of the bus with him, trying not to cause any further injury to his ankle. Again, the young lad got out first and slowly they eased the old man, feet first, through the window. As soon as he was out, David and the young lad took him up the steps and sat him down next to the unconscious woman. The young girl was sitting on the step with the woman's head in her lap.

The old man looked at the girl. "Where are you from, love?"

"We… from… Bulgaria," haltingly, she replied.

"You're not very old, are you?"

"I… Sixteen," she said. "My brother… Eighteen," she added.

Back in the bus, David and Jackie found it more difficult to extricate the passengers on the lower deck. It was going to be necessary to lift them up through the broken window. Both of the men, despite their injuries, said they would do what they could to help, but the woman was still unconscious. David considered the problem and decided that the only way would be for him to lift the woman's body. Fortunately, she was slightly built.

Crouching down, he pulled her arms up and over his shoulders. He then pushed upwards with his knees until he was standing with the woman next to him, supported by

Jackie and the lad. David now bent forward, keeping her arms in front of him and allowing the woman's body to be draped over his shoulder. He bent his free arm as far back as he could, until he could hold her round her thighs. He could now manoeuvre her body onto his shoulders in a fireman's lift.

Jackie and the lad, seeing that the woman was now secure, climbed up the seats and through the broken window. The man with the wrenched shoulder stood up. He was obviously in a lot of pain, but he was able to support David as he started to climb up the seat towards the broken window. Jackie and the young Bulgarian boy were lying spread eagled on the side of the bus and on either side of the window. Slowly David climbed higher until they were able to get a grip on her clothes. As he felt the woman's weight lessen, David was able to climb faster and, pushing upwards from below, the three of them were finally able to get the woman through the gap, until her body was lying on the side of the bus.

"That was hard," David muttered. He could feel his thighs shaking with the effort.

"Are you OK?"

"Will be in a sec." He panted his reply, before climbing up next to them. "Right, we've now got to get off the bus and then up the steps. Think it might be best if I get down first and then you can lower her down to me."

Together, Jackie and the teenage boy pulled the woman to the edge of the bus. David looked up at them. "Can you let her come down legs first but keep holding her arms until I've got her safe?"

"OK."

Jackie pulled the lady closer to the edge and then rolled her body onto her front, before pushing her so that her legs extended out over the back of the bus. As they pushed, the lady's legs slowly began to bend at the hips, until her knees hit the back of the bus. They pushed some more and then took a firm grip of the lady's arms, as her body inch by inch disappeared over the side.

Down below, David reached up to locate her feet and then her legs and thighs. He took a firm grip of her waist as Jackie called that they were now holding her only by the hands and would have to let do.

"Let her go now!" David braced himself for the weight and all of a sudden, the woman was down, in his arms. He carried her dead weight to the steps and laid her down next to the other passengers.

When he was back in the bus, he turned Jackie's light onto the man with the wrenched shoulder.

"Are you OK?"

"You'd never have got her out on your own," he replied. "And, yes, I'll live. But the pain is increasing."

"I'm going to have to ask you to help me again."

"I realise that. Anyway, when you've freed his leg," the man indicated the other passenger, "He's going to have a much greater degree of discomfort than me."

"I expect you're right."

David crouched down to look at the leg. It was under water but bent under the man's body. David was no expert, but it appeared that the man's thigh was broken. There would be no easy way of lifting him without causing intense pain, but they couldn't leave him in the bus.

"Jackie, his thigh appears to be broken. Before we do anything else, we've got to get it splinted."

"How can we do that?"

"First, we must lift him to free the leg and that will be intensely painful. Then we've got to support the leg with a splint."

"I'm sure I've seen a shopping bag near here," Jackie muttered. "Maybe there's an umbrella inside. Here it is! No, sorry, there's nothing here."

The lad pulled David's arm. "I get branch from outside." And with that, he climbed up the seat and disappeared.

"Don't you think it would be better to leave me here?" The man looked pleadingly at David.

"No. I don't." David looked him full in the face. "The tide is still coming in and the water is still rising. If we leave you here, it is very likely that you will drown."

"Right." The man looked frightened and disorientated. "So what are you going to do?"

"I'm going to lift you, with my girlfriend's help, until we can straighten your leg. That will be extremely painful for you. Then, we are going to splint your leg. After that, I will lift you in a fireman's lift onto my shoulders, like I did with the unconscious lady. With this man's help, I will climb up to that window and we will pull you out. After we've got you down onto the ground, we will carry you up some steps to the other passengers where you will be well above the surface of the water." David paused and looked at the man's frightened face. "I'm sorry. It's not the best plan, but I don't think that we have any alternatives. But first, we need to find something to put your thigh into a splint."

Suddenly, the lad was back. He had a branch, which he had broken off a nearby tree. It was about three feet long. More importantly, he also had a belt.

"Put branch next to leg and then tie belt round both legs." The teenage boy tried to explain in halting English. "We need another belt."

"That woman's coat on the top deck has a belt. Will that do?" Jackie said.

"Can you see if there are any others on the dead people?" David asked, in a somewhat matter of fact manner.

"I help."

Jackie and the boy disappeared and quickly returned with three additional belts.

"Right." David said to the man. "We're ready to get you sorted. First, we've got to lift you, so we can straighten your leg."

"Yes, I understand. Please be as careful as you can."

"Come on, Jackie. Let's get to it."

He squatted next to the man and, gently, lifted the man's arm onto his shoulder. "Jackie, as I stand up, can you try to get under his other arm, so that as little weight as possible is being put onto his broken leg?"

"Yes. I think so."

"Are you ready?" David asked the man. The man nodded.

David took the strain in his own thighs and slowly began to rise. As his bodyweight lightened on the broken leg, the pain returned and the man let out a blood-curdling scream. Jackie now got under his other arm and the lad took hold of the man's leg, straightening it. The scream suddenly stopped as the man passed out.

"Right! Let's do this as quickly as we can," David said.

With Jackie keeping his head above water, David grabbed the branch and, helped by the Bulgarian boy; he placed it next to the broken thigh and passed the belt around both thighs. He quickly pulled it tight and made it firm using the buckle. He then tied one of the extra coat belts around both legs, just above the knees, while the lad tied another coat belt just below the knees. Finally, he used the last belt to tie both ankles together. The man's legs were now completely immobilised.

"OK. Let's lift him up, so he's standing and then get him on my shoulders."

They repeated the process they had used with the unconscious lady, although it was considerably more awkward trying to work with the man's immobilised legs. Finally, after a lot of effort, he was lying across David's shoulders.

"You'd better get up top and be ready to pull him up through the window." David panted.

Jackie and the lad climbed up the seat and disappeared through the window. With the help of the other man, David began to climb up the seat.

"David, we'll have to ease him out with his head and shoulders first," Jackie said. "He's too tall with the splint on."

"OK," David panted. "I'll do my best."

He pushed the man's upper body up and was relieved when he realised that his body was being pulled up from above. Slowly, it disappeared from his view and David was able to climb out.

"Are you sure you're all right?" Jackie looked at him with some alarm.

"I'll just catch my breath." David stayed in a kneeling position with his head hanging down, until his heart rate returned to normal. He turned to the boy. "As soon as we've got him off the bus, you'll have to help me get him up the steps."

"OK. I understand."

They pushed the man to the back, turned him round so he would go down feet first and then rolled him onto his front. David got off the bus and Jackie and the lad began to lower the man. As soon as David had him secure round the waist, the lad quickly joined him and, together, they supported him under the shoulders and half carried and half dragged him up the steps before laying him gently on the ground next to the others.

After that, the last guy should be quite easy, David thought.

The two lads quickly re-entered the bus and, together with Jackie, dropped inside where the last passenger was patiently waiting for them.

"I've been thinking about your shoulder," said Jackie. "When you are climbing out, you must protect it as much as possible. We don't really have anything to support it, so we'll have to disable it somehow."

"How do you mean?"

"Well, if you slip and it moves or if you fall on it, you could make your injury much worse. So I suggest that we take off your coat and then, with your arm held across your stomach, we'll put it on again and do up all the buttons. That should disable your arm pretty effectively."

"OK. But how are you going to get the coat off?"

"Very carefully," Jackie replied.

Gently, she reached up and undid the buttons, before easing the sleeve down the uninjured arm. It was then quite a simple task to take the injured arm out of the other sleeve. She carefully placed his arm across his stomach and put his good arm back into its sleeve, before wrapping the coat round his back so that it was lying correctly on his shoulders. She pulled it tight across his chest and belly and did up all the buttons.

"How does that feel?" she asked.

"Much better, thanks." He nodded. "Surprisingly so!" he added.

"Good," said David. "I'll push from below, as you climb up the seat. As soon as she can, Jackie will get hold of your good arm and will pull you up, as I push from here."

As a plan, it was pretty basic, but in its execution, it was brilliant. In no time at all, the man was through the window and ready to be let down onto the ground. Very soon, he had joined his companions on the steps, where the two Bulgarians were finally reunited.

David surveyed his small group of refugees and muttered to Jackie, "We've got to move these people up to the main road. No one will ever see them here."

"I don't think that's going to be easy. Two of them are still unconscious."

"I know. I've been thinking about that. I can carry one of the women and I was hoping that you and this lad's girlfriend could help the guy with the broken leg. The old man and the chap with the wrenched shoulder should be able to help each other. That'll just leave the other unconscious woman."

"The boy's not strong enough to help her on his own."

"I realise that. But he could wait here until I get back. We could move all the others to the top of the steps and I could then come back down to help him."

"That'll work." Jackie looked at David with admiring eyes, wondering where his strength and ability came from. She realised, with a sudden intense internal shock that she loved him intently and would never want to let him go.

They explained the predicament to the group and how they planned to resolve it. Slowly, except for the two unconscious women, they got to their feet. With difficulty, Jackie explained the plan a second time to the Bulgarian girl and together they helped the man with the broken leg to his feet. His legs were still firmly bound together and to the splint. Standing either side, they each took one of his arms over their shoulders and holding him firmly around the waist, started to lift him step by painful step, to the road above.

In a similar fashion, the man with the wrenched shoulder, which was still immobilised by his jacket, with his free hand assisted the old man to his feet. The old man put his arm around the younger man's good shoulder and, together, they slowly followed the girls. The Bulgarian boy helped David to lift the first unconscious woman onto his shoulders in a fireman's lift and he followed on, rather more easily than his companions. He reached the top first and walked a little way towards the Strand before putting the woman down.

There was no traffic at all on the approach road to Waterloo Bridge. David gently put down his burden and, as the others arrived, they all settled down next to the woman. David trotted back down the steps, where he found the Bulgarian boy talking to the second woman.

"Has she come round?" he asked.

"Sorry, what … you … mean?"

"Is she awake?"

"Yes. Just after you leave, she groan and sit up. I help her. She ask where she is and I explain when you come back."

David looked at the woman who was sitting with her knees drawn up to chest and her head bowed over them. "How do you feel?"

"Bloody terrible. What the hell happened? And who are you?"

"The river's flooded. There was some sort of a tidal surge, which has flooded both sides. I think a boat has been freed from its moorings and come over the river wall. It must have hit the bus and knocked it over."

"But you weren't on the bus."

"No, my girlfriend and I were in Somerset House. When we came out, we saw the bus and came down to help. All the other passengers are on the road at the top of the steps." He looked more closely at the woman. "Do you think you can walk?"

"I don't know. I think I'm going to be sick." And with that announcement, she leant over to her left and was sick onto the steps. When she had finished, she looked up at David and asked, "Did you bring out my briefcase?"

"We didn't see a briefcase. I'm sorry."

"I'll have to get back in to look for it."

"You'll never find it. The bus is on its side and partly under water. Any papers will have been destroyed."

"You don't understand. The briefcase is waterproof and the documents inside are really important."

"Surely nothing is as important as saving your life."

"Without that case, my life will be finished anyway. Where's my handbag?"

"That'll also be inside the bus."

"My mobile and my house keys are inside it. I can't leave without them," she stated.

She started to look round her and then struggled to her feet. She saw the Bulgarian boy, standing behind her. "Who's he?"

"He was another passenger."

"What's he doing?"

"He has been helping me to get the injured passengers out of the bus."

"OK. I see." The woman turned back to face David.

"Right!" she said decisively, "I've got to get back down there and find the briefcase. I'll either do it with or without your help."

David turned to the lad and explained quickly that he should go to the others and explain to Jackie what was now happening. He had no choice but to help her find her things. The boy turned and ran up the steps. David put out his hand to help the lady back down to the bus. In her late twenties, she was quite short, with red hair and a pretty face.

As they reached the bottom of the steps, he turned to her and said, "I'm sorry, I can't remember. Were you on the top deck or the bottom?"

"On the bottom. Why? Does it matter?"

"Yes. To get into the bottom deck, we have to climb up onto the side and drop through a broken window."

"Oh! I see." The lady waded through the water to the back of the bus. "God, this water's cold!" she exclaimed.

"You need to climb up, using the top deck emergency exit. I'll help you. Put your foot into my hands and then pull yourself up. When you've got both feet up, I'll climb to the top and pull you up the last bit."

He bent down and as she placed her foot into his clasped hands, he realised that she had no shoes and he could see that her stockings were torn and laddered. He boosted her up and then clambered up, past her, to the top. He turned back, took her hands and pulled her up onto the side of the bus. He took her arm and helped her towards the broken window. As she stepped up to him, he also noticed that, under her jacket and coat, her blouse was torn and dirty. He suggested that he should go in first and then he could catch her if she should slip. He climbed down the chairs and into the water. Looking up, he watched her as she carefully followed until, finally, she was standing next to him with the water round their waists.

"Where were you sitting?" She closed her eyes.

"On the left, near the back. I could hear that lad and his girl talking to each other in a foreign language, behind me and to my right. There was a man on the other side of the aisle and someone else in front of him."

"We've got all of them out."

"My briefcase must be quite near here then." She bent down and started swishing about in the water.

"Hang on!" David pulled out his mobile and turned on the light. "This might help."

"Thanks. Can you shine it there?" She indicated with her finger. The water was dirty, muddy and smelly. They couldn't see through it. The woman knelt down and the water made her skirt balloon around her waist. Methodically she searched below the surface.

Kneeling up straight, she announced, "I've got something." She bent forward again and moving slightly forward on her knees, she suddenly straightened up with a handbag in her hand. "Well at least I'll be able to get into my house." She smiled triumphantly at David, as she passed him the leather bag, before bending forward for a third time.

The water was cold and, now that he was basically standing still, David began to shiver. The adrenalin rush that had sustained him throughout the rescue, was rapidly draining away leaving him cold and indecisive. He kept his light shining just in front of the woman, who was soaked, dirty, but exultant. With a triumphant "Yes!" she again knelt upright but, this time, she was holding a silver style briefcase in her arms.

"Come on," she said. "Help me up and let's get out of here."

David put his mobile into his pocket and took hold of her arms. Her clothes were soaking and clinging to the curves of her slight body. Once again, he made a step with his hands for her to be helped up the chairs and through the broken window. With great difficulty, because she refused to let go of the briefcase, she clambered up, David helping by firmly pushing her bottom. When she reached the top, she lay full length, reaching back to help David. Once again, he suggested that he should get off the bus first and then be able to catch her, should she slip. He told her to come down, on her stomach, feet first. As she slid off the top side of the bus, David reached up first for her feet and legs and then for her waist. At that point she slipped, but David caught her with his arms round her chest and one hand cupping her small but shapely breast. As her feet touched the road below the surface of the water, she turned and, smiling broadly, she kissed him firmly on the lips.

"Thank you. You will never know how important it was to recover this." She indicated the briefcase. "But you're shivering. You must be really cold."

"Not as cold as you. Your clothes are all soaked. We must find some shelter and quickly. Come on! This way. Up the steps."

David gave her the handbag, took her free hand and pulled her up across the road. They waded to the pavement and started to climb the steps. As soon as they were clear of the water, she stopped. Very quickly she took off her coat and jacket before unzipping her skirt. Standing there in her lacy black bra and matching panties, she twisted her skirt to get rid of the excess water. She then shook it out and the put it on once more.

Spellbound, David watched this exercise, having never seen a lady wearing stockings and suspenders before. Even in the moonlight, he could see that the panties were very sheer and, despite his shivering, he could feel his masculinity stirring. It was the same with her bra through which David could see the shape of her hardened nipples. The white silk of her blouse was mouldered to her body, leaving nothing to the imagination.

"Hold these." She passed over the jacket and coat before quickly stripping off her blouse. Just as quickly, she squeezed out the excess water, before putting it back on and tucking it into her skirt. After repeating the twisting actions with her jacket and her coat, she put them back on, picked up her handbag and the briefcase and started to walk briskly up the steps. David followed behind, hardly believing what he had just witnessed.

Chapter 15
Thursday Evening – After High Tide

The weather slowly continued to improve. The wind slackened and the rain stopped. The clouds cleared and a bright moon was shining. High Tide in London came at 10 minutes to 5, after the sun had finally disappeared. Ordinarily, this would cause little comment, but on that Thursday, it was of considerable importance. If it was possible to observe the river from above, the familiar snakelike bends of the Thames had disappeared and been replaced by an enormous wedge of water, rather like a massive slice of pizza, extending from Brentford in the west to the open sea beyond Southend.

The land on either side of the river rises and falls in a series of low hills and valleys, in some places allowing and in others denying the inundation of flood water in equal measure. In central London, the water covered all of Lambeth, Bermondsey and Deptford as far south as Camberwell, but there was very little flooding on the north bank at Holborn and the city. To the west, however, the reverse was the case in that Chiswick, Hammersmith and Fulham were under water, but on the south bank much of Richmond Park, Mortlake and Putney were left unscathed. The floating containers created mayhem in Barnes and Battersea, but left Kensington and Chelsea untouched. Opposite Waterloo Station, Westminster and Pimlico were under water, causing enormous damage and disruption to Government, the Civil Defence and the communications networks.

Further east, beyond the city, it was the same story. As the river approached the sea, the wedge of sea water widened. Poplar and the Isle of Dogs, as well as the City of London Airport and Barking sewage works were flooded, but because it lies on a small hill, Woolwich was broadly untouched. Thamesmead and all the industrial lands eastwards to Erith were completely overwhelmed, as were Tilbury, Corringham and Canvey Island on the north bank. The Isle of Grain was totally under water.

The damage to the river's infrastructure, the piers, the wharfs and the gantries lining both banks, was devastating. The empty containers swept from the container ports by the gigantic wave as it travelled up river, caused most of the destruction.

All power throughout the capital was severed and the city was in darkness. The only light came from vehicles gridlocked on all roads leading away from the river and that massive wedge of water. Because all the traffic lights had failed and there was no street lighting, most drivers were trying to avoid the main roads. One by one, a number of buildings were coming back to life as their emergency generators kicked into action.

Across the rest of the country, the confusion and interruption to ordinary life was less accentuated with the levels of disruption differing from area to area. Because of the severe snowfall and gales in Scotland and the North of England, every Local Authority north of Sheffield remained at a complete standstill, while they grappled with the enormity of the task of helping their areas return to some semblance of normality. All attempts were severely curtailed by regular disruptions to the power supply but, with weather conditions swiftly improving, engineers were already surveying the damage and working to restore the necessary connections.

The change in the weather was having a surprising and unusual effect in the Pennines. The two weather fronts, which initiated the unique sea surge up the river Thames, abutted each other in a line across England and Wales from Anglesey in the west to Kings Lynn in the east. To the north, the weather was cold with northerly gales and snow. To the south the wind was warmer, bringing prolonged rain. With both depressions now drifting to the east and filling, this dividing line began to move slowly northwards, raising temperatures and melting the snow much more quickly than was normal.

In West Yorkshire, the snow was deep and lying on land which was already saturated. The rivers were already in spate from the unrelenting autumnal rains. The rising temperature was very quickly melting the snow, where it was lying in deep drifts on the hills. The meltwater was now flowing off the hillsides down into the valleys. This was to become a considerable problem.

In Huddersfield, Cllr Christine Sykes was watching the television. Suddenly, yet another power cut plunged not only her house but also the whole of Huddersfield, into darkness. The news from London was reporting some sort of a major incident. Her husband, Robert, was cooking in their small galley kitchen. Fortunately, the cooker was powered by gas and the saucepan of vegetable ragout remained gently simmering. He reached for the matches to light the two candles that he had found earlier that afternoon, during a previous power cut.

"Not again," he grumbled. "This is really irritating!"

"I know," Christine replied. "It's cut off the News."

"Anything interesting."

"I'm not really sure. They were saying something about some flooding in London, but it all disappeared before there was any detail."

"Well, I've just bagged up the potato peelings so I'll pop them in the bin."

Robert opened the kitchen door. In front of him, his back garden was at least a foot deep in snow. He went through the door and down a couple of steps. Carefully he made his way to the dustbin, leaving a trail of deep footprints in the drifts. He knocked a foot of snow off the grey wheelie bin lid and placed the sealed waste bag inside, before making his way back to the kitchen.

"It's quite strange out there."

"What do you mean?"

"There's over a foot of snow in the back garden, but the air feels really warm. I can't see this snow lasting too long."

"What do you mean?" Christine repeated. "What's really warm? How long?"

"If it stays as warm as it is now, it could all be gone by tomorrow morning."

"Don't be silly. It's far too deep." Christine sat back and thought a bit more. "Mind you, if it does melt as fast as that, the water coming off the hills will cause some difficulties. There could even be some local flooding. I wonder what effect it'll have on Butterley Dam."

"I was wondering when you were going to mention that."

Back in 2012, Yorkshire Water plc had announced its intention to remove and replace an iconic Victorian stone spillway with a concrete overflow. The objections of the local people in Marsden had fallen on deaf ears and, finally, the popular tourist attraction had been dismantled and removed. The new concrete spillway looked like a hideous scar on the hillside and, despite promises to the contrary, it appeared that none of the original stone had been incorporated in the new structure. The melting snow would be a severe test. The water level in the reservoir was already full, so a sudden inflow of melt water could really test the dam wall and the new spillway might come under severe pressure.

"Have you got any signal on your phone?" Christine asked.

"Dead as a doornail," he replied.

"I wonder if the roads are clear to get to Marsden."

"You're not thinking of going out, are you?"

"I need to make sure that people know that the dam will be under severe pressure throughout the night. Are you really sure about the warmth of the air outside?"

Robert shrugged. "Go and see for yourself."

Christine got up and went to the door. Once outside, just like King Wenceslas' page, she stood in the footsteps made by her husband only five minutes earlier. She immediately realised that he wasn't exaggerating. The air was warm! She looked up at the weight of snow on the roofs of the houses that stretched down on either side of her small back garden. She was aware that a number of her neighbours had not taken advantage of previous Government initiatives to get their homes insulated. As she was idly considering their indifference, she saw a crack appear in the snow on a roof to her right. And, suddenly, as she watched spellbound, the snow slid gracefully down the roof and over the gutter, before landing with a loud 'plop' on the ground.

She now realised that the compacted snow below the soles of her shoes was actually quite slushy. She turned to go back into the house, as she heard snow sliding down another roof. *Robert's right*, she thought. *This thaw will be quick and that could well spell disaster.*

"We need to get up to Marsden," she announced as she re-entered the kitchen, kicking snow off her shoes.

"Thought you'd say that, so I nipped out to the car and checked the road. A few other cars have gone past and the road is driveable, with care. Do you want to try to get up to Marsden now?"

"Yes. I'll get my coat."

After turning off the gas, Robert locked the back door, put on his coat and opened the front door for his wife.

"This won't be easy," he muttered, half to himself, as he opened the car door for Christine. After she was settled, he got behind the wheel and started the engine. Checking that they both had put on their seatbelts, he gently eased out of his parking space into the tracks already left by other vehicles. Although the snow was lying about a foot deep, he was surprised that the tracks were easily drivable.

They turned onto the main Manchester Road which was already ploughed and clear. The road surface gleamed wetly at them but, surprisingly, it was completely clear of snow and compacted ice. As they drove along, Christine glanced at the roofs of the terraced cottages on either side of the road. They were heavy with snow, except where the warmth from inside the houses had caused the snow to slip. The only lights that they could see were from their car's headlights. They passed the chicane at Slaithwaite without seeing any other traffic at all. All of a sudden, they were in the country, passing West End Garage.

"Where exactly do you want to go?" Robert asked. "Remember, there will be no power and people might not welcome the idea of being visited at this time."

"You're right about that," she replied. "But this is an emergency and we need to spread the word one way or another. I suggest we try to get to Mary, Stephen and George. They all live on main roads. Mary has three teenage children, who can walk to their neighbours. Stephen is the local scout leader and can organise his troop. George, of course, is the local doctor.

"I'm going to ask Mary and Stephen to alert the people living in the town centre and alongside the river that comes from the dam. They'll have to do it door to door, for obvious reasons. Stephen will also have to alert the people on the new estates alongside the upper river Colne and the old folk in Wessen Court. They'll all have to be persuaded to go upstairs to the first floor. When we've contacted George, he'll be able to open the medical centre and be ready for people who won't be able to get transport to hospital.

"If the dam overflows," she continued, "The flow of water down that small stream, will cause havoc. It'll rip out all the trees and flood out at the bottom of Mount Road, before joining the river Colne in the centre of Marsden. The flood water will then flow down to Slaithwaite. It'll be joined by all the other streams which'll also be swollen from the melting snow. We'll have to knock on some doors there as well."

"You've really been thinking about this, haven't you?"

"Ever since Yorkshire Water started on their barmpot scheme. Do you remember their first public presentation? It was so awful that it made me believe that whatever they wanted to do, it wouldn't really stop or reduce the effects of a real disaster. If the spillway is able to cope with the increased levels of water, it won't reduce the probability of a flood in the town centre, because that amount of flood water will still be there. If the spillway can't cope and the overflow starts to erode the dam itself, it may give way and that really will be a disaster."

"What happens after Slaithwaite?" Robert asked.

"There's no real problem until the flood water reaches Milnsbridge. Mind you, there will be local structural damage, especially to the businesses alongside the river and the canal. But in Milnsbridge, the bridge could well be damaged as well as all the housing down George Street. When the flood water gets to Longroyd Bridge, it could damage that bridge as well and that'll make the main road impassable. So we must hope that it won't be as bad as that and that we can alert as many people as possible."

Robert stopped the car outside Mary's house.

Sebastian returned from Soho at about four o'clock. Before Andy dropped him off, he asked whether Sebastian had yet had an opportunity to consider using the portfolio he was building up for Alice.

"Not so far, Andy," Sebastian replied. "But it's rather strange, because I know the girl."

"What do you mean?" Andy feigned complete ignorance.

"The girl. Is she called Alice? Well, she works for my banker."

"Of course she does!" Andy exclaimed. "I thought I knew her from somewhere, but I just couldn't place her."

"Don't be so bloody disingenuous," Sebastian remarked. "I don't doubt that when you first met her, she was a complete stranger, but she has stayed here twice and each time arrived in your cab. So, I know that you know perfectly well who she is." Somewhat taken aback, Andy just nodded. "You'll find, if you keep working for me, that I know a lot of people and I have excellent connections. It's extremely difficult to pull the wool over my eyes."

Quietly, Andy replied, "OK, Mr Fortescue Brown. I'll never make that mistake again."

"You'll also find that it's far better to volunteer information rather than wondering whether I might find it out later from another source. Be under no illusion, I will find out and you will rue the day if I learn that you have been hiding information from me."

Sebastian got out of the cab. All the windows were dark, but he could see the glimmer of torches and candles. He turned back and spoke through the passenger window.

"Andy, when I have information that can enhance Alice's career, I'll let you know."

"Thanks. I appreciate that."

Andy drove away, back onto the Cromwell Road. The traffic was thick with slow moving traffic. He turned into a side road, trying to make his way southwards towards the river. With no street lights and no traffic lights, he thought it might be more sensible to use back doubles wherever possible.

As he drove through South Kensington, he heard the sound of breaking glass and saw a couple of young men walking down the street, carrying a big television screen between them. They scurried away into the darkness of a side street. In the dark, it was impossible to identify them.

Just short of Sloane Square, a man walked into the road in front of the cab, holding up his hand to stop him.

"What's the problem, mate?" Andy asked, leaning out of his cab window.

"You can't get through here. The river's flooded and everything's under water further down there."

"Are you trying to get somewhere?" Andy asked.

"Well, I do need to get back to the city. My apartment's in the Barbican."

"Hop in. I'll take you. All the roads are pretty grim with traffic, so it'll take some time. I've already been into the West End this afternoon and that was a nightmare, but there's no flooding there."

"No, there won't be! It's too high up. Everyone thinks London's flat, but it's not. On both sides of the river, it's just a series of low hills all the way from the sea to Richmond."

"Don't I know it? Some of those inclines can be real bottlenecks."

Andy drove along Eaton Square and turned up Grosvenor Place. The traffic conditions forced him to go round Hyde Park Corner and into Piccadilly. Slowly, he worked his way past Trafalgar Square, down Duncannon Street and onto the Strand. Even though the traffic was nose to tail, it was moving as, one by one, drivers turned northwards up any convenient side street to get away from the river and the congestion.

At a snail's pace, Andy drove along the Strand past Aldwych and up Fetter Lane to Holborn Circus and the Barbican, where he dropped his fare.

He checked the time and as it was now six o'clock and because he had no other fares to consider, Andy decided to go back home, with the idea of crossing the river over Waterloo Bridge.

Waterloo Station was a mess. After rescuing the woman and her baby, Pamela and Milton went back to the main concourse and started to organise the people into teams to help with the injured and to deal with the dead. Most people were simply milling about aimlessly, as though they were waiting for an announcement or for someone to take charge. In the darkness of the concourse, it was difficult to see how best they might assist the aimless crowds. They decided to split up and Milton left Pamela talking to a number of passengers who were already discussing what they could do.

Milton now walked down to the end of each platform, where he noted a number of bodies floating in the water. At the same time, Pamela got hold of a couple of old oil drums and, with those few volunteers, she was able to start fires in them both, using some wood that she found in a shop that was being renovated. As soon as the fires were burning, she helped the woman with her baby to sit next to it, to dry out her clothes. The ladies in one of the cafes, brought across some biscuits.

"What we really need is blankets or warm clothes," Pamela commented.

"I'll knock on the doors of some of the shops to see if they've got anything," one of the ladies replied.

"It might be an idea to get hold of the pharmacist from the chemist's shop as well." The lady disappeared into the gloom of the station.

When Milton returned, in the gloom, he looked over the frightened crowd. Rather than calling for volunteers, he asked a number of them to organise themselves into two teams. He explained that they were to try and fish the bodies out of the water. The first team reluctantly started to do so, laying out the bodies on the platforms. The water was, at last, beginning to recede and Milton knew that they must do this unpleasant task now, before the bodies simply drifted away.

His second team comprised just one woman and two men. He took them down the stairs to check the state of the roads around the station. Not surprisingly, the whole station complex was completely surrounded by water. Basically they were marooned, although the water seemed to be quite shallow between the station and the BFI Max. In the moonlight, they could see a number of bodies gently drifting in the water. As the water had already receded a little, Milton decided to wade out and retrieve them. As in the station, they laid the bodies where the authorities would easily be able to retrieve them. Milton noticed that the water was beginning to drain away quite quickly. With his helpers, they all returned to the station concourse, where they found that the first team had started to try to get down the steps into the underground.

There were so many people squashed into the tunnel leading down to the underground platforms that no one was able to move. In and amongst that crush was a mixture of dead, injured and trapped people. Working slowly and methodically, they extricated the bodies. Those needing medical treatment were escorted to Pamela, who was managing a temporary reception area near the pharmacy. After opening his premises, the pharmacist was dispensing drugs and medicines as required. He recruited two burly assistants to keep order at the door to his shop, ensuring that his drugs were protected. Under Pamela's direction, they were at last beginning to make an impression on the crowd that was still milling about, seemingly lost and without direction.

Milton quickly assessed the overall situation. He suggested to Pamela that he should try to direct the crowd into three distinct groups. He now called for volunteers. The first group would deal with the dead, laying them out neatly in rows, down the platforms. The second group would help those still living to areas on the concourse where they would not be a hindrance. The third group, a smaller but more active group, went to organise and help with the retrieval of the bodies from the entrance to the Underground.

They worked in this manner for over two hours, during which time the water steadily drained away from the platforms until, at last, pedestrians were able to walk out of the station, under the bridge which carries the trains to Charing Cross and onto the road leading up to Waterloo Bridge. There was a significant exodus as the realisation struck them that they would probably find better facilities at their places of work, than in the station itself.

In the city, the panic, which had overtaken so many people earlier in the day, now subsided leaving the roads and alleyways quiet and deserted. Michael Varley ventured out of the office at about half past four, to see for himself what was happening outside. First, he walked to Moorgate station, to find a crowd of people standing around at the entrance. There were two Underground staff explaining that the platforms were flooded.

He turned round and walked to Bank station, where the crowd was bigger, but the situation was the same. The station was closed. He had no idea what he was going to tell

Alice apart from the numbers of people standing around the Underground stations, which were closed. Other than Moorgate being flooded, he was unable to find out any other information. He was already feeling depressed from his inability to make love to Alice the previous evening. Because it was praying on his mind, he was not really interested in the problems facing the people at the stations. His lack of enquiry did little to help. Just a few questions would have elicited the information that very few people were returning to the surface and that no one was able to go down because of the crush of men and women clogging the stairways and escalators leading down to the platforms.

The river water, after entering the underground system south of the river, blasted its way into the Northern Line tunnels at London Bridge and Borough stations. From there it flowed under the Thames northwards to Bank and Moorgate. At the same time, it flowed southwards to the Elephant and Castle, where it split and turned northwards towards Waterloo and where it also entered the Bakerloo line. Both the Northern and Bakerloo lines acted as conduits for the flood water from Waterloo making its way northwards under the river to Charing Cross and even as far as Piccadilly and Baker Street. The Waterloo and City Line under the river gave access for the flood water to inundate Bank station. Being so deep, Bank station is very vulnerable.

The loss of power throughout London caused the flood defences to fail and water, under considerable pressure, was able to blast along the tunnels. At Bank, the flood water entered both the Central and the District and Circle lines. With little hindrance, it now blasted along the tunnels both east towards Stratford and west towards Oxford Circus and Ealing Broadway. Any trains that the water encountered were forced towards the nearest station, where the platforms were already completely filled with people. As the trains emerged, like toothpaste out of a tube, they buckled and were swept onto the platforms, mowing down everyone in their path. And as soon as the trains exited from the tunnels, pressurised water followed which simply sluiced away the dead to the far end of the platforms and into the tunnels, as well as up the stairs and escalators. The water pressure was greatest in the deeper lines, like the Central and the Northern, making the death toll even greater.

The irony of this mayhem was that, on the surface, the city itself and those parts of the West End served by the Central Line were well away from the flooded riverbanks. The people, who heard the message put out by the Environment Agency that morning and decided to leave work early, started a massive and panicked exodus. This, in turn, placed an intolerable burden on the public transport system so that the flood, when it hit, came with such speed that many of the flood defence systems were simply overwhelmed.

What Michael didn't know, therefore, was the total devastation on the platforms at Bank Station. The water surged into the underground system just after three o'clock. The press of people, trying to get out of the city, caused death and injuries to others who fell on the stairs and were simply trampled underfoot. Others were suffocated and many suffered heart attacks and strokes brought on by stress and anxiety. This pattern was repeated at station after station. Even those lines, unaffected by the flood water at the surface, were subjected to panic driven crowds showing a total lack of consideration for others.

At around ten past three, the people already on the platforms at Bank station, could hear a rumbling sound coming from the tunnels that run under the river. The force of air hit them with such power that several people near the tunnel entrance were knocked off their feet. The cause of the rumbling noise suddenly burst out of the tunnel. A train, packed with people eyes wide with fear, screaming, scrabbling at the doors, was forced from the tunnel, dragging behind it yards of cabling like a bridal train. It was already off the lines, sparking and squealing in protest as it was forced against the walls of the tunnel.

The edge of the driver's cab hit the platform breaking the concrete lip, making broken bricks and tiles fly through the air like shrapnel from an exploding shell. The debris hit the crowd, injuring, maiming and killing. It all happened so fast, that there was no time even to turn and run before the pressurised flood water followed.

Still pushing the train, half on and half off the platform, the pressure of the water swept round the obstruction sluicing the platform clear of all the people, living and dead, before entering the tunnel at the far end. The water also burst into the side tunnels and up the stairs. The lights flickered, dimmed and went out. There was no escape, as the tunnels were now completely filled with water. All those people that escaped the crush on the platform, the train bursting out of the tunnel and the pressurised water surge, simply drowned. Inexorably the water rose up through the connecting tunnels, the stairways and escalators, until it finally reached its equilibrium. For a moment there was complete silence.

As he retraced his steps back to the office, Michael was still unsure as to what was really happening. The only lights he could see were from passing vehicles which, as they negotiated their way through the crowds, lit up their faces drawn and frightened. The office blocks looming over him were dark and inert, like the cliffs of some man-made diabolical canyon. As he looked up to the sky, Michael noticed that the clouds were parting and he realised that it was no longer raining. He slowly trudged back to London Wall, wondering what had happened and how on earth he was going to get home.

As he entered the reception area, Alice was there to greet him. She had found a couple of candles and in their glimmering light, she saw fear in Michael's eyes.

"Are you all right?" she asked, somewhat needlessly.

"No… Not really," Michael stammered his reply. "It's not so good out there." He glanced apprehensively over his shoulder.

"How do you mean?"

"Moorgate and Bank stations are closed and there are people just sort of milling about. I can't begin to imagine what's happened, but it's obviously caused a massive disruption to the Underground. Someone said that Moorgate station was flooded."

He walked unsteadily towards his office, with Alice following behind, carrying a candle to light their way.

The rescue operations organised by Fred Shemming were beginning to bring considerable relief to the people living on the devastated estates in Millwall and Cubitt Town on the Isle of Dogs. Using the fire station as a command HQ, Fred firstly ferried all the children with their teachers as well as Rajinder Singh across to the Queen Victoria Seaman's Rest on the East India Dock Road. Following his phone calls before the wave struck, he was pleased that the management and the staff at both the Salvation Army Citadel and the Seaman's Rest were already organised.

To get down to Millwall and the Isle of Dogs, it was necessary for his boats to cross a number of roads and his firefighters were already bringing back a continual stream of wet, cold and unhappy people, who were telling tales of ruined homes, dumped sea containers and drowned people. Slowly the water was receding and, as the roads became passable once more, the traffic slowly returned.

On his first recce from the fire station, Fred realised that he needed hi-visibility jackets and light sticks, in order to control the traffic. He stopped a car driving towards London from Canning Town.

"How far have you come?"

"From Plaistow," the driver replied.

"Isn't it all flooded up there?"

"Well, yes! It is. I've had to skirt round the worst parts on Prince Regent Lane until I reached Newham Way."

"What's the state of the road?"

"Everything to my right seems to be under water. I guess that Bow Creek will have burst its banks. But a lot of Newham Road is elevated and most of it's clear. When I was stuck in traffic at the Canning Town flyover, the bloke in the car next to me said that the river had burst its banks and flooded the City Airport. He had been trying to get to the university campus in North Woolwich but couldn't get very far."

"Thanks. That's really helpful. How far are you going?"

"Hoping to get to Whitechapel."

"With the tide now going out, you should be OK." Fred informed him that he should find the road free of water from Limehouse onwards but suggested that he should proceed with great care.

In considering his options, he realised that the Salvation Army Citadel and the Seaman's Rest would quickly fill up and might only be useful on a temporary basis. It would be necessary to organise a more specific destination for all the people that he and many others would be bringing northwards from the flood. Without light and without telephones, it was rather like punching in the dark. He knew that Newham General Hospital was not far and he considered trying to utilise Leyton Orient Football Club at Brisbane Road and the old West Ham ground at Upton Park. He would have to organise transport, drivers and carers, until someone else arrived to take over operations.

It was now half past seven. The tide was ebbing fast and the river banks were returning to normal. Fred decided to return to his HQ at the fire station to assess the overall situation. When he got back, he was advised that because the water had receded the inflatables could no longer be used. Instead, his team were using the station's fleet vehicles as well as commandeering the school's minibus. They were bringing back far more people. He went to the Seaman's Rest, where found the staff well organised, handing out warm blankets and drinking water. He saw that Dinah was assisting the warden. She excused herself and went over to Fred.

"Hi, Fred. How are things out there?"

"Improving. But there's still no light and there's an enormous amount of rubbish strewn about all over the place."

"Is it hampering the rescue parties?"

"Well, the big sea containers that have been dumped on the roads by the wave aren't helping. So, we're having to drive about quite slowly. There's also a lot of dead bodies just lying about!"

"That's dreadful," Dinah responded.

"Listen, Fred!" she continued. "Very soon, we'll be inundated with people. Mary is running things at the Citadel. It's basically the same over there. You're going to have to take these people somewhere else very soon."

"Yes, I realise that. I'll have to make contact with Newham General Hospital. We'll have to requisition some buses and start the transfers immediately." He stopped and looked at his wife. "What's the situation towards the river?"

"Your guys have told me that many houses have been totally destroyed. It's almost as though something big has rolled through the estates like a combine harvester. I expect containers from Tilbury and Thameshaven have been swept into the water by that wave and they've just destroyed everything in front of them. It's difficult to tell in the dark, of course, but already the guys have decided to ignore the bodies floating in the water. At the start, they pulled them to the boats, but each one they got was dead, some with horrific injuries. Arms or legs ripped off, one with its head completely missing."

"That's awful," Fred muttered. "Are the guys OK?"

"Not really, but they are coping. But the good news is that the teams who were waiting to come on shift have all arrived early and are already staging those that were on the boats."

"Thanks, Dinah. I know this isn't really your job, but I do appreciate what you're doing." He checked his watch and was surprised to see that it was already nearly eight o'clock.

"The tide will be flowing out very fast now."

"What are you thinking?"

"The teams will have to take extra care, because the water will also be draining off the land. Look around. Very soon, these guys will be able to walk up the A12 and that'll relieve the pressure considerably."

As Fred and Dinah were talking, the lights flickered and then came on.

Martin Havers and his family, together with a few of their neighbours, gathered near the gate next to Hadleigh Castle. They made up an odd collection of vehicles. Landrovers, tractors and trailers piled high with metal sheeting and corrugated iron, two diggers and more trailers crammed full with wooden posts, electrical cable and generators. They met at the gate just before six o'clock. In the moonlight, they could see that the river was flowing out very fast. The water was also draining off the land and Martin reckoned that they would be able to assess the damage to the seawall in about an hour. In the far distance, on the Kent side beyond the river estuary, they could see traffic moving on the main roads. The lights of the vehicles were the only indications of human activity.

"I'm not sure whether we'll be able to cross the railway line through the bridge. We might have to drive up the embankment and go over the top. If we have to do that, I suggest we try, over there, where the land rises up a little." Martin pointed a little way to the west of the bridge. "On the other side, it will be very boggy and we must keep to the grassy edge of the fields, especially when we turn towards the sea wall."

"What about the neighbouring farms?" James, ever practical, was already wondering whether his father's neighbours would also be gearing up. "I hope it won't be necessary to build a dyke between us."

"I don't think so." Martin considered carefully. "The further up Hadleigh Ray, the less damage will have been done. I doubt there'll be much flooding beyond Benfleet Yacht Club."

"Anyway, we'll soon know," said Charlie. "The tide's going out very quickly."

As they watched, they saw parts of the seawall slowly re-emerge from under the waves. The water was quickly draining off the land, but in the moonlight it was difficult to observe anything with any real clarity.

"Come on," said Martin. "Let's drive down the track to the railway line and check out the situation. And drive carefully!"

They started up the vehicles and slowly the convoy drove down the track, towards the railway embankment. The track leading under the bridge was still under water, but it was only about two feet deep.

They all stopped and Martin got out. Behind him, James was driving a tractor and trailer piled high with corrugated iron. He got out and joined his father.

"Do you think we can get through the bridge?"

"I'm not sure." Martin got his flashlight and walked through the muddy water to the bridge. "James, come over here!" he called his son.

"What do you reckon, Dad?"

"Well, you can see that the water has come through here with some force. Look there!" He pointed the flashlight at the brickwork foundations.

"They seem OK to me, Dad."

"Maybe. But I thought they looked rather bashed in," Martin replied, moving further under the bridge. "If the foundations have moved then the whole bridge will be unstable." He pointed his light upwards, where they both saw a large crack. "That's new."

They waded further and finally emerged on the far side, where they saw that the water had eroded some of the embankment itself. James pointed to the damage and said, "I don't fancy driving down this side of the embankment and finding it disappearing under my wheels. I'd rather take my chances with the bridge."

"Yes. I agree with you, but the first vehicle must be clear before the next starts through. I realise that will take time, but it'll be better to get all our equipment through now, rather than driving all the way round.

"And we must carefully watch the walls and the roof to make sure that the vibrations from the vehicles don't cause any further damage."

Before wading back through the bridge, Martin looked over towards the sea wall, planning the route for the vehicles. Even during their time assessing the bridge, he saw that the level of the water had reduced.

One by one, slowly and very carefully, they drove under the bridge and then, following Martin's instructions, turned right to follow the edge of the field alongside the embankment. Soon they came to the western edge of the first field. They continued to drive straight on, keeping as close to the railway embankment as possible. They came to and drove round a wooded, marshy pond, until they finally reached the far side of the second field. Here, Martin now turned left towards the sea wall. On his right, he knew that there was a drainage stream. Tonight, in the moonlight, he could see that it was still full of fast running water, but he remembered that, just before the stream reached the sea wall, it flowed into the long open ditch which runs parallel with the sea wall all the way from Benfleet to Leigh on Sea.

At the bottom of the field, there was a bridge on their right leading over the stream. In the next field, there was a second bridge built over a narrow part of the ditch, giving direct access to the track next to the sea wall. As he drove slowly down the slope of the field, Martin could see across the ditch where a powerful outflow of water was continuing to erode the wall. He knew that they wouldn't be able to do anything to close that gap until the force of the outflow of water had abated.

By the time the last of the vehicles reached the bridge over the ditch, the outflow of water was already reduced to a trickle. Charlie checked the generator and the electrical cabling, ready to set up as soon as his father crossed the ditch.

Martin walked up to the bridge over the ditch and, with his flashlight, carefully assessed whether it was still capable of bearing the weight of the other vehicles. He gingerly walked across but detected no adverse movement. He called James to come across to him.

"What's up?"

"I'm concerned about this bridge. It's always looked a bit flimsy. After all, it's only old concrete beams laid across the ditch. They seem firm enough to me and, if we can use it, we'll save an enormous amount of time. So, you're the practical one! What do you think?"

James took the flashlight and walked across the bridge. He noticed that the concrete beams were actually quite substantial and deeply embedded in the ground on both sides. Even though they had been immersed in the flood, they did not appear to have moved.

Looking to his left along the sea wall, he saw that the outflow had almost stopped and that they really needed to get on with the repair work.

"Dad!" he called over the ditch. "It looks OK to me."

"I'm glad you agree."

"The vehicles should take a good sweep round so that they approach the bridge straight on. That might be difficult, because the field will be very muddy."

"OK. We'll do that," his father replied.

Martin got back into the Landrover and engaged 4 wheel drive. Driving forward he took a long loop to his right until he was facing the ditch and the bridge. James was still there and guided him safely over to the other side. He detected no movement of the concrete beams. The other vehicles, tractors and trailers copied Martin's manoeuvre and followed on behind.

Now on the south side, Martin turned to his left and drove towards the breach. He was surprised to see that the concrete pipe, which allowed the stream to flow under the track and the sea wall through a special sluice, was still firmly in place. He parked and got out, in order to climb up to the path on top of the wall. It was very wet, but it all seemed to be holding firm. From the top, he was able to see to his left that the breach was about fifty yards long. The sea wall had simply disappeared. He tried to see whether there were any other breaches, but although the moonlight was bright, he was unable to see with any clarity. He decided that he would drive along the track as soon as the repair work to this breach was underway.

The plans to repair the breach were already thought through. Martin knew that it was his responsibility to give precise instructions to the team. It would be vital to ensure that the edges of the wall, at both ends of the breach, were made as solid as possible and to be tied into the remaining wall. He was also aware that the repair across the gap would be very flimsy at first, but it was even more important to stop the sea from flowing back onto his land when the next tide came in.

He looked at his watch. It was now after seven o'clock. By midnight, the tide would have turned. He reckoned that they had a maximum of eight hours before the sea would be making its way across the mud flats towards the sea wall. If the breach was closed, then they would still be able to keep working from the landward side of the wall.

As he was finalising his plans, all the other vehicles slowly arrived. Charlie started the generator and connected the lights. The immensity of the task suddenly seemed to be overwhelming.

"Right!" Martin faced them all. "This is going to be a hell of a long night. It'll be dirty, cold, tiring and pretty miserable. The breach is about fifty yards wide. Fortunately that massive outflow of water doesn't appear to have damaged the track between the ditch and the wall.

"The first job is to drive stakes into the ground, evenly spaced, right across the breach. The stakes must be close enough to allow the metal sheeting to be laid up against them.

"Next, we'll lay the metal sheeting against the stakes on the seaward side. When the tide comes in, the pressure of the water will force the sheets against the stakes and they'll act as some sort of initial barrier.

"From the landward side, we will then build up the soil and mud against the metal sheets. You must be really careful not to knock the sheets over and remember, any earth that is put on the seaward side of the breach will just be washed away.

"James, can you organise the stakes? They are vital. Remember you must keep them close enough. Charlie, I want you to ensure that as much light is made available wherever it's needed. Can you run a second string from here to light the far end of the breach?"

"No problem, Dad."

"Good. Please do that. Are there any questions?"

They set to their tasks with a will.

Very soon row of stakes began to snake across the breach. Martin ensured that the first metal sheet was laid upright, mimicking the angle on the wall itself. He hammered it into the ground. Because the earth was very soft and wet, he was able to force it at least eighteen inches down into the ground.

He laid the next sheet crosswise against the upright, solid sheet and the first post. Helen was driving one of the two diggers. It had a big scoop. She began to back fill the space behind the metal sheet. As he watched her taking earth from the ditch and dumping it next to the metal sheet, Martin suddenly realised that the original sea wall must have been built using the earth from the landward side, which was how the ditch was made in the first place. Helen was now doing exactly the same, creeping slowly forward, as the stakes and the metal sheets were put into place.

Martin drove along the track to the far end of the breach. He had already concluded that the water had swept over the top of the sea wall, just at that dip which he and the boys noticed earlier that morning. Pouring over the top with an unstoppable and growing force, it had simply eroded the back of the sea wall, until the weight of earth was no longer able to keep out the sea and it had collapsed. He recalled the height of the wave as it rolled majestically up the river. He realised that the dip in the wall didn't really matter, because the wave had come over the wall along its entire length. The dip would simply have indicated a weakness, which was quickly exploited by the sea.

He knew that it was vital to seal the far end of the breach as well. Just as Charlie connected a second string of lights, Martin collected a metal sheet and again laid it upright, before hammering it into the soft ground. A second team joined him and began to hammer in more stakes and the second digger started to back fill as soon as the sheets were laid against the stakes.

Martin climbed up the wall to check on their progress. It was dreadfully slow. They had been already been working for about an hour and a half and the stakes had only covered about 30 yards. It would be quicker, of course, now they were working from both ends simultaneously, but the back filling was not keeping pace with the sheet laying.

Realising that he was now somewhat surplus to requirement, Martin decided to drive further along the track to check out whether there were any further breaches in the sea wall. Although the track was wet, he was able to drive its length to his boundary. There were no other breaches, but the fields were very wet and he fully understood that they would be contaminated. He returned, somewhat relieved, to the breach.

At ten o'clock, Jennifer Havers arrived with sandwiches and coffee. They all took a very welcome break.

"How did you find us?" Martin asked.

"I just followed all the tracks," she replied. "It really wasn't difficult. Oh! And you'll be pleased to know that power has been restored to the farm."

Once again, Martin climbed up the wall. Standing on the footpath, he looked over the river Thames towards Sheerness on the north Kent coast. As he stood there all was in darkness when, magically before his unbelieving eyes, the street lights came on. He looked to his right, but Canvey Island still remained dark. He slowly turned round and realised that power had been restored to Benfleet and Leigh on Sea. Away in the distance, he could see the lights of London creating a glow in the western sky.

"OK, everyone." He looked round at his dirty, tired family, friends and neighbours. "We must get on. It's quarter past ten. In an hour and a half, it will be Low Tide and then the water will start to come back in. We've got to speed up, especially with the back filling. Are you OK, Helen?"

"I'm fine, Dad," she replied and then pointed towards Hadleigh Castle. "Hey! Look over there! Someone else is coming."

Two sets of headlights were making their way down the slope from the ruined castle towards the railway line. They didn't wait to see who or what was coming, but went back to their back breaking work, in the full knowledge that if the tide came in before the breach was closed, the water could simply wash everything away. Scoop up, dump, scoop up, dump, flatten down; scoop up, dump, scoop up, dump, flatten down. It was monotonous, repetitive and mind numbing.

And then the cause of the lights appeared. Another two diggers had come to assist!

By midnight, all the stakes were in place and the metal sheets snaked across the gap. They looked very flimsy in the moonlight. Now that they were working with four diggers, the back filling was progressing much faster, but progress still appeared to be painfully slow. The extra diggers were placed in the middle of the breach and each began to work backwards towards either end of the breach. Even with this additional help, it would be a close run race between completion and the tide's return. The next High Tide was due at about six o'clock, but Martin knew that the gap must be closed at least two hours before then. Although he knew that the stake bashers and the metal sheet handlers were tired, he gave them all shovels, to ensure that the back filling work would speed up as much as was possible.

With their shoulders aching, their backs breaking, their legs trembling and their minds numb with cold, the gap slowly closed. There were insufficient of them, for anyone to have any significant rest so, each hour, Martin called a ten minute halt for the shovellers. Then, once more, he encouraged them back to work.

Slowly the line of earthworks extended across the gap until, unbelievably, at half past two in the morning, the far gap was closed. Although it was the middle of the night, Martin now tried his mobile and was somewhat surprised and relieved to find that he had a signal. He phoned the farm, where Jennifer immediately answered.

"How are you getting on?" she asked, as she answered the call.

"It's depressingly slow. I think we've closed about forty yards, so there are still ten to do. But the tide's coming in. With High Tide at about six o'clock, we must get the gap closed latest by half past three. That's in an hour."

"That's going to be tight, Martin. Are you OK?"

"We're all fine. It's cold and the work is really hard. I really need some hard core now, to bolster the earth works that we're building."

"Where on earth are you going to get that in the middle of the night?"

"Do you remember meeting that young chap at the Christmas Social? He's new round here, but he told me he was the manager of the Builder's Merchants in Benfleet."

"Yes, I do. His name is Wayne Maltravers."

"He gave me a business card. I put it into the office. I think I slipped it under the corner of the blotter pad."

"Yes. You did. It's here! His telephone number is a mobile."

Martin breathed a sigh of relief. "I thought it might be. I know it's nearly three o'clock in the morning, but can you get him up. Please ask if he can open up his site and provide any hard core that he might have available."

"I'll do my best." She rang off and Martin returned to the back breaking work of shovelling earth and helping to back fill the repaired sea wall.

175

After dropping off his passenger in the city, Andy swung his cab round and started his return journey towards the West End. He decided to drive down Aldersgate and was surprised to find that the intensity of the traffic was considerably reduced. He had a virtually clear run around St Paul's Cathedral south to Cannon Street, where he turned left. Because there were no street lights, nor traffic lights, he turned down Friday Street and then onto Queen Victoria Street and Blackfriars where, finally, he was able to turn right onto the Victoria Embankment. As he dropped down the slip road, he couldn't help but notice that the river was still exceptionally high and had obviously flooded over the river wall onto the road ahead. There was still water lying on the road and, with some horror, he realised that HMS President had been lifted from its moorings, as though by a malignant giant's hand, to be deposited partway over the road in front of him. The trees on the river bank had prevented the vessel from being pushed further across the road.

He stopped to consider his options. There was no traffic behind him. The road on his right was blocked by an abandoned lorry. He decided to carry on and, carefully, he drove past the wrecked vessel. Two hundred yards later he was approaching Temple Place with the Victoria Embankment Gardens on his right. He knew that HQS Wellington should be moored in the river just on his left, but it was no longer there. In his headlights, however, he could see that another boat was straddling the road ahead. Slowly, he drove forward to find the one of the pleasure boats from Temple Pier with its bow stove in, pointing into Temple Place with its stern still hanging over the broken river wall. The river water was still flooding over the road.

As he was carefully manoeuvring around the vessel, he saw four people sitting at the side of the road. He stopped.

"Are you guys OK?" he shouted.

"Not really." One of them, a burly man with a bushy beard, turned to Andy. "I've got three ladies here who are bruised, wet and dirty. We were all on this boat when it was swept from its moorings and into the road. It hit something really hard and then just settled here.

"There are still six other people on board, but we checked and they're all dead. Can you get us to a hospital?"

"There's no electricity in London at the moment, mate. The whole area is completely blacked out. But I might be able to get you all to a safer place where you'll be looked after."

"Cheers, mate!" The man waded through the water to open the back door of the cab, before helping his companions to get settled. "Where is this place?" he asked.

"A client of mine has a small hotel in Kensington. I'm going to take you there."

As Andy drove off, he looked at his watch. It was seven o'clock. He drove up Temple Place before turning left up Arundel Street towards the Strand. Near the junction with Lancaster Place, he saw another group of bedraggled pedestrians. One of them stepped out into the road to stop him.

Andy pulled over. "What's up?"

David leant into the cab and said, "I've got a small party here who were trapped in a bus. It was hit really hard by something from the river and knocked on its side, before being washed almost under Waterloo Bridge.

"Anyway, one lady is still unconscious, one old guy has a twisted ankle and another has broken his leg. This man's got a badly wrenched shoulder. There are three other ladies and another young lad besides me. We're all cold and really need to get some shelter quickly. You're the first car to have stopped. Can you help?"

Andy gestured in the back. "I've already got four, but I could take another couple."

"Where are you going? I mean it's getting really cold out here."

"I can see that! The Gloucester Palace Hotel. It's near Gloucester Road tube station." Andy looked at the lad and considered. "Listen, lad. Tell you what I'll do. I'll take the unconscious lady and the bloke with the broken leg and then I'll come back for the rest of you."

"Will it be helpful if we walk in the right direction?"

"Yeah! I guess it will." He pointed westwards down The Strand. "Keep walking that way. You'll finally get to the big roundabout near Trafalgar Square. Go under Admiralty Arch and keep walking along the Mall towards Buck House. I'll be as quick as I can."

After they loaded the man with the broken leg and the unconscious lady into the cab, with David leading, his dirty and bedraggled party started to walk slowly down the Strand towards Admiralty Arch. Andy drove off with his extra passengers, in the same direction. Within half an hour he arrived at the Gloucester Palace Hotel, where he stopped, got out of the cab and ran up the steps into the hotel. There was no one at the reception desk, so he walked down the corridor past the dining room to Sebastian Fortescue Brown's office. He could see a sliver of pale, flickering light under the door. He knocked.

A muffled voice called, "Come in," and Andy entered the room. Sebastian was seated behind his desk. The room was lit by four strategically placed candles. Seated in a chair on the near side of the desk was Fred the handyman.

"Hello, Andy. I certainly wasn't expecting to see you."

"No, sir. I've got a bit of a problem. It's absolute madness out there." He pointed dramatically to the door.

"Calm down. Take a deep breath and tell me why you're here," Sebastian interrupted.

"Thank you, Gov." Andy did as he was told.

"The river has burst its banks on both sides. I haven't been on the south side since I dropped you off earlier, but I have driven back into the city with a fare. The traffic was awful because there's no street lights and all the traffic lights are out.

"Anyway, on my way back, I was driving from Blackfriars down the Victoria Embankment. Stupid really, because of the water still on the road. Two of the boats that are moored in the river have been washed onto the road. I've no idea where HMS Wellington is, but it's not at its mooring.

"There were four people sitting on the banking above the pavement at the side of the road. They had been on one of the pleasure boats. It was washed out of the river onto the road. I've picked them up. Obviously, I should have taken them to a hospital, but with the blackout, it's really difficult to know what to do for the best. So I decided to bring them here because I thought you might have some room for them?

"Because of the mess on the road from the pleasure steamer near Temple station, I had to work my way up to the Strand where another group waved me down. They had an unconscious woman and a man with a broken leg. I've got them with me as well." Andy's report slowed to a halt as he looked at Sebastian.

Sebastian sat back in his chair and considered carefully what he had been told. He didn't particularly relish having his own sanctuary invaded by a load of strangers, over whom he would have no control. But, on the other hand, he could hardly turn them away. He was also canny enough to realise that he might even be able to gain a suitable degree of decent publicity, which might further enhance his growing reputation and also help to keep him out of the direct focus of the Authorities.

"Well, if they are outside in your cab, you'd better bring them in." Andy thanked Sebastian and left the office.

"Fred," Sebastian addressed his handyman. "You'll have to get Betty organised and we must see whether one of the girls might work the reception desk? We must also lock the door leading down to the cellar. I don't want anyone wandering down there. We'll need to know how many bedrooms we can use, as quickly as possible. I'll ask Chantelle to see if she'll help. I expect she will."

They both left the office and went up the stairs, Fred to his apartment and Sebastian to the second floor to knock on Chantelle's door. She answered the door very quickly. She was dressed in a blouse and skirt with a dressing gown to keep warm.

She smiled at Sebastian when she realised who was at the door. "Hello, Mr F B. What are you doing knocking at my door?"

"Good evening, Chantelle," Sebastian replied somewhat formally. "I wonder if you can give me a hand."

Very quickly, Seb explained the situation and, just as quickly, Chantelle understood. Even as he was explaining, she turned into her apartment and slipped on her shoes. She took off her dressing gown and replaced it with a warm cardigan. Quickly checking her hair and makeup in the mirror by her door, she followed Seb to the stairs.

As they emerged onto the ground floor, they saw Andy, with one of the pleasure boat's crew, struggling up the steps with the unconscious lady. They approached the reception desk and Chantelle passed over a registration card and a pen.

"Is that really necessary?" Andy asked.

"Yes, Andy, it is. Not necessarily for our records, but more to assist the emergency services when they arrive." Seb turned to the girl and said, "Chantelle, as well as listing the names, addresses and other contact points, you must make a specific note of the allocated rooms and the potential injuries. Ah! Here's Fred."

Sebastian took Fred away from the desk and they discussd quietly the availability of the rooms. He quickly made a note on a piece of paper and passed it to Chantelle. Fred also reported that Betty was already making sure that the rooms were open and available. He also advised Sebastian that he would nip down to the cellar and secure the door.

"Right, Andy!" Sebastian returned to the desk, as the other bedraggled passengers from Andy's cab made their way through the front door, half carrying and half dragging the man with the broken thigh.

"We've got no power, so the lift doesn't work," he announced. "I'm afraid the injured are all going to have to be carried up to the second floor. If you want to make use of the lounge rooms, behind the reception area, that's fine. I'll leave you to sort that out yourselves. I expect that you'll want to get the lady into a bed as quickly as possible."

"Thanks, Gov," Andy replied. "This guy here will organise all that." He indicated the man who had flegged him down on the Embankment. "I've got to get back to pick up those other people that I left on the Strand."

He turned, left the hotel and got back into his cab. As he turned it round, several street lights suddenly flickered and lit up. Driving towards the Cromwell Road, he glanced in his mirror at the hotel and saw that its lights were working. His journey back to Knightsbridge and Hyde Park Corner was without incident. The traffic was virtually non-existent and, very soon, on the Mall he saw the rest of the group walking slowly towards Buckingham Palace.

Huddersfield was in a real mess. With the ambient temperature rising rapidly, the snow was quickly turning to slush. Where it was lying on the roads and pavements, the car tracks and the footprints first compacted the snow to ice. Following the temperature rise, a film of water covered that ice and this made the roads lethal. On the major arterial roads, there were a number of accidents and these, in turn, caused major blockages.

On the positive side, however, power was now restored.

In the hills surrounding Marsden, the snow was rapidly melting. As the ground was already sodden with the continuous autumn rain, the meltwater simply flowed over the surface and collected in the small streams. These quickly built up into raging torrents, emptying into the three reservoirs situated to the south of Marsden. The most southerly, Wessenden Reservoir, was already full and Wessenden Brook was hardly able to cope with the outflow, especially when it was joined by the increased torrential meltwater in Blake Clough. This joint inflow created a significant increase in the level of the water in Blakeley Reservoir. A wave, some three feet high, passed down the length of the reservoir.

The amount of meltwater flowing off the hillsides into the Wessenden valley was now converging on Butterley Reservoir, which had recently been subject to the upgraded concrete slipway. Following all the autumnal rain, it was already full. As with Blakeley Reservoir, a wave some three feet in height, now swept down Butterley Reservoir to the clay dam wall and the new slipway. This sudden increased weight of water was too much for the slipway to carry. Water is a massively destructive force and will always seek an outlet in its attempt to flow downwards. A slow trickle appeared between the new concrete slipway and the dam itself. The increased pressure of water forced its way into that small crack, which widened and deepened, until there was a stream of water jetting through the dam wall itself.

The snow was lying several feet deep all over the whole of Marsden Moor and the meltwater continued to flow into the Wessenden valley, maintaining an intolerable pressure on the dam wall. Without warning, a complete section of the wall gave way and the water immediately flowed out through the new gap, eroding the dam wall even more, before sweeping into the valley below. The breach widened and the wall of water swept down the valley between Mount Road and Binn Road, sluicing away the sheds of the old derelict textile mill, carrying that debris across the roundabout at the end of Carr Road. With no respite, the water flowed over the Marsden Football Club and the derelict land behind the old fire station.

After crossing the main Manchester Road, the wall of water swept down Peel Street and across Brougham Road, before finding the river Colne itself. Many houses in the town centre were flooded and some even received structural damage, before the floodwater found its way into the river. The flood water now followed the course of the river Colne in the valley bottom eastwards from Marsden to Huddersfield. Trees and natural vegetation were ripped away and the river banks were badly eroded.

The flow of water, however, was basically contained by the main road, the A62 on the south side and the Huddersfield Narrow Canal and the Manchester to Leeds railway line to the north. As the valley naturally widened at Sparth Reservoir, the intensity of the flood lessened somewhat as the water spread right across the valley. Here it even inundated the Huddersfield Narrow Canal.

The flood waters divided and flowed to the north and south of the derelict Cellars Clough Mill and again at Holme Mills, before reforming as the valley narrowed once again. As the river reached Slaithwaite, the valley narrowed considerably, forcing the flood water to deepen and flow even faster. It thundered into the western part of the village, dividing once again as it reached and flooded the ground floor of Upper Mill and the houses lining the banks of the canal. Forcing its way across Britannia Road, causing considerable damage to the road bridge as it passed, the wall of water inundated the timber yard, before washing away the council's entire winter salt reserves. Timber, washed free from the timber yard, was now floating down the river in the flood water, breaking through the fence surrounding the chemical works, before destroying large storage tanks, adding a toxic mix of chemicals to the water.

Once again, the valley widened as the flooded river swept past Titanic Mill in Linthwaite, before narrowing significantly, as it reached Milnsbridge. Although the overall intensity of the flood was slackening, the water was now badly contaminated. Trees, timber and other debris flowed past the Aldi supermarket in Milnsbridge, where the flood undermined the supports to the road bridge, before sweeping on towards Longroyd Bridge and Huddersfield.

Back at Butterley Dam, the wall, although badly damaged, still held back the greater part of the water in the reservoir. The breach was thirty feet across and some twelve feet deep. The intensity of the outflow quickly slackened as the water level in reservoir lowered, but the meltwater from the hills surrounding Marsden, however, would sustain local flooding throughout the length on the Colne Valley from Marsden all the way to the outskirts of Huddersfield for several days. Once the initial intensity of the flood had swept through the township, the local Marsdeners were able to mop out their cellars and to divert the rest of the water away from the town centre.

Fortunately for Christine and Robert Sykes, they were already driving away from Marsden before the dam was breached. Their successful intervention was ensuring that their contacts were busily knocking up their neighbours and, by word of mouth, the urgency of the situation was brought to most householders living under the dam wall and in the immediate path of possible danger. The surgery was open and all the old folk in Wessen Court were now safely upstairs.

Their job done, Robert turned the car round and drove back down the valley towards Slaithwaite. Christine reminded Robert that they should go into the village and try to warn people on Howgate Road and in the centre of the village. Once again, they were willingly helped by local people who promised to pass the word to their neighbours.

After knocking on a couple of doors on Bridge Street, Robert got back into the car. He could hear a muffled roar as the wave of destruction entered Slaithwaite at the western end of the village. They could hear the noise getting closer as he started the car and drove over the canal bridge up towards New Street. As he glanced to his left, he saw the wave of flood water coming towards him. He gunned the engine and drove up Cross Street past the Town Hall. As he reached Carr Lane, the floodwater started to lap at his rear wheels, but as quickly as it had come, the water began to recede.

"Bloody hell!" he exclaimed. "That was right close."

"We'll have to go home," Christine replied. "There's nothing more we can do now."

"We're on the wrong side of the river." Robert turned left to Slaithwaite centre. "I'm not too sure that the Britannia Road Bridge will be safe. I'll have a look, but I expect we're going to have a bugger of a journey home."

Chief Superintendent Bleasdale sat at his desk in Scotland Yard. After returning from his visit to Mr Chao, he wrote up his report. He still believed that, despite assurances to the contrary, Mr Chao was well aware of the people involved in smuggling illegal immigrants into the country. He fully appreciated that Mr Chao, himself, would not be directly involved. After all, Kevin knew Mr Chao's history and his abhorrence of people smuggling and slavery. Even so, Kevin did believe that Mr Chao was most unlikely to turn down an opportunity to turn a profit.

Over the previous thirty years or so, their relationship had blossomed. In his early days in the Metropolitan Police, Constable Bleasdale made it plain to Mr Chao that, if he kept his business legitimate, he would receive little interference from the police. Indeed, for a reasonable and regular consideration, PC Bleasdale himself would ensure a degree of protection for Mr Chao and that he would be treated somewhat differently from the rest of the Soho underworld. Consequently, Mr Chao was able to build his empire in real estate with little attention from the authorities. In addition to his quarterly consideration, whenever the opportunity arose Mr Chao was also expected to feed Kevin with accurate and appropriate information.

To their mutual satisfaction, this arrangement continued to flourish through the years. It was somewhat ironic that Chief Superintendent Kevin Bleasdale's career prospects were so much improved that he was now the senior officer leading the police inquiry into illegal immigration, asylum seekers and modern human slavery.

Nevertheless, as Kevin Bleasdale gained promotion through the ranks, he found it increasingly difficult to maintain both the necessary professional contact with Mr Chao, as well as collecting in person his quarterly pay off. This dilemma began to weigh heavily on his mind. With his career blossoming, the secret payments were becoming somewhat difficult to collect. Kevin fully realised that, should he be found out, his whole career would be over and that he and his family would be thrown to the wolves.

It was rather fortunate, therefore, that he was able to resolve his disquiet when a newly employed, young Woman Police Officer was seconded to his department in Scotland Yard. A minor indiscretion on her part had been brought to his attention. She was short, with dark red hair and sparkling blue eyes. Her uniform set off her slight figure to perfection and Kevin had been captivated from the moment he first saw her.

Her indiscretion involved the non-reporting of a personal parking ticket but, in order to resolve it, Kevin inappropriately pulled rank, took her into his office and threatened her with dismissal. Although WPC Elizabeth Drury was young, she was also very canny. She immediately realised that such a trivial incident was being blown out of proportion and that made her believe that there must be some other underlying reason for his behaviour. There was! Like a thunderclap on a warm, sunny summer's day, the penny dropped for Kevin when he realized that WPC Liz Drury was the answer to his problems.

Thereafter, every three months or so, WPC Drury would travel by bus and in plain clothes to Soho, where she exchanged one locked metal briefcase for another heavier one with the receptionist in Mr Chao's office. On her return to Scotland Yard, she would deposit the case in the boot of Chief Superintendent Bleasdale's car. She was instructed to use public transport for this mission, so that no trace of the journey would be logged.

Naturally, she didn't know the contents of the briefcase and was sensible enough never to enquire about them. On the first occasion, however, her natural curiosity overcame her inherent caution but when she tried to open it, she found that the case was locked. After completing that first mission, she was carefully questioned by the then Inspector Bleasdale whether she had looked inside the briefcase. She brazenly lied, saying that it was none of her business and that she was quite content simply to do as she was bidden. During that exchange, Kevin Bleasdale watched her very closely and concluded that she had indeed tried to open the case but, finding it locked, she was able to remain calm and relaxed and, consequently, was able to lie convincingly. For her part, she resolved never again to try to open the case. That evening they went to dinner, followed by a show and afterwards Kevin stayed over in her small apartment in Fulham. That was the start of a relationship which, although it never developed into anything deeper, was continued to their mutual satisfaction and convenience.

On that Thursday, neither Chief Superintendent Bleasdale nor his catspaw WPC Drury could have known that her bus would have been side swiped by a tourist boat and then swamped by a freak wave, the result of two intense, colliding sea surges way out in the North Sea. It was, perhaps, somewhat fortunate that WPC Drury recovered consciousness before David and Jackie started to move the passengers up the steps to Lancaster Place and then towards the Strand. Not knowing the whereabouts of his junior officer, Kevin Bleasdale busied himself, finalising action plans for the protection and rescue of the public that would be rolled out as soon as conditions around Scotland Yard were sufficiently improved. He would have been really amazed to know that his junior officer and part time lover had been saved from drowning by his own daughter and her boyfriend.

He was sitting at his desk when, all of a sudden, the lights flickered and came on as power was restored. He walked to the window and looked down at the road below. He could now see that the iron gates and fencing at each end of Richmond Terrace were severely damaged. All the cars, parked so neatly earlier that afternoon, were now piled up in a small mountain of buckled metal and broken glass against the gates near the junction with Whitehall. He strode to the door of his office, opened it and turned left into the corridor. At the far end, he entered an open office where the teams were busily re-booting their computers and other communication equipment.

"Listen up!"

As soon as he had their attention, he began to issue instructions to the teams for the immediate protection of London. Links were to be established at once with the office of the London Mayor and the various Borough Councils; details were given for the patrols to seek out and extract people in danger; above all instructions were given for their own protection.

"We need to assess the damage to the river banks as quickly as possible. Where there is obvious damage, the breaches may well have to be shored up before the next tide. This is not, I repeat, not a time for following all the normal protocols. This is a time for action, for using your initiative to make immediate decisions based on the facts as presented at the scene; for the saving of lives; and for the protection of property. Requisition whatever you need and, for the love of God, keep as complete a record as you can of all that you do and see.

"Report back here by radio and mobile phone as often as possible. A log will also be kept of each and every conversation.

"Make no mistake, as soon as they realise that there are easy pickings out there, every towrag in London will be on the streets, nicking, looting and causing problems.

"I cannot tell you when you will next get off duty but, rest assured, you will be joined by as many other officers as I can muster. A complete record will be kept of all the hours that you do and I will ensure that no one will be out on patrol longer than is necessary before being relieved. I will also despatch to you any relevant information that is received here.

"You'll have to do all this on foot, of course. All the vehicles parked on Richmond Terrace have been smashed up against the Whitehall gates and I expect that all other vehicles in the garage will be flooded. Teams will be sent down to extract them and make them roadworthy as quickly as possible.

"Finally, I don't want to lose any of you. Do not work alone. Stay in pairs and watch each other's backs. Be careful! This flood will have left weakened walls, unsafe road surfaces, as well as undermined buildings. Log them all, however insignificant, and report them back here."

Forty officers left immediately, using the stairs because they were still unable to trust the lifts. Outside, two teams of fifteen turned down Richmond Terrace towards the river, while the third team of ten turned left towards the cars piled haphazardly against the gates leading into Whitehall. After exiting Richmond Place, that team turned then left down Whitehall, walking swiftly towards Parliament Street and the Houses of Parliament.

As the last officer left the room, Chief Superintendent Bleasdale returned to his office, thinking, *I wonder where on earth Liz has got to. She would have been on her way back from Soho when the wave struck. I hope to God that she's OK.*

The tide continued to ebb, leaving in its wake stranded containers, beached vehicles and tons of unidentifiable debris. As the water drained from the housing estates of Fulham, Chiswick and Pimlico, the devastation caused by the floating containers became frighteningly clear. Slowly, area by area, power returned to the street lights and, as the survivors opened their doors, they witnessed scenes more in keeping with Dante's worst nightmares. In the stark street light, they could now see the indiscriminate nature of the destruction. In one particular street, all the houses on the left hand side were completely demolished from one end to the other, while on the right hand side there was no damage at all. In another, two containers had been swept across all the side roads that lead towards the river from the New King's Road in Fulham. The destroyed houses were completely missing with no sign of any household goods, or even rubble, as it had simply been sluiced away. Some of the remaining houses were in a precarious state, having received side swipes from passing detritus, bringing down parts of their walls. All the cellars and basements were flooded. Two containers had even come to rest in the gardens between Foskett Road and Cristowe Road, Fulham, ironically next to the office of Kensington and Chelsea Property Maintenance.

On the south bank, as the wave arrived carrying the heavy sea containers from the docks at Tilbury and Thames Haven, it caused great devastation to the housing estates around Abbey Wood, where the housing is a mixture of traditional terraced streets and more modern brick homes. The water inundated the land from Erith to Thamesmead, as far south as Abbey Road and the railway line. As in Fulham and Putney, the heavy containers, turning over and over at the front of the wave, had mown an indiscriminate swathe through the housing estates, leaving some houses completely untouched whilst others were totally wrecked.

Now that the water was receding, in the moonlight the damage was plain to see. There are many tower blocks on the south bank, some of which were built years ago, in the 1960s, as part of London's slum clearance programme. Their foundations were not as strong as might be expected today. Over the years, many of these towers had been poorly maintained and, as a consequence, they were unable to resist the power of the flooding water and the continual pounding of heavyweight detritus. Several collapsed completely while others, after their ground floors were compromised, collapsed slowly around the central column.

Further west, however, the disastrous effect of the floating containers was considerably diminished by the main railway lines coming into London from the south east. The Thameslink line, from Bromley and New Cross, joins the main line from Bexley just to the east of The Den, home of Millwall Football Club. The lines are already elevated from ground level and they cross innumerable road bridges as they approach London Bridge and Cannon Street stations on the north side of the river.

After passing Deptford and leaving it predominately unscathed, the surge swept across Southwark, Walworth and Vauxhall. The railway line, however, effectively filtered out many of the heavy containers, leaving them scattered, with no sense of order, on top of but mainly alongside the embankment from Tooley Street in the north to Deptford Park in the south. The wave, however, was high enough and strong enough to wash a few over the railway lines themselves, but much of their destructive momentum was diminished and they sank.

The water itself, of course, was forced through the bridges under such considerable pressure that many of the uprights were simply washed away and, in some cases, this allowed the actual weight of the bridges to sag, fall in on themselves and break up. Cars, vans and other debris were then swept through the gaps, where they caused considerable damage to the infrastructure in and around the Elephant and Castle.

Water was now draining rapidly from the flooded areas on both sides of the river, leaving behind a trail of devastated buildings, dumped vehicles and abandoned containers. In addition, there were thousands upon thousands of drowned bodies.

Chapter 16
Friday Morning – Before Dawn

The weather, after the high winds, snow and rain of the previous few days, was now calm. An anticyclone had formed over much of the British Isles, although the country was still being affected differently in Scotland and in England.

The temperature across Scotland was cold, with a gentle northerly breeze bringing with it cold Arctic air. This was resulting in ice and frost in all exposed areas. In England and the south, however, the anticyclone was drawing warm air from the Mediterranean and North Africa. The temperatures were unseasonably high and all the lying snow was rapidly melting. From Yorkshire in the north to the Channel coast in the south, there was local flooding as rivers were simply unable to cope with the amount of melt water. They burst their banks, making local roads impassable and many low lying housing estates were inundated.

Huddersfield experienced its first major flood in over 100 years. The breach in the Butterley Dam in Marsden created a flood wave which left behind severe structural damage in the centres of Marsden, Slaithwaite and Milnsbridge. All the bridges crossing the river Colne were damaged, as well as many of the bridges crossing the Huddersfield Narrow Canal. The water flooded the cellars of shops, offices and houses along the length of the river from Marsden, through Huddersfield and to its confluence with the already swollen river Calder at Cooper Bridge near Bradley.

Where the river Colne turns north and skirts the east side of Huddersfield, the engineering works on St Andrew's Road were overwhelmed, as was the relatively new football stadium, home to Huddersfield Town Football Club and the Huddersfield Giants. The surge water followed the river valley north easterly until it reached the river Calder, which was already in spate from the melting snow on the hills above Halifax, Hebden Bridge and Todmorden. The conjoined rivers now flooded all the low lying land from Mirfield, as far as Dewsbury and Wakefield.

In London, Low Tide arrived just before midnight, with the next High Tide scheduled for six in the morning. The sun would rise just after seven o'clock.

Martin Havers, with his children, neighbours and friends, laboured throughout the night. The breach was finally closed at just after half past three in the morning. Glistening in the moonlight, Martin could see the tide returning. It was already washing over the mudflats below the breach and creeping inexorably towards their puny row of stakes and metal sheets.

Soon after the breach was closed, Charlie called his father. "Dad! There are five or six more vehicles coming down the track." Martin turned to see the first set of headlights disappear below the railway embankment. As he watched, he saw the headlights reappear through the arch of the bridge. In the stillness of the morning, they could all hear the throbbing of the diesel engines, but the lead vehicle didn't appear on the near side of the railway line. For some reason it had stopped.

Martin stared and tried to make sense of what was happening. James walked up to him.

"I think these must be the trucks with the hard core."

"Yes," Martin replied. "But why have they stopped? And why is the driver revving his engine so much?"

"It looks as though he's stuck. But how?"

Suddenly it all became plain as, with a terrifying rumble, the rest of the bridge collapsed onto the truck. The obstruction to the truck was obviously freed, because the driver was now able to drive out from under the tracks. He came through slowly but steadily. As the dust cleared, they realised that there was a new, wider gap in the embankment, through which Martin and the others could see all the other trucks lined up, waiting their turn to come through.

"Come on, James. We'll have to get up there to see what's happened."

Martin turned to the nearest Landrover and got in behind the wheel. James was only just able to slam the passenger door before Martin set off. After his earlier inspection of the sea wall, the vehicle was already facing towards the bridge across the ditch. Once back on the landward side of the ditch, he turned right and crossed the bridge over the stream before turning left up the track to the railway line. A couple of minutes later, the cause of the problem was clear to them both. The top of the jib of the truck's crane, used for lifting bags of material on and off its flat bed, had caught the roof of the bridge. Not realising that it was already unstable, the driver had simply tried to force his way through, only to get stuck. As he revved his engine, at first the crane only dislodged a couple of bricks, but these made the roof that much more unstable so that more bricks were dislodged until, finally, the whole bridge collapsed.

Martin and James got out and hurried over to the driver's cab. The driver was already pulling the truck clear of the destroyed bridge, leaving behind a huge pile of rubble, effectively cutting off all the other vehicles.

"Is anyone hurt?"

"Nope. My cab was already clear this side. Mind you, it took some effort to get through, with all that rubble. And it's now blocking access for all the other trucks."

"Is Wayne with you?"

"Yeah. But he's still on the other side, mate."

Martin turned to James. "Get hold of Helen. We need her digger here, right now, to clear all this rubble."

"OK, Dad."

"And it's really important that this truck and its hard core get to the breach to offload, as quickly as possible. The extra rubble on the truck can also be used as extra hard core. This truck must come back straightaway to get loaded with more of that rubble from the bridge." He pointed at the remains of the bridge. "Hopefully, that'll soon allow the other trucks to get through. Go with this driver and make absolutely sure that he gets over the ditch OK. After that, you must stay to supervise the offloading. I was hoping to start off loading in the middle of the breach but, with this lot here, we'll have to start at the near end because I need this truck back here as quickly as possible."

"Right, Dad." He raised his hand. "Helen's answering now." James repeated all the instructions to his sister and they heard, while he was still talking, the digger start up and they watched it move towards the bridge. "She's on her way. I'll get off." With that, he climbed up into the passenger seat of the truck.

Martin began to make his way through the dusty destroyed bridge. Only the railway lines, with some sleepers still precariously attached, remained and they were sagging rather disconcertingly. As he emerged on the other side, he saw Wayne Maltravers.

"Wayne." Martin shook his hand. "I can't thank you enough for turning out."

"That's OK, Mr Havers." Wayne turned to look at the gap where the bridge had been. "How the hell are we going to get through there?"

"My daughter, Helen, has been using a digger to scoop up earth to back fill the temporary sea wall that we've built across the breach. She's now on her way back here. She'll dig her way through the rubble, dumping it on the back of the truck that's already got through. The truck should nearly be at the wall by now. One way or another, we'll get all your trucks through here and, into the bargain, we've gained all this extra rubble."

Wayne chuckled. "You certainly know how to look on the bright side, Mr Havers."

"It's Martin. Call me Martin, Wayne." He smiled grimly. "The problem we've really got is time. The tide is already coming in, so we've only got a couple of hours at most to shift this lot."

"Well I've got a digger coming as well."

"Really? How far away is it?" Martin looked up the hill towards the ruined castle,

"I expect it'll be another ten minutes or so."

The dust had now dispersed and one of the other drivers, who had climbed up the embankment, called down, "Jack's on his way back, Wayne." At the same time they heard the engine of Helen's digger as she arrived back at the bridge. She immediately assessed the situation and began to clear the pile of rubble, dumping it behind her on the field itself. She also used the shovel to knock down and break up the concrete sleepers.

As soon as Jack returned with the flatbed truck, he turned it round ready to be loaded before the return trip to the seawall. Helen now loaded the rubble onto the truck, trying to spread the load as evenly as possible. The rubble was a mixture of broken bricks, old black cement and the coarsely crushed limestone from the rail track. It seemed to be an impossible task to complete before the tide was back. However, Jack had also come back with three of the Martin's neighbours, together with their shovels.

As soon as Jack's flat bed was full once more, he set off back to the wall. While the shovellers enjoyed a brief rest, they heard Wayne's digger arrive. The driver started to work at once clearing rubble from the north side and began to make an immediate impression because his digger shovel was twice the size of Helen's. Within twenty minutes, he was able to drive through the shattered bridge, with a load ready for Jack's next return. Behind him, one by one, the other trucks drove through the cleared bridge and made their way down to the sea wall.

Martin looked at his watch. It was quarter to five and High Tide was due in an hour. He scratched his head and phoned James.

"Where's the tide?"

"It's already part way up the temporary wall, Dad. We need more hard core, urgently. The other trucks are just arriving. They will offload from the centre to the far end."

"OK." Martin turned to Wayne. "I've got to get back to the wall. James says they need more hard core. Is there any chance that your guys can get more down here? If we can keep the sea water flowing over the top to a minimum, we'll still be able to keep dumping more rubble, even as we approach High Tide."

"Thought you might ask that, Martin. My depot at Benfleet is already cleaned out, so I called my mate at Chelmsford. He's rousted out at least eight more trucks and they should be arriving very soon."

As he was speaking, they all heard a truck's bull horn from further up the hill, beyond the ruined castle. They could see the lights of a new convoy on its way down the track from the farm. Martin put his hands to his head and muttered, "Thank God for that."

Just after ten o'clock in the evening, the two military columns entered London one from the M3, the other from the M4. They were in constant radio contact with each other and with their bases. Arriving at broadly the same time, they were confronted with no street lighting nor traffic lights. It was rather fortunate that virtually all of the civilian traffic was driving out of London, so neither column had any real obstruction until they reached their initial objectives.

The column from the M3 was deployed to the southern bank and instructed to assess the damage to the river defences from the Thames Barrier westwards to Waterloo. The column from the M4 was deployed to the northern bank and instructed to assess the damage from the Thames Barrier westwards to the city.

The two commanding officers, already in close contact with each other, could see each other's columns across the river as they set up their temporary headquarters, one on the north side in the now ruined Thames Barrier Park, with the other on the south side at the Barrier Control Building. The Barrier itself was still in place. Both HQs were up and running by 02.00 hours and their work was considerably eased when, within an hour of arrival, power was connected.

The immediate assessment, made in the dark, was that the inundation had washed away much of the park itself. The Control Building on the south side, however, was still in place, but only because it had deep, solid foundations.

Inside the Control Building, they found Barrier staff marooned on the top floor. The first task was to make an urgent assessment of the Barrier itself. Teams on both sides of the river broke out inflatables and, together with Barrier staff members, set out from both river banks to check the piers. After each inspection, the individual barrier between each pair of piers was lowered. They immediately reported that the Thames Barrier was still in good working order but that each individual barrier had received a considerable battering during the flood. This information was forwarded to the Ministry of Defence and to Downing Street.

Both teams also observed the large number of sunken containers littering the river bed. On the seaward side, until they could all be cleared, they would remain a considerable hazard to shipping. On the London side, even in the moonlight, they could see individual containers that had been washed over the Barrier itself, lying higgledy-piggledy in the mud of the river bed.

Acting on the advice of the Barrier management and with the agreement of the Environment Agency, it was agreed to keep the Barrier raised until after High Tide scheduled at just after six o'clock that Friday morning.

Both teams were now tasked to assess the river banks. The Barrier staff overrode the original instructions from the Ministry of Defence and insisted that it was necessary to check the flood defences on both river banks below the Barrier. From the Barrier to the Woolwich Ferry, for many years both banks had been protected with iron pilings. The sea surge had completely washed over these, so it was now important to confirm whether they were still in place, how badly damaged, or even destroyed. Much of the domestic housing on both banks suffered flood damage from the inundation as well as specific and massive structural destruction from the rolling, tumbling containers. On the north bank, just down river from the Barrier itself, the Tate and Lyle refinery was unable to avoid being totally destroyed, as was the London City Airport just to the north at Silvertown.

As both teams of soldiers worked their way down river from the Barrier to the Ferry piers, they quickly realised that the iron pilings were basically still in place and had suffered no specific damage. The piers for the Ferry, however, were no longer in place, as they had been completely swept away. With the water now draining rapidly off the land, the stench of kerosene from the devastated airport was a confirmation of the damage done both to the aircraft and the fuel storage tanks. After making their reports, both teams were instructed to return to the Barrier and start their assessments of the river defences westwards towards the centre of London.

Slowly, led by David and Jackie, the bedraggled group walked down the Strand, towards Trafalgar Square. As they approached the cobbled square outside the Amba Hotel at Charing Cross, the street lights started to come on. They could now see Admiralty Arch beyond the statue of Charles I sitting proudly on his horse. A few minutes later, they passed through the arch into The Mall, where they could see and smell the mud and other detritus on Horse Guards Parade and in St James Park. Now that the water was receding, they noticed more and more drowned bodies deposited with no dignity whatsoever all over the grass. Their progress was painfully slow, because the old man with the injured ankle needed to be supported. When they set off, Jackie and the Bulgarian girl put his arms over their shoulders and half carried him between them.

David was at the front with the other lady, whose briefcase they had recovered, while the man with the wrenched shoulder walked behind the group with the Bulgarian boy.

"We should be checking to see whether any of these people need our help." The lady commented to David, as they walked down the Mall.

"I know, but I think it's best if we get this party to shelter first and then we can reassess the situation."

"I expect you're right. Anyway, why are you in London this evening?"

"I'm revising for my 'A' levels at the moment and to attempt a decent General Studies paper, I've been tracking these recent storms as they crossed the Atlantic. When I read the message put out by the Environment Agency I realised that there would be problems today and I just wanted to see it for myself. I suggested to Jackie that we bunk off school and come here."

"So what has caused all this?"

David explained about the two weather fronts and the creation of the sea surge.

When he finished, he added, "But, I had no idea that it would be as big as that." He turned to the lady and asked, "Anyway, what do you do?"

"I'm a Woman Police Constable, working out of Scotland Yard."

"Oh! That's interesting. You might know Jackie's father." David remarked.

"Is Jackie your girlfriend?"

"Yes." David thought about it for a further second and repeated, "Yes, she is. And she's been really fantastic, helping me get all these people out of the bus."

"So, who's her father?"

"Chief Inspector Bleasdale. Do you know him?"

"Well, he's well known at the Yard for his work in the Illegal Immigrant Department," she replied somewhat disingenuously. She quickly changed the subject. "How soon do you think the taxi will come back?"

"If it comes back at all."

Just as David was responding, Andy's cab did a U turn next to them and drew up besides the kerb. They all squeezed into the back. The man with the wrenched shoulder and the man with the damaged ankle sat on the pull down seats with their backs to the driver. The WPC, Jackie and the two Bulgarians sat on the main bench seat, while David sat on the floor between Jackie and the policewoman.

"Won't be long before we get there," Andy announced cheerfully. "There's very little traffic about, but I suppose that'll change as people realise this part of London has mainly missed the flooding."

"Have there been any news announcements yet?" the WPC asked.

"The radio's still dead and I haven't had an opportunity to check my phone."

"Hang on," said Jackie. "I've got mine in my pocket." She wriggled closer to Liz Drury and finally dragged the phone from her jeans. "There's still no signal."

As they began to warm up, the smell of the river water in their clothes began to fill the cab. The windows misted over and blocked any further view of the outside. Andy drove as quickly as he could and within twenty minutes, they had arrived at the Gloucester Palace Hotel. David and Liz quickly got out of the vehicle so that they could help the others. Between them, they organised the Bulgarian boy and girl to help the man with the ankle, while Jackie assisted the other man. David and Liz held open the doors, as they all traipsed into the lobby.

Chantelle was behind the desk and began to fill in the registration cards. Betty was also hovering in the background, to help them to their rooms. It was decided that they would have to share with three to a room. They would all have an opportunity to shower or bathe, but more importantly get warm. With the power restored, Betty was also offering to wash and press any clothes, during the night.

Jackie and Liz took the Bulgarian girl upstairs, while David and the Bulgarian boy helped the man with the ankle to a second bedroom. The unconscious lady was lying on a settee in the lounge behind the reception area with a second settee occupied by the man with the broken leg. The three ladies from the tourist boat were allocated the third bedroom, while their companion was in the fourth.

As Jackie and the Bulgarian girl walked into the bedroom, they were both rather surprised that Liz immediately turned to Betty to ask how quickly she could get her clothes back if they were washed straightaway.

"The wash takes thirty minutes and the drying and pressing will be a couple of hours after that. Mind you, with all the extra people coming in, it's bound to be a bit longer," Betty replied.

"I'll be very grateful if you can start on mine as soon as possible."

"Well, yes. That's no problem at all. There are dressing gowns laid out for you, if you want to get changed."

With that, Liz started to strip. She took off her coat, followed by her jacket and skirt. She then took off her blouse and underwear, revealing a toned body which was obviously in very good shape. She slipped on one of the dressing gowns and looked at the other two girls.

"Come on! I suggest you do the same as me, because those at the front of the queue will get their clothes back soonest."

"That's quite right," agreed Betty.

Jackie immediately took the hint and took off her coat. She stripped off her jumper and jeans, followed by her blouse. She was not wearing a bra, nor tights, but she had a pretty pair of knickers, which has been soaked when she was in the bus. As soon as she was naked, she saw the Bulgarian girl watching them both, with her eyes wide in amazement.

She walked over and explained, "This lady will wash your clothes and dry them." She looked at the girl. "Do you understand?" The girl shook her head as her eyes began to fill with tears.

Jackie started again. "Your clothes all wet…from the river. Yes?"

"Yes. I understand."

"This lady," pointing at Betty, "Will wash and make clean. OK?"

"Yes. I understand."

"Well, take them off quickly," added Liz, handing a dressing gown to Jackie.

"I can't. Not with you both."

Jackie put her arm round the girl and turned her away from Liz. "What's your name?"

"Ivelina."

"Ivelina, is this the first time you have been without clothes in front of strangers?"

"What do you mean?"

"Have you ever taken off your clothes with other people there?"

"No. Never," she replied haltingly.

"There is nothing wrong." Jackie was now putting on her towelling gown. "We will all get our clothes cleaned." Ivelina nodded. "And dried." Ivelina nodded again. "And then you can be dressed again."

"OK." She took off her coat. Underneath she was wearing a T shirt and jeans with typical eastern European boots. She took off her underwear and Jackie noticed that her pubic area was unshaved. Her breasts were quite large for a girl who said she was only sixteen. Jackie handed the dirty clothes to Betty and then helped Ivelina to put on the third dressing gown.

As Jackie was assisting Ivelina, Liz started to fill the bath. The taps were half way down the side of the bath. She settled down in the soothing water and considered the extraordinary coincidence of being in a hotel room with the daughter of her boss and part time lover. Jackie stuck her head round the door.

"Do you mind if Ivelina gets a shower. She's absolutely freezing."

"She can get in here with me, if she wants. There's plenty of room and that'll warm her up quicker and better. After all, I don't take up too much room!" She added, jokingly.

"I'll try to persuade her." Jackie immediately saw the sense in what Liz was saying.

Liz heard Jackie explaining to Ivelina through the open doorway. They both came into the bathroom and Ivelina took off her dressing gown. She lifted her leg to get into the bath and then her second leg until she was standing there facing Liz.

"Tell her to turn round and sit down."

"Ivelina. Turn round and sit down," Jackie said to the Bulgarian girl. She turned slowly and started to sit down and as she lowered herself into the hot water, Liz opened her legs to allow the teenage girl to sit between them. She put her hands on her shoulders and gently pulled the younger girl back until she was resting her head on Liz's shoulder. Liz gently moved her legs closer together, until she was holding Ivelina firmly between her knees.

"You're right!" She looked up and saw Jackie watching them. "She's absolutely freezing." She took the soap out of the recess in the wall and began to wash the girl, starting with her shoulders and arms. Her skin was unblemished and of an attractive creamy tan colour. She lifted her right arm to wash her body and ribs underneath, feeling the girl move between her legs. She lifted the left arm and repeated the process, before rinsing away the soap.

"I think our young Bulgarian friend has fallen asleep," Liz commented. "Can you wash her legs?"

Jackie tried to roll up her sleeves, but found it impossible, so she slipped off the terry towelling bath robe and knelt on the bathroom floor. Liz passed her the soap and Jackie lifted and washed first the left leg and then the right. As she soaped the legs above the knee, Ivelina once again moved and murmured contentedly.

"Well, she seems to be enjoying this!" Liz looked at Jackie enquiringly. "I think you're old enough to warm yourself! But before you can get in, we've both got to get out, so I think we should wake her."

Jackie shook Ivelina's shoulder until she jumped slightly and opened her eyes. She looked at Jackie and smiled.

"Thank you … for saving my life." She slowly realised that she was in the bath, lying between the legs of another woman and turned to see Liz smiling gently at her.

"Why am I in here…? With you?"

"We had to get you warm as quickly as possible. You were also very dirty and we had to wash you. I suggest do the rest yourself. I'm going to get out to let you do that on your own."

Liz made sure that Ivelina's arms were on the sides of the bath, before pushing herself backwards and then standing. She was pink with the warmth of the water and her red hair was wet. As she stood up, she lifted her left leg over the side, followed by her right. She turned and knelt down next to Jackie. She looked directly at Ivelina.

"You must wash yourself. Jackie has the soap. Wash your hair, as well." She put her hand onto Ivelina's shoulder. "You've done well today. You're young and you've seen many horrible things. You are very brave. When you've finished in here, you must get some sleep. Don't take too long."

Ivelina looked at Jackie, who was putting the bathrobe on. "You get in bath now?"

"When you've finished washing." Jackie explained that the river water was dirty and carried much contamination. She had to say this slowly and carefully, until Ivelina fully understood, before she finished washing herself. She then washed her hair. Finally, Ivelina arched her back and put her head under the water to rinse out all the soap. Jackie gazed admiringly at her breasts. Although Ivelina was two years younger, her breasts were fuller and heavier.

As soon as the young Bulgarian girl finished rinsing her hair, she got out of the bath and Jackie gave her a big bath sheet. Jackie now let out all the dirty water before running in more hot water. They continued talking together, haltingly, slowly making their words understood. Jackie explained that she was at college and hoping to go to university in the autumn. For her part, Ivelina said that she and her brother had arrived in England only six weeks before. They had made contact with their older brother, who was living with an uncle, but the work they had been given was very badly paid and people took advantage.

In the bedroom, Liz could hear the younger girls talking together. She wondered whether the Bulgarian brother and sister were illegals, without papers. *Well, they're not likely to have any papers now, are they?* she thought. *And this flood will be a real godsend to thousands of people, if they aren't already drowned. We'll have to be really on our toes to ensure that records aren't compromised.* She made a mental note to discuss her thoughts with Chief Superintendent Bleasdale.

As Jackie got into the clean, warm water, Ivelina went into the bedroom. Liz was already in the bed. She beckoned the young girl to join her and as she hesitantly approached the bed, Liz folded back the duvet, showing that she was quite naked. The girl took off the gown and got into bed with the older woman.

"You are nice and warm now."

"Yes, thank you."

"You must now sleep. Everything will seem much better in the morning."

Liz pulled Ivelina closer to her, towards the centre of the bed. As the younger girl's head touched the pillow, her eyes began to close. Liz turned her onto her side, before snuggling closer to her. They were both in the foetal position, Liz's knees touching the back of Ivelina's knees, her body moulded to the younger girl's and her arm lying over the younger girl's waist. Ivelina, as she fell into an exhausted sleep, took hold of Liz's hand and placed it gently between her breasts. When Jackie came out of the bathroom, she saw that they were both asleep. She was warm and clean, but so very tired. She turned out all the lights, slipped off her bathrobe and got into the bed behind Liz.

At Waterloo Station, Milton and Pamela continued to help the teams separating the living from the dead. The station was free of all flood water by eight o'clock that evening, but still Milton kept the teams working. Their task was made much easier when power was restored and Milton decided that they should concentrate on clearing the bodies away from the stairs leading down to the Underground.

They made excruciatingly slow progress, such was the sheer press of bodies. As they slowly descended lower and lower, the number of survivors dramatically reduced. The work was hard, with very little respite and it was increasingly unrewarding.

Soon after midnight, a platoon of soldiers entered the station's concourse. The commanding officer, a young lieutenant, immediately observed that the disaster was already being addressed. He strode over to a blonde, middle-aged lady who appeared to be assessing the state of some of the survivors.

"Who's in charge here?" he asked.

"Well, I am, I suppose," replied Pamela. "With my boyfriend who's organising the removal of bodies from the entrance to the Underground."

"Is there anything you need?"

"Warm clothes, hot drinks, hot food, doctors and medical equipment."

"I'll radio that in."

He turned to his men and repeated the information before making a brief report on the radio to his HQ and requesting further instructions. As he now read the situation, with the water predominantly drained away, most of the bodies left on land were already dead. On their trek from the south side of the Thames Barrier, they had logged every corpse that was encountered. Every quarter hour, a radio report of their progress was made to Headquarters

At the command post, there was an immediate and brief discussion. As far as could be ascertained, although there was some damage to the river banks, most of the flooding had been caused by the height of the sea surge, simply flowing over the Barrier and the river defences. As the water later flowed back into the river, they could see in the moonlight that the river defences were still mostly intact. Intelligence was now building up, detailing the exact locations of a small number of breaches, as well as the position of the drowned bodies and the heavy, dumped detritus. Men and equipment were being diverted to those locations.

The secondary task of the army columns, was to assess the state of any and all survivors and how best to deal with them. The task, at first, seemed to be overwhelming. Specific contact was made with Scotland Yard and the London Fire and Rescue Headquarters. By the early hours of Friday morning, with power now restored to most of London, there were various teams working hard to move survivors to safety and to reopen the roads. The track of the massive wave, that had caused so much damage after washing over the river's defences, was now seemingly etched onto the landscape with all the abandoned sea containers randomly deposited across roads and embedded in houses and shops. There were also a number of collapsed tower blocks adding to the chaos. Progress was at a snail's pace and there was an increasing number of requests for heavy lifting equipment.

The army patrol at Waterloo Station was able to give much needed assistance to Milton and his teams as they extracted the bodies from the stairway tunnels leading down to the Underground. All the dead bodies being removed had either suffocated or simply been squashed to death. Hour after hour, the teams descended the stairways, while the stench of death increased around them.

The water on the platforms had also receded to some degree. With the tunnels being completely inundated, however, the water would have to be pumped out and the sheer mass of drowned bodies would make that a particularly delicate task. Every station in the centre of London was facing exactly these same difficulties.

On the north side of the river, the army patrols had encountered Fred and his colleagues ferrying survivors from the isle of Dogs up to the Salvation Army Citadel and the Seaman's Rest. Fred had been able to requisition a car and drive to Newham Hospital, where the staff immediately commenced preparations for a massive influx of people.

The army patrols, with their equipment and vehicles, assisted with this work which immediately speeded up the evacuation. The soldiers were also able to move westwards into the city, where they found very little structural damage. They did encounter a large crowd around Bank station which reported that it was impossible to access the station itself because of the press of bodies.

With reports now coming in of the flooded road tunnels at Dartford, Blackwall and Rotherhithe, it was fast becoming apparent that movement north and south across the river would be severely curtailed. The Army was the first to report that, because all bridges would have to be assessed for structural damage, it was strategically vital to reopen the tunnels as soon as possible.

In Downing Street, the Prime Minister held an impromptu meeting with senior ministers at half past two in the morning. Since power was now restored, he was able to receive updates from Scotland Yard and the Army with increasing regularity. All over London, although all the Emergency Services had firstly experienced immediate difficulties coping with the lack of electricity and communication, this had not stopped their activities. Throughout the flooded areas, Fire and Rescue personnel were joined by ambulance responders, off duty police officers and a growing number of individual people helping the public to safety. Their work was considerably eased when power was restored, soon followed by the re-connection of the mobile phone networks.

Slowly but surely, the work of so many disconnected groups, either professionally led or just local volunteers, began to be coordinated and central controls were formed which began to direct operations, rather than simply compiling information.

All this information and more was relayed to the Prime Minister, but it was still dark outside and until the Army patrols began to report the state of the river defences at around midnight, no one really knew how disastrous the next tide might be.

"Colleagues, the situation facing us is very grave. To present the overall position, I have invited the Chief Executive of the Environment Agency to brief us."

A middle-aged man stood up and removed his glasses. After briefly polishing the lenses, he looked at the members of the cabinet.

"Prime Minister, ladies and gentlemen. I cannot underplay the disaster that has overtaken London over the past twelve hours or so. You will all be aware of the cause of the sea surge up the river Thames. Those weather fronts have now passed from the United Kingdom and are diminishing in force as they drift eastwards over Northern and Central

Europe. It is, perhaps, somewhat fortunate that the current weather is now giving us clear skies with a full moon. This has allowed some degree of observation to take place.

"Certain parts of London have been severely flooded. I am aware of the difficulties experienced here in Westminster. However, our local problems are nothing compared with those areas where the river banks were overwhelmed allowing sea containers to be washed into housing estates, industrial estates, London City airport and elsewhere, causing massive structural damage. The contaminated sea water has also inundated all the riverside sewage treatment works, as well as flooding foot, rail and road tunnels. There has been almost complete destruction of the river side infrastructure.

"I appreciate your first question will be: 'Why were the river defences so inadequate?' I do not believe that this is the time for apportioning blame, but it must be said that this Agency has been increasingly vocal in expressing its concerns over global warming, rising sea temperatures and the increasing ferocity of winter storms."

He stopped and looked around the cabinet room. Very few caught his eye.

"I have brought with me the Executive Director of Flood and Coastal Risk Management. He will be able to answer specific questions as to where the flooding has occurred. He will not be open to interrogation as to the efficacy of the flood defences."

The Prime Minister frowned slightly. He looked directly at the Chief Executive as he thanked him for his brief overview.

"Can you tell me why the flood defences failed so spectacularly, on both banks of the river, from the sea to Teddington in the west?"

"Thank you Prime Minister. The Thames Barrier was opened in 1984. The primary cause for its construction was the inundation of Canvey Island in 1953. It took various Governments over 30 years to recognise, plan for and finally construct a Barrier to control the flow of water in the river Thames. Even when it was built, there were those who stated that it was too low, but that was over forty years ago.

"From the Barrier to the sea, all the sea walls have been reconstructed. All are higher, many are of concrete and they tie in with the requirements of the Barrier itself.

"Further north, the sea walls have been strengthened and heightened on a regular, rolling programme and this work can be seen to have been successful as the flooding in East Anglia over the past two days has been negligible in comparison with the Thames Estuary and Northern Europe.

"The actual sea surge, caused by the two specific weather fronts, was of a height never witnessed before. We all talk glibly about 'Once in a Lifetime Events'. Indeed, at the Agency, we plan, often in the face of considerable public opposition, to put into place appropriate protection. This surge was much more than a 'Once in a Lifetime Event'. Statistically, it is unlikely ever to happen again." He now looked directly at the Prime Minister. "It remains to be seen whether the flood defences have failed or whether they were simply overwhelmed by these specific meteorological circumstances."

"Excuse me," the Home Secretary interrupted. "You aren't answering the Prime Minister's question. You aren't even addressing it."

"I'll endeavour to be more candid, Home Secretary." He looked at the Home Secretary and then round at the Chancellor and other ministers. "The sea is dangerous. When combined with hurricane force winds and spring tides, it is lethal. Any sea surge reaching land will rise higher and water will always try to find its level.

"The sea defences are too low. The Barrier is too low. The sea surge was too high – much too high."

"One moment." The Chancellor raised his hand. "Can you clarify the financial implications in your comments? Are you suggesting that higher sea defences would have saved London?"

"Actually, I'm not." The Chief Executive looked at the Chancellor. "It is obvious that there will be an enormous cost to recover and rebuild the infrastructure. It will certainly run into billions. The sea surge, however, was of such an immense proportion that it would have inundated London whatever puny defences might have been put into place. Look over the North Sea at Holland. Communications have now been re-established and we are hearing that the coast from Amsterdam northwards has been completely washed away. The Zuider Zee gone. The polders gone. All the islands off the coast of Holland and northwest Germany – all gone.

"Here in Britain, we have always looked towards Holland for advice and leadership in respect of protection from the sea but in comparison, this event has probably been more disastrous for the Dutch economy than for the British. The loss of life in this disaster will be much more of a problem than any damage to the infrastructure."

"Indeed it will." Again the Home Secretary caught his attention. "It would appear that all the road tunnels under the Thames have been completely flooded. Why?"

"The methods of protection for the road tunnels are a matter for the Highways Agency. But from what we can ascertain at this time, it would appear that the sea surge came up river so quickly and was of such intensity that there was no time for the automatic protection systems to fully engage."

As the discussion continued, the tide was flowing up the Thames, once again, with High Tide scheduled at about six o'clock. The sun would rise about an hour later.

By half past five, Martin and his family were well past breaking point. After clearing the rubble from under the bridge, access for the trucks carrying bags of hard core eased considerably. The breach was already closed and the metal sheeting, snaking across the breach, was increasingly well bolstered with bricks and hard core. Wayne and his colleagues were bringing even more with increasingly regularity down the track and through the ruined bridge.

The tide was almost full and the sea had already reached the top of their temporary structure. It was another spring tide and, in places, the water was already slopping over the top of the temporary wall. However, the sea was calm and there was no wind.

As the next truck arrived, carrying eight large bags of hard core, Martin realised that they could now start to build a third layer, which would make the wall higher than the sea. He called over to Wayne.

"Look! I think we've done it." He pointed to the truck offloading the hard core.

"You're right. Mind you, we'll have to complete this new level. The water slopping over the top is making it trickier for the trucks to turn."

"Yes. I'm not sure what to suggest." Martin watched as the last bag was swung into place. The driver brought back the jib and drove forward six feet, before reversing towards the ditch. "Hey! I don't think he should be doing that just there. The ground's too wet."

"Watch out!" Wayne shouted, waving his arms. "Stop!" He was too late. Slowly and gently, the truck slipped backwards, down the muddy bank into the ditch, which was now quickly refilling with sea water. Wayne ran to the driver's door.

"Johnny, are you OK?" The driver looked up, somewhat bewildered.

"Yes, boss. Bloody hell, that was a bit careless."

"Bit careless, my arse, you daft prat! We can't pull you out now. We'll have to do that after the tide has turned."

The driver of the next truck in the line had stopped and watched open mouthed as the vehicle slipped into the ditch. Wayne walked up to the cab.

"This is now going to get messy and much more difficult. I think it'll be best for you to drop off your bags and then drive forward well past the breach. Find a dry spot with enough room to reverse and make sure you reverse towards the wall and not the ditch."

"Yes, boss," the driver replied.

"You'll find a suitable place to turn just round the next curve in the wall," Martin added. "I turned round there earlier on and it was fine."

"There's not many places to pass another wagon." The driver remarked.

"As soon as you've turned, wait until the next wagon arrives to turn round. You can then pass him, come back to the bridge and cross over. We'll make sure the way is clear before we let the next truck across."

"OK. Got it!"

And with that he drove his truck to the wall where he started to off load his big bags of hard core. Water was already seeping through the wall as well as slopping over the top, making the track very slippery. When the last bag was in place, he drove off and Martin waved the next truck into place, as James took up position on the other side of the bridge over the ditch. He was explaining the problem to the next driver, as the first truck returned and crossed the bridge. James now waved the fully laden flatbed across. It made its way to the wall and unloaded his bags of hard core without mishap, before disappearing round the bend in the track. Immediately the second empty truck reappeared and drove over the bridge. The system seemed to be working, as James was explaining the problem to the next driver.

Wayne helped his driver of the stricken truck out of the cab and onto the track.

"High tide will soon pass. It's nearly six o'clock. When the tide has turned and when we've got these bags all in place, we'll pull you out."

"Thanks, boss."

"Listen Johnny. We're all knackered and we're all working on adrenalin. You made a simple mistake and we're all just going to have to live with it. As soon as the sun's up, we'll be able to assess the situation more carefully. If we can get you out without too much difficulty, we'll be able to put it all down to experience."

Martin looked towards the east and realised that a mist was forming, hiding the coming dawn. There was no wind and the air was surprisingly warm. As he looked at the flood lights, he could see the tendrils of mist wrapping themselves around the lights. He climbed up the wall to look over the river. He could no longer see lights in any direction and realised that the river mist was already well formed. He turned and looked to the north, towards the railway bridge. It too had disappeared in the mist.

At Waterloo Station, when Milton and his teams were joined by the soldiers, they were able to leave to the military the grim task of extracting the rest of the bodies from the entrances and stairways to the Underground. The silence, as they worked, was depressing. Slowly, one by one, the bodies were extracted and, equally slowly, the teams were able to descend step by step. When they reached the first bend, they came across their last living casualties. A small boy had lost his footing on the stairway and his mother had caught hold of the handrail to form a barrier over her son. A second person, a man, immediately grabbed the handrail behind her and together they were able to force the crowd away from the child. The man linked both his hands around the handrail and dipped his shoulder into the crowd, bracing his feet adding further protection to the child. The boy's mother knelt over her boy to form a protecting bridge. But the weight of the press was too much.

As more and more people pushed up the stairway, the man first felt his wrists break before his breath was forced out of his lungs by the sheer weight of people behind him.

His final screams of agony were lost in the noise and bedlam all around him. Because his fingers were interlinked, his hands remained locked around the hand rail. The press was so great that he was unable to breathe in and he suffocated to death, but in that death his body continued to protect the mother and her son.

The soldiers found them forced into a corner of the stairway. The mother was barely alive when they reached her. She was breathing with difficulty and, as the soldiers carried her to the surface, she wept uncontrollably. Her young son walked by her side holding her hand as they climbed up the steps and emerged onto the platform.

As they reached the surface, they saw a military medical unit that was already in operation. They were immediately ushered inside the temporary accommodation that had been erected on the concourse. Communications with local hospitals were now up and running, but the Accident and Emergency Departments were already completely overwhelmed. Plans for a tented facility to be set up on Clapham Common were already being executed, because the three more local parks, Kennington, Burgess and Southwark were all flooded.

Already, the army had flown in the necessary infrastructure to create the appropriate departments from wards with beds to operating theatres, from waiting rooms to treatment rooms. A team of ambulances, buses, cars and taxis were already transferring the injured from Waterloo Station to Clapham.

On the north side of the Thames, the army had linked up with the police and the Fire Service and, together, they were setting up a similar facility in Hyde Park. Through the night, more units joined the original Army HQs on either side of the Thames Barrier. High Tide came at six o'clock and the various units that previously assessed the river defences were now ready to deal with any further flooding. Because the weather was now calm, it was regarded as a miracle that the expected weak points remained firm with no further damage and as each hour passed, the critical danger receded.

Chapter 17
Friday Morning – at Dawn

The weather was no longer uppermost in people's minds. The news channels were again broadcasting and after a brief description of the conflicting weather fronts which created the sea surge up the Thames, the newscasters were concentrating on the scenes of death, destruction and mayhem. It was still dark when the first reports were transmitted and the accompanying pictures were unrepresentative of the catastrophe which would unfold at dawn.

The weather fronts themselves were disappearing to the east. The intense depressions were filling and, in their place, an anti-cyclone was producing an atmosphere of calm with unseasonal warm air. This was creating intense fog, across the whole of England. Over the border in Scotland, the air remained cold and, with the wind speeds having dropped, there was a severe frost, which was restricting the repair work to the electricity grid. In addition, the gritters were experiencing long stretches of black ice, curtailing the clearance and re-opening of the roads.

On the River Thames, following the disastrous flooding the previous afternoon, the tide finally turned at six o'clock. As it ebbed and the flood water drained off the land, it swept down river carrying away much of the damaging debris. Containers, boats, barges and cars, anything and everything still retaining some buoyancy was now carried downstream causing further damage to any remaining riverside infrastructure as well as the uprights of various bridges. It was perhaps fortunate that HMS Belfast was stuck fast under London Bridge. Had the ship broken free, it was quite possible that it would have demolished Tower Bridge. During the surge, after crashing into London Bridge, its stern was swept into south bank and grounded in the soft mud. As the tide ebbed, the vessel was caught between its grounded stern and its bow, which was embedded in the bridge itself.

Many containers and vehicles slowly filled with water and sank. They were now strewn over the whole length of the river bed from Teddington in the west to the Thames Barrier and beyond in the east.

At the Barrier, in order to assist the outflow of flood water, the decision was made to open the gates. Although this allowed the water to flow downstream, the gates themselves acted as a giant sieve and captured the floating debris. Slowly a mountain of cars, buses, containers and boats of all sizes built up, creating a steel dam, through which the water still continued to flow, albeit at a decreased rate. This enormous pile of scrap metal acted, in its turn, as a strainer, capturing many of the drowned bodies. The weight was so great that it began to put pressure onto the foundations of the Barrier itself.

At seven o'clock, the sky lightened but the mist, which now pervaded the country from the Channel coast to the Scottish border, filtered the light making the landscape eerily gloomy. Both army teams forwarded messages to their central Headquarters that any overflying would be impossible as, in some places, the mist was reducing visibility to as little as fifty yards. Although this additional meteorological complication was unwelcome, it did not impede the build-up of resources.

In Downing Street, the Prime Minister finally dozed off in his office at about five o'clock in the morning. His staff decided to leave him. At dawn, two hours later, he was roused and updated with all the latest despatches. Glancing through them at speed, he read that High Tide, just one hour earlier, had caused no additional damage; that the army patrols were continuing to assess the damage to the flood defences plus the road and rail infrastructure; that temporary tented hospitals were now established in both Hyde Park and on Clapham Common; that power was restored to all parts of the capital and the hospitals were functioning. Further reports indicated that the damage to housing, roads and businesses on both sides of the Thames was catastrophic; that army patrols were now pushing further down river from the Thames Barrier to assess and evaluate the structural damage and potential loss of life; that the country was blanketed in fog which was expected to remain throughout the morning.

He was further advised that the situation in other parts of the country remained very mixed. In Scotland, the teams on the ground were slowly re-establishing the power grid, but that it would be several days before that work would be completed; snow drifts, black ice and freezing temperatures were still curtailing transportation and communication; there had been flooding in Huddersfield following the failure of a local reservoir wall causing considerable structural damage, but no loss of life; local flooding around the east coast was being contained and structural damage from the hurricane force winds along the south coast was being addressed.

The Prime Minister placed the last report on his desk, stood up and went through the door to find his private secretary.

"I'm going to shower and freshen up. This will be a long and arduous day. Can you advise me when the Meteorological Office is forecasting that the fog will lift?"

Martin Havers stood on the sea wall and, in the gloom of the new day, looked closely at the wall he and his family and friends had constructed. It snaked away from him to the east. The mist was so thick that he was unable to see the far end too clearly. The water was still high on the seaward side, but they had managed to close the gap and build the new wall sufficiently high to deny any significant ingress. Water had slopped over the top when the tide was at its peak, but now it was on the ebb and any danger of a collapse had passed. He turned to look at the truck which had slipped into the ditch and slowly began to plan in his head how best to extract it. He suddenly realised that Wayne had joined him.

"How're you feeling, Martin?"

"Pretty bloody knackered," was the uncompromising response.

"When did you last sleep?"

"Last night. No! Wait on a sec. The night before. Well, I suppose that was Wednesday night."

"Martin, you've just led us through the most intensive night of our lives. We're all knackered, but we're all much younger than you. It's time for you to get off home and get to bed."

"Thanks, Wayne." Martin looked at the younger man. "We wouldn't have been able to do all this without you, but I can't leave now. We've got to get your truck out of the ditch and I'm not leaving until that's done."

As he turned to walk down the side of the wall, he realised that James was standing just behind, listening to their conversation.

"Come on, James. We've got get this truck out of the ditch."

"Yes, Dad. But you should listen to Wayne and get off home otherwise you're going to be useless over the weekend."

"What the hell are you talking about?"

"It's your wedding anniversary, Dad. That's why we're all at home."

Martin stood still for a moment and put his hand to his forehead. "I'd completely forgotten about that."

"Not for the first time, I understand!"

"Well, that is true. But anyway, we've still got to get this truck out and all this talk is only taking up time. I'll get off home as soon as it's out."

"OK. But mind that you do."

"Yes, yes. Come on. We've got to do this before it sinks any further. What I think is that we need one truck on the far bank with a chain attached to its jib. The other end should be attached to the rear of the truck. That'll be a really mucky job – and cold. On this side, both diggers should have chains attached to the front of the truck. As the diggers pull the cab up the bank, the truck on the other side can lift the trailer and suck it out of the mud.

"Once the suction is broken, it should be a simple task to drag it out." He stopped, to consider what he was saying. "Mind you, the truck driver over on that side must make sure that he releases his chain at the right time. We don't want another truck in the mire."

"I don't think there's enough room for both of the diggers to work side by side." In his own mind James was carefully working his way through his father's plan.

"I realise that. They'll have to be driving one in front of the other, the rear one with a shorter chain and the front one with a much longer chain. Have we got all that kit here?"

Johnny the truck driver had been listening carefully to the plan.

"Boss, as soon as the suction of the mud is broken, I could start the engine and try to drive out, to relieve stress on the chains."

"What do you think, Martin?" Martin shrugged.

"It's worth a shout, I suppose."

Charlie produced the various lengths of chain from the back of the farm truck. The two diggers lined up on the seaward side of the ditch. There wasn't too much room to manoeuvre and it was lucky that the flat bed wagon was angled, facing slightly towards the west. Charlie volunteered to connect the chains to the front of the truck. The first was connected without too much difficulty. He then wrapped the second in a big loop around the first, ensuring that it wouldn't slip and in such a way that, as the digger pulled, it would tighten. He now looked at the rear of the vehicle.

"Wayne! Do your flat beds have a towing hook?"

"'Course they do. They're on the near side. But I don't think it'll be much use, because as you lift the trailer, the chain will slip off the hook."

"Thought you might say that. I've also been thinking that when the diggers on this side start to drag the truck out, we've got to be able to release the chain at the back, otherwise your other truck could be pulled in."

"I was wondering how to slip the chain off the hook of the jib. I don't think we'll be able to release it from the rear of the truck."

As he was talking, Charlie was stripping off his coat, jacket and trousers. As soon as he was undressed to his shirt and underpants, he put his boots back on. Wayne had walked over the bridge to direct the driver of the truck with the jib, to ensure it was in the right place. Finally it was parked parallel to the ditch, but close enough for the jib to extend over the water itself. James had driven the farm truck with all the chain over the bridge.

"I'll attach the chain to the truck first." Charlie slipped down the bank into the cold water. "Blimey, that takes your breath away!" he quipped as the black, dirty water covered first his knees, then his thighs and finally up to his waist.

On the bank, Wayne looped the chain over the jib and the driver then swung it out over the water, before lowering it sufficiently that Charlie could reach it. He took one end and pulled down a sufficient length, before disappearing under the water. Working with his eyes closed and by feel alone, he wrapped the chain round the axle, pulling enough of the chain to make a big loop. When he resurfaced, he gulped several breaths.

"James, I now need that big locking pin. Quickly. It's bloody cold in here."

"Right!"

James waded out into the water and passed the pin to Charlie who attached it to the chain, closing the loop. Wayne now crawled along the jib until he could drop onto the the stricken truck.

James helped Charlie out of the water, where he rubbed himself dry with some spare sacking before dressing once more. As Charlie got back into the land rover, Wayne grabbed hold of the chain. He pulled the slack over the hook of the jib until it was as taut as he could pull it. He then attached a second locking pin.

"Right!" said Wayne. "Let's do it."

Johnny the truck driver got back into his cab. Helen and the other digger driver both moved forward slowly taking up the strain. Wayne indicated to the jib operator to try to lift the rear of the truck. As the chain took up the slack, there was a creaking and slurping noise from the rear. Slowly the truck was lifted up about a foot. Johnny started the truck's engine and the noise of bubbles coming to the surface from its exhaust added to the creaking and slurping. The diggers now slowly began to drag the truck as they held their chains taut. As the truck was slowly pulled forward up the banking, the jib was slowly swung out further over the water slowly becoming increasingly extended.

When the jib was almost at its fullest extension, Wayne shouted to Johnny to engage first gear and gently start to drive. The diggers were still taking the strain, but to everyone's surprise and relief, the wheels caught traction. *Now for the difficult bit*, Wayne thought.

He shouted to the diggers to stop dragging forward, but to hold position and to Johnny to stay completely still. With everything stopped, the jib was fully extended across the water. Wayne directed the truck driver to lower the jib until the chain was slack once more. He now removed the locking pin, freeing the chain from the jib. As soon as the jib was free, the diggers started to move forward and Johnny again engaged first gear. Slowly, inch by inch, the truck came over the bank of the ditch, followed by its trailer and a vast amount of black muddy water. When it was safely and completely on the track, the digger drivers stopped and their chains were released. Having watched the whole extraction, James now drove Charlie back to the farmhouse for a hot bath and breakfast.

For the first time since the previous afternoon, Martin now felt that he was able to relax and he sat down on the base of the sea wall. Almost immediately, his head drooped onto his chest as he was fighting off sleep.

Suddenly, he felt a hand on his shoulder. He looked up to see Wayne standing in front of him, with Helen just behind. He realised that the day was much brighter and looked round.

"The sun's out and the mist has gone," he said, wonderingly.

"That's right, Mr Havers." Wayne gently sat down next to him. "It's gone half past ten and we've let you sleep for the past couple of hours."

"What?" Martin now struggled to get up. He looked at the temporary wall and then across the field to the embankment and the bridge. All the vehicles had gone and all the spare equipment. Only the Land rover, Helen and Wayne remained.

"Come on, Dad. It's time to go home."

Martin sat down again and buried his face in his hands. "Thank you. Thank you for all that you've done." As he looked at them both, his eyes filled with tears.

Michael Varley had spent a most uncomfortable night in his office chair. Alice fared little better but was able to relax in the knowledge that there was absolutely nothing she could do to assist the situation and therefore there was no point in worrying about it. She was sure that everything would finally work out fine. After the power was restored, the heating in the building returned, so they were able to keep warm, albeit in their separate offices.

Alice woke just before dawn and after a trip to the ladies' toilet where she had a stand up wash, she applied a minimum of makeup and put a comb through her hair. She checked the latest news on her computer and now felt able to face whatever the day might throw at her. She went into the kitchen and put on the kettle to brew coffee, wondering whether there would be any shops open. She would have to go out to forage for supplies, but she knew that the early bird catches the worm and after her coffee, she set off.

At first, she thought that the streets were completely deserted but, after walking a few paces, she realised that there were people sheltering in shop doorways, huddled together to keep warm. She walked northwards up Moor Lane towards the Tesco Express. As she approached, she could smell croissants baking and her mouth started to water. *Just as I thought. Everything is fine*, she said to herself.

She entered the sanctuary of the warm shop, collected a basket and slowly meandered around the gondolas, picking up other items for their breakfast. There were two or three other people, with haunted looks in their eyes, wandering aimlessly through the mini market. Alice realised, looking at their dishevelled appearance, that they must have spent the night on the streets. Besides appearing shell-shocked, they were dirty and shivering. They avoided her as she approached, as if embarrassed. They then shuffled away from her. Alice now realised that they were only in the shop to keep warm.

After paying for her goods, she returned, as quickly as possible, to Le Grove Investments, realising that Michael would be awake and wondering where she was. As she entered the office door, she saw that the light to his office was on and she could hear the television news. She put down her bags and went to his office.

"Good morning, Michael," she said brightly. He raised his head from the armchair where he had spent the night. He was unshaven and his clothes were all wrinkled.

"What's good about it?" He asked belligerently.

"There's a bit of mist about but the sun is trying to shine. I've got breakfast and I'm going to brew fresh coffee. You should get a shower and have a shave. While you're doing that, I can freshen up your suit and press your trousers. I think we might be very busy today."

"Why? The whole world came to an end yesterday. Haven't you seen the news? London was flooded and thousands, perhaps even millions of people are dead." He spoke roughly as though he was seeking an argument.

"Yes, I know," she replied gently. "I've checked my phone for updates and I've already seen the news on my computer."

"Well, there you are then. I'm stuck here and I have no idea whether my wife and son are safe."

"Is there any reason why they shouldn't be? Have you tried to phone them?" Alice was fast losing patience with this shadow of a man. "Or have you just been wallowing here with no sense of direction or thoughts as to what we now need to do."

"You can't speak to me like that," he complained.

"Well, I just did and I'm going to say more. You are a respected banker. Out there!" She pointed dramatically through the window towards the river. "There will be massive re-construction jobs needing finance. You are so good at raising solid finance, that this could be an extraordinary opportunity for you and Le Grove Investments to get in on the ground floor, not only make a whole pile of money, but possibly to be the controlling influence. Do this right and you will be lauded up and down the city and the country. But get it wrong, or even worse, don't do it at all and you will forever wonder 'what if'. We can do this together, if you want but, right now, you've got to get a grip."

Alice turned on her heel. She stopped at the door and turned back. Michael was still looking at her with his mouth agape. "And you can stop looking at me in that gormless manner. Call me as soon as you get into the shower, so I can deal with your clothes," she instructed.

Slowly, Michael stood up and shuffled towards the private bathroom. He was now thinking about Alice's major rant. She's right, of course. There's a fortune to be made here. After going to the lavatory, he stripped to his underwear, went to his office door and called Alice.

"I've got another suit here," he advised her. "And a clean shirt and socks. I think I'll just send this to the cleaners, rather than you do anything with it."

"Good idea," she replied. As she looked at him, she wondered whether his assertive self was returning. "I'll warm up the croissants."

"Bring yours in here as well," he suggested. "We can have breakfast together and discuss how best to implement your plan."

"I suppose that's the real meaning of a 'breakfast meeting'!" she quipped as, once again, she left his office.

Michael shaved and showered before dressing in his clean clothes. He already felt better, even on top of his world, as he emerged from the bathroom. He walked to the window and looked out over the city. Although it was still murky, the sun seemed to be trying to burn off the mist. Between the office blocks, he could see the Shard, on the south bank near London Bridge station. He was oblivious of the catastrophic devastation at the station, on the roads throughout Southwark and in the Underground network. He could only glimpse the river Thames itself and as he looked first west and then east, he could see no evidence of flooding.

Alice arrived with the warmed croissants, butter and jam plus piping hot, fresh coffee. She had also brought her notebook.

As the sun slowly burnt its way through the mist, it was only now that the appalling devastation of Waterloo station could be evaluated. The pillars holding up the roadway were severely compromised and the road itself had collapsed in a number of places. The shops on the ground floor were all flooded with the stock completely ruined. All those people inside at the time of the inundation were either crushed to death or drowned.

Inside the station itself, because the main concourse is built above ground level, the major problem was in dealing with the enormous crowd of people which, during the long hours of the night, was gently but specifically marshalled into two distinct groups – the deeply traumatised and the rest.

Before the arrival of the military and the creation of a tented medical facility on Clapham Common, Milton and Pamela recruited some of the more able bodied people, to maintain order and to assist those who were obviously unable to cope. In this way, they were able to continue with the important work of trying to save people from the water or trapped in the entrance to the Underground. A fleet of vehicles, taxis, buses and army trucks was already transferring large numbers of these people to Clapham Common for registration and assistance back to their homes.

As order was slowly restored, all the self-imposed responsibilities slowly lifted from Milton's shoulders. With the dawning of the day, he realised how tired he was, especially when Pamela pulled him to one side and suggested that they should go home.

"There's nothing left for us to do here," she said. "There's really no more that you can do."

"I know," Milton replied. "But it would feel like we're running away."

"No one could have done more than you, Milton. There is no one on this station who could deny that your actions have saved lives – many lives."

"I only did what anyone else would do," he muttered. His head sagged forward until his chin was on his chest. His shoulders slumped forward. After a moment's reflection he said, "Actually, I'm rather concerned as to what we might find at home."

"What do you mean?"

"I can't get it out of my mind. You know. When we watched that colossal wave come towards the station. You remember, when we were above the pedestrian bridge? Well, we didn't really watch what happened after it passed the station because we went straight down to the main concourse to help the survivors."

"What do you think happened?"

"The surge from the river was so high it was carrying all those sea containers, big buses, trucks and so on. We already know that extensive damage has been done to the houses and buildings between here and London Bridge. But that wave extended much further south and will have swamped the housing estates southwards to Kennington and Walworth. If the containers and other debris were swept through those areas as well, then they'll have knocked down houses, maybe even tower blocks. The roads will be blocked and I suspect that looters will be out on the streets."

"Oh Milton. That sounds awful," Pamela replied. "Really depressing. I think it'll be best if we get off as quickly as possible to check it out. After all, if what you say is correct, my place will be affected as well."

Milton turned to the army lieutenant who was now coordinating the work in the station to tell him that he was leaving. The officer nodded his agreement, recognising how close Milton was to the point of exhaustion. Pamela took him by the arm and led him away.

Outside the day was still misty and damp, with the sun breaking through intermittently. As they walked southwards towards Kennington, all around them they could see the damage caused by the flood. They were not surprised to encounter some very large pools of water, as though the drains in the roads were blocked. All the roads were still wet and muddy. At first, they noticed odd vehicles abandoned in weird places – cars in front gardens, trucks on their sides blocking road junctions, containers embedded in buildings. As they looked more closely, they realised that some houses were completely missing, as though a giant hand had malevolently scooped them up and swept them away. At first, Milton couldn't understand why there was no rubble, until he realised that the flood had been so intense and so powerful that all the broken bricks and tiles had simply been washed away.

As they approached Milton's street, their footsteps slowed as though they were reluctant to discover what awaited them. Finally they reached his corner and turned towards his home. Much to their surprise, the street appeared to be unscathed. As they looked down the road, the sun was finally burning away the last of the morning mist. They could see the neat terraces on both sides, which encouraged them to walk a little faster. Reaching the garden gate at the front of his house, Milton suddenly stopped and pulled Pamela closer to him, preventing her from walking up the short path to the door.

"What's the matter?" she asked.

"Hang on a sec," he said. "I think I saw something move in my front room. Just stay here while I check."

He walked up to his front door and, very carefully, inserted the Yale key. After turning the key round to disengage the deadlock, he twisted it a further quarter turn, releasing the lock. Taking a deep breath, he pushed open the door and burst into the house. In the hallway, he was confronted by a young, dark man, who was obviously not expecting anyone to arrive through the front door, at just that moment. Frozen to the spot, his eyes widened and his jaw dropped. He was carrying Milton's television screen. The momentum of bursting through the door, carried Milton right up to the intruder. He wrapped his arms round the lad, before clamping his hand over his mouth. Close on his heels, Pamela relieved the youngster of the screen. Milton propelled the lad back into the front room.

"How many of you are in my house?" he whispered into the young lad's ear. Tears began to well up in his eyes and he shook his head, refusing to answer. They heard movement in the bedroom above them, just before someone from the kitchen, in a stage whisper, said, "Hurry up! We've got to get out of here!"

Milton shook the lad and whispered, "Two others?" The lad nodded. Pamela took the boy's right arm and twisted it up his back, as Milton went to the door and carefully looked around the door jamb, down the passage past the dining room, towards the kitchen. Just as he saw a second man leaving through the back door into the garden, Milton noticed a pair of legs wearing dark jeans and trainers start to come down the stairs. He ducked back into the sitting room and hid behind the door, until the owner of the legs had passed the doorway. Through the crack between the door and the door jamb, he could see that this second lad was carrying the music centre from his bedroom.

After glancing quickly at Pamela, to confirm that she had the first lad secure, Milton went after the second and caught him as he entered the kitchen. He put his left arm round the lad's body, pinning his arms, and clamped his right hand over the boy's mouth.

"What the fuck are you doing in my house, you little bastard?" Milton whispered in his ear. The surprise was so great that the boy's bladder was overwhelmed and he peed himself as he was roughly dragged back to the front room. "Put my music centre down gently on that armchair." The boy did as instructed, realising that his friend was already restrained by Pamela. Milton ushered the boy behind the sofa and pushed him until he was bent over the back. He then twisted one arm up his back, indicating to Pamela that, from the front of the sofa, she should take hold of the arm. As soon as the boy was secure, Milton relieved Pamela of the other lad and took him to the rear of the settee where he was similarly restrained. Pamela was now able to control both lads without too much difficulty for, as each tried to squirm free, all she needed to do was to pull the hand of the twisted arm further up the back, creating considerable pain in either lad's shoulder.

"If they struggle, pull harder and hurt them," he instructed quietly.

He left the room and darted down the passage to the kitchen. Somewhat bizarrely, the third lad was still on the terrace, sucking on his e cigarette as he surveyed the garden. Milton could see that the gate to the track at the back of the houses was open. With complete malice aforethought, Milton jabbed the boy hard in the kidneys. He went down, face first onto the wet lawn, as though pole axed. As he writhed on the ground, Milton looked closer, realising that the boy was son of one of his neighbours.

"Good morning, Randy." The lad twisted his head and looked up.

"That really hurt," he whined.

"Not as much as what I've got in store for you."

"What do you mean?"

"You'll see. Now get up."

"I can't. I think you've broken my back."

"Unlikely." Milton chuckled grimly. "And if you don't get up, I'll carry you inside and that could really hurt."

"OK, OK."

The boy got onto his knees and, as he started to rise, he tried to make a run for the garden gate, not realising that Milton had already moved to cut off that escape route. He stuck out a leg and the boy went tumbling down once more.

"Now," said Milton. "That was just silly and has made me really angry." He grabbed the boy by his hair and pulled him upright. Instead of marching him straight inside, he undid the boy's jeans and pulled them down to his ankles, seriously restricting further movement. Slowly, Milton made the boy shuffle to his shed. He produced the key and the boy unlocked the padlock, before opening the door.

"On the shelf at the back you'll see a ball of thick cord. Pass it to me."

The boy shuffled into the shed and found the ball. He passed it over his shoulder to Milton.

"I'm now going to show you what happens to little shits like you, who take advantage of innocent people like me and decide to loot and rob. Prison is too good for you but, I promise you, what I have in mind will stay with you for the rest of your miserable lives. Pull your trousers up."

They entered the house and found Pamela still holding the other two boys, over the sofa. While they were still restrained, Milton took the cord and tied it to the left wrist of the third boy. He twisted the boy's left arm up his back and then passed the cord over his left shoulder, across his throat and back across his right shoulder, before twisting up his right arm. He then tied the cord to his right wrist. As the arms tired and the boy tried to relieve the pain in his shoulders, the cord tightened over the throat. He made the boy sit in one of the armchairs, before repeating the process with the other two.

He then took a permanent marker pen and wrote on the forehead of each boy, 'Looter'.

"Right. That'll do. Now, I want you all to stand in a line against the wall." As they moved across the floor, Milton took out his iPhone and photographed them. "That's going straight onto as much social media as I can find. You see, with this flood, the police won't have the time or the resources to come and arrest you. So, instead, I have arrested you, charged you, found you guilty and sentenced you to public humiliation. Now, I'm going to tie you to that tree outside Randy's house, so your family, your friends and your neighbours will all see what you've been up to. I don't know who these two boys are, but I reckon they will also live locally. It'll be interesting to see how quickly or how slowly the local people will release you."

With that, he pulled them to the front door and, with Pamela bringing up the rear, they were marched outside, down the road to the appropriate tree. Milton made sure that they had their backs to the tree before looping some more cord over their hands and around the tree. After making sure that each was secured by the hands one to the other and that they were able to sit or stand, he cut the cords around the neck of each boy. He then photographed them again, standing in the sunshine and in their own humiliation.

As they walked back to his house, Pamela mentioned that the house was really wet, throughout the whole of the ground floor.

"I noticed that as well. It seems that the water almost came to the top of the internal doors."

"I suppose every house will be the same."

"Bound to be. The sadness is that the TV screen those boys were nicking is probably ruined anyway, so taking it would have been a bit pointless."

"That's what I thought," Pamela replied.

As they re-entered the front door, the smell of damp carpets hit them. Milton went to the kitchen. He tried the gas cooker which, to his surprise, not only worked but, once alight, started to warm up the room. He went out of the back door and, after closing the rear gate, he stood on the terrace, looking up and down the rows of gardens. To his left, back towards Kennington, he noticed a large shape some seven or eight gardens away. He went back inside, where he found Pamela already cleaning the kitchen. Without saying a word, he walked through and up the stairs, to the back bedroom.

Leaning out of the window, he could now see that an upturned lorry had been swept down the track between the two rows of houses, those on his street and the next on the adjacent street. It had demolished all the garden fences for the first ten or twelve houses, before coming to rest against a big horse chestnut tree. *That'll take some shifting*, Milton thought to himself.

David woke before dawn. Although it was past three in the morning before he finally got to his bed, the events of the previous day continued to prey on his mind and he had slept only fitfully. He was in a bedroom with two of the crew from the tourist ship that had been swept onto the Embankment. There was one double bed and a single, which was left for David.

He quietly slipped out of bed. By the door to the bedroom, he noticed a neat pile of clean clothing which had been washed and ironed by Beryl during the night. He extracted his own and took them to the bathroom, where he indulged in a long, hot shower, before drying himself and dressing. As the steamy water cascaded over his head, he could feel the intense pressure of the previous evening being washed away. Afterwards, he felt so much better that he decided to go down to the dining room to check out the possibilities of breakfast. He was halfway down the stairs when he suddenly thought about Jackie. He doubled back and climbed the extra flight to the floor where the girls were accommodated.

He stopped and listened at the door to their bedroom. Hearing nothing amiss, he quietly opened the door and peeped inside. The room was at the front of the hotel and a streetlight was shining through a gap in the curtain. In the gloom, he could make out that Jackie, the Bulgarian girl Ivelina and the woman police officer were all in the same bed. Jackie was on the side nearest the window and furthest away from the door, with the Bulgarian girl in the middle. He tiptoed round the bed towards Jackie, who was lying on her back. He knelt by the bed and gently shook her bare shoulder.

"Jackie?" he whispered. "Are you awake?"

He watched Jackie's eyes open slowly and then, when she saw David there, her arms came from under the covers and encircled his neck. She kissed him long and hard on the lips, as though she would never let him go.

"I am now," she whispered.

"You are what?" asked WPC Liz Drury.

"Oh!" Jackie jumped. "David's just come in to see if I'm awake."

Liz sat up, the thin duvet dropping to her waist, revealing her pretty breasts. "Good morning, David." She made no attempt to cover herself. "Did you sleep well?"

"Not really," he replied, hoping that he sounded really casual. "I was sharing a room with two other guys, who obviously know each other really well." Jackie noticed that he couldn't take his eyes off Liz's breasts, so she sat up as well, swinging her legs out from under the duvet. David now realised that she was completely naked.

"I'm off to the bathroom," she announced before standing up and walking across the room.

"Don't take too long."

"You can come in when you hear the shower," Jackie said over her shoulder from the bathroom door.

"Thanks." Liz got out of bed and stretched. As she lifted her arms, David watched her breasts lift and flatten, before returning to their normal shape. "Do you know what the time is?"

"Yes. It's just coming up to seven o'clock," David replied.

Despite himself, he could feel his heart hammering in his chest and the butterflies fluttering around his groin. Liz picked up a dressing gown and slipped it over her shoulders, before sorting out the washed and pressed clothes that had been left on a chest of drawers next to the bedroom door. "I wonder how soon breakfast will be."

"Last night, they said it would be available from seven," David said helpfully. "As I came up the stairs, I could smell bacon cooking."

"Good. I'm feeling really hungry." Now that she could hear the water from the shower, she disappeared into the bathroom. There was a sudden gasp from the bed.

"Why you in here?" Ivelina asked, looking at David.

"It's OK," David replied, holding up his hands, palms outwards. "I've only come to get Jackie." He looked at the girl in the bed. She had pulled the duvet up to her chin and her frightened, dark-brown eyes were staring out at him. "Please tell Jackie that I'll be waiting outside." He went through the bedroom door are disappeared.

Very soon, Jackie emerged from the bathroom, wearing just a towelling robe. She turned on the light and saw Ivelina cowering in the bed. She looked completely terrified.

"Are you OK?" Jackie went over to the bed.

"There was a man, David, in here."

"Oh that! Yes, I know. He came to wake me up so we could go down for breakfast together. Are you hungry?"

Ivelina shook her head.

"Well, I think you must be. So I reckon that you should get up and have a shower and then get dressed in your clean clothes."

"No ... No! I wait ... after you go."

"Don't be silly. We all had a bath together last night and then slept with each other in this bed. There's no need to be ashamed." Ivelina, in reply, pulled the duvet over her head, lay on her side and curled up in the foetal position.

"Listen, Ivelina." Jackie knelt down next to the bed and put her hand onto the younger girl's shoulder. "After you've had a shower and got dressed, we can all go downstairs and find your brother. But first, you must get up!"

"No! I can't." Her answer came, somewhat muffled, from under the duvet.

From the bathroom door, Liz was watching this exchange.

"Jackie's right," she announced. "We can't wait here all day. Here, take my robe." Liz let it slip from her shoulders and threw it onto the bed, before picking up her clean clothes from the chest of drawers by the door. First she stepped into her panties and then put on her bra. Ivelina's head emerged from the duvet to pull the bath robe to her. She was crying.

"Come on, Ivelina. It's not all that bad," Liz said.

"Actually, I guess it might be. I think her period has started," Jackie suggested.

"Well, that'll be a bit inconvenient," Liz agreed. She went to the bed and sat down. "Are you bleeding?" Ivelina nodded. "Right. That's OK." She picked up the robe on the bed and put it on over her underwear. She turned to Jackie. "Try and get her to the bathroom. I'll be back in a couple of minutes." With that, she left the room.

"Can you get to the bathroom?"

"I think … OK."

"Here, I'll help you."

Jackie drew back the duvet and helped Ivelina to sit up. She slipped off her own bathrobe and put it around the Bulgarian girl's shoulders. Drawing the duvet further back, she noticed some spots of blood on the bottom sheet. She helped the younger girl to swing her legs over the side of the bed, before gently pulling her upright.

"Do you have stomach pain?" she asked.

"Yes. Always. But will be OK in two, three hours maybe."

"You'll feel better after a hot shower, as well, I expect."

Jackie put her arm around Ivelina's waist and, together, they walked to the bathroom. Jackie made her sit on the toilet, while she started the shower. There now seemed to be a lot of blood. Soon she was under the shower and washing herself properly. Jackie washed and dried her hands and went back into the bedroom, where she quickly dressed. She opened the bedroom door to find David waiting outside. He rushed to her and they kissed each other hungrily.

"Blimey! Love's young dream!" Liz was back, carrying a box of tampons and some pads. "Is our young friend all right?"

"She's in the shower."

"I'll see if she's feeling any better."

"Hang on. I'll come as well." She turned to David. "Can you wait just a bit longer?" He nodded.

They could hear the water was still running. Liz went to the bathroom door. Inside everything was very steamy, but she could see Ivelina standing under the shower.

"How are you feeling?"

"A little better."

"I've got some tampons and some pads for you. Whichever you prefer."

"Thank you."

"I'll leave them here for you."

Liz went back to the bedroom where she finished dressing. Her stockings were missing, but that didn't really matter as they were very badly torn. Her blouse, however, had been expertly repaired. The jacket and skirt were pressed and clean. *That's really rather impressive*, she thought. Jackie had thought the same as she was dressing. Liz looked at Jackie.

"Why don't you go down with David?"

"OK."

"I'll hang on here for Ivelina and then we'll come down together."

"OK." Jackie repeated, before disappearing through the door.

Liz pulled the duvet off the bed and bundled up the bloodied bottom sheet before replacing the duvet. Ivelina came out of the bathroom, looking rather pale, but definitely brighter. She went to her clothes and started to dress.

"Who make them clean?" she asked.

"Staff from the hotel, I expect." Liz simply presumed that laundry maids would have done the work, not realising of course that, these days, there was only Betty. She looked at the young Bulgarian girl. "Whereabouts are you from?"

"Bulgaria."

"Yes. I know that. Which town or city."

"A little village, called Balsha, near to Sofia."

"Do you miss it?"

"Oh yes. It is very pretty and everybody is very friendly."

"Why are you here?" Liz asked her disingenuously.

"My brother is to look for work. I asked to come with him. He is trained, how you say, as carpenter? With wood. I want to learn better English before I return home. We have uncle who lives in Will…es…den."

"Why were you in the bus? That's nowhere near Willesden."

"Our uncle is to work in day, so we went to see London Tower. Then we went on bus to see river and boats."

"Do you have any travel documents?" Ivelina looked up sharply, suddenly realising that she had been under interrogation. "Why you ask? Who are you?"

"Oh. I'm sorry." Liz returned the look. "I should have said. My name is Woman Police Constable Elizabeth Drury. I work at Scotland Yard. I am currently working in the Illegal Immigration Section…"

Ivelina nodded slowly, looking carefully at the other woman. "My brother has all the necessary documents," she said slowly.

"That's OK, then." Liz broke the tension. "Are you ready? Come on! I'm starving."

She opened the bedroom door, to find Jackie and David standing outside, holding hands. "We're off for breakfast."

"We've been waiting for you."

Together they all went downstairs to the dining room, where they found the other refugees from the bus and the boat. Ivelina went over to her brother where she spoke to him in their own language. He stood up and hugged his sister, while he surveyed the room. He noticed WPC Liz Drury watching them from the doorway, before following Jackie and David across the floor to an empty table.

In a demonstration of normality, Chantelle was taking the orders and both Jack and Sebastian were serving the breakfasts as they arrived in the dining room. Down in the kitchen, Betty was cooking the hot breakfasts to order. The speed with which the breakfasts arrived seemed to demonstrate that this was just another day in the hotel, albeit somewhat busier than normal. Outside the sun was trying to break through the mist. They had all heard the news. Each succeeding bulletin was increasing the detailed information about the disaster. Nothing had been experienced in London like this since the Blitz, nearly a century earlier.

Fred Shemming climbed up the training tower just before dawn. The long night slowly and somewhat reluctantly was turning into a misty, grey day. There was little wind and visibility was very poor. He could hardly see beyond Canary Wharf and down to the Isle of Dogs. After a few minutes standing there alone, Dinah joined him.

"What are you doing up all by yourself?" she asked.

"I'm so bloody tired, I just needed to get away from all the activity downstairs."

"It's not like you to use bad language."

"I know." He slowly shook his head. "But in the circumstances, I think it's absolutely appropriate. We've been relatively lucky here on the Isle of Dogs. That wave was so high, it should have been far more destructive. We haven't really surveyed all the damage

211

to the housing estates down in Millwall and I guess there must have been extensive damage out in Canning Town and Beckton, but our teams have only brought in twelve dead people so far."

Dinah put her arms round her husband's waist. "Even before the wave arrived, you were thinking what to do for the best and you made sure all the children and teachers evacuated. Was that prescient or just good sense? Your actions have done more for this community than anyone could have expected."

"I'm not so sure," Fred replied. "All I do know is that it's been a hell of a long night and now we've got a river mist hindering the work."

"I don't think it'll last long." Dinah looked up at the grey sky. "There's no wind and the air is really quite warm. I expect the sun will burn it away by ten o'clock."

"You may well be right. But until then, we've still got plenty work to do."

Just to the east, a mile downriver, a motorized army patrol on the north bank was driving rapidly eastwards along the A13 towards the Hornchurch Marshes and the Queen Elizabeth II Bridge. The mist over the river seemed to be lifting and the sun was already trying to break through.

After passing Barking and Dagenham to its left, the road turned south east towards the Rainham Marshes. All the soldiers were looking towards the river and, as the mist cleared, they could see sea containers, vehicles of all types and bodies scattered haphazardly between the road and the river. In the direction of the Bridge, there were columns of black smoke, mixing with the mist and drifting idly away, down river.

Just before Aveley, the road crossed over the railway and turned more southerly towards the river, in order to skirt around the township. There were no obstructions on the road and soon the column was leaving Aveley behind. It turned first to the north and then eastwards before approaching the M25 at the Mar Dyke Interchange.

Here, the column halted to survey the roads and the land to the south along the London Orbital Motorway towards the river. The approach road to the Queen Elizabeth II Bridge was raised well above the surrounding land on concrete pillars but, although it was still closed, all three southbound lanes were completely blocked with traffic. To the east, they could see that the oil depot on the south of the Thurrock Trade Park was burning, creating an enormous pall of oily, black smoke, which was mixing with the remains of the sea mist and slowly drifting down river towards the sea. Every so often, they could hear the whump of a muffled explosion as more oil caught fire.

After carefully assessing the situation and formalising the most suitable route, the column continued east along the A13 to the next junction, where it turned south down the A126. Moving slowly and carefully through the devastated streets, it made its way into West Thurrock, before finally entering the Trade Park.

It now turned back towards the Bridge along Oliver Road and entered the oil storage depot. The roadways were covered with spilt oil, making them virtually impassable. Many of the storage tanks were leaking and there were regular explosions, as the fuel oil caught fire. It appeared that, before the blackout had plunged London into a frightening and disorientating darkness, power cables had been snapped apart by heavy containers floating in the flood water causing short circuits and starting a number of fires. These spread to other storage tanks which were still burning, creating the choking, black smoke.

They reported back to HQ all that they could observe, as well as forwarding videos of the damage and devastation in the oil storage depot. The column turned northwards, before reaching the fence at the end of Oliver Close that separated the road from the railway line. After cutting the metal links, two jeeps were deployed to drive eastwards along the tracks in order to assess the state of any damage at the tunnel entrance where the railway disappeared under the river. When they returned, they reported that the tunnels were full of water. The column turned back along Oliver Close to drive under the railway bridge to the roundabout on the north side of the tracks, before proceeding up St Clements Way.

Before it passed under the approach roads to both the Bridge and the Dartford Road Tunnels, the column waited for the other two jeeps to return. Once again, it turned north up Stonehouse Lane, until it came to the roundabout where it was able to access the slip road coming off the north bound lane from the road tunnel. There was no traffic moving northwards at all, so the column was able to drive the wrong way down the slip road, heading back towards the road tunnels. Unlike the Bridge, there was no traffic on either the southbound or the northbound lanes. Very soon, the column reached the tunnel exit and parked.

Two platoons were deployed, one to the northbound tunnel exit and the other, across the central reservation, to the entrance of the southbound tunnel. Both teams immediately reported that the tunnels were completely flooded and full of smashed vehicles. The cars nearest the entrance had been forced back by the weight of the water into the vehicles behind them, completely crushing them. All the drivers and passengers were dead. As far as they could see, the tunnels were full of vehicles and because access to both entry and exit lanes were blocked, the immediate assessment was that the surge of water, after overwhelming the Thurrock Trade Park, had swept into the approach roads, not so much because the defences had failed, but simply because of the immensity of the wave.

That enormous amount of water then forced itself into the tunnel, demolishing those first few vehicles near the entrances, before inundating all the rest deeper in the tunnel. Without appropriate cutting and lifting equipment, it would be impossible to enter the tunnels or even extract any vehicles. In fact, it would take many days of heart breaking work to clear and drain the tunnels and it would take even longer to identify all the travellers.

The soldiers wondered why there were no vehicles on the approach roads themselves, before reaching the conclusion that the wave must have been so massive, it simply scoured the roadway of all vehicles. Any that were on the approach road would have simply been swept upriver and dumped onto the Rainham Marshes and beyond. There was even a possibility of some survivors, but each vehicle would have to be searched individually and that would take both manpower and time.

A third platoon was now despatched to assess the state of the Bridge's concrete pillars. Some containers, after being swept into the river from the container port at Tilbury, were carried across West Thurrock and the Thurrock Trade Park, before crashing into the concrete uprights of the bridge. Some simply sunk next to the bridge, although others were swept further west onto and beyond the Rainham Marches. Each of the concrete pillars would need a careful assessment. Although the Bridge itself was closed, all the lanes leading south were full of standing traffic. As the mist continued to clear, the soldiers could see the lines of traffic snaking southwards, even out and over the river itself.

A similar military column, despatched to the southern end of the Bridge, was reporting the same level of death, devastation and destruction. In addition, it was able to explain the non-movement of the traffic from the Bridge. As the wave swept over the fence and into the tunnels on the south side, it also carried vehicles southwards along the carriageway until it met the toll booths where there were now many vehicles piled up in a mountain of twisted, broken metal. Soldiers were already searching for survivors, but with precious little reward.

After reading the reports from the Dartford crossings, civil servants at the Ministry of Transport, liaising with the Police, deployed officers to help clear the Bridge of traffic and to turn the queues around. The Bridge would be closed for the foreseeable future, until its foundations were thoroughly checked and passed 'fit for purpose'. The Minister for Transport was also advised that every bridge over the river Thames, from Dartford to Teddington, would be subjected to a similar survey and that, until this task was complete, London would become a city split east/west by the river.

In Downing Street, after freshening up, the Prime Minister called an emergency cabinet meeting. At ten o'clock, as his ministers filed into the Cabinet Room, he faced them looking pale and drawn. Although impeccably dressed, he appeared to have aged several years. His whole demeanour made him look as though he had worked through the night, which, of course, he had.

"Colleagues. I have no simple words to describe the catastrophe which has struck London. We have an immense disaster on our hands which is immediate, overwhelming and defining. You are all aware that, yesterday afternoon, a sea surge, created by whatever malevolent meteorological forces, flooded vast swathes of London, on both sides of the river Thames. To put this into a wider, more European context, that same sea surge has overwhelmed Holland and caused widespread flooding throughout northern Europe from France and Belgium, through Holland, Northern Germany and Denmark. The loss of life has been immense and widespread.

"Here, in London, my office is receiving regular updates of the structural damage and loss of life. The Metropolitan Police and the River Police are working closely with the Army. The Ambulance Service is working in tandem with the Fire Service. Together with innumerable members of the public, each service has already worked through the night and many lives have been saved. They are also engaged in recovering and identifying the dead, a task of immense difficulty.

"The immediacy of this disaster is that the wave struck with such force and such speed that many, if not all, crossings of the Thames – bridges, ferries, tunnels – have been affected. The main railway tunnels are full of water, but I am assured that no trains were actually underground at the time the wave struck.

"Sadly, this is not the case with the London Underground. I am advised that the water overwhelmed the passenger entrances to London Bridge station so swiftly that the flood defences were not deployed. After entering the railway tunnels, the flood water proceeded both north and south and under enormous pressure. Both the Bakerloo and the Northern lines are out of action and will be for some time to come. There are unconfirmed reports that the flood water has also entered the Central Line system, through the connecting tunnels and through other stations."

The Prime Minister paused, as his words were digested by his Ministers. Hearing these details for the first time, some of the Ministers raised their hands to seek further clarification, but the Prime Minister shook his head and raised his right hand to stop their potential interruptions.

"Colleagues, there will be time for questions later. Please let me continue. As far as can be ascertained, all bridges over the Thames, from the Queen Elizabeth II Bridge on the London Orbital Road, as far west as Teddington and even Kingston on Thames, have received some damage. Although the damage only appears to be superficial in many cases, in others it is severe. As a case in point, I am advised that the wave ripped HMS Belfast from her moorings at Southwark and she struck London Bridge with such force that masonry was dislodged and the bridge was almost cut in two. There are deep cracks across the entire road surface. Her bow was lodged in the bridge just to the south of the first piling and her stern was then forced by the weight of the water into the river bank, by the London Bridge Hospital.

"Somewhat surprisingly, Tower Bridge appears to have received very little damage at all, save for water ingress.

"I regret that the position with the road tunnels is far, far worse. As with the railway tunnels, the wave struck so quickly and with such force, that every road tunnel has been flooded. Because the water entered the tunnels at both ends simultaneously, the chances of any survivors are negligible. Just before this meeting commenced, I received reports from army patrols in Dartford that the water has completely filled both of the tunnels. The vehicles nearest the surface are crushed beyond recognition from the force of the flood and there are no survivors at all. Because the bridge was closed due to the very high winds, the traffic on the tunnel approaches would have been very heavy. There are no vehicles on the approach roads, leading to the presumption that that they have all been swept away.

"It is also reported that the ferry terminals at Woolwich have been destroyed, as have the ferries themselves. Indeed, army patrols have reported that much of the river infrastructure has been swept away as though by a giant scouring pad. Again, somewhat surprisingly, they also report that the river defences themselves are predominantly in place and, indeed, when the early morning tide came in, there were no reports of further flooding, despite this being the season for spring tides.

"Much damage has been done to the businesses lining the river on both banks. Full reports will follow.

"I can also advise that housing has suffered a terrible onslaught. The flood swept away all the empty sea containers from the container ports at Thamesmead and Tilbury. Once these were in the river, together with many cars, vans and trucks from the various storage facilities on both banks, they were simply washed over the river defences and into the housing and trading estates, where they swept indiscriminately across roads and through the buildings causing devastating destruction. Wherever there were people in the houses that were destroyed, it is expected that there will be few survivors, if any. However, where the housing estates were only inundated, I have been advised that there are many thousands of survivors and all the services are liaising with each other to provide whatever assistance and shelter might be required."

Once again, the Prime Minister paused. He looked down at his notes and took a deep breath. He then lifted his head and squared his shoulders, before looking left and right down the cabinet table. No one tried to intervene.

"At the beginning, I said this disaster is immediate, overwhelming and defining. I have described the immediacy of the disaster, as the wave struck with such destructive power and extraordinary speed. I have also given you a sense of the overwhelming catastrophe this has created. I now wish to make comment as to why I say this disaster will be defining."

He looked round the room.

"This country has faced disasters in the past and from them we have emerged stronger and more determined. It is our duty, colleagues, to lead the way in whatever manner possible. The country will be expecting strong leadership and because this disaster is so widespread across northern Europe, I rather feel that it will not be appropriate to seek assistance from Brussels. After all, we spent too many years over the process of leaving the European Union in order to face our own independent future, whatever that future might be. We must, therefore, be prepared to raise the necessary finance ourselves, to recruit the necessary expertise, to assess and address the necessary work. This will not be a time for committees, interminable discussion and careful assessment, even though we all know that such attributes are all so important. Colleagues, this is a time for action!

"The army is already carefully assessing the defences along both banks of the river. We will be building on those reports and all such information will immediately be passed to any and all agencies who can utilise the information to help in returning this city, as well as this country, to normality as quickly as possible.

"We will need capital. We will need volunteers. We will recruit from the job centres, the universities and the voluntary sector. Anyone who is able, fit and capable of lending assistance will be welcome. It will be everyone's job to work alongside the unions and the opposition parties. This is not a time for petty political differences and in-fighting.

"However, I wish to make it absolutely plain that, when these events are re assessed from a historical point of view, any decisions made now must be capable of standing up to public scrutiny. Be assured, every decision, every action will be picked over for years to come and this government, my administration, your work will be defined by this event."

Unbeknownst to the Prime Minister, in her office at Le Grove Investments, Alice was thinking along very similar lines. She and Michael Varley discussed the disaster, in as much as what they knew from the news on the television, over their breakfast meeting. It was already emerging that damage was widespread and loss of life immense. To restore London to anything like normality would take an immense amount of investment. Michael was of the opinion that a fund should be raised with government backing, similar in many respects to Government Bonds and Gilt edged investments but administered by the private sector and controlled from the city.

He saw the need for the immediacy of capital and available distribution and that it should be broadly and initially immune from excessive Government control. In time, however, he recognised that central control would most assuredly be incorporated, as normality returned but, for the immediate future, there was a greater need for funding, rather than nit picking compliance control. The detail, as is invariably the case, would be in the record keeping.

He and Alice talked round how best they might pursue his vision before she returned to her own office to type up her notes of the meeting. Michael started to make some calls and, to his surprise, not only did he find colleagues and friends available to talk, but more than willing to listen warmly to his suggestions and proposals. Slowly, he spread his net wider and wider.

In her own office, Alice completed her task, saved it in a new file on her computer and returned to Michael's office, with two printed copies.

"Thanks for doing this so quickly." Michael appeared vigorous and more in control than he had for the past few days. "I've already made some calls. Everyone I've spoken to, without exception, has been most supportive. So, we now need a structure to ensure this plan will not only work but will also receive the blessing of the Treasury."

"How do you mean?"

"Although this funding will be firmly created within the private sector, the Government will demand a say in how it is organised and spent. And rightly so, I suppose. But for it to work quickly, we must endeavour to restrict Government control as much as possible, especially in the short term. I foresee that the primary clients for this funding will actually be various Government departments, especially the Ministry of Transport and the Ministry for the Environment. They've been starved of funding for years. There must be a reasonable level of return for the investors and this return must also take future economic changes into consideration."

"This will need additional staffing and careful records."

"Correct!" Michael looked carefully at Alice. "And I want you to step up to the plate."

"How do you mean?"

"When you brought in our breakfast, you instigated all this. I remember exactly what you said to me about wallowing in self-pity. You were right! So, now's the time for you to demonstrate your own talents and come on board with me."

"What exactly do you mean?" Alice repeated.

"I want you to become a director of Le Grove Investments. That's easily sorted. Then I want you to direct the manner in which the fund will be raised and administered. I will assist in whatever way I can. Once our consortium is in place, we can approach the Treasury and put our proposals to the Chancellor. My first few calls have been very positive and we already have three banks ready to work with us – Well with you."

"Do you really think I can do this?" Alice asked wonderingly.

"Yes. I do!"

Alice felt a warm thrill start in her chest and slowly work its way down her stomach and into the cleft between her legs. She forced her face to remain absolutely passive, but knew that, very soon, she would have to leave the room. As she stood in front of Michael, her legs began to weaken and her head felt light, as though she was about faint. With some concern, she realised that the intensity she was now feeling was just like her very first orgasm and, as she willed herself to maintain control, she wondered whether men felt such a degree of intensity in similar circumstances.

"Michael, will you excuse me for just a couple of minutes. I just want to check something on my desk."

"Of course."

Alice turned away and walked slowly to the door. She turned back and said, "I'll bring back fresh coffee, when I return."

"I won't be expecting you to be doing that sort of stuff in the future, you know."

"Well, there's no one else for now!" she quipped.

She left his office and went straight to her own, where she quickly lifted the skirt of her dress to remove her panties. She knew that she had orgasmed and now she found that her knickers were completely soaked. She used a couple of tissues to dry herself, before sitting in her chair. She pulled out the lowest drawer of her desk and put her left foot onto it, before lifting up her skirt so that she could masturbate herself. She orgasmed again very quickly and, at last, felt that totally unexpected degree of intensity begin to recede. She dried herself once more, closed the drawer, stood up and readjusted her dress. Already, she felt totally in control.

Gosh, that was rather intense. I'll have to ensure that I maintain a far better control over my emotions from now on, she thought to herself.

After making the coffee, she re-entered Michael's office to find him on the telephone with a list of names in front of him. He had put a tick alongside most of them. She poured the coffee and sat down in the chair on the opposite side of his desk.

At the Gloucester Palace Hotel, breakfast was finished and the various refugees from the previous evening were making their plans. Some had already left the hotel, in an attempt to make their way back home. They faced long and frustrating journeys because Transport for London had closed all operations on the Underground, as well as cancelling all bus services. All bridges over the river were now closed, with the police re-directing traffic accordingly. All mobile communications were now restored, of course, so David was able to contact his mother.

"Where are you?" She asked, trying hard not to display the anxiety she had suffered through the long night. "The school has been on the phone asking why you weren't in Assembly this morning."

"Yeah. I thought they might be." Like his mother, David was also trying very hard to play down his emotions. "So what did you tell them?"

"What could I tell them? I didn't know where you were. Nor who you were with. The radio and the television came back on at about eight o'clock yesterday evening, but of you and your father, not a sign."

"Listen, Mum." David decided it would play better if he was absolutely straight. "You know I've been tracking the storms coming across the Atlantic?" He waited for a response, but there was none. "Well, with the wind staying so strong on Wednesday and Thursday, I was pretty sure in my own mind that there would be an event in London, so I phoned Jackie. We cut school and went up to Waterloo. There were thousands of people milling about in the station all trying to get trains out of London. We forced our way over Waterloo Bridge. There were thousands of people trying to get across the river. The crowd was so big that it forced the traffic to stop.

"Anyway, we finally got into Somerset House. It was open, but all the staff had disappeared. We found a room overlooking the river. We could see all the way down the river to Tower Bridge and as far as Vauxhall Bridge in the other direction. While we were there, we watched as the big wave came bursting through Tower Bridge, surging all over the south bank." He stopped, as the memories of that awful moment came flooding back. Jackie was standing next to him and she linked her arm with his. He turned to look at her, with tears streaming down his face. He shook his head from side to side and took a deep breath."

"David, are you all right?"

"Hang on a sec, Mum." Seeing that he couldn't continue, Jackie took the phone from him. "Hello, Mrs Varley? This is Jackie."

"Where's David? What's happened?"

"He's here and he's OK. You must understand, though, we've both been through a pretty difficult time. There was this bus that had been knocked on its side by the flood water from the river. David organised the rescue of all those that had survived, but were trapped inside. He was brilliant, but now it's all catching up with him."

"What on earth do you mean?"

"Look, Mrs Varley." In her turn, Jackie took a deep breath. "I don't think it'll be very easy to tell you everything on the phone. It'll be best to leave the details until we see you. We're going to get a cab now and come home. I've no idea how long we'll be. The roads are difficult and some are blocked, but we do have a guy here who has already been very helpful to us."

"Whereabouts are you?"

"Oh! Right! We're at the Gloucester Palace Hotel in Kensington."

"Have you heard anything from David's father, Michael? And have you spoken with your family?"

"I spoke with my mum just before David called you. We haven't heard from your husband. Have you tried to call him?"

"Yes. Of course I have," she replied rather testily. "And his phone is constantly engaged."

"I guess you should keep trying," Jackie advised. She turned off the phone.

She turned and put her arms round David. He took another deep breath and leant his chin on her head as she squeezed him tight. He was leaning with his back to the reception desk as he watched WPC Liz Drury came through the door at the bottom of the stairs.

218

Despite the trauma of being knocked unconscious and then having to find and recover her briefcase, this morning she looked absolutely wonderful in control, poised and well rested.

"Hello, you two," she greeted them, brightly. "Have you seen the Bulgarians?"

"No. Not since breakfast." David looked up and shook his head as he replied.

"I have," said Jackie. She gently pulled away from David to turn and face Liz. "Just before David came downstairs, they went through the front door and into the street. They haven't come back."

"Did they say where they were going?" A frown crossed Liz's face which, for an instance, made her look hard and mean.

Somewhat taken aback by the look on her face, Jackie replied, "No. I'm sorry. They just said 'Thank you for looking after us' and went out."

"OK. That is a pity." The frown had gone and her face had returned to normal. "I just wanted to have a chat with them." She shrugged. "No matter. I suppose I'd better get off myself." And with that she returned through the door to go back upstairs.

David looked at Jackie. "Do you know where they've gone?"

"Not really. Ivelina mentioned something about Willesden, but they'll have a hell of a walk to get there."

"You mentioned that we are going to get a cab. Is Andy still here?"

"He spent the night here."

"Would you mind if we went to the city first. To see if I can find my dad."

"Now that is a good idea! And then we can call in at Scotland Yard on the way back, to see if mine is OK."

David looked at her to see if she was joking and decided that she wasn't.

"Do you have anything upstairs?" he asked.

"No. I've got everything right here." She picked up her coat and slipped it on. "I think Andy's gone down there." She added, pointing down the passage leading to Sebastian's office. "Come on. Let's dig him out."

They found the office door and knocked on it. A disembodied voice called to them to come in. They opened the door and went into the room, to find Sebastian behind his desk and Andy sitting in a chair with his back to the door.

"Can I help you?"

"We were wondering whether Andy could drive us to London Wall." David explained that his mother had been trying to phone his father, but that his father's phone was constantly engaged. "And then to Scotland Yard."

"Why on earth do you want to go there?" Sebastian raised both his eyebrows, being so surprised by Jackie's comment that his self-control briefly slipped. He quickly regained his inscrutable attitude.

"My Dad works there." Jackie explained, without reacting to the sharpness of his question.

"Over to you, Andy." Seb waved his right hand in the direction of the cabbie.

"That's fine with me. Do you want me to get you home after that?"

"Well, yeah! That would be great," replied David

"Right then. How soon do you want to go?"

"As soon as you're ready, if that's OK?"

"Sure. Give me a couple of minutes with Mr Fortescue Brown and I'll be right with you."

The two youngsters thanked Sebastian for opening up his hotel and left the room. They walked back to the front door, joining hands in a show of mutual respect and consideration. Back in his office, Sebastian finished his conversation with Andy and then commented that David's father was Michael Varley at Le Grove Investments.

"That's a bit of a coincidence, Gov," Andy remarked.

"Yes. It might well be. But, there's no need to let on that you know that."

"No, Gov."

Andy left the office and after collecting Jackie and David, they all climbed into his cab for the journey to the city.

At much the same time, Alice gently knocked on Michael's door and entered with a piece of paper in her hand.

"What's that?"

"I've started drafting up the office requirements. We will need a minimum of three executives, each controlling a team of two managers, one secretary and one computer operator. In addition, we must have an overall IT specialist and, in due course, there will be a need for a compliance officer. All this will require space. Apart from my own office, each team will need its own accommodation. I wondered about open plan but, on balance, I feel that separate offices for each team will be better. The secretaries will need a separate room and the compliance officer will need a private office. In addition, we'll need a sizeable meeting room. Taken all together, that will virtually fill a complete floor of this office block."

"So now you can see, Alice, why I felt that you could head up this operation. I've been thinking, in very broad terms, on much the same lines. I don't suppose you are aware that the floor below us is also retained by Le Grove Investments. It has been sub-let in the past, but it's completely empty just now."

Michael continued. "To set all this in motion, I suggest we set up a new company and Le Grove will lease the appropriate space to that company." He shrugged. "I will also have to find a replacement for you!"

"And what am I supposed to use for capital?"

"In the short term, you can leave that with me. As a partner in this venture, I can assist with the capitalisation."

"How soon do you think that we will obtain some form of short term understanding from the Treasury?"

"I am hoping to have some confirmation of that around lunchtime."

"Well, I need to contact electrical contractors, IT hardware companies and a builder who can create the space and rooms we need." Alice looked at Michael. "Without wanting to ask a silly question, how soon do you want this operation up and running?"

"And without giving you a flippant answer, this afternoon would be good. However, I think we'll all have to work over the weekend to be ready first thing Monday morning. I've also prepared three lists for you. The first is a list of financial institutions that have already agreed to support our venture, together with the appropriate contact names.

"The second is a list of potential executives, to run your teams. There are five names in all, two of whom are already signed up. You'll have to select the third from the balance.

"Lastly, there is a list of potential managers. I would advise that you work closely with the new executives to complete your teams.

"I'll leave the other employees to you. I'm sure you'll be able to pick up very suitable people pretty easily."

Alice took the lists and left Michael's office, feeling more empowered than ever in her life. As she walked down the corridor to her own office, the discreet front door bell rang, making her start. She opened the door to find Andy the cab driver together with two teenagers outside.

"Can I help you?"

"Good morning!" David greeted her. "I don't think we've met before, but I am David Varley, Michael's son."

"Please come in." Alice opened the door for them all to enter the reception area. "But, why are you here?"

"It's a bit of a long story. Is my father here?"

"Yes. He's in his office, but he is really very busy. Hang on a sec. I'll buzz him." She picked up her telephone, which was answered very quickly.

David could hear his father say, "What is it Alice? You know I'm waiting for calls."

"Your son, David and a young lady, as well as Andy the cabbie, are all here in reception."

"You'd better send them all through to me. And I wonder if you can make some coffee?"

"Of course."

Alice turned to David. "His office is at the end of the corridor on the right."

"Thanks. But please don't make any coffee. We only want to make sure that he's OK before we track down Jackie's dad at Scotland Yard."

David, holding Jackie's hand walked towards the office door and gently knocked, before opening the door. Michael was behind his desk, talking on his iPhone. As they entered, he cut the call and looked at the pair questioningly.

"Hi, Dad. This is Jackie, my girlfriend." Michael nodded. "We were in London yesterday afternoon and got caught up in the flood. We had to spend the night in a hotel in Kensington. Anyway, I spoke to Mum this morning who said that she had been trying to call you but that your phone is permanently engaged. She's very worried and has left you a number of messages."

"You're right!" David lifted his right hand to stem the flow of words. "We'll discuss later why you were in London and not revising for your exams." He stood up.

"Jackie, it's a pleasure to meet you." He came round his desk to shake her hand. "Strange circumstances, of course. But that's why I'm really busy. This flood has caused enormous damage and the country will require immediate access to funds in order to rebuild. But, you're right! I should have phoned your mum and I'll do that straightaway."

"We've only come in to check that you're OK."

"Well, you can see that I am. But you'll have to let me get on. I'm waiting for calls from the Treasury as well as other colleagues and I really shouldn't miss them."

"OK, Dad. We'll get out of your hair. Anyway, we've got to go the Scotland Yard now, to check on Jackie's dad."

"Why Scotland Yard?"

"Because that's where he works."

"Oh! OK." Michael was somewhat surprised and his mind was quickly assessing and storing that information. "Well, don't let me keep you. And you can tell your cabbie to bill me for the fares."

David, followed by Jackie, left Michael's office as he was dialling his wife. They collected Andy from reception and after saying good bye to Alice, they all returned to the taxi for the journey to Scotland Yard.

As the roads were unusually quiet, especially with the temporary cancellation of all public transport, within ten minutes Andy was driving down the Embankment. He slowed down before he reached the junction with Temple where the pleasure boat was still stranded. He pointed out to the youngsters in the back the place he had picked up the

221

other refugees, before driving up Temple to the Strand. He continued down the Strand to Trafalgar Square and turned down Whitehall. When the cab reached Richmond Terrace, they saw all the police vehicles crushed up against the gates. A policeman was on duty at the pedestrian entrance.

"Off you go, you two," Andy said cheerily. "I'll wait here until you get back."

"OK. Thanks." David got out and then helped Jackie. Together they crossed the pavement to the policeman.

"Good morning," David said politely. "Can we come in?"

"Not really." The policeman explained that, "Everything's in a bit of an upheaval, what with the flooding an' all."

Jackie fixed him with a stare and said that she wanted to see her father.

"And who might he be, miss?" the policeman replied, somewhat patronisingly.

"Chief Superintendent Kevin Bleasdale."

"Oh! Right. I'll call through."

He turned to a small box, just inside the gate and dialled a number. It was answered almost immediately and after a brief conversation, he ushered Jackie and David inside the gate, pointing to the door where he said they would be met.

Even before they had reached the door, it opened and a fresh faced constable emerged.

"Are you here for Chief Superintendent Bleasdale?"

"Yes."

"Please come this way, miss."

"Thanks."

"I'm afraid we're avoiding the lifts until they've been thoroughly checked, so we'll have to climb the stairs. Your Dad's on the fourth floor."

"That's fine. We've done worse."

They climbed up the four flights, with the constable chatting about nonentities all the way until, finally, they reached Kevin Bleasdale's door. It was already open and he was already walking from his desk by the window to greet them.

"Hello Jackie." She rushed to him and hugged him. After a little while, he took hold of her shoulders and held her at arm's length. "Are you all right?" He looked over at David. "Both of you?"

"Yes, sir!" David replied. "For reasons that are too complicated to explain, we were both in London when the wave came up river and flooded all the south bank and parts of Westminster. We spent the night in a small hotel in Kensington and spoke to Mrs Bleasdale just after breakfast. She advised us that she hadn't heard from you since yesterday, but she realised that you would be busy with organising your teams." David stopped.

"Now then, young fella," Jackie's father responded. "I'm not too sure I like the sound of my daughter staying in a hotel with a young lad and for it to be talked about so casually."

"Daddy." Jackie decided to take control of the conversation. "After the flood, David and I saw this bus that had been washed onto its side. He organised the extraction of all the survivors and when we had got them all onto Waterloo Bridge Road, he flagged down this taxi. We were then ferried to this hotel where the staff looked after us. I shared a room with a Bulgarian immigrant and a Woman Police Officer. I think you know her – Liz Drury?"

"It all seems highly irregular to me but, here you are, large as life." He hugged his daughter once more.

222

"Yes, Daddy. We are. And we've come here to tell you to call Mummy and let her know that we're OK."

"All right. All right." The Chief Superintendent knew that he would get no more out of his daughter.

"Anyway, we're going home now."

"That'll be difficult. There's no public transport and no trains."

"Doesn't matter, Dad. We've got a cab waiting downstairs."

Chapter 18
Friday Lunchtime and Afternoon

As the deep depressions slowly filled and drifted away over northern Europe, the weather in Britain turned unseasonably warm. Although it was still only February, the birds were singing and there was a detectable heat in the sun. The anticyclone that followed in the wake of the two vicious storms brought clement weather northwards from Africa, across Spain and the western Mediterranean. New weather fronts in the western Atlantic were forced much further to the north towards Greenland and Iceland and the forecasters were firmly predicting fair weather for as much as the next two weeks.

The peak of the spring tides passed and the job of clearing up the flood damage all around the south and east coasts commenced. Nowhere, however, was that damage as great or as grave as in the Thames Estuary and London.

After his two-hour catnap at the sea wall, Martin was finally persuaded to follow his family, neighbours and friends back to the farmhouse. His eyelids were so heavy that it was a conscious struggle to keep them open. He felt bone weary but strangely exultant. Helen helped her father into the back of the Landrover and, with Wayne sitting next to her in the passenger seat, she set off. They crossed over the ditch before driving up the fields towards the railway embankment. The land was now deeply rutted with the tyre tracks from all the trucks that had driven down through the long night. The track itself was quite slippy but after engaging four wheel drive, Helen made good progress. She and Wayne were chatting quietly in the front, while Martin sat on the backseat alone with his thoughts. As they drove up the field towards to railway bridge, he could feel the warmth of the sun on his right arm.

"Now we can see clearly, can we stop and look at the damage to the bridge?" He asked.

"Righty oh!" Helen replied.

She stopped the vehicle in front of the wrecked bridge and they all got out.

In the sunlight, it was frightening to see how much of the embankment had been eroded by the flood of sea water. The brick bridge was completely destroyed. Except for the hard core track through the embankment itself, all the bricks had disappeared. Rubble infill was now falling onto the track. The bricks from the walls and the roof of the bridge had been transported during the night down to the sea wall breach there they now helped to form a key part of the rushed and temporary repair. As they looked at the bridge, they could see above them that the only the rails remained, twisted and buckled. All the concrete sleepers had gone and of the original bridge only the foundations of the arch remained.

"And to think that all your trucks came through that gap," Martin muttered to Wayne.

"I know. I'm really sorry about the jib knocking the bridge itself down." Martin turned the younger man to face him and put both hands on his shoulders. He looked straight into his eyes.

"I suggest you don't mention that ever again to anybody. As far as I'm concerned, the flood did that and our diggers had to force a passage through the rubble. I made the decision to knock off the sleepers before we cleared the rubble out of the way, because of the potential danger to the drivers of the trucks driving through the gap.

"Mind you, I'll have to speak to the Environment Agency, but I expect they'll have their hands pretty full today." He turned to his daughter. "Thank you, Helen. I always knew that you were dependable, but I never appreciated the real depth of your spirit. I rather feel that your mum and I have created three really special children."

With tears in his eyes, he turned back to the Landrover.

"Come on," he said over his shoulder. "I need some breakfast."

Helen glanced at Wayne and lifted her eyes to the sky. He smiled at her and mouthed 'And I agree!'

"Stop it," she whispered, as they walked back to the vehicle.

As soon as they arrived at the farmhouse, Jennifer very quickly had hot coffee and a full breakfast waiting for each of them. No sooner were they sitting down at the big family kitchen table, than Martin's two sons and their wives drifted into the room.

"How are you feeling, Dad?" James asked. "Helen told us to leave soon after you had nodded off. Are you feeling rested?"

"Actually, I feel really elated as though we have achieved something quite remarkable," Martin replied. "If you boys and Helen hadn't been here, the sea would have reclaimed the land. And without Wayne and his team and our neithbours, we would have been completely stuffed. You must all be exhausted. I know that I am."

"And as soon as you've finished your breakfast," Jennifer said as she put her hand on his shoulder, "It's a hot bath and bed for you, Martin."

"Well, there is something else I've got to do first." He stood up and left the kitchen. He returned after a couple of minutes with a small package and an envelope in his hand.

"Today is a very special day," he announced. "We have our complete family with us and I'm really pleased that Wayne is still here. Today is our fortieth wedding anniversary and this is a small token of my love for you, Jennifer." He handed her the envelope together with the package that had been gift wrapped in the store.

Jennifer sat down at the table to open the card and slowly read the inane poem. She then removed the wrapping paper from the display box and opened it. The rubies on the necklace twinkled up at her. She gasped and felt the blood running up her neck and into her face.

"Where on earth did you find something as beautiful as this?" she asked. "And the earrings match the necklace. They are truly wonderful. I really don't know what to say."

"Don't say anything at all." Martin put his arms around his wife and kissed her fondly on the cheek. "You have been my rock for all these years and, together, we have produced three exceptional children. This family is a strong family and we are so lucky to have them all with us, Helen, the boys and their wives of course. This damned flood has been a bit of an intrusion, but I now realise that they are all here to help us celebrate our forty years." He shrugged. "And they said that it wouldn't last!"

"I'm sorry, Dad, but the Regiment has been on the phone and I've been recalled from leave." James quickly explained that the Army was now fully committed to organising the relief and clear up in London and elsewhere. He and Megan would have to leave very soon.

"Of course I understand. I expect that there will be plenty of other breaches in the sea wall as well. All the way round the coast as far as Norfolk, probably. A lot of work to be done." His voice tailed off as fatigue began to take over. He sat down. "I'll just finish this coffee and get off upstairs."

Fred Shemmings and his firefighters were now slowly and methodically checking every house and street for survivors, gas leaks and other damage. Most people were refusing to leave their homes and were already hard at work clearing out their damaged furniture and cleaning the mud and dirt off the floors and walls. That special spirit of community, so typical of the British when facing insuperable odds, was beginning to emerge as younger people helped their older neighbours; groups were organising themselves to shift heavier items; the more able bodied were sifting through the damaged houses for potential survivors. Even the children, recognising the seriousness of the situation, were helping their families and neighbours.

There was a persistent stench of kerosene in the air from the devastated London City Airport where the damage to the standing aircraft had been extensive. As the sun warmed all those outside, Fred realised that it wouldn't be too long before the sun started to sink in the sky and the day would be over. He knew that the coming night would be long and would throw up many difficult and varied challenges. The Army was already bringing in basic supplies and queues were forming at street corners to collect whatever provisions were available.

The flood had destroyed virtually everything up to the first floor of every building and, closer to the river bank, even higher than that. Where houses had cellars, these were full of dirty, smelly water and the owners were slowly bailing them out with buckets. Fred deployed all his pumps and slowly but surely his teams began to make a significant difference.

Dinah maintained contact with all the local schools where the teachers were organising the children, keeping them busy cleaning up the debris and helping to clear away the mud. Everywhere, there was a coating of mud. Older children were helping with the distribution of food and water to the housebound and the infirm. Slowly and inexorably the death toll was rising, as more drowned bodies were found in the flooded houses. Where the houses had been demolished, the bodies had been washed away in the flood and some were now being discovered in surprising and unexpected places. Some had been caught in the branches of the trees, others in telephone lines. One was even wrapped around a street lamp.

Fred and Dinah had now been on the go for a full thirty hours and their exhaustion was beginning to affect their judgment. However, they were both reluctant to return home, because they both knew that their own house would be flooded just like all their neighbours'.

As Fred and his team slowly made their way along one of the streets off Westferry Road, a local resident stopped him.

"Hallo Fred. I thought that was you."

Fred stopped and looked at the man standing in front of him. "Richard! Blimey, I've not clapped eyes on you for, what, twenty-five years?"

"Must be. Anyway, I can see you're busy, but you do need to know this."

"What?"

Richard took hold of Fred's arm and pointed him towards a container that had been swept out of the river, but its progress had been slowed by some trees at the end of the cul de sac, where they were standing. It was now on its left hand side, wedged between two houses.

"Yeah! OK. So what's so special about that one? There are containers like that all over Millwall."

"Yeah! I know. But I bet they aren't all making knocking noises, as though someone was inside."

"What? Bloody hell! You sure?"

"Wouldn't have stopped you, otherwise!"

They ran to the container and, sure enough, there was a definite knocking coming from the inside. Fred could see that the door was padlocked and because the container was on its side, even if they could get the padlock off, it was doubtful whether they would have the strength to lift the door up, because of its weight.

Fred spoke into his mobile phone. "Where's the nearest cutting and lifting equipment?"

"We've been advised to keep all the gear in readiness before taking it to the Dartford Tunnels, Gov," came the reply.

"Well, that'll have to wait a bit longer. Can you get one of the lads to run the kit down here?" He turned to Richard to ask for his postcode and then spoke it into his phone.

"Be with you in ten minutes, Gov," came the reply.

However, only five minutes passed before they heard the sirens of two approaching Fire and Rescue trucks. Fred directed them to the cul de sac. He had already assessed the situation and decided that the container would have to be dragged from between the two houses, before it could be lifted upright. The door would then swing open normally, as soon as the padlock was cut. He instructed the team, who attached light chains to the front end of the container and, after slightly lifting the front end, the truck slowly dragged it into the street, leaving a deep rut through the garden and across the pavement. The knocking stopped.

Now for the tricky bit, though Fred.

He made sure that the rescue trucks left sufficient room for the container to be lifted along its full length, so that when it was turned to more than 45 degrees, its own momentum would help to carry it into an upright position. To ensure no one was further injured on the inside, Fred positioned the chains from the second truck in such a way that it would take the strain at that point and gently lower the container to the ground in an upright position.

This plan was executed without a hitch and soon the padlocks were cut, allowing the door to be swung open. Sunlight flooded into the interior where the rescuers could see a number of people cowering at the far end. The smell inside was overpowering. Fred entered with his flashlight and, in its beam, he could see blood stains on the walls and the ceiling. He now realised that only a few of the people cowering in the far corner were moving.

"Does anyone speak English?" he asked.

"Little." A small woman raised her hand.

"We are going to get you out and give you food and water."

"Thank you." The woman shook her head. "Most are dead."

"How many are alive?"

"Four, maybe five."

"How many dead altogether?"

The woman lifted three fingers on her left hand and five on her right.

"Where are you from?"

"Cambodia."

"OK."

Fred went outside and called both the police and the ambulance service. The lifting teams and equipment were already clear and on their way to the Dartford Tunnel. His team was already helping those that were still alive to leave the container and sit on the ground in the sunshine.

Milton and Pamela were only able to sleep until Noon. The smell of damp finally wakened them. They got up and immediately realised that there was no food because it had all been destroyed by the flood.

As soon as Milton got out of bed he walked to the window and glanced down the road. He was surprised to see the three young lads were still tethered to the tree. He went to the bathroom and washed quickly. He was followed by Pamela. They dressed.

"What are we going to do about food?" she asked.

"I'm not sure." Milton tried to consider the situation rationally and came to the conclusion that all the local food shops, including the supermarkets, would be closed as all their stock would have been ruined. Apart from food and water, they would also need to buy a good quantity of cleaning materials, especially bleach and disinfectant.

"I think that best thing will be to go back to Waterloo."

Pamela considered this and commented, "All the people there were being transferred to Clapham Common. Don't you think we should try to go there, instead?"

"Mmm! I don't know. That's a bit of a hike and I doubt there'll be any public transport. At least we'll get some sort of a lift from Waterloo."

"You're probably right."

Milton turned on the radio, part of his saved music centre. Very soon the announcer advised the listeners that a Government Message was to be broadcast in a few minutes. The Band of the Coldstream Guards played 'Land of Hope and Glory' and as that faded away a taped message came from the Prime Minister.

All through the night the civil servants in the Cabinet Office had been working flat out. No one could remember a time when any degree of urgency had been greater. From one of the despatches, timed 10.15 am, that landed on the Prime Minister's desk, he learned that Transport for London had suspended all public transport for the foreseeable future. He immediately picked up the telephone and asked to be connected with the London Mayor.

"Good Morning, Mr Mayor."

"Good Morning, Prime Minister."

"Can you advise me why Transport for London has suspended all public transport across London?"

"I imagine it's because all the tunnels under the Thames have been flooded."

"Mr Mayor." The Prime Minister took a deep breath. "As far as I have been informed, that is not the case. I am advised that the flood defences to both the Victoria and the Jubilee lines prevented any ingress of water and all the connecting tunnels to other parts of the system were automatically sealed.

"In addition, I was unaware that buses make use of the same tunnels," he added somewhat sarcastically.

There was no reply from the London Mayor. He could hear a number of papers being shuffled about, as though he was looking for a specific despatch.

"Prime Minister." Finally, he returned to the telephone. "You are correct in both comments."

"Thank you, Mr Mayor." The Prime Minister took another deep breath. "Mr Mayor, I realise that since your election we have had our differences, predominantly from a political perspective. Despite that, I hope you will now join me in a spirit of cooperation to resolve the difficulties that now face both the capital and, indeed, the country as a whole. Whatever decisions are taken today, including your own, will obviously have long term ramifications. I recognise that we won't get everything right but, I'm sure you will agree with me, there is little point in aggravating an already catastrophic situation by playing petty politics.

"Can I suggest you have a word with your contacts and colleagues at Transport for London and get the buses moving once more?" He replaced the telephone, leaving the London Mayor wondering why the transport management hadn't reached the same conclusion several hours earlier.

He now made two calls himself. The first was to the Leader of the Opposition who confirmed that political hostilities were temporarily suspended until London was, once again, functioning. The second call was to Transport for London. The call was short and to the point. Within half an hour, buses were leaving the garages and a skeleton transport network was quickly re-established.

Just before eleven o'clock, the Prime Minister re-entered the cabinet room to advise his senior cabinet colleagues that the buses would soon be back on the streets. Wearily he sat down, realising that he was very hungry. He expected that his colleagues were feeling the same. He turned to the Cabinet Secretary and asked whether there were any provisions available, even if that might be just tea and coffee. The civil servant disappeared.

"What's the current situation?" He looked at his colleagues.

"Prime Minister." The Environment Secretary looked up. "The army patrols have now established that all road tunnels are completely flooded and blocked with vehicles. A start has already been made on pumping out the water at Dartford, but this is being impeded by the crushed vehicles and their dead passengers that are blocking the tunnels. I have been advised that it will be better for the pumping and the extraction of vehicles and passengers to proceed in tandem, rather than to leave the extractions until all the water is clear."

"Why?" he interrupted.

"Well, it is felt that it may well be several days before all the water in all the tunnels can be cleared. The decomposition of the dead bodies is expected to become an increasing problem and it is thought that if the bodies are under water, the rate of decomposition will be slowed." The Prime Minister nodded.

"The major stumbling block to this work is manpower," he continued. "And equipment. I will need a considerable boost to my budgets if we are to make any meaningful inroads to that particular work.

"In addition, there are problems building up concerning the road network, but I will allow my colleague to cover that."

The Minister for Transport looked up and nodded. "I can only repeat my colleague's comments concerning manpower, equipment and finance." He turned and looked at the Chancellor. Surprisingly, the Chancellor was looking intently at his electronic notepad, although such devices had long been banned from cabinet meetings.

"Prime Minister. I have some timely and welcome news."

By half past eleven, the new teams that Michael wanted were already in place. They all agreed that they would be happy to come to Le Grove Investments immediately and to work through the weekend if necessary. Alice, much to her surprise, was able to track down both a builder and an electrician. They arrived late in the morning and were already at work on her planned office refurbishments. She was now endeavouring to obtain furniture and computers with a view to having them installed overnight.

Also to her surprise, the level of cooperation was excellent.

More importantly, Michael had already obtained the promise of £100 billion of potential capital, which could be used as soon as the Treasury gave its backing to his proposals. When he telephoned the Treasury, he was asked to put his proposals in an email.

He wrote:

Dear Chancellor,

You will recall our meeting yesterday morning when you attended and opened the Financial Symposium at the Guildhall.

Following the extraordinary events of yesterday afternoon and evening, with so much of London and its infrastructure being destroyed by the sea surge up the River Thames, the city appreciates that there will be a need for vast sums of capital to be made available to the Government so that the country and its capital can be returned, as quickly as possible, to some semblance of normality.

Since dawn, I have been working with colleagues here in the city to set up a fund to be made available for the Government so that this work can commence immediately. Obviously, the Government will require some degree of control over the usage of this capital, but my colleagues and I also recognise the need to commence work at the earliest opportunity, without incurring unnecessary bureaucratic encumbrances.

We also recognise that some of the damage will have been insured and it is hoped that the Government will be able to persuade the Insurance Companies to reach early settlements.

Can we meet, today, in order to discuss and finalise a pragmatic methodology whereby the city's funding can receive Government's support at a sensible and reasonable level of interest?

Yours ever,
Michael Varley

This was the note that the Chancellor read on his notepad during the impromptu cabinet meeting. By nature a cautious man, he read the email out loud to his colleagues. *Is this too good to be true?* He was thinking. He passed the notepad to the Prime Minister, who looked up, when he finished reading the message for the second time. There was silence in the room.

"I wonder how much capital he's talking about?" he murmured, as though to himself.

"We'll only find out by talking with him," the Chancellor replied.

"Colleagues." The Prime Minister looked at his cabinet. "Earlier today I said that these events would be defining. Defining for this government and defining for each one of us. Our decisions will not only make or break this Government but will also make or break this great country. We must talk with this man and discover whether he can do what he says." He looked at his Chancellor. "This could just be the opportunity to demonstrate to the world that Great Britain knows exactly how to look after herself."

The Chancellor immediately left the cabinet room so that he could telephone Michael Varley without interruption from the other ministers. It was just after Noon when the call was received at Le Grove Investments. Alice immediately put it through.

"Chancellor, good afternoon." Michael formally greeted the Chancellor of the Exchequer before reminding him that it was only the previous morning that they had met. "As soon as the flood passed by the city in the afternoon, I realised that there would no opportunity of travelling home. My secretary and I were cut off, here in London Wall and soon after dawn we began planning how best we could assist the government."

"Your call has been well received by the Prime Minister and the Cabinet," the Chancellor replied. "Indeed, if you can make available the appropriate levels of capital to set the necessary renovations in motion, I am sure that the Government will be able to demonstrate a degree of understanding how best this can be achieved in the short term."

"Thank you, Chancellor. I would suggest that we meet, immediately if that's possible, in order to set up the basic ground rules and how soon the Government will want to take over full control of the funds and their distribution."

"I can make arrangements to come to your office within the hour, if that's convenient to you, Mr Varley?"

"I fully appreciate the necessity for urgency. We will be able to demonstrate to you how we are already able and capable of controlling this extraordinary situation."

"Mr Varley, it is already past mid-day. I can be at your office by two."

"Chancellor, it will be a pleasure to meet with you again. Thank you for responding to my email so positively. I am sure that, working together, we can indeed demonstrate to the world that London is already using this catastrophe to build for the future rather than allowing it to knock us back."

As soon as the call was complete, Michael leant back in his chair and breathed a deep sigh of relief intermixed with empowerment. From the other side of his desk, Alice had listened to the conversation and realised that she had less than just over an hour to prepare for the visit.

At the Dartford Tunnel, the Army was now working closely with the London Fire and Rescue Service, the Ambulance Service, the Police and a number of Undertakers, under the control of the Coroner's Office. The task facing them all was immense. Both tunnels being full of water, it seemed that the pumps were making very little impression. Requests were despatched for more powerful pumps and the troops on the ground were reassured that various organisations from the mining industry and elsewhere were responding with immediate effect.

The first vehicles were already being extracted from the tunnels. As soon as one vehicle was disentangled and cut free, it was pulled away from the tunnel entrance and powerful cutting equipment used to demolish it on site. This was done to extract the bodies as quickly as possible and these were immediately identified if that was possible, before being taken away in an ambulance to a local mortuary. Very soon, as the numbers of the dead continued to increase rapidly, it became apparent that bodies would have to be taken some distance. It is extraordinary to note that, in the event, mortuaries as far away as South Wales and County Durham were pressed into service, alongside cold stores and warehouses as well as refrigeration plants. The police were keeping the records of all the vehicles and identified bodies.

As soon as practicable, the dismembered vehicles were removed from the slip roads, to be stored elsewhere.

At Dartford, this work was continuing at both the north and the south ends of the tunnels. Very soon, similar teams were in place at Blackwall and Rotherhithe, as well as the Greenwich Foot Tunnel.

Transport for London was now facing the appalling task of accessing the flooded stations and tunnels. The logistics of removing the hundreds of thousands of bodies, after identification wherever was possible, were already exercising the minds of both the senior management and the rescue teams on the ground. With the exception of the Victoria and Jubilee lines, in every station in the city and the West End, there were dead bodies in the stairwells, the foot tunnels, on the platforms and on the tracks. Some were obviously crushed to death by the sheer weight of other bodies, some electrocuted where they had fallen or been pushed off the platforms and onto the tracks, many were drowned and still others were rendered almost unrecognisable after being hit by the trains as they were swept by the pressurised water out of the tunnels, off the tracks and onto the platforms.

The army was coordinating the removal of people from various places where they had congregated during the flood. Many had gathered together in stations, open parks, housing estates and in the upper floors of tower blocks. They were all taken to processing centres on either side of the river. Here they were given a medical check, their details were recorded and, if they had no home to return to, temporary accommodation was arranged. Such accommodation was rapidly becoming difficult to find within the London area, with the numbers of homeless growing very rapidly. Early decisions were made to transfer people to holiday camps, large hotels, and disused services' camps. As far as possible, families were kept together but, inevitably, there was considerable confusion, made worse by officials who were working without proper direct training or accurate information.

Reports and messages between the Emergency Services and Downing Street were also increasing rapidly as Friday afternoon slowly descended into Friday evening. The sun sank in the clear winter sky, giving way to the dusk of early evening. Although the day had been surprisingly warm, the coming night would be cold and frosty.

Just as the terrible and difficult work was now assisted at the entrances to the tunnels with temporary flood lights, so the activity in Government continued unabated. Ministers snatched sleep wherever they could, but major decisions still had to be made. The Prime Minister made an early contact with the Local Government Association in the old Transport House at Smith Square. All County, Metropolitan and Borough Councils were asked to offer whatever services they could bring so that order and control could assist with the overwhelming tasks facing the teams operating on the ground.

Teams of volunteers were arriving in many parts of the flooded areas asking how they could assist. At first, they appeared to be more of a hindrance than a help, as no one seemed to be in a position nor had the knowledge as to how to deploy them, because no one on the ground really knew how bad the overall situation was. However, as information slowly began to emerge throughout the day, the army was able to take control of these volunteers and they began to be directed to those areas where they could be the most effective.

Information also began to emerge about the devastation in Holland and northern Europe. The French and Belgian coastlines and the Danish and German coastal areas were all inundated, but not to the same degree of intensity or catastrophic damage as in Holland.

The Environment Agency had produced, many years before, predictive maps of potential flooded areas of the River Thames, should the Thames Barrier fail. These were now updated in the form of a report and presented to the Prime Minister at four o'clock. In addition, photographs were included of the devastated housing estates, some collapsed tower blocks and the catastrophic condition of the various road and pedestrian tunnels. Some early proposals in respect of renovation and reconstruction were added, with very broad indications as to cost, which already well exceeded one billion pounds and the report's author indicated that the final cost was expected to exceed that figure many times over.

As soon as he read this latest report, the Prime Minister called a further Cabinet Meeting, which would be followed by a COBRA meeting. In Cabinet, he distributed photocopies of the Environment Agency report. As soon as his colleagues had read and assimilated the contents, he started asking questions.

"How is the liaison between the Army and the Police and other Emergency Services?"

"After a few initial hiccups, it is working very well," the Armed Forces Minister replied. "I am advised that overall command lies with the Ministry of Defence and direct lines of communication between Whitehall and Scotland Yard have been organised. Basically, the Police are centralising all the work of the civilian Emergency Services and together they are bringing in the specialised pumping and extraction equipment. This is being supplied by the private sector, where Local Authorities are unable to assist."

"Where are the displaced people being housed?" The Prime Minister looked at the Home Secretary.

"After they have been processed in the central processing areas, they are given a medical check and are then despatched to specific and logged addresses. All names, original home addresses and temporary addresses are being recorded and cross referenced with Local Authority records. Although my teams are confident that every person who passes through a processing centre will be recorded, we are conscious that the records cannot expect to be one hundred percent accurate. We have already come across a number of anomalies where it appears that illegal immigrants have been found. These people are being detained in separate accommodation. The major problem will be in uniting families whose members were spread over London when the flood occurred." The Home Secretary paused.

"And how are they to be fed?" the Prime Minister asked.

"We are working closely with the Army and the Police to get all the major supermarkets cleared of all contaminated stock as quickly as possible. The supermarket chains have all supported our proposals that their stores should be cleared, cleaned and restocked as quickly as possible. It is already recognised that cleaning products will be needed in considerably increased quantities. In addition, increased amounts of basic staple foods will be available in all major outlets by Sunday morning and we also recognise that there will be considerable pressure on the public throughout Saturday.

"In order to keep public order, the Police have cancelled all leave and officers will be on the streets to assist and direct the people."

The Prime Minister finally turned to the Chancellor. "And how is the government to pay for all this?"

"Fortunately, Prime Minister, some of the immediate costs will be covered by insurance, but those funds will not be made available until the Insurance Companies have had an opportunity to assess the damage, the causes of that damage and whether there were any contributing factors by the insured. This will all be done in the future and I have asked all such companies to speed up their processes as much as possible, to assist in the general programme of regeneration.

"More importantly, as you will already know, I have already been in discussion with certain bankers in the city who have offered a specific relief fund, which is already totalling as much as £100 billion. A new company has been created specifically to organise this fund and to liaise directly with the Treasury. It has been put to me that the Government itself will be the first beneficiary of this fund as it will need hard cash to assist in the removal of the damaged vehicles, the rubble from collapsed buildings, making the roads safe, assisting the payment of the Emergency Services and the Army and so on.

"Fiscally, this Government has been running a very tight economic ship and this catastrophe cannot possibly be addressed by Government finance alone. Although I appreciate that there will be a need to control this degree of outside finance very carefully, I am willing to proceed with it in order to assist those who are wanting to move forward rapidly in the reconstruction programme."

"This fund isn't going to come back to haunt us, is it?" The Prime Minister voiced the question that was in the minds of the other cabinet members present.

"I have just returned from an initial meeting with Le Grove Investments. This is a small, well respected investment bank with excellent contacts through the financial industry both here and overseas. Mr Varley, with whom I have been speaking, has already shown me some of the details with regard to the backers of the first £100 billion.

"The new company will be working singularly and specifically in administering the fund whilst liaising with the Treasury. At this stage, the only records I have seen will cover the amounts invested and the amounts distributed. In the current ethos of getting things moving, I am more minded to make the capital available and, in due course, to tighten up the necessary and appropriate regulatory requirements. We are in discussion with regard to the interest payable on the funds and how the exact details will work. Their new offices will be in place on Monday morning with all the necessary communication links set up and working. I am advised that the necessary personnel has already been engaged."

This statement was met with a stunned silence, each cabinet member wondering how their somewhat dour Chancellor could have achieved so much in such a short time.

"Prime Minister, by way of a personal explanation, I met Mr Varley at the Financial Symposium on Thursday morning." He stopped and looked at his notes. "Yes indeed. It's somewhat surprising to note that it was only yesterday morning." He shook his head. "So much has happened since then.

"Anyway, Mr Varley opened the Symposium and, obviously, I met him then for the first time. He must have recalled our meeting before setting up this fund and telephoning my office. This proposal could and should be an excellent example of Westminster and the city working closely together for the benefit of the people overall."

"I completely agree." The Prime Minister echoed his Chancellor. "This is just the type of defining decision to which I referred earlier this morning."

After leaving Scotland Yard, Andy was forced to drive David and Jackie via a most circuitous route to get back to Richmond. With all the bridges over the River Thames now closed with both the Army and the Police manning the road blocks, Andy had to drive as far west as Brentford, before he could turn south and work his way down to Walton-on-Thames where he crossed the river over Walton Bridge. Once on the south side it was a simple task to drive up through Kingston and then on to Richmond. They arrived home after four o'clock and it was already dark.

During the journey, Jackie spoke with her mother to assure her that her father was safe and well but would be staying in London while the emergency continued. David also spoke briefly with his mother and was similarly comforting with regard to his father. When they arrived at David's home, much to their surprise, they saw that the small drive to the house already had two cars parked in it.

"I wonder what's going on," commented David as the cab approached the house.

"That's my mum's car," Jackie replied, pointing at a light blue Corsa.

"She must have come round to take you home."

"Suppose." Jackie took hold of David's hand and squeezed it. "David, thanks for everything. I know we've seen some horrible things but, in a funny way, I'm really glad you called me yesterday. It was a lot more interesting than just revision."

"You've been brilliant!" he replied quietly. "There's no way I could have got those people out of the bus without you. Come on, we'd better go in."

As they got out of the taxi, David's mother came down the drive to the road.

"I was beginning to wonder where you'd all got to," she said. "Then I heard that all the bridges have been closed from the city all the way to Kingston. Did you have to come over Hampton Court Bridge?"

"No, ma'am," Andy replied. "That's closed as well. We've been all the way to Walton."

"That is a long way round. Please come in. I expect you'll all want a cup of tea. Hello, Jackie. Your mum's here. Oh, and, David, Mr Smith is here from school."

"What does he want?"

"He mentioned that he volunteered to come to see you, when the headmaster was asking him about your non-attendance this morning."

"Am I in trouble?" David asked as he and Jackie went through the front door into the hall.

"No more than you should be, skipping off school, like that," his mother replied.

They went into the dining room, where Annabel Bleasdale was chatting with Mr Smith. They both looked up as the young people entered the room.

"Jackie, are you all right?"

"Yes, Mum."

"But you've been through such a traumatic experience."

"Not really. We've only done what anybody would have done in the same circumstances."

"And you, David! What on earth did you think you would achieve by persuading Jackie to leave college early in such dangerous circumstances?" Annabel Bleasdale's voice began to rise as she struggled with her emotions.

"Oh! Just a second, Mrs Bleasdale," Mr Smith intervened, in his best school masterly and reassuring manner. "As I understand things, when David and Jackie caught the train from Richmond, there had been no official warnings issued that travelling to London could be dangerous. All that happened later."

"Are you condoning their behaviour?"

"Not at all. I'm just trying to keep matters in perspective."

"Well. That's easy for you to say. You aren't a parent."

"Well, as a matter of fact, I am." Mr Smith walked across the room to David. "And, if you'll excuse me, I do have some questions to ask David."

He took David's arm and steered him out of the dining room and into the sitting room across the hall, muttering to himself, "I really don't want to be in there if she's going to lose control."

"I'm sorry, sir. I didn't quite catch that."

"It isn't of any consequence," Mr Smith replied. "David, you already realise that cutting school yesterday is bound to have some repercussions and I am here, this evening, to give you the official verbal warning. I volunteered to do this because, in some way I feel partly responsible. Nevertheless, you must realise that, had you sought the school's permission to travel up to London, this would have been refused on two grounds. Firstly, you have your exams in three months and secondly there is the overriding matter of safety."

"Excuse me, sir," David interrupted.

"Yes? What is it?"

"Well, sir! I think you should know that I contacted Jackie on the spur of the moment. I knew that the weather was creating a specific and possibly unique situation. Jackie is fully aware of my interest in such things and agreed to come with me. But the overall responsibility for the trip is completely mine."

"It's good of you to say that, David. And because you have immediately and voluntarily taken the blame, I will ensure that this will go a long way to mitigate the level of punishment that will subsequently be decided."

A silence now fell between them. After a few seconds, David looked up to see his teacher closely looking at him. It was almost as though he was being scrutinised in a completely different manner than ever before. In fact, Mr Smith was reaching the conclusion that David had changed. He was no longer the polite, bright schoolboy, struggling with that awkwardness of changing from teenager into adult. He realised that the last 36 hours themselves had taken this intelligent pupil through that process and produced a young adult, confident in himself and in his surroundings. No longer would David suffer fools quietly. Mr Smith now regarded him in the realisation that David was now his equal and, although he might not quite realise it just yet, he would expect to be treated as such.

"Can we sit down, David?"

"Of course, sir."

"For my own part, I am much more interested in knowing what occurred when you were both in Town. Can you tell me in your own words where you were, what you saw and what you did next?"

David took a deep breath. After gathering his thoughts, he related everything he had seen and observed as soon as he and Jackie had arrived at Waterloo Station. Mr Smith was not particularly interested in the state of the crowds that had been running across Waterloo Bridge, as though their lives depended on it. Nor, indeed, did David consider it important to describe the rather more intimate details immediately following the recovery of WPC Drury's briefcase. It became more obvious that Mr Smith's primary interest lay in the state of the weather and the massive surge of water up the river Thames. When David finished with the disappearance of the Bulgarian teenagers earlier that morning, Mr Smith decided to intervene.

"When did you first see the wave of water, David?"

"At first, we could only hear it, but we didn't know what the noise was?"

"What did it sound like?"

"When we first looked out of the window in Somerset House, everything seemed to have gone quiet. Then Jackie nudged me and asked me what the strange noise was. It was coming from our left and sounded like a low growling or grinding sound. Perhaps like an overgrown kitten purring. But there were other noises as well."

"What were they like?"

"Well, sort of like an underground banging or clanging. Like an enormous bell being rung under water. Only it wasn't just one big noise. It was like happening all the time."

"When did you first see the wave?" Mr Smith repeated.

"The rain had stopped and we were both looking towards Tower Bridge in the distance. Suddenly the wave just crashed through the bridge. We could see that the bridge was already closed to traffic because the roadway on both sides was lifted up. The water seemed to rear up on the far side of the bridge, before bursting through. It was also coming through on both sides of the towers as well. We could see the walls of the Tower of London and they just disappeared as the water went over the top and into the moat. On the other side of the river, we watched the wave pick up that big ship that's moored there. It was lifted up like it was a toy and washed up river to London Bridge where it crashed into the bridge itself, ripping up the roadway.

"The wave now came towards us. I realised that it was already washing through all the buildings on the south side of the river because behind it there was just water swirling about, with all sorts of rubbish floating on the surface. It became obvious that the banging noise was coming from the sea containers that were being swept up the river by the flood. They were banging into each other and into other obstacles on the river banks"

David suddenly frowned and looked at Mr Smith, as he broke off his narrative.

"Why are you asking these specific questions, sir?"

"David, as well as being a science teacher at Richmond Academy, I have also studied Meteorology for many years and have already written a number of papers which, I'm pleased to say, have been well received by colleagues. Together with a small group of like-minded people, we have been urging our various Governments all around the world to observe more closely the changes in weather patterns in all our different countries."

"So you already knew that London was facing a specific problem."

"Yes. I was already aware that two storms were coming across the Atlantic. It's quite rare to have two storms of such intensity so close together. Your comments on the progress of those storms only confirmed my own thoughts and conclusions. If I had known that you were planning to skip school, I might even have come with you. To observe a sea surge of such height and intensity coming up the River Thames right into the centre of London and beyond would have been utterly astounding. Such an occurrence would only happen once in a lifetime."

"I realised that you had more than a passing interest, sir, but I can't understand why you didn't tell me the rest."

"Two reasons, David. Firstly, I doubt that you would have believed me. Secondly, it's a hobby that I tend to keep separate from my career as a teacher.

"So, tell me," he continued. "How fast do you think the wave was travelling as it went past Somerset House?"

"It seemed to be moving pretty fast. You know those pictures that are mocked up of spacecraft re-entering the atmosphere, creating the wave patterns in the air? Well, it was a bit like that. On either side of the river, the water seemed to be just welling up and the wave was moving more slowly the further it was away from the river itself. As it went past us, though, we weren't able to see any flooding on our side near Somerset House. But we did watch it swamp over the river walls after it had surged past the railway bridge leading to Charing Cross. Although we couldn't really see it clearly from our window, we know that the wave swept into St James Park.

"As to the speed, it seemed to be rather like a bus. Fifteen miles an hour, perhaps. Maybe twenty." David shrugged. "We did watch it sweep all the boats from their moorings on our side of the river, one of which was washed onto the Victoria Embankment near the Underground Station."

"What else did you observe from your vantage point?"

"We saw the London Eye fall down into the river. There were no people in the cabins because of the high winds, I suppose. The strange thing is that the height of the water after the wave had passed by seemed to stay higher than it was before the wave happened. I didn't really think about it at the time, but when you throw a pebble into a pond and create a ripple, the water level tends to return to what it was. I don't think it can have been much higher, but the land was all flooded on the south side. And when we went down towards the river, we found that the Victoria Embankment was as well. That's where we found the crashed bus. And the water was still rising. I suppose the tide was still coming in."

"When was High Tide yesterday afternoon?"

David thought a moment. "Around five o'clock, sir."

"And have you thought about the time the wave passed Somerset House?"

"It must have been about a quarter past three. So there would still have been almost two hours before High Tide. That's why the water continued to rise."

"Does anything else come back to you?"

"Thinking about it, watching the water flood through Tower Bridge, the height of the wave must have swamped the river side of the Tower of London. We could see the effect on the other side of the river, as the water approached the Shard. But when it came opposite us and was about to hit Waterloo Station, it seemed to be lagging much further behind the main wave in the river itself. It didn't seem so intense somehow, as though something had held it back. The water level still rose and we were able to see that even the American Embassy was flooded. We left pretty soon after that and went down to the Embankment where we found the bus lying on its side."

"Thank you, David. It would be really useful if you could write down all that you have seen. Your observations will be of immense interest to my group. Based on your evidence and that of other people, we will be able to present to Government specific proposals that will help to protect London in the future, should such a freak weather phenomenon strike again."

"What's the likelihood of that, sir?"

"Difficult to say. But as weather patterns change, all previous comments about 'Once in a lifetime' or a 'Fifty Thousand Year Event', they must be consigned to the dustbin."

David and his science teacher returned to the dining room, where Mrs Bleasdale was ready to take Jackie home. She turned to face David as he came through the door.

"I am so angry with you!" she started. Jackie tried to intervene, but her mother turned and slapped her across the face. Suddenly realising what she had done to her daughter and in front of David, his mother and school teacher, she gasped and froze. She sat down and buried her face in her hands. "I'm sorry, Jackie. I'm so sorry."

Jackie half turned away, but David quickly crossed the floor and knelt on one knee at Mrs Bleasdale's side. He put his hand on her shoulder. "Mrs Bleasdale?" he murmured. "Mrs Bleasdale, you have every right to be angry, but not with Jackie. None of this was her fault. It was all mine. I persuaded her to come up to London. But in everything we have done, she has supported me every step of the way. Those people on the bus would have drowned if she hadn't been there. I couldn't have helped them just on my own." He took a deep breath.

"Look, Mrs Bleasdale. I know we are very young and that this coming year will see many changes in our lives, but I love Jackie and I sincerely hope that we can see a lot more of each other until we go to university. After that? Well, who knows? What I can say is that neither of us will ever forget the experiences we had together."

Annabel Bleasdale lifted her head and looked into David's eyes. "Thank you," she whispered. "You really don't know what it's like." She shook her head slightly from side to side. "All my married life I have been worried about Kevin, Jackie's Dad. He never rings to say he's going to be late and I just thought Jackie was now doing the same." She put her hand gently onto David's face and repeated, "Thank you."

David stood up and helped Annabel to her feet. He looked across at Andy, who was standing in the corner of the room. "Can you take Mrs Bleasdale and Jackie home, please? I think they'll be OK now."

Jackie came across, a red mark on her face, but smiling at him. She put her arms around his neck and pulled his face to hers until their lips met. Her eyes sparkled and he could feel the hair on the back of his neck lifting as though it was electrified. When she broke the kiss, she whispered in his ear, "I'll see you very soon. Tomorrow?" David nodded.

In the city, Alice was empowered, but feeling utterly exhausted. She knew that she must have a shower, sleep and a change of clothes. But she also knew that she would forever be judged by all her actions and involvement over the next twenty-four hours and that these would either make or break her. She now had all her necessary teams camped out in the Le Grove Investments offices, waiting until they could move downstairs.

The builders in the new office were moving forward very quickly. The walls and doors were already in place. The wiring in the ceiling cavity was also coming together and Alice could see that by midday Saturday, it should all be functioning. The IT experts were already on site connecting the new computers to the internet and installing the necessary programmes and spreadsheets. In and amongst all this activity, painters were putting their finishing touches to the walls and doors.

Alice was standing in the doorway of the main entrance, legs apart, arms akimbo, watching all the activity in front of her. A voice behind her murmured, "I bet you never realised that you had it in you." She heart missed a beat, as she turned round to see Michael standing there with a big grin on his face.

"You look pleased with yourself."

"I am. The Treasury has just telephoned to advise that the Government has given its blessing to our new venture. Now we need to get the capital together and set this operation in motion."

"These offices will be fully operational at midday tomorrow."

"Really? That's brilliant. Well, it's more than that. It's really unbelievable." Michael paused and looked at her. "How do you feel?"

"Completely exhausted."

"Well, you don't look it."

"I need a shower, a power nap and a change of clothes. But I can't leave these guys."

"Let me take over."

"Michael, this is my baby…my responsibility."

"I know. But if you fall down because of exhaustion, you'll be no good to anybody. Have you a change of clothes here? Use my office to freshen up. I don't suppose you've got such facilities down here."

"Well, that's where you're wrong! But ours can't be used yet as the tile cement is still drying. And ours will be available for all the employees not just the odd director or two," she added tartly. "I realised very early on that everyone would be putting in long hours and it would only be right to make such facilities available to us all."

"When did these guys last have a break?"

"About an hour ago. The next is due at seven o'clock when pizzas and drinks will be delivered. These guys have really earned their money and, broadly, they're doing it for me."

What on earth do you mean?"

"I've told them that this is my new business and that they will be in for substantial bonuses if they complete all the work before their contractual times. Early in the operation, one of the plasterers started to get a bit fresh, taking the mickey and making inappropriate remarks, so I fired him. They all realised then that I was completely serious."

"Bloody hell! I've got a tiger working for me!" Michael exclaimed.

Alice turned to him. "No, no! Hang on a second. You told me that this was my operation and that you would simply be here in an advisory capacity. By no stretch of the imagination does that make me 'working for you'. And, remember, I am not a tiger, rather a tigress." She smiled. "Right! It's twenty to seven. I'm going to take up your offer of that shower. I'll be back here when the food arrives."

She turned and walked through the doors to the stairwell. As soon as she arrived at the Le Grove offices above, she went first to the wardrobe in her own office where she found a clean dress and fresh underwear. Next she went to Michael's office and walked through to the shower. Inside, she stripped and looked at herself in the mirror. Her face was looking drawn, but that was nothing a bit of makeup wouldn't put right. For the rest, she was surprised to note her back was straight, her shoulders back and her head upright. She really did look good!

The shower was invigorating and restored her more quickly than she thought possible. She dried her body, thinking about the long list of things that still needed to be done. After wrapping a towel round her hair, she started to dress. Her underwear was lightweight, cream and virtually transparent. Her dress was figure hugging in off-white. The shoulders were slightly padded and the skirt fell to just short of her knees. When the zip was fastened, it showed off her figure beautifully. The waist was tailored to fit properly and there was a modest split in the skirt at the back. She decided not to wear pantyhose.

After applying her makeup and tidying her hair, she took the dirty clothes back to her own office and put them in a bag ready to be taken home. She picked out a pair of high heels to match the dress. It was now five to seven and time for the pizzas. Returning downstairs to the newly refurbished office below, she found Michael talking on his mobile. She recognised the name Sebastian and realised that he was talking with the owner of the Gloucester Palace Hotel. They were arranging to meet later that evening. Michael turned, as he finished the call and his jaw dropped as he saw her standing in the entrance. She was carrying an armful of serviettes and a roll of kitchen paper.

"Come on, guys. The pizza man is on the stairs. It's time for a break and an assessment of where we are, what's to be done and how soon it'll all be finished."

They all downed tools and walked across the office floor. She turned to Michael and steered him away.

"Who was on the phone?"

"Sebastian Fortescue Brown. You know, the owner of the hotel in Kensington."

"What did he want?"

"I called him. He has capital to invest and I believe he can bring in more capital from his contacts. I think we might be able to offer him a great facility here."

"Are you meeting him here?"

"No. I can't get hold of the taxi driver, so he's coming across himself to pick me up. We are going to meet a couple of his contacts in the West End."

"This evening?"

"Yes. I'm being picked up at eight."

"As this is my venture, shouldn't I be with you?"

"I thought you wanted to keep an eye on your workmen."

"I do. But I have a feeling that your activities will be rather more important and I must keep an eye on all that is going on."

"That's fine with me. You'd better bring a laptop with you as well."

And so, by Friday evening, as the hour hand slowly turned towards midnight and the latest tide ebbed away down river, London was already returning to some degree of normality. The massive displacement of people was causing the biggest headaches because they all needed to be cared for. The extraction and identification of the dead continued through the night, as it would do for many days to come. The enormity and reality of the catastrophe was only now beginning to seep into the consciousness of most people.

Early decisions began to bear fruit. The flooded supermarkets were quickly stripped of all provisions, cleaned and restocked with basics. The Government announced that, until Monday morning, basic staples of food and water would be available at all such outlets, where the army and the police would be on hand through the night and the following few days to help those in need.

The disruption to daily life would continue for many months and the long list of the dead continued to rise. The Government, working closely with the Army and the Police, drafted many of the unemployed from all corners of the country and brought them to London to help with the clean-up. For many, this was their first experience of work and being away from their home comforts. To the surprise of many, a large number became enthused by this activity and many resolved never to go back into the Benefits System.

In the Underground, following instructions from the Government, given with the full support of the Opposition, the work to clear the affected stations started and as the night progressed the work continued with a growing intensity. Slowly the comments about funding began to filter into the boardrooms and management offices raising the levels of confidence for the overall organisers to get to grips with the necessary work. The equipment needed to cut up the ruined trains into transportable sizes made its way through the darkened tunnels. The dismembered trains were then removed the same way. In the face of the appalling death toll a surprising degree of harmony developed between Transport for London and the Government.

Because of the heat that is generated in the Underground, there was an intensity of activity to remove the dead bodies as quickly as possible. Initially this work was hampered by the inaccessibility of the system with tunnels, stairs and escalators being crammed with dead bodies, many of which had been crushed and asphyxiated in the panic. It was quickly realised that these access points had to be cleared as quickly as possible, so that power could be restored to the escalators. Engineers began to work on the destroyed lifts with a view to bringing them back into service at the earliest opportunity.

On the surface, where the flood had devastated the housing and business estates, clearing the dumped sea containers was the primary task, thus ensuring the reopening of the road networks. At first, because of their size and weight, the work to remove them proceeded very slowly. To assist with this, lifting gear was requisitioned from wherever it could be procured. The Government quickly realised that the closure of all the bridges over the Thames was exceptionally unhelpful, although there was a realisation that all of them had to be surveyed. Very soon, it was suggested that a temporary system of traffic flow could be introduced, ensuring that vehicles flowed only one way over each bridge. The congestion charge was also lifted for a limited period.

Very soon, those people who were flooded out of their homes, said that they wished to return to start their own clearing up. Where houses had been destroyed, the Government pledged to rebuild them irrespective of any insurance policies being in place. Removal of the rubble from destroyed buildings, tower blocks, offices and warehouses commenced very early on, as soon as there was access on the roads. Much was dumped alongside the river, bolstering up the river defences.

During the first week following the disaster, new bricks were brought in for rebuilding, but the major drawback was a lack of available bricklayers. To combat this shortage, the Government arranged for every tertiary college across the country to release its students and tutors so that they could assist the emergency re-building work in the devastated housing estates.

Underwriting all this activity and more was Alice's consortium. Funds continued to flow in, when it was understood that the Government would agree to cover all the loans over a twenty-year period and committed itself to pay one half percent interest per annum on all the monies thus raised. It was, perhaps, inevitable that a proportion of these funds would be illegitimate, but there was an understanding from the very first day that the more urgent need for the capital outweighed such niceties.

But the most extraordinary reaction to the disaster was the demonstration that the human spirit will forever overcome the most insuperable of odds. According to the old myth, Hope was the last item to emerge from the box when Pandora removed its lid. Out came war, pestilence, disasters and destruction, but following them all came Hope. And it is that Hope which enables all of us to work together to create a better future.

Epilogue

The weather, following the London Flood, became far more settled. It turned colder at the end of February, but by the end of March the sun was high enough in the sky to herald an early spring. The persistent rainfall over the previous summer and autumn gave way to light showers and with the coming of April and May, the weather turned warm and the crops in the fields began to grow. The summer was forecast to be warm and dry.

In August, the railway bridge was finally rebuilt and the railway line from Liverpool Street to Southend was reopened. There was a ceremony at Liverpool Street Station and a commemorative journey to Southend. Martin Havers and his wife Jennifer were invited to attend in recognition of the work he and his family had done overnight following the Thames inundation. They graciously accepted and Jennifer took the opportunity to wear her new rubies. Their sons were, once more, back in their own homes, but Helen now seemed to be spending much more time in Essex. Both Jennifer and Martin were delighted with her blossoming relationship with Wayne.

As the train made its way along the new track from Benfleet, Martin could see the contractors hard at work, raising and strengthening the sea wall. All their intensive work, on that terrible night, had finally been replaced by a new wall, with new sluices to regulate the outflow of water from the land. Martin's improvised wall had kept the sea at bay with much greater success than anyone might have expected. So much so, he had decided to plough the flooded fields, once they had dried out, and plant them with grass. Much to his surprise and, indeed, to the amazement of all his neighbours, a decent crop had grown, on which his cattle were now feeding.

"Jennifer! Look over there." He pointed to the fields. "The cattle look really healthy and sleek in this sunshine. You would never believe that all those fields were flooded only six months ago."

"I know. What you did that night was remarkable and I am so very proud of you."

She slipped her arm into his and held him tight to her. A warm feeling of well-being flowed through them both and, once again, Martin reflected that he must be one of the luckiest people alive.

The devastation of the housing estates, industrial sites, container ports, roads and tunnels had fed the media for many weeks. The tabloids, after the sensational headlines of the flood itself, had busied themselves with negative comments and stories about the Government and its apparent laggardly response to the disaster. To everyone's surprise, however, the agreement between the government and the opposition to work together continued to hold firm for the six months following the disaster. A Joint Working Party was created to oversee the reconstruction of the Capital. At the top of the agenda for the Working Party's attention was a determination to reopen the tunnels and bridges at the first possible opportunity. Initially, the Army helped with the survey of the bridges over the River Thames but, very quickly, it was replaced by teams from the Ministry of Transport.

It was an enormous relief to learn the Thames Barrier was declared free of all damage. The Report from the Environment Agency, however, went on to remark that the sea surge had been so high, it had simply flowed over the top of the Barrier, enabling a massive inundation of water together with sea containers and other heavy debris to flow up the Thames, which had caused so much damage to the riverside infrastructure. The Report concluded not only that the Barrier should be replaced with a new construction, built higher and stronger and more in keeping with current sea levels, but also that the sea walls from East Yorkshire all the way round the east coast to the Thames Estuary, should be raised and strengthened.

The damage in the housing estates was exacerbated by the tons of mud that had been dumped by the inundation. As soon as it became clear that the sea defences themselves were broadly undamaged by the flood, the local people who had been evacuated began to return to their homes. At first, the Joint Working Party felt that this drift back home should be discouraged until a more practical consideration suggested that the local people would be far more likely to get on with the job of clearing up their own localities and provide local protection and security, than could be offered by the Government or the Local Councils. In an extraordinary demonstration of good sense, the Joint Working Party set up a sub-committee to work closely with the Local Borough Councils. Instead of opposing the desire to return home, an active policy was put in place to encourage local residents to return and to assist in the drafting of the lists of people that were missing, buildings that were destroyed and roads that required clearance and renovation.

At first, the plethora of all this information appeared to be overwhelming, but slowly the officials in the Local Councils began to make sense of it all and were able to direct the teams dealing with the clearances to the most appropriate places. The sea containers, buses and cars that had been randomly dumped blocking roads and railways, together with those in housing and industrial estates, were all removed within three weeks. The clearance of the demolished houses and tower blocks took longer because, in many instances, further demolition was necessary. Somewhat surprisingly, the Local Councils willingly sought the advice of their local people in order to save as much personal property as possible. It was also agreed, following advice and direction from the Environment Agency, to dump all the rubble from the many destroyed buildings alongside the riverbanks, thus acting as hard core for the planned improvement of the river defences.

Slowly, the 'quality' press began to support the Government, as it continued to work in conjunction with the Opposition. By the spring, when reconstruction of the new houses commenced, even the tabloids expressed some surprise that so much was being done. The cooperation between the city and the Treasury continued to work extremely well. As soon as the final details of the financial arrangements for the raising of the capital loans had been agreed, the money started to be released against specific and logged applications. The capitalisation of the reconstruction fund, now known as 'Re-build London', originally came from many and varied quarters. At the very start, in those first few weeks before the compliance processes were put into place, Michael Varley was able to arrange for a substantial inflow of funds generated by and through Sebastian Fortescue Brown. This immediate access to cash was a boon to the Government, as it allowed for the clearance work to commence immediately. Michael realised, however, that this window, which was allowing him to receive and utilise some rather dubious capital, would be very limited and by the middle of March, it was already closed.

Sebastian Fortescue Brown, using his close links in the underworld, was able to raise several millions of pounds of illegal cash, which were washed through the system. The surprising and beneficial knock-on effect of this illegal movement of funds was to generate immediate employment in the flooded areas. Several new companies were formed specifically to employ the available labour from the Job Centres. A Government Initiative was also announced that these companies, working closely with the Home Office and the Treasury, would be allowed, for a limited period of time, to employ temporary labour without paying National Insurance. The drop in the rate of unemployment was remarkable and, again to the surprise of many people, a growing number of these temporary labourers went on to seek training, thus enabling them to move into more skilled and better paid areas of work.

The loans to the fund generated by Sebastian were of a particularly short term nature and, of course, as soon as repayments were made the returned capital became completely legitimate. In a very private meeting between the Chancellor, Michael Varley and the head of The Securities and Investment Board, it was agreed that no action would be taken to review the legitimacy of these loans for the initial three months, so long as the necessary work of clearance and reconstruction continued to increase in intensity. After that amnesty, all the necessary checks as dictated by HM Treasury would be imposed, but Alice had been anticipating this crack down and her records were already impeccable.

It was a massive task to clear the affected tunnels in the London Underground. To keep the public transport system working, the London Mayor introduced additional overground bus services and to enable these to run unimpeded, he banned all other traffic, other than reconstruction vehicles, between the hours of 7.30 am to 10.00 am and again from 4.00 pm to 7.00 pm. Although this was not particularly popular it was generally accepted in the spirit of getting London moving. The unaffected parts of the Underground were quickly reopened thus allowing access into the Capital from the suburbs.

The bodies from the flooded platforms and tunnels were slowly cleared with the help of battery powered trains with specially constructed flatbed trucks. Identification became increasingly difficult as the bodies continued to decompose and finally local identification was abandoned. The mortal remains were initially taken to cold storage facilities all over the south east of the country and then further afield, until the problem literally overwhelmed all the available resources.

Because the numbers of the dead were so vast, it was suggested that the bodies should be buried in large communal graves. Slowly it became apparent to the public that, however much individuals might be opposed to this, there simply weren't the facilities to store the bodies pending identification. It was recognised, of course, that families and loved ones were more than likely to seek their lost family members and friends. To assist with this, therefore, a DNA register was created, which included the information as to the place and time the bodies had been found and extracted.

The last bodies were removed from the Northern and Bakerloo lines ninety three days after the sea surge had devastated the Underground. As soon as the tunnels and the stations were clear, work began on the necessary renovation and, where necessary, reconstruction of the infrastructure, including its flood defences. It was already well known how vital a resource the Underground is to London. Transport for London was encouraged by the Government to increase its flood safety features as well as protection from terrorist attacks. This considerably lengthened the time taken before the Northern and Bakerloo lines became fully operational but, in order to comply with the public's travelling needs, a system of rolling renovation was introduced whereby stations were closed in turn, but still allowed the lines to be used.

Elsewhere in London, the necessary civil engineering surveys of all the bridges were quickly completed. Most were allowed to reopen to normal traffic within thirty days, but because of the damage caused by HMS Belfast, London Bridge itself was closed for much longer while it was substantially rebuilt. In August, the King himself reopened London Bridge with much fanfare and London was declared to be effectively 'back to normal'.

The bridge surveys demonstrated that the damage to Queen Elizabeth II Bridge was only superficial and it was re-opened very quickly. By the middle of March, the London Orbital Motorway was, once again, operational.

Sadly, this was not echoed by the clearance and renovation of the tunnels. The ingress of water had damaged all the electrical cabling and the removal of all the vehicles and the bodies took far longer than was first anticipated. Indeed, a full ten weeks had passed before all the road tunnels were cleared and work could start on the necessary repairs and renovations. Between Dartford and Purfleet, the loss of the Dartford Tunnels was temporarily resolved by opening the Queen Elizabeth II Bridge to two way traffic.

The rail tunnels had only suffered water ingress and after this had been pumped out, rail services were quickly restored. Work immediately commenced on additional protection for the entrances to all tunnels so that, in the event of a future failure of the river defences, the access to the tunnels would still be protected. The additional protection not only included higher protective walls, but also systems of automatic doors that could slide down and effectively seal the entrances. Failsafe facilities were also included to ensure that the trains would be halted, either inside or outside the tunnels, before the new sliding doors were activated. Similar failsafe systems were introduced at the entrances to the road tunnels, which were also protected with higher and stronger walls, in addition to the generally improved river defences. The cost for all these repairs, renovations and improved defences were underwritten by the Government but the initial work was completely dependent on the funds being generated by Michael Varley's new finance company.

David returned to school and buckled down to the necessary revision for his 'A' levels. To his relief, as well as the delight of his parents, his results confirmed his place at Sheffield University. He and Jackie continued to see each other during the spring and summer. Jackie was offered her place at Bristol University and, suddenly, they both realised that the coming September would be a big challenge to their relationship.

As soon as the exams were completed, they were hardly out of each other's company, even spending two weeks in Cornwall on holiday in a chalet. Although the weather was beautiful and the sun was hot, they were unable to ignore completely their forthcoming separation. Slowly, David became increasingly withdrawn and Jackie, noticing this, became falsely jolly. Neither had the experience to recognise that both desperately wanted to remain together but were unable to work out how to make this happen. The desire for instant results and resolutions, so common in the young, is not a suitable training ground for impending separation. Both realised that they were growing apart, even though neither wanted this to happen, but neither was able to talk about it and to propose any satisfactory solution.

On their return to London, both fit and tanned, David's mother immediately noticed the new distance between them. David was withdrawn and spent an increasing amount of time in his room. For her part, Jackie sought out her mother and tried to talk with her about her unhappiness. Annabel, however, did not immediately appreciate how deeply saddened her daughter was becoming. Instead, she put it all down to the forthcoming move to Bristol and all the changes that would follow.

Jackie and David celebrated their exam results together, but although the evening started with all their friends at the tennis club, slowly and steadily the evening changed and, for them, it became increasingly sombre. A wrong word here, an inappropriate gesture there and the gulf inexorably widened between them. Suddenly there was no laughter between them, no secret smiles, no touching, nothing. Two days later, after spending an agonised and sleepless night thinking it all through, David texted Jackie suggesting that they should meet at the Costa Coffee where they had met all those months before.

Desperately hoping that the spark might re-ignite, she agreed. As before, David was sitting at the back in the secluded corner when Jackie arrived. It was a cold, wet day for the end of August and Jackie was dressed exactly as she had been on that exciting day back in February. He stood up as she walked towards him and they kissed each other on the cheek. David bought a latte for her and an Americano for himself.

"How are you?"

"Fine."

"I'm just finishing all the packing and stuff before getting off to Sheffield."

"Thought you might be. I'm doing the same."

"Jackie?" David looked at her. "What's wrong with us?" He watched as her eyes began to fill with tears.

"I don't know. I've thought and thought, but I just don't know."

"I couldn't sleep last night, thinking about you, about us. I don't want us just to drift apart and not be friends. We've seen and done too much for that. I love you so much and I will always deeply cherish the times we have had together." His voice caught as he saw the tears slowly falling down her cheeks. "But I know that we have moved apart over the last few weeks and, if this isn't working, it would be wrong of me to try to find ways to bind us closer together. I don't know why this has happened, but it has. I still love you and I do want you to stay my friend, but…"

His voice drifted off as he watched Jackie silently crying in front of him. She reached out her right hand and, taking hold of his left, she squeezed it. She coughed gently to clear her constricted throat.

"You are such a lovely person, David. You are kind, thoughtful and generous. You always seem know when to do the right thing. I have loved my time with you and I wish that it could go on forever. I don't know how we have come to this, but we have."

Through her tear filled eyes, she watched David's face slowly crumple as his own eyes filled. But he then squared his shoulders, lifted his head and took a deep breath.

"Of course I want to stay friends with you."

As she replied, she squeezed his hand tighter. "I want to know everything about you. Who you meet. Who you go out with. How well you are doing in your course. Everything."

"Thank you, Jackie," he replied simply. "Thank you."

Sebastian Fortescue Brown had enjoyed a remarkable six months. On the same day that he was invited by Michael Varley to invest in "Re-build London," he contacted Mr Chao. A meeting was quickly arranged and suitable conduits were set up to raise funding. Both Sebastian and Mr Chao immediately appreciated that an unmissable opportunity was being presented to launder considerable amounts of dirty money. They were completely aware that the capital they could raise might not be strictly legitimate, but this new fund was an obvious facility to bring millions of off colour pounds back into acceptable circulation. In fact, 'Re-build London' might even be regarded as some sort of amnesty.

This ready supply of capital from such unexpected quarters had caused Michael Varley a degree of disquiet but, following an unrecorded yet realistic conversation with the Chancellor, a time limit of one month was set before any serious compliance scrutiny of the fund was instigated. Consequently, all records from the middle of March were to be scrupulously documented and maintained. Alice was aware of this arrangement and ensured that she knew exactly what finance was completely legitimate. She set up exemplary records and kept an increasingly watchful eye over her domain.

Prior to March, the records simply demonstrated receipts of funds, payments for specific work and repayments to lenders. The mere fact that there were ample funds available, to allow for the reparations to commence within days of the disaster, became the overriding reasoning not to delve too deeply into the exact legitimacy of the source of the funds. In addition, the immediate capital was raised as short term loans much of which were to be repaid by the Fund before the end of April. The repayments of many of these loans, of course, legitimised the returned capital.

With Michael's advice and knowledge, Sebastian set up a trading and investment bank, based in Guernsey, which acted as the recipient of the cash coming from the underworld. He was then able to transfer that capital to 'Re-build London' and, when each loan was repaid, he was able to return the now legitimised money, less a suitable commission, back to the original lender. With the fees he received for these transactions and with his own rapidly expanding wealth, he was able to open six other hotels which were operating in exactly the same manner as the Gloucester Palace Hotel. Four were in the London area, one in Birmingham and the last in Bristol.

During the weekend following the disastrous flood, Mr Chao's workmen started work on the secret access from the basement into the cellar of the hotel. The doorway at the bottom of the stairwell was reinstated and it became the first part of Sebastian's security system. This door opened to reveal a descending stairway, just as on the other floors, but at the bottom of the first flight, there were no more steps beyond the half landing, only a hatched access to the bottom of the lift shaft.

The wall facing the stairs appeared as a perfectly normal wall, but on activating the electronic key, it silently moved back six inches, before sliding to the right. Automatically, a light came on and a newly constructed half landing, behind the rear wall of the original lift shaft, was revealed. A stairway now descended to the right to a second half landing and, turning right once more, there were more steps leading to a second brick wall which was the second secret door. This was activated in a similar manner.

Beyond the second door was a short passage leading to an ordinary wooden door with a mortice lock. When opened, a well-appointed office was revealed, with all the necessary and expected office equipment. It was richly carpeted and along the left hand wall was a bookcase filled with collectibles and first editions, a veritable antiquarian's dream. Because the room was well below ground level with no natural light and because of the value of the library, it was blessed with excellent air conditioning, maintaining the humidity at the most appropriate level.

Sebastian had rationalised that, if the two electronic doors on the stairway were breached, then his office, his *sanctum sanctorum,* would be searched and his computers taken for analysis. He even expected that his library would be seized. Consequently, in that office, he only retained information that, although sensitive, was ultimately disposable. A further access, therefore, had been constructed behind the bookcase.

The bookcase was split into three sections and the central section acted as the doorway. Behind this section was yet another brick wall, constructed in old London brisk, so that should the bookcase be removed, a natural wall would be revealed. However, when this was activated, it also moved back six inches and then slid silently to the left. There were two rooms beyond, in the first of which Sebastian stored the proceeds of his hotels and in the second the proceeds of his other activities. All the appropriate computer records for these additional activities were maintained in these two rooms and behind very secure firewalls.

Already, he had realised that the growth of his illicit cash was creating a growing problem and 'Re-build London' was a most welcome opportunity to legitimise it and more. The opening of his other hotels required a considerable outlay of capital, but he planned that the income would quickly see the new acquisitions returning satisfactory dividends.

And because there now appeared to be a suitable and secure place to launder their money, an increasing number of 'clients' approached Sebastian to make use of his facilities. The future looked really good.

Despite the difficulties facing the Underground, the media, at first somewhat sceptical, continued to support the Government in its endeavours to bring London back to normality as quickly as possible. Naturally, there were some complaints concerning the rebuilding of London Bridge and the time taken to clear and repair the tunnels of the Northern and Bakerloo Lines.

Pamela soon returned to work at Waterloo and, as the weeks passed, the horrors of that night slowly receded from her memory. In the first couple of weeks she suffered from sleepless nights and decided that the best therapy would be to work through the trauma. She did not discuss her difficulties with Milton, particularly as he was increasingly involved with the extraction of the bodies from the tunnels and the stations on the Northern Line.

The air temperature in the tunnels is always higher than on the surface and, consequently, the bodies began to decompose within a very short time. Each day the smell was increasingly overpowering. Identification of each corpse became more and more difficult and, finally, the authorities agreed that this work would proceed much faster if the position of each corpse was accurately logged, with a specific attempt to finalise identification at a later date. DNA identification was also logged. Following this decision, the speed of extraction increased considerably, but it was still 93 days before all the tunnels and stations were clear.

As the bodies were cleared, the job of cleaning and disinfecting started. The pervading stench of corruption made all this activity exceptionally difficult and it was necessary to introduce incentives to get the job done at all. At last, the teams of workers were able to commence the reconstruction work in the tunnels and the stations themselves.

Alongside this activity, the failed flood gates were all removed and replaced with new, state of the art flood defence systems. These were electronically linked to the Thames Barrier so that, in the event of a recurrence of such a storm and subsequent sea surge, the flood defence system would be activated much earlier. In its turn, the Thames Barrier was connected to surge sensor indicator stations further downstream, three on either bank of the Thames, so that a continual stream of information was made available for regular and constant analysis. Based on the understanding that any detected surge at Shoeburyness and Sheerness would not reach the Thames Barrier for thirty minutes or more nor central London for over an hour, it was decided that this would be sufficient time for warning sirens to sound and verbal announcements made that the flood doors would be closed.

Once all the bodies had been removed, Milton began to notice that the oppressive odour of death and decay slowly receded, being replaced by the cleaner smell of disinfectant and bleach. The repairs to the cabling and the track in the tunnels, especially under the Thames, were now prioritised.

As soon as the cabling repairs were complete, power to the tracks was reinstated, making it possible to use specially converted trains for the transportation of bricks, tiles, sand and cement. The repairs to the platforms started and, once again, there was a noticeable increase in the work rates of the repair teams.

The work continued day and night, with consistent pressure being exerted from the London Mayor and the Government. In turn, Transport for London put its own pressure on the Unions and staff members to raise their work rates. With the memory of that awful day receding from the forefront of the public's mind, there was a growing irritation that the repair work was taking far too long. Because she was more involved with the public, Pamela was forced, more and more often, to face up to much of this mounting criticism.

Each evening, after returning home, Milton's conversation was now becoming increasingly positive, as he recounted that the rate of progress was speeding up. Initially, like Pamela, he had been so despondent that she was concerned for his mental state. She believed that he was suffering from depression. His demeanour deepened even further in those first few weeks, while the bodies were being extracted, but as soon as the work commenced on the reconstruction, he experienced a lightening in his mood.

For his part, Milton observed that Pamela was becoming increasingly withdrawn. Her normal, friendly behaviour was being replaced by a quietness and a separation. Before the flood they were growing to learn about each other, but now it increasingly appeared to Milton that they were acting like two strangers living in the same house. Because they rarely talked about that night, neither realised that the other was deeply troubled, although endeavouring to cope with the stress by increasing their work load.

At first, while Milton was facing up to his own demons, Pamela took on the role of looking after the house. As time went by, however, Milton's black mood lifted and his whole being became more positive. Somewhat surprisingly, Pamela's thoughts became more depressed and slowly Milton took over the household chores, leaving Pamela alone with her thoughts. He realised that she was reflecting on the events in February and as the months slowly passed into May and June, he appreciated that by working through her own trauma, Pamela had not actually come to terms with the enormity of the devastation. Rather, she had compartmentalised it all, but it was now becoming apparent that she was increasingly unable to accommodate those memories.

Gently, he tried to engage her in conversation to see whether he was able to assist, but she rejected his well-meaning overtures. When Pamela started to demonstrate mood swings, Milton decided that she should visit her doctor. It took a certain degree of persuasion, but finally she agreed. At the end of July, she commenced a programme of mental rehabilitation, supported by Milton and her work colleagues. The prescribed drugs kept her mind on a satisfactory level, to such a degree that, on the re-opening of the Underground, she was able to celebrate that London was finally returning to normal.

Milton now suggested that they should take time away from work and Pamela's final hurdle of recovery was to organise a three week holiday in the Caribbean. This became the real basis of the recovery for them both, as they actively planned their holiday. It brought them closer so well that Pamela soon felt she could dispense with the tranquillisers and start to plan for the future of their lives together. At last they were both looking to the future rather than dwelling in the past.

The junior football team in Poplar thrived over the three months following the disaster. Fred Shemming very quickly realised that the amount of time he was putting into coaching and organising the team was an excellent therapy for his own mental state.

Diane had noticed a weariness and despondency immediately following the flood. She had quietly spoken with Brigade Headquarters and together, they hatched a scheme which took Fred away from the immediacy of his responsibilities at the Poplar Fire Station. This gave him the time to concentrate on his forthcoming promotion.

Fred, having a well-tuned and canny nature, realised that something was being resolved for him behind the scenes but, being both a thinker and a strategist, he decided it would be for the best if he kept his own thoughts to himself. It soon became apparent to him, however, that he was being placed in a position of rehabilitation without actually being given the time off and, rather than being angry at being so manipulated, he realised that it rather suited his own plans. He was able to concentrate on his reading and, much more pleasurably, coaching the football team.

Each boy's home had been inundated so Fred, in those early days immediately following the flood, worked hard to harness their energy and enthusiasm to help to clean up their own houses and neighbourhoods. In their turn, the boys then encouraged their school friends to join them in setting up proactive teams to help with a general clean up and improvement of their whole locality.

Slowly they watched their estates recover from the devastation caused by the sea containers. The bricks and rubble were removed from the destroyed streets and houses and dumped next to the original river defences where they would form the hard core base for the planned renovations.

They watched as the randomly dumped sea containers were removed. The estates were cleared of these very quickly, leaving behind the mud and mess.

They watched as the old destroyed homes were rebuilt. It was slow work as first, but as soon as the new foundations were in place, the walls and roofs followed on much more quickly. A serious attempt was made for these new homes to replicate the destroyed buildings so that, by blending in, the memories of that awful night would be encouraged to recede as quickly as possible.

They watched the new roads being installed and, like all children before them, they delighted in the smell of the asphalt.

The weather following the Great Storm was mild and benign. The ground dried out and the team was able to train regularly and to play matches against other similar teams. With Fred's coaching, his boys quickly gelled together and, by the end of the season, the team remained unbeaten. Big plans were being discussed for the future.

As she sat behind her desk in New Scotland Yard, WPC Elizabeth Drury slowly finished her report of the flood and her personal involvement. She reported in detail the activities of David Varley and his girlfriend Jackie Bleasdale. She paid particular tribute to the manner in which they had selflessly entered the crashed and flooded bus and saved the lives of all the occupants, including herself. She included in her report the assistance that was given by the two teenagers but decided to omit that she believed them to be illegal immigrants. She spent some time reflecting on her stay at the Gloucester Palace Hotel and although she felt that something was a little odd about the place itself, she was unable to specify exactly what it might be. She also included the active role played by the cabbie.

Her report formed part of the overall report that was prepared by Chief Superintendent Keith Bleasdale, which finally found its way to Downing Street.

In the weeks that followed, Elizabeth decided that she would re-visit the Gloucester Palace to see whether she might be able to deduce what it was that she found unsettling about the hotel. It was some weeks before she was able to find the time. She found her visit rather strange, particularly as there was no one immediately available on reception. There was a bell and, after ringing it three times, a lady appeared down the stairs.

"I'm so sorry," she said. "I was upstairs and didn't hear the bell."

Elizabeth looked closely at her.

"You were on duty that night when London was flooded," she said.

"That's right." The girl looked more closely at Elizabeth. "You were here that night as well. You came in with those people injured in the overturned bus."

"I did. I know it's a bit of an off chance, but I just wondered whether you ever heard from the Eastern European teenagers again. I remember that she wasn't well the next morning and it's been preying on my mind whether she was OK."

"Never another word. She and her brother just left the next morning and they've never been back."

"Pity!" Elizabeth stepped back from the desk as though about to leave. She then stopped and turned back to the girl. "Is the proprietor in today?"

"I'm so sorry." The girl shook her head. "He's out on an appointment this afternoon."

"Oh well. Another time, perhaps."

Just as the front door closed behind Elizabeth as she left the hotel to return to the Yard, Sebastian appeared from the corridor leading to his office.

"Who was that?"

"She didn't say. But she stayed here in February on the night of the flood."

"I thought that I recognised her. Did she say what she wanted?"

"Not really. Only to ask whether those Eastern European teenagers had been in touch."

"Thanks."

Elizabeth's next encounter with Sebastian appeared to be completely coincidental but, in fact, it had been completely set up by Elizabeth outside Mr Chao's office in Soho. During one of her regular pick-ups for Chief Superintendent Bleasdale, she had seen Sebastian walking towards the office as she was leaving. She wasn't sure whether he had seen her, but she stopped in the doorway of a café on the other side of the road, simply to observe where Sebastian would go. Much to her surprise, he entered the door from which she had just exited.

Hmm, she thought. *I wonder what's going on there.*

She was fully aware that Mr Chao sailed very close to the wind and she now had her suspicions about Sebastian. All the instincts of a police officer now took over, except that she decided not to report the chance sighting. Instead, she decided to watch and wait and to see whether anything would develop.

Several weeks went by, until she saw Sebastian once again, walking towards Mr Chao's office. This time, she walked over and stepped in front of him.

"Hello! Aren't you that chap from the Gloucester Palace Hotel?"

Sebastian stopped and looked at the short, pretty and well-dressed young lady in front of him, wondering who on earth she might be.

"And who might you be? I don't think we've met before."

"There's really no reason why you should remember. After all, it was a very confusing evening. But I shall never forget your generosity when you opened the doors of your hotel on the night of the flood."

"My word!" Sebastian exclaimed. "I do remember! You came in with the injured passengers from the crashed bus. I remember thinking that you controlled the situation and the other passengers admirably." He smiled amiably at her and looked at his watch. "I'm so sorry, but I do have an appointment."

"I'm keeping you! Perhaps we could meet up on another occasion. Would it be possible to visit you in Kensington?" Elizabeth turned her head very slightly and, with a slight smile on her lips, she looked up at him with eyes full of promise.

"That would be lovely. Please get in touch."

And following that chance encounter, Elizabeth and Sebastian met several times during that summer, but at no time did she reveal that she worked at Scotland Yard, nor that she collected a mysterious briefcase for her boss from Soho on a regular basis.

London had definitely returned to normal.